Homecourt Advantage

HOMECOURT ADVANTAGE

A NOVEL

Crystal McCrary

and

Rita Ewing

AVON BOOKS NEW YORK

This is a work of fiction. Except for passing reference
to real celebrities, all characters are entirely imagined
and any resemblance to real persons or events is purely
coincidental. Although reference is made to real celebrities,
their dialogue, actions, and the context in which they are
portrayed are all products of the authors' imaginations.

AVON BOOKS, INC.
1350 Avenue of the Americas
New York, New York 10019

Copyright © 1998 by Rita Ewing and Crystal McCrary
Interior design by Kellan Peck
Visit our website at http://www.AvonBooks.com
ISBN: 0-380-97663-3

Library of Congress Cataloging in Publication Data:
Ewing, Rita.
Homecourt advantage : a novel / Rita Ewing and Crystal McCrary—1st ed.
p.   cm.
1. Basketball players—Fiction.
I. McCrary, Crystal.   II. Title.
PS355.W54S33   1998   98-18175
813'.54—dc21   CIP

First Avon Books Printing: November 1998

AVON TRADEMARK REG. U.S. PAT. OFF. AND IN OTHER COUNTRIES, MARCA REGISTRADA,
HECHO EN U.S.A.

Printed in the U.S.A.

QPM   10   9   8   7   6   5   4   3

Acknowledgments

Biggup' to my husband, Patrick Ewing. Without you, I'd just be an innocent bystander.

A huge "thanks" to all my NBA partners—current and ex-wives, fiancées, and girlfriends. Stay strong!

For all my friends (and you know who you are)—thank you for all the insight and support.

Thanks go out to my family (Mommy, Daddy, and Kelly)—without your support I still would have done this, but it wouldn't have been as much fun.

To our editor, Carrie Feron, and our agent, Denise Stinson: I thank you both for believing in our story and making it happen. Sandi Gelles-Cole, a huge thanks for helping us tighten this up.

Jeanne Moutousammy-Ashe, an amazing photographer and beautiful friend, thank you! You captured our good sides (with a little help from Angel).

Thank you Terrie Williams for your friendship, advice and unlimited resources!

And the BIGGEST thanks of all to my true partner in crime and best friend, Crystal McCrary-Anthony. Without you, girl, this would still be just another good idea.

R.E.

I want to thank God. Much love and respect to my family and friends; Kyra, my uplifting positive best friend, I'm so thankful there are people like you in the world; Dominique Sims-Lash, Nikki Doss, Leslie Danley, Carla Diggs—thanks for giving the first draft read; Lisa Handley Bonner, Shaun Robinson, Dena Dodd-Perry, Shauna Neely, Marcia Mackey and the whole Detroit crew, Jay Norris, Peter Simonetta and Patrick Orr, Kery and Samantha Davis, the Wu Clan, Fran Rauch, Tonya Lewis-Lee, Nikki Skalski, wherever you are, Sheree Carter-Galvan, for your friendship and great legal advice; Nancy Taylor Rosenberg, you've been a friend and mentor; Nick Ellison; Denise Stinson, for believing in the book; my editor, Carrie Feron, for your enthusiasm throughout the project; Sandi Gelles-Cole, for teaching me more about writing; Jeanne Moutoussamy-Ashe, it was an honor and a privilege working with you; Angel Raphael Gonzalez, for fabulous make-up; Rita, we got it done with commitment, vision and professionalism. To My Friend up above for everyday guidance. To Monga, my first angel. To Vikki, for life.

C.M.

Homecourt
Advantage

Prologue

Casey Rogers squinted her eyes against the white glare as the sun's rays reflected off the still waters. Spectacular was the only way to describe it. The ocean surrounding the small French Polynesian islands of Bora Bora created a magnificent tranquil lagoon ranging in depth from two to thirty feet of crystal clear aquiline water.

Casey felt the strong brown arm around her squeeze even tighter. Peeking up at her husband, she smiled as he placed one hand across her forehead, shielding her eyes from the sun.

Just like my mother used to do when I was a little girl, Casey remembered.

"How's my gorgeous wife doing?" Brent asked her as he bent over and kissed his bride.

Casey could not get enough of him. And now they were on their honeymoon. Her long awaited dream of marrying Brent had finally come true. She opened her mouth and greedily accepted her husband's probing tongue as he sucked her full soft lips and explored her mouth with a burning intensity matched by her own mounting passion. Pulling Brent down beside her, she still could not believe they were actually married.

The newlyweds were lying side by side on the *Indigo Warrior*, a large private white catamaran provided by the Hotel Sofitel, the exclusive, private resort they had chosen for their honeymoon. The captain of the vessel, a short, sundrenched Frenchman named Dominique, had taken Casey and Brent on a shark feeding excursion, stopping at a small remote island to serve them a freshly prepared lunch of quiche, salad, baguettes and chilled chardonay.

Casey leaned in even closer to Brent and had to restrain herself from climbing on top of him. She pulled back from her handsome husband and breathed deeply.

"I better stop before we give Dominique a real show," Casey murmured as she twisted around to see where their guide was standing.

"You better not stop woman. I don't ever want you to quit," Brent began as he grazed Casey's neck with his full lips. "You're Mrs. Rogers now. Nothing is off limits for you. The world is yours if I have anything to say about it."

"Sure, I bet you say that to all the girls. I've seen your teammates in action, even the married ones," Casey teased as she ran her hands over her husband's smooth head. "You better put some more sun block on, you're about to . . ."

"Casey," Brent said as he raised up from her neck and stared directly in her eyes. "Casey, I wouldn't say that to anyone but you. As far as other women are concerned, that's all behind me. I'm serious. That's not what I want for us, baby. I want you by my side forever, just you and me. When I took my vows, I dedicated my life to making you happy."

Tears of joy welled up inside of her.

"And what about you Brent," Casey replied softly. "What is it that you need?"

"Just you Casey. You and your love." Brent cupped her face in his hand and lightly stroked her cheek with his fingers.

Brent's words tugged gently at Casey's heart. One of the qualities that initially attracted Casey to Brent was his honesty. He had a way of expressing himself to her with a naive sincerity that made Casey fiercely protective.

"Do you hear me, Mrs. Rogers?" Brent asked as he lifted Casey's face so that they were eye to eye.

She felt butterflies in her stomach and a love so intense that she actually ached. A memory flashed through her mind and Casey wondered what she would have said if someone had told her just three years ago when she first met Brent in an upper west side antique shop that she would end up loving this man more than life itself.

"I hear you and you know something?" Casey asked her husband. "What?"

"I love you," Casey stated, kissing her husband's fingers as he continued tracing her tanned face with his protective hands.

"I love you, too," Brent said returning her kisses.

Noticing the Frenchman's stare, Casey lightly pushed him away. Brent followed Casey's gaze as she averted her eyes.

"Relax, baby, don't worry about ol' Dominique seeing us," Brent said.

They both turned to each other and tried to hide their laughter as they noticed the captain dangling awkwardly from one of the masts as he tried to get a better view of the couple.

"Maybe we better wait until we get back to the hotel," Brent said keeping one arm wrapped around his wife's slim, toasted-brown waist.

Casey snuggled down against her husband once again and sighed. She had never before in any of her twenty-four years fathomed that being with any one man could make her feel so happy and complete. It scared her to imagine a life without Brent. She was at home and as far as Casey was concerned, he was the perfect fit to her being.

Greenwich, Connecticut, in mid-April was quite a sight, thought Casey Rogers as she climbed the winding driveway to Alexis and Mike Mitchell's estate. This morning Alexis, the coach's wife, was hosting a play-off celebration breakfast for the wives of the New York Flyers basketball team. And as wife of Brent Rogers, the team's star forward, Casey had been summoned not just for the breakfast but also for a prebreakfast chat with Alexis.

Should be a *great* time, Casey thought glumly.

Both Alexis and her husband were used to living more than extravagantly; that much was clear. But Casey also knew that Alexis had not a drop of her own style or creativity: Every inch of the estate was purposefully decorated to allude to some sophisticated place she and her husband had traveled to during the off-season—usually some exotic enclave in Europe. For example, the cedar trees imported from Allegheny, Pennsylvania, lining the driveway created a tableau reminiscent of Tuscany, a favorite off-season vacation spot for the Mitchell family. Casey shook her head. Despite the grandeur of the Mitchell estate and grounds, it lacked warmth. As did Alexis. The sight of this place made Casey yearn for her childhood neighborhood with its green hills and unplanned trees. She could remember playing among the rose garden and cherry trees in her backyard.

But New York was where she lived now, and surprisingly, she liked it. She and her husband lived in a penthouse apartment on Central Park South, and from her city window Casey had a view of the park's trees, lakes, and ponds. She had become used to the noisy city sounds below.

Everything Casey had accomplished in her youth—from being a musical virtuoso, to studying prelaw at the University of Virginia, earning her law degree at Columbia, and achieving partnership at one of New York's most prestigious law firms—had been in order to arrive at a place like New York City so that she could compete with the best in her field. And she'd been a great success professionally.

Then she'd met and married Brent Rogers. The Brent Rogers who was quoted in every morning's sports section. The Brent Rogers who scored an average of 28 points a game. Over the last eight years, her own career had been swept aside in the wake of the life of a superstar athlete's wife. This was not exactly part of her plan. Sometimes she wanted to laugh at the word *plan*. Certainly the coach's wife wanted to believe everything could be planned and controlled. Casey knew differently. The basketball schedule fastened by a magnet to her refrigerator both at home and on her desk at work determined not only each day of Brent's life, but also hers. Her husband's ever-growing celebrity had only increased Casey's lack of control over her own life. They'd become prisoners in their home, hiding from fans, reporters, the ubiquitous paparazzi, venturing out at night only if there was a game or for the occasional outing in the country.

And soon it would get worse.

The one thing Casey hadn't banked on when marrying Brent was that *she* would be forced to make the sacrifices, *she* would be the one to leave her job at the firm and the fancy partnership. Brent needed for her to be available to him and Brent Jr., his son from his college girlfriend who visited them on occasion. Finally she'd cut back hours and offered her expertise privately to clients, many of whom couldn't afford to pay three hundred dollars an hour for a few phone calls. She began working part-time at Volunteer Lawyers for the Arts where she could come and go as suited her husband's schedule. Lately, though, in the last month, she seemed to be back to her seventy-hour work week with two new demanding clients whose cases left her up to her ears in paperwork. What was going on with her? She had a stack of case law to read through and numerous phone calls to return. Why had she consented to meet with Alexis of all people, and at a hectic time like this?

As coach and queen of the New York Flyers for going on nine years, Alexis and Mike were touted not only by the sports media but also by the society papers as New York's Golden Couple. They were both beautiful blondes, and many believed that he was even prettier than she. In his early fifties, he was a more attractive version of Robert Redford, if that was possible. Mike stood a full six feet six inches and had the lean, muscular build of an athlete in his early twenties. Alexis was slender and striking, with wide-set, almond-shaped blue eyes. What really struck Casey was Alexis's unnatural interest in her husband's endeavors. She was obsessed with the Flyers' records and her motto (which, of course, was an echo of her husband), was "Win at all costs." Neither Mike nor Alexis seemed genuinely interested in any aspect of their players' lives; rather, the games took precedence over all else. The Michells had made the team a true partnership: Coach handled the players and Alexis handled the wives.

Two days before, the Flyers had ended the regular season with the best record in the Eastern Conference for the second year running. Now with the play-offs about to start, the real test for the team would begin. Would they finally win it all? But though the Flyers had advanced to the finals for the last three seasons, easily beating all of the other teams along the way, they had never won the championship. Bringing home the NBA championship trophy was the one goal that continued to evade the Flyers.

This would be the subject on Alexis's mind.

"What do you have up your sleeve this time, Ice Queen?" Casey asked aloud in her cobalt blue Jaguar convertible as she finally made her way up the endless driveway and arrived in front of the French Normandy Tudor estate.

Alexis came out the glass doors. "Casey! You look gorgeous, as usual. How *are* you? It seems like *forever* since I've seen you. Take your coat off!" Alexis spoke in a rush as she embraced Casey, withdrew even more quickly, and turned with her coat to an older black servant who had appeared out of nowhere.

As usual, Alexis looked stunning in her ice blue silk Escada blouse and matching slacks. A gold Chanel belt rested against her flat stomach. Her sparkling stone-encrusted Cartier watch and the ten-carat emerald-cut diamond on her finger kept flashing in Casey's eyes as Alexis gesticulated with her hands. Casey still marveled at the sheer extravagance of Alexis's trinkets. It was difficult to discern the woman Alexis really was beneath all of her adornments.

Alexis didn't look a day over thirty-five, though she was actually in her early fifties by Casey's reckoning. Though she was not overdressed, there was something too perfect about the way Alexis was put together; she looked like she was prepared for a tea at the White House. Not a hair moved from her French twist—even the honey color looked natural. Casey was certain that Alexis was not a natural-born blonde: her two brunette daughters gave her away. And Casey suspected that Alexis must have had a hairdresser on call twenty-four/seven.

Once Alexis ceased her flurry with the servant, she turned her blue gaze on Casey, who could feel Alexis's eyes all over her. In true Alexis form, she began at the feet, gazing at the shoes, then made her way slowly up to the clothing, with a slight hesitation at the midsection to determine whether a gut was developing, then to the face to check out the makeup application, and finally to the hair. For those who did not know Alexis's modus operandi, they would think she was either rude or trying to pick them up.

"Lovely. Casey, you just look lovely . . . without ever really trying. How do you manage to constantly pull it off?" Alexis asked, completing her once-over. Casey simply smiled in response. She hadn't yet summoned the energy to deal with Alexis or her verbal barrage.

"Thanks, but I'm actually exhausted. I'm sure I look a mess. I haven't been getting much sleep lately."

Casey had always been uncomfortable receiving compliments, even as a child, especially since she was often referred to as the beauty of the family. The praise somehow made her feel guilty. Now, being married to Brent, she was constantly scrutinized by everyone from his employees to his fans, and she hated being sized up.

"Casey, I know how you feel. The games are so stressful for all of us, but you must get your rest. Brent depends on you to be strong."

"It's not the games, Alexis," Casey said, marveling at Alexis's total fixation on basketball. "It's my job. I've been working long hours lately dealing with my clients and some pretty complicated legal issues."

"Casey," Alexis said, shaking her head. "I don't know why you even bother to work outside of your home. It's obvious that you don't have the time, and I'm sure Brent could use your one hundred percent undivided attention. It's such a crucial time."

Casey's voice didn't change. "Brent will have to settle for what I have to offer. I like what I do, Alexis. I didn't go to college and law school so I could sit home and be Brent Rogers's personal cheerleader. Besides, Brent likes that I have a career of my own."

"Well, I suppose as long as it's acceptable to Brent, it shouldn't pose any problems for the two of you."

Casey shook her head, realizing that it would be futile trying to get Alexis to understand her point of view. Plus, she was far too tired to even try and convince her of anything.

In reality, it would take a great deal of work for Casey to look a "mess" even after three and a half hours of sleep, a scenario becoming even more frequent for her lately. Casey had a fit, long-limbed frame, standing five feet ten inches tall. Her caramel skin was flawless, and her high cheekbones offset her full, pouty lips. Casey had classic smiling eyes set below a thick mane of jet black curly hair. She was apt to underdress in a retro conservative uniform consisting of turtleneck, slacks, and Gucci loafers or boots for almost every occasion.

Casey stifled a yawn. Between the work that she brought home and the nights waiting up for Brent to get home, she was beat. She still had a difficult time sleeping if Brent was not home. She hated to admit—even to herself—that part of her sleeplessness was due to her worries of where Brent was spending his time. His affair a few years ago was still a sore spot, and though Casey told Brent that she'd forgiven, she hadn't forgotten.

As Casey tried to suppress another yawn, she promised herself to make more of an effort to trust Brent. She had to, not only in fairness to their marriage but to herself. If she didn't stop obsessing, she was going to run herself ragged.

"Why don't we go into the morning room where it's more comfortable," Alexis suggested as she led Casey through several lavish yet tastefully decorated period rooms.

Casey felt a bit dizzy as she was led through the maze, each connecting room lovelier than the last. Although she had been to the Mitchells' home before on several occasions, Casey was still astonished at the elegance and aura of her surroundings. When they finally reached the morning room, Casey almost gasped. There were four enormous new eighteenth-century oil paintings on each of the four walls. The ambience made her feel like she was in a museum even if the paintings weren't bona fide treasures. Even the frames were gilded.

The sun highlighted the deep tones of the paintings, as well as the warm yellows and creams of the other furnishings in the room. The cumulative effect of the decor was masterful—both soft and gentle. The brown velvet sofas seemed to be overflowing with down fill, and the window treatments were canary-and-cream-striped works of art made of Scalamandre silk. There was a white marble mantelpiece, adorned with Limoges cherubs which housed roaring fires during the cold winters. Resting also on the fireplace was an exquisite floral arrangement consisting of fresh wild orchids, lilies, and baby's breath. Casey felt intoxicated, despite the cold, harsh presence of Alexis.

"Alexis, this room is exquisite," Casey said.

"It was a labor of love for me. Each room in my home is like an extension of myself," Alexis said, clearing her throat as she motioned for Casey to sit beside her on the sofa, a sure indication she would change the subject quickly. "Casey, we've known each other, what . . . five, six years now, and I feel that I can *trust* you. You've always made Coach and me proud to have you in the Flyers family. You carry yourself well, you're intelligent and articulate, and you're an excellent envoy for your husband."

Alexis dropped her voice conspiratorially. "Now, we both know how important this championship is to the boys." Alexis paused and refolded her hands in her lap.

Casey's toes curled at the description of her husband as a "boy" or any of the players as "boys." The connotations were demeaning and never sat well with her, no matter how often the term was used to describe grown men, especially black ones, as were most of the Flyers players. Casey didn't know how much longer she could take this little tête-à-tête, and she was having a difficult time concentrating on Alexis's pitch. She was about to explode.

"Casey? Casey? Are you following me?" Alexis asked, interrupting her thoughts.

"Yeah," Casey said, trying to hide her distaste.

"Well, do you agree with me?"

Casey shook her head, clearing her thoughts before she answered. "I agree that it's important to carry myself in a dignified manner, but not only for my husband and his team—there are more important reasons." *Like myself,* she wanted to say.

"Of course, Casey, but *my* concerns pertain to a few of the other wives and significant others who are not so—how shall I put it—aware of the delicacies of being involved with a professional athlete. Do you follow what I'm saying?"

"I hear you, Alexis, but I'm not so sure that I know what you're getting at."

"Well, let me put it this way: This is a crucial year for the Flyers for a variety of reasons. With the acquisition of the new players, especially Michael Brown, we are under a lot of pressure to win. We had to give up our top three draft picks for the next four years. But in order to pull it all together we need the cooperation not only of all the players but also their *partners.*" Alexis paused again.

Casey was totally aware that the real reason for her being there in the overstuffed, overgilded room had still not been mentioned.

"I'm not supposed to tell you this, and none of the boys know it yet either. Brent is finding out today at the meeting, but . . ." Alexis stopped in midsentence and looked around the empty room as if someone might be eavesdropping before she continued. "The Flyers will be sold and moved out of New York City if they don't bring home a championship this year."

"What?" Casey looked at Alexis in amazement. Was this one of her tricks?

Alexis continued. "It would be the worst for all of us, *especially* since the lurking buyer is Hightower Enterprises."

Casey knew that not only was Leonard Hightower a bigoted, right-wing zealot, he was also known for acquiring sports teams as if they were toy trains. He treated his players like machines on a southern plantation.

"We've got to bring home the championship! Our boys need complete concentration during the play-offs. They get enough distractions from outside sources; they don't need to get it from home too! We need to be on our jobs."

"What exactly are you saying, Alexis?"

"It's really quite simple, dear. The Flyers women need to stay out of the way. We should not be asking to meet our mates on the road for away games. You know how that can be such a distraction. And at home, the women need to stay in the background, and, Casey, I need your help to get through to them on this. You can teach them better than I can. I'm hoping you can help them get involved with activities of their own. Maybe then they won't be so eager to disturb the boys. Do you think you could handle that, Casey?"

"Boys" again! Who the hell did Alexis think she was?

Casey swallowed hard before she answered, reminding herself that she was talking to her husband's boss's wife. Very carefully she said: "First, I don't know how I can motivate the other wives to get involved in independent activities. That's a personal decision; I can't be responsible for their lives. Second, I have a career, Alexis, and I don't have time to play house mother."

"I know you can't change their outlooks on life, Casey. That would be like getting water from a rock, but they admire you. If you could just get them to understand that this is a do-or-die season, then maybe they'd be willing to cooperate," Alexis said in her syrupy voice.

"What are you proposing?"

"I want to encourage the ladies to arrive at the home games on time dressed in presentable attire, and I want to make sure that no outbursts occur with any of the fiancées or girlfriends during the play-offs. I want to ensure that the ladies are up to par on their etiquette. We'll have a few public engagements, and I want to avoid any embarrassments. Whatever their personal problems may be, they can wait until after the season has ended. I think that's a small price to pay for a championship title and the team remaining at the Mecca Arena where it belongs. I think you know better than anyone how to get through to them."

Casey was speechless at her audacity. She knew that Alexis was prone to outrageousness, but this approached the ridiculous. Everyone was supposed to forget that they have a personal life and instead center their lives around the Flyers. *Yeah, right.*

"Excuse me, Mrs. Mitchell." A servant appeared, interrupting them. "A few other ladies have arrived and the parlor is properly prepared."

Casey watched as Alexis jumped from the sofa and straightened her clothing. She then readjusted her diamond charm bracelet. Casey followed suit, feeling disgusted and defeated knowing that Alexis held all of the cards. That was usually the case with her and Coach.

"Casey, I need to know if you're with me on this."

Casey reluctantly nodded her head before she answered Alexis. "I'll see what I can do," she said, feeling as if she had made a pact with the devil. But what could she do? Her husband, her marriage—both were involved.

"Wonderful!" Alexis beamed, changing face once again. "Oh and there's one more thing. I'm glad to see that you and Brent have finally worked out your problems, especially about the little girl."

"Excuse me?" Casey said.

"I saw Brent with the little girl and, I believe, her mother in Boston."

"What?" Casey felt the floor dropping beneath her.

"She's really a precious little thing. Brent looked so proud. He really dotes on her. I'm glad you can be generous enough to let him involve her in his life. You're a fine example." Then Alexis walked away to greet the other women as they filed into the living room.

Casey found her way into the circular parlor and requested a cup of espresso from one of the women dressed in black and white. How was she going to make it through the breakfast? Alexis had just told her, basically, that Brent had violated his promise to her: he'd seen Nikki and her mother, Shauna—Casey's nemesis.

Casey stared at the large round mahogany table with lace place mats. The table was decorated with a silver candelabra and set-tings for a nine-course meal. Freshly squeezed orange juice had already been poured into each glass at the table, and a fruit bowl was sitting in the cen-ter of each setting.

A buffet of delicacies was spread across a marble server: salmon, tuna, poached eggs, bagels, muffins, and croissants circled an ice sculpture shaped like a giant basketball. Casey was not sure how many women were coming, but she was certain that even if they stayed for breakfast, lunch, and dinner, they could not put a dent into this spread of food.

At the entrance to the parlor, Casey watched the familiar faces file in. All of the women were wearing Rolex watches and tennis bracelets, with Gucci or Chanel purses draped across their shoulders. Most of the women also wore some sort of massive diamond ring. This included Casey, to her sudden embarrassment. A couple of them were tiptoeing around as if they were afraid they might break something.

All of the mates were decked out in the latest designer fashions, ranging from Prada dresses to Armani pantsuits. All except Trina Belleville. Of course, she was the wife most out of place. She obviously could care less about the tags inside her clothes or the style atop her head. Trina's slightly graying hair looked like she had just removed the sponge rollers moments before and had forgotten to comb through the clumps. Casey could only imagine what Alexis was thinking about Trina's appearance. It was only a matter of time before she commented on it.

Casey felt sick. She was not in a particularly sociable mood as she sorted out her feelings about Brent and his daughter, Nikki, and Nikki's mother, Shauna. Casey watched as Alexis worked the room. She knew when to pat a hand and when to nod, albeit condescendingly, as she feigned interest in some conversation or another. The coach's wife had a plastic smile glued on her face as she sauntered around the parlor, directing her staff and entertaining her guests. Casey wondered if the other women noticed. They all seemed to stiffen when Alexis neared them, fearful of making one wrong move. Casey knew how they felt. And yet, against her better judgment, she was about to follow Alexis's plan for these unsuspecting victims. She really had no choice. Not as long as Brent was a Flyer and under the thumb of Alexis's husband, known simply as Coach.

She thought again about Brent and his affair. When he had confessed to having had a one-night stand with some anonymous groupie weeks after the fact, Brent had seemed genuinely remorseful. And after a few months, Casey had finally gotten to the point that she was willing to forgive him. Then suddenly he'd been hit with a paternity suit. Brent tried to convince Casey that this kind of thing happened all the time to professional athletes; there were women out there who pur-

posefully got pregnant in order to go after an athlete's money. Casey knew this was true, but it wasn't a compelling defense for his major screwup. Though Shauna might have targeted him, his actions were unjustifiable.

The blood tests had proved with 99 percent certainty that Brent was the father of the little girl. Fearful that the woman would go public, Brent had settled to keep her quiet. Throughout the entire debacle Casey stuck with Brent despite feeling as if her heart were being ripped to shreds. Out of respect for Casey and their marriage, he had promised not to have any contact with the woman or the child other than providing financial support.

Casey still loved her husband with a fierceness she did not know was possible, but it was a daily challenge for her to believe in him again. Sometimes she longed to be back in Virginia, the home of her childhood and young-adult memories, and escape from the feelings of pain and betrayal she had been confronted with during her New York years.

Casey's mama had always said, "A cat may stray, but it always comes back home." And as long as they were willing to genuinely rectify their wrongs, her mama felt men should be given another chance. Undoubtedly this was why Casey's mom had always been called the Queen Settler, a title Casey was not eager to inherit. If her mother had any idea of some of the bad choices Brent had made, Casey wondered if she would be so quick to forgive. Her mother obviously assumed that Brent's faults were as harmless as forgetting to put the toilet seat down or not cleaning up the kitchen after himself. And even though her mother might imagine that Brent had been unfaithful, she would never believe that he had fathered a little girl by a random groupie. She would be shocked.

Casey wished she could recapture the sense of hope that she had had when she married Brent six years ago. Lately, Brent was always, it seemed, either out late at meetings or on the road. Since his affair, she had a problem trusting him during these times. Whenever he traveled to an away game, Casey could not completely shake the feeling that he might cheat on her again. She longed for the serenity of when they were first together. It used to be a given that he would be faithful. Now she was constantly plagued with doubts. It had gotten better, but there was always that lingering fear in her mind that Brent might slip.

And what was worse, after the hell Casey had experienced, she realized how little she knew about herself. Brent's indiscretion had brought out Casey's hidden "paranoia," her insecurities. Inside herself she discovered previously unexplored weaknesses—some of them not so pretty. Casey longed to be at peace.

Brent stepped off the elevator and glanced down at the platinum Cartier hanging loosely on his wrist. Swearing softly to himself, he walked quickly down the Mecca Arena's long hallway. This was one meeting Brent did not want to be late for, especially if the topic of discussion had anything to do with his contract with the New York Flyers. When Brent had opened the FedEx letter late yesterday afternoon, he had immediately paged his agent, Jake Schneider, demanding to know if any trade rumors had surfaced. Although Brent knew the trade deadline had already passed back in February, he was also well aware of the workings of the NBA. The player was usually the last person to know about decisions made that would affect his career. And the place he lived. At first Brent had wondered if the meeting had anything to do with the play-offs, like the meeting his wife, Casey, was attending this morning at his coach's house. Then, to Brent's surprise, Jake had informed him that he had also received an invite to the meeting and assured his star client that he had no idea why the Flyers' owner, Hal Hirshfield, wanted to meet with them.

The smell of fresh paint in anticipation of the play-offs combined with stale lingering food aromas permeated the air of the Mecca hallways. Brent could feel the anxiety building within him as he approached the doors to the Arena's office suites.

The Hirshfield family had owned the New York Flyers for the past fifty years. The Mecca had been built in 1948 and was the team's first and only home. Although Brent had never played for any other NBA team, he had heard the horror stories of other teams and appreciated the style with which the Flyers were run. The Flyers management techniques were clearly a reflection of Hal Hirshfield. Hal was in charge of his family's estate and was the key decision maker for the Flyers' daily operations. As Brent was ushered through Hal's private suites, he admired the paneled oak surroundings and was reminded of the grace of the Hirshfield family.

Hal Hirshfield was the patriarch of a multigenerational family of Eastern European Jews. Hirshfield loved to tell his family's stories, usually after a few Scotch and sodas on those rare occasions when he traveled with the team. His grandfather had been a Lower East Side peddler, selling anything customers would buy, "on time." Fifty cents held a lot of merchandise on layaway. Brent had seen Hal in action enough times to know that Hal Hirshfield was a true gentleman in every sense of the word, and he respected Hal's uncanny knack for making those around him feel important. He gracefully held himself high above the manipulative male chauvinism inherent among the other NBA league owners. His respect for the players and fans alike, coupled with his genuine love for the game, made Hal Hirshfield the ultimate team owner.

Brent glanced at his watch once again as he stepped into the conference room. It was 11:30 sharp. He was right on time.

"Brent, come on in. How are you?" Hal stood up and walked around the table to shake Brent's hand.

"Hello, Hal. It's good to see you." Brent gave Hal a quick hug and clapped him on the back.

"Hey, Coach. How's it going?" Brent reached across the table and greeted the Flyers' coach, Mike Mitchell, with an easy high five.

"Jake, any room over here?" Brent asked as he pulled out the chair next to his agent.

Jake looked like a caricature with his thick toupee and tortoiseshell glasses as a puff of smoke from his Cuban cigar rose above him. He gave Brent's shoulder a quick squeeze. "There's always room for my favorite client."

"Yeah, yeah, that's what they all say until the new guy comes along," Brent responded, only half jokingly.

"Brent, you remember Tom Lenko, the Flyers' attorney?" Hal asked, pointing at the suave man with the slicked-back hair neatly parted on the side.

"Of course. He made you look like the nice guy while he did all your dirty work renegotiating my contract last year. How could I ever forget? Jake was there, he can testify; you guys even made him look bad." Brent laughed. Every man there knew nothing could be further from the truth—no one could "make" Jake look bad.

"Come now, Brent," Hal said with a wink. "You don't have to worry about your contract for years to come. I think it's fair to say that you got everything you asked for."

"Touché, Hal," Jake said, adjusting his glasses.

"Listen," Hal said, obviously anxious to get down to business. "I asked each of you to come here today because there's something extremely confidential and important I need to discuss with you. I've already mentioned some of this to Coach and I trust that what I say here today will go no further than this room." Hal stopped talking and looked around the table, making sure everyone met his eye. "If what I'm about to tell you gets leaked to the media, the Flyers could lose all of their corporate sponsors overnight."

Brent had never seen Hal so somber. The other men looked as confused as he was.

"I'm sure you're all familiar with Hightower Enterprises," Hal said as he looked around the table.

"Isn't that the group that just made an offer for TCI?" Coach asked no one in particular as he stood up from the table and nonchalantly walked toward the buffet.

"Actually, it was a joint offer to TCI and ITT, and though neither company has accepted as yet, they haven't rejected the offer either," explained Tom, looking every bit the Ivy Leaguer Brent knew he was.

"Wait a second, is that the same Hightower Enterprises that owns the Wolverine football team?" Jake asked, putting his cigar down.

"Yes, it's all one and the same. Apparently Hightower is now interested in owning a basketball team. They've approached Hal with an offer to buy the Flyers."

Coach Mitchell and Jake focused their attention on Tom at the head of the table as his words began to sink in. No one stared harder than Brent.

He felt as if his world were rocking around him.

"You can't be serious, Hal. Sell the Flyers? The New York Flyers? You and your family have owned the team for fifty years. Why would you want to sell us—especially to Hightower?" Brent demanded. "The players, hell, the entire team, the Hirshfield history, would get lost in a conglomerate like Hightower Enterprises. And," Brent continued, "let's not fool ourselves; we've all heard the rumors about the racist asshole who runs that show. What's his name? Leo or something like that."

"His name is Leonard Hightower," Hal said. "Listen, please be patient with me while I explain everything. There's no way to make any of this look any better than it is, so just hear me out and try to understand exactly what is going on here. The Hirshfields have always supported ownership of the Flyers. Over the years the team has proved itself to be much more than just a fanciful whim of my grandfather, God rest his soul. The team turned out to be a damn good investment. But times have changed and so have many of the tax breaks and city financing programs. Today the team is barely running itself, and the operating costs are eating up whatever profits the team generates. I'm really left with few options."

The conference room was thick with silence. The young Ivy League attorney cleared his throat and pushed his chair back from the table.

"This is really difficult for Hal. Maybe I can help put some of this into perspective. There is no way for Hal to continue operating the Flyers without a profit margin. The Hirshfield estate is subject to numerous trusts. Each trust has relevant conditions stipulating the rules and guidelines for using the funds. The funds allotted for ownership of the Flyers are regulated by the Flyers management, but only if the team operates at a profit. The moment the Flyers begin to cost more than they're worth, the trust mandates the present owner to place the team on the auction block. In other words, even if Hal wanted to help run the team with his personal funds, the trust guidelines would not allow for this. This was done to protect all future Hirshfield heirs from having the principal of the Hirshfield estate invaded."

"I don't understand, Hal. This is ridiculous. I'm not about to sit back and let this happen. Maybe Hightower can manipulate you but he can't touch me or my team." Brent, usually cool and collected, was visibly upset and not willing to accept the idea of selling the team . . . the team he was captain of, the team he helped build into a championship contender.

"How much money are we talking about here? Can't the players chip in and help out?" Brent looked to Coach for backup, but he seemed to be lost in his own thoughts.

"Sorry, Brent," Tom replied, "but your union rules don't allow for active NBA players to have ownership of any NBA team. You're either a player or an owner. You can't be both."

"Hal." The agent waited for the older man to look at him. "Isn't there some other viable option here? We've all heard rumors about Leonard Hightower. He's an asshole and he doesn't have an ounce of respect for athletes."

Everyone in the room did a double take at Jake's last comment, especially Brent. Even though Jake was one of the finest negotiators in the business, he was notorious for treating his basketball players like childrens in virtually every aspect of their lives. Brent was one of the few athletes who didn't tolerate being Jakized.

"And," Jake continued as he adjusted his Hermés tie, "he treats his other employees worse. He dictates to those around him and could care less about his employees or their families. Remember when the papers ran that story a couple of years ago about the coal miner from West Virginia who died in an accident in one of Hightower's mines? Hightower got away with paying his widow a cash payment of ten thousand dollars in exchange for her signing away her rights to that poor guy's survivor's insurance policy, which was worth over a million dollars. And what about the two Wolverine football players that were waived from the team when they leaked those rumors to the media about Hightower's support of the Southern Christian Coalition and David Duke? If you must sell, can't you at least solicit other offers?"

Brent stared at Jake as his glasses shifted down on his nose and wondered why he seemed so concerned. It was not like him to take things such as personal or ethical issues into account. Brent had often found his agent ruthless—sometimes more than he felt comfortable with—and although Jake was not a racist, at least not overtly so, Brent knew he held his own stereotypes regarding athletes and the business of professional sports.

Then it hit Brent. Jake was dead set against a Hightower takeover because Leonard Hightower was renowned as a hard-ass negotiator. Since Jake currently represented four of the Flyers' top players as well as Coach, he was protecting his own selfish interests. The last thing Jake wanted was a lethal battle when he went up to bat for his clients.

"Jake, actually a couple of other offers have floated our way, but each time we acknowledged receipt of the offers, they were withdrawn," Tom explained. "We heard from a reliable source that Hightower has put the word out on the street that the Flyers are his and if anyone dares to get in his way, he'll crush them."

Coach cleared his throat, drawing everyone's attention. "This all seems like a bad movie. Who does this guy think he is, the Godfather or something?"

Brent found the whole situation unbelievable. "I don't even see why a good ole southern boy like Hightower would be interested in an urban, Yankee team like the Flyers. It just doesn't make sense."

"It does if you have money to burn and an ego that requires constant nourishment." Hal clasped his hands together firmly and looked around the table with intense wizened eyes that were weighted down with more than the layers of age. "The bottom line is, I cannot afford to continue running the Flyers under the city's present terms, and believe me, Hightower knows the position I'm in. Let's face it, owning and operating a professional sports team in the Big Apple is big business. I'm certainly not getting any younger, and aside from a few spoiled nieces and nephews whom I love dearly, there's not even a Hirshfield in line who would be interested enough to take on owner-ship of the Flyers. I believe it's time to hand over the reins and let the team be run the way it deserves."

Brent was shocked. He couldn't accept Hal throwing in the towel, not on something as crucial as this. "Come on, Hal," Brent began in des-peration. "What if we could get all the guys to defer some of their salaries? Give you time to get things taken care of?"

"Brent, that's very kind of you, but I would never ask any of the players to do something like that. You guys deserve every penny you get for what you bring to the city, and I know I shouldn't admit this in front of Jake, but a few of you deserve even more than what you're get-ting paid. I'd be doing you guys a disservice to hold on to the team, because there would be little room for expansion or increased salaries under the salary cap rules."

Even though Brent held a B.A. in business from Duke University, he didn't need it to know that his agent was ultimately concerned with the best business deal, no matter how it affected his players' private lives. Brent watched Jake perk up at the mention of increased salaries and was not surprised when Jake asked Hal to explain the exact terms of the offer.

"Well," Hal began, "Hightower Enterprises has offered an obscene amount of money for the team. And as much as I hate to admit it, as far as my attorneys and advisers are concerned, that's really the bottom line for them pushing me in this direction. But from what I've heard, Hightower plans on building a brand-new state-of-the-art arena, buy-ing a new team jet, and offering a chauffeured car service for each player to and from the home games. We all know the Mecca is way past its day. We've needed a major renovation for the past twenty years."

"Well, that sounds like the first good news I've heard today," Coach Mitchell said with wide eyes. "I think he did that with the Wolverine football team."

Hal looked over at the lawyer, and Brent noticed the silent com-munication between the two. Tom accepted his cue and once again performed Hal's dirty work.

"There is one last part to this offer," Tom began. "It's probably the only negative part of the deal."

"It can't be any worse than having to work for Leonard High-tower," Brent muttered.

"Hightower Enterprises plans on relocating the Flyers to Albany, New York," Tom said, taking a deep breath.

"Oh, hell, no!" Brent shouted as his temples throbbed. He shot up from his chair and turned to Hal, enraged. "This is un-fucking-believable! Move the team? Hal, come on! It's one thing to put us up for sale, but move the Flyers to Albany? You can't even be considering that asshole's offer. The fans would never forgive you and every local sponsor would pull out so fast, they'd leave our heads spinning. And you know what else. I can guarantee you, the players would never forgive you either. The Flyers are New York. You might as well ship us off to Siberia!"

"Brent, Brent, come on, that's enough," Jake said. "Let's not get too upset. The Flyers haven't been sold yet, and you know Hal would never do anything to hurt you guys," Jake said in an obvious attempt to smooth things over.

"It's not about whether or not Hal's trying to hurt us. Nobody said Hal is trying to hurt us." Brent jammed his hands in his pockets and started pacing back and forth behind the table.

He knew he had to regroup. The Flyers were not going to be sold. It couldn't happen, not to his team. Brent began to feel fueled by his anger. Nobody was going to move the New York City Flyers. The city would be devastated by the loss. And although it wasn't Brent's main concern, most of his teammates would be hit hard in the pockets. Brent, as the captain of the Flyers, knew that he spoke for his teammates, who were conveniently excluded from this private meeting.

"How could it not hurt all of the players?" Brent started. "Besides the whole team's life being turned upside down, which is hurtful enough, most of us have endorsement deals, some worth millions of dollars, that would be yanked away the moment we left Manhattan. Hell, we're in the marketing capital of the world, and you think our being moved to Albany won't hurt us? Think again . . . And what about the city? How much money does the city stand to lose if they no longer have a pro basketball team attracting thousands of people into the city three to four days a week?"

"If the city cares that much, then they should cut the Flyers some breaks, but they're not doing that, Brent," the lawyer said. "The city will only step in when it's going to work in its favor and improve its public image. Hightower, on the other hand, has some major holdings in Albany. Hell, he probably owns the city. He's guaranteed to make a fortune even if the Flyers' profits suffer."

Brent saw Coach come to attention at the mention of public image. Everything was about perception to the debonair Flyers coach, whether it be the image the ruthless New York City sports writers depicted of Coach Mitchell or how the other coaches in the NBA viewed him. Coach wanted to conduct his orchestra in only one way— his own. And he had to look perfect doing it.

"Improve its image, huh?" Coach began, running his manicured hands through his curly grayish blond hair. "So has the city offered any type of . . . of financial assistance?"

Tom looked again at Hal, but this time Hal spoke first. "Look, everyone, if I don't turn a profit with the Flyers soon, my family estate will take any decisions about the team out of my hands. What Tom was referring to came out of a meeting with a couple of city officials last week. There's no guarantee in it, though."

"Hal, if there is something, anything, that the Flyers could do to avoid being sold, then damn it, tell us . . . please!" Whatever was in his power to keep the Flyers together in his city, Brent knew he would do.

"If, and some might consider it a big *if*, the Flyers were to bring home a championship this year, the city would be amenable to financing fifty-five percent of the Arena's operating costs and would issue a couple of municipal bonds to the Flyers which would decrease some of our major tax-related expenses." Hal sat back in his chair and placed his hands on the table.

"As much business and revenue that we've brought to the city already, you mean to tell me that the city will only help us out if we win the championship this season, as in at the end of this season's play-offs?" Brent asked.

"Afraid so, Brent," Jake began. "It's politics . . . The city might be nice enough to help us out of the kindness of its heart, but minus a championship, every department in the city would have something to say about it. Housing would be pissed off because they'll claim that the funds should have gone to a housing development project. Welfare would cite their statistics and point out all the unemployed people the money could have gone to. Education will cite the ten city schools it had to close down last year because of insufficient funding, and so on. On the other hand, if we bring home the ring, we make enough people in other departments happy, like in transportation and tourism."

"Hal, you know better than anybody what kind of team we have this year. It's the best squad we've had in years . . . hell, since I've been a Flyer. I think we can really do it this year. I'm confident enough that we have the best team in the NBA. Can't you wait until the play-offs are at least over to give Hightower his answer?" Brent asked, looking at Hal hopefully.

The weary owner of the Flyers locked eyes with Brent. "Listen, I don't have to respond immediately to Hightower Enterprises, but I do know that the longer I take to accept their offer, the more risk I run of them withdrawing it. At least under Hightower's ownership I could rest assured that the Flyers would have everything the team deserves."

"Maybe in your eyes, Hal. But from a player's point of view, this sucks. Working for someone like Hightower would be a nightmare. His ego is gigantic. And Lord knows we already have enough big egos in this business," Brent said, envisioning Hightower's abuse of them already. "Hightower would probably expect us to be at his two-year-old's birthday party dressed in our uniforms shooting baskets with his drunk racist friends who'd call the police on us if they spotted us in their neighborhoods on any other occasion. It won't work, Hal. People will get hurt and more than a few careers will be ruined before someone like Hightower tires of us and moves on to his next project. You know it just as well as I do. Stop trying to fool yourself into thinking you're making the right decision."

Hal looked down at his age-spotted hands. Brent noticed once again how old and tired Hal actually was. The lines in Hal's face showed every one of his sixty-eight years, and Brent found himself feeling sorry for the owner. Hal had always been there for him ever since the Flyers drafted him nine years ago. Unlike most of the other team owners, Hal had extended friendship to each and every New York Flyer. He had always maintained an open-door policy with the players. He even helped some of them out with personal problems.

But Brent couldn't allow his concern for Hal's health to override his concern for his teammates. "Hal, I'm begging you. Just hold off for a little while and let Coach and me take care of the team . . . please."

Brent caught Coach's eye for backup, knowing this added challenge would be right up his alley. Winning was everything to Coach, especially with such high stakes.

Hal looked hard at Brent and turned to Mike Mitchell. "Mike, are you with him on this?"

"Winning an NBA championship isn't a new goal for me or Brent. Have a little faith in us. We might surprise you."

Hal looked at his lawyer, who shrugged his shoulders.

Hal covered his face with his hands and took several deep breaths. Looking up, he said, "Brent, Mike, I'll give you some time. I can't say just how much time. Hightower is putting pressure on me to close the deal right away. But I'll keep him and his sharks at bay for as long as I can." Hal looked doubtful as he continued. "In the meantime, I wish you luck. You have a difficult task ahead."

The next six weeks would be hell.

Kelly was on fire. How dare Steve try to shut her out!
Everyone knew the Flyers reserved their tickets to play-off games for
their nearest and dearest. How did he expect her to see the game without giving her a ticket? She couldn't simply go to the box
office and purchase a ticket—play-off tickets to
the Flyers games were the hottest items in
New York City. Be- yond that, even if she
bought a ticket, her name would have to
be on a special list in order to get into the
Flyers Family Lounge— after all, she was still
Steve's fiancée!

At least she still boasted the rock he'd given her. She
comforted herself with this thought for a moment, then her anger took
fire again. What would the other wives think if she didn't show up for
the first game of the play-offs? Everyone was probably already wondering why she hadn't been at Alexis's breakfast. It would be doubly
humiliating if she wasn't at the first play-off game.

Steve was going to have hell to pay when she caught up with him!

She stood in front of her floor-to-ceiling, wall-to-wall mirrored closets, alternately pacing and staring at her own reflection—the face and body most men would kill to have for themselves. She needed to look especially hot tomorrow night. That was for sure. Steve was up to something. Probably he had invited one of his bitches to the game and he didn't want to risk Kelly running into them and ruining their evening. Well, she had a surprise for him! She'd get into the Mecca if it was the last thing she did.

She was not going to let him get away with dissin' her like this. After all, there was Diamond to consider. Besides, Kelly knew she was fine as hell. If Steve had any sense, he should recognize that she was more than enough woman for him. She would be a prize to most guys with her glowing complexion and large ebony eyes.

Kelly made weekly visits to a tanning salon to enhance her already cocoa-colored skin with a bronze glow. She kept her thick, wavy hair in a close-cropped fade that accentuated her swanlike neck. She slaved at the gym with a personal trainer to maintain her perfect size-six figure, working out five times a week, combining an hour of weight lifting with an additional hour of aerobics. Though no one would consider her a Barbie doll beauty, she knew her one real attribute was her raw sexual appeal. She was capable of seducing almost anyone, man or woman, with a lick of her full, sensuous lips and a wink of her teasing eyes.

It stung that she had not been invited to Alexis's play-off commencement breakfast. Kelly was forced to hear about it three days afterward from another player's wife.

She'd been included in the last gathering at Alexis's house for the wives' annual X-mas gift-wrapping party. Kelly didn't know who was responsible for this slight, but she did know that it was not the type of disrespect she would tolerate for too much longer.

Was it *possible* that Steve told Alexis not to send her an invitation? Were they conspiring against her? If he had gone that far to ensure that she was excluded, the only reason could be that he had someone else substituting for her—or worse, taking her place permanently. No way! Kelly became enraged envisioning someone else being with *her* Steve Tucker of the New York Flyers. Whoever that woman was, she couldn't possibly know Steve like Kelly knew him, nor would she ever, if Kelly could help it.

Steve's patterns were usually predictable to Kelly, especially when they involved other women, but this time Steve had gone off the path of their comfort zone. He was trying to exclude her from a world she helped him enter. A world she had a right to. She should be at the Mecca Arena tonight enjoying the fruits of their labor with him.

Despite her anger, Kelly was truly concerned. Though Kelly and Steve had been engaged for two and a half years, and had been together for five more, no wedding date was in sight. And the way things were going, she wasn't sure there would be one. Steve owned a mansion, which Kelly took care of, though at any given time, if Steve chose, he could force her out with no warning. Not that he'd ever have the nerve to do that. He might have threatened her with eviction every now and then, but that was as far as it went. He didn't have the balls. Just in case, Kelly had been putting away some of the weekly allowance Steve had been giving her over the years, and she now had saved a sizable mad-money account. But Kelly knew enough about her taste; the cash she saved would not be enough to sustain the lifestyle she had become accustomed to. Kelly had an additional cushion: her daughter, Diamond. No matter what happened, Steve was crazy about the little girl. Kelly did not believe that she was using her daughter, she simply looked at it as watching her back—she had to. As far as Kelly was concerned, Diamond would attend only the very best schools and have all of the opportunities she never had. And Steve would help her.

Reluctantly Kelly thought back to their last meeting over a month ago. Steve had stopped by the house. Kelly had prepared a romantic candlelit dinner, put on her sexiest lingerie, and was ready and waiting to reel him in again. But Steve had only accompanied her upstairs to tuck in the sleepy-eyed Diamond and kiss her goodnight. "This is how it could be every night, if you'd just let us get married and move in here for real."

"I told you, Kelly, that's not going to happen. Drop it."

"You just need more time."

"No, Kelly, I don't need more time. My decision is final. I'm not marrying you—ever. I told you that you can stay in the house until the end of the year and then you'll have to find your own home."

"But what about Diamond?"

"I can love Diamond and still leave you."

As quickly as Kelly replayed the conversation in her mind, she pushed the scene away. She'd figure out what to do about Steve. He just needed to come to his senses, and he would.

Kelly had been with him since the beginning when the only *Air* in his gym shoes came through the holes. Now that he was rich and famous, he had forgotten where he came from and who had climbed with him up that ladder of success, with Kelly sometimes carrying him on her back. She and Steve had their share of troubles, but all couples went through ebbs and flows. Didn't he remember what she'd done for him?

Kelly had dropped out of the community college she was attending in Atlanta after only one semester to make extra money working full-time to help out Steve's family. The National Collegiate Athletic Association regulations had prohibited Steve from working, and the money he received from his scholarship was not enough to help his physically disabled mother and younger brothers and sisters. Kelly was the one who'd taken up the slack in order to help make ends meet for all of them. She'd treated his family like her own until Steve was drafted by the Flyers five years ago. Never had she questioned her role in his life until now.

Kelly paced back and forth over her plush taupe throw rug, stomping a foot in rage with each stride, thinking about how Steve was dogging her.

He could hit her with his best shot, but Kelly was going to be at the Mecca tomorrow night. She knew what to do. Casey would get her a seat. Kelly knew what a softy Casey was when it came to children. She was going to go over to Casey's this morning, with Diamond on her hip. Casey wouldn't have the heart to refuse Kelly and the baby. And with Casey's thousand-dollar seats at the Mecca, there Kelly would be, front and center—play-off opening night! Steve couldn't stop her.

"He's not going to squeeze me out like this! No way! I'm going to that game, and he better not have some young ho in his seats." Kelly scowled at her reflection in the mirror.

She started going through her racks of clothes, throwing designer ensembles on the bed. She held up a black Gianni Versace sleeveless zippered jumpsuit that exposed her most generous assets: surgically enhanced breasts and a taut rear end.

Kelly had relied on her sexual power for years, and if that failed her now, then she'd think of something else; she always did. But what she would not do was lose her lifestyle or her man. She had invested too much hard work pushing them both to the top. If he chose to cut her loose, she wouldn't go without a fight, and she definitely had no intention of going down by herself.

"Oh, I guess you don't even need to be announced, with your late self," Casey said between mouthfuls of cake as she removed Remy's vintage leather jacket.

"I guess not," Remy shot back, as she stepped off the elevator into her friend's foyer. "Besides, I'm not that late. It's only two-thirty," she said, glancing at her watch.

"Humph, I guess some of us just got it like that, huh."

"I guess so," Remy said, quickly cutting her eyes at Casey.

"I know I didn't see you roll your eyes at me."

"And what if you did? You gonna sic Alexis on me too?"

Casey couldn't stop herself from bursting into laughter. The two women were on the same wavelength concerning Alexis's meddlesome presence in their lives, but they also recognized the role she played in both their men's livelihoods.

"Damn right; you had no business missing Alexis's breakfast. You know she was educating us poor ignorant souls on the ways of the civilized world."

"Oh, daahhling, do forgive my faux pas," Remy began, switching to a mock English accent. "Sometimes my social skills regress so, but thank goodness we all have Mrs. Coach to enlighten us."

"You should be grateful to her."

"Yeah, just like the pimple on my ass," Remy said, dropping the fake accent.

Hanging up Remy's jacket, Casey continued to smile thinking about their relationship. She knew the two of them had to air all of their most vile thoughts about Alexis, and anything else, for that matter, before they joined the rest of the women in Casey's library. Lorraine, Trina, and Dawn were not privy to the private conversations Casey and Remy regularly shared. Casey felt she had an image to uphold as the quasi-leader of the wives of the New York Flyers, and Remy Baltimore, being on the cover of *People* every six months, had a difficult time letting her guard down.

Casey and Remy were each other's best friends. They both turned to one another for refuge from their own harsh expectations as well as the world's. Together they were completely at ease, and no topic of discussion was off-limits. Nothing was taken personally between the two women as they both knew every word exchanged was coming from a place of love—even when they mercilessly teased one another.

Casey crossed her arms over her chest and began tapping her Gucci-clad foot on the marble floor as Remy ran her fingers through her jet black straight hair.

"Would you come on, girl? Aren't you late enough?" Casey said, grabbing Remy's arm.

"I told you I had rehearsal for my "Happiness Is Divine" video. You should be glad I made time for y'all," Remy said, flicking her wrist in front of Casey's face.

"Oooh, so it's like that now," Casey began, giggling as she turned toward the long corridor that led them through her fourteen-room Central Park South penthouse. "I'm gonna tell them what you said. You know they already think you're a prima donna as it is."

"Casey! Don't you go in there playin' around and embarrass me."

"Whatever are you talking about, dear?" Casey said with a wicked grin.

"You know exactly what I mean."

As the two ladies walked through the wide hallway with the marbleized walls adorned by original Ernie Barnes paintings and Romare Bearden collages, Casey knew exactly what Remy meant. She had come to realize over the years that Remy avoided talking about her work with most people. Remy never basked in her own limelight. She regularly rubbed elbows with more stars than all of them combined would ever meet in their lifetimes, but she would rather discuss Trina's latest recipe or Lorraine and Dawn's work at the hospital than even mention her video shoot with the four hottest young male models in the industry.

As Casey and Remy entered the library, all of the women looked at Remy's slender physique silhouetted in the doorway. Trina had gotten comfortable and kicked up her thick, shoeless feet on the brown leather chaise lounge. Dawn and Lorraine were sitting around the mosaic tile coffee table on the suede sofa, drinking coffee, undoubtedly swapping hospital stories. The samplings of sweets Trina had baked were almost gone.

"Hello, ladies. Sorry I'm late. You know how midtown traffic can be this time of the day," Remy said, walking toward Lorraine and Dawn as they stood up.

True to form, Remy mentioned nothing about the video. Casey watched Remy kiss the two women and then head over to a stretched-out Trina, who made no effort to budge from her seat. Trina looked bloated and exhausted leaning back in the chaise as Remy bent down and greeted her in kind.

"Don't even worry about it," Trina began, sounding every bit like the wise fourteen-year NBA veteran wife she was. "You know what your girl brought everyone here for; you're not missing anything."

Casey had already briefed Remy on what she planned to talk to the women about, swearing her to secrecy when she told her about the threat to sell the Flyers. Her best friend knew what a precarious position Alexis had placed her in. Remy, Dawn, and Lorraine had been no-shows at Alexis's breakfast meeting three days ago, and Casey now had been assigned to pass on Alexis's message. Although Trina *had* attended the gathering, Alexis had been mortified by her appearance, pulling Casey aside to say that Trina looked "slovenly and tacky." She believed Trina was in dire need of extra "coaching" on improving her image.

"Mrs. Coach's breakfast was a waste of everybody's time," said Trina. "I heard her and Coach been playin' those trifling mind games for years, especially at play-off time. Now she's just tryin' to get Casey to do her dirty work."

It wasn't as if Casey could blame Trina for feeling that way, but then again, Trina wasn't in her position. Of course, Casey was still trying to figure what exactly her position was. She knew her concern for Brent's career was a major part of it, but she was beginning to wonder if even that was worth manipulating her friends.

"God, Casey, no matter how many times I come over here, the view always amazes me, especially on a day like this," Remy said, walking toward the library's large picture window.

Casey realized Remy had made that comment for her benefit in an effort to change the direction in which Trina was taking the conversation.

"Yeah, it's gorgeous, Casey," Dawn said, standing up and moving toward the window herself. "The view of Central Park up this high is spectacular. We can see all the way up to Harlem."

"I don't know how y'all can stand to look out that window. I got dizzy when I was over there," Trina said, waving them off, sounding disgusted.

Casey grabbed one of the large suede throw pillows resting in front of the grand oak mantelpiece of her fireplace and threw it on the floor next to the coffee table. Taking a seat cross-legged, she tried to figure out another angle of attack to broach the topic for today.

"Well, listen, ladies." Casey cleared her throat. "I know nobody is really interested in hearing this, but I did tell Alexis that I would fill in everyone who missed the breakfast."

Casey noticed Trina roll her eyes again and she realized that Trina was probably wondering why she had been invited today since she had actually attended the breakfast.

"So it wasn't just a social gathering to kick off the play-offs?" Dawn asked, looking back and forth between Casey and Trina from her spot at the picture window.

"Ha! Social gathering, my butt!" Trina sardonically laughed.

"Dawn, I know you're new around here with Michael being a rookie and all," Lorraine began in her usual diplomatic manner. "But in case you haven't noticed, nothing is ever as it really seems with Alexis or Coach. There's a secret motivation behind everything they do, but hey, in all fairness to them, maybe that's a part of their winning formula, and that is the idea isn't it . . . to win?"

Dawn returned to the sofa and sat down next to Lorraine with a quizzical expression on her face. It was obvious to Casey that Dawn's confusion was probably a result of her medical background where things were black or white, not somewhere in between.

"Well, there's not exactly any secret motivation here," Casey said. "Alexis was fairly straight about what she expects from the wives and significant others during the play-offs."

"What she expects?" Dawn asked with raised eyebrows.

Casey helplessly looked up at Remy, who was still standing at the window. It was going to be more challenging than she thought, especially with Trina there heading her off at every pass. And Dawn was very perceptive, although she was the youngest of the fivesome at twenty-five years old. Of course, she was in her first year of her medical residency in psychiatry.

"Maybe 'expects' was the wrong word to use. Maybe . . . a better way to describe it is that she's hoping to get our cooperation to help ensure the image of the Flyers during the play-offs is . . . is flawless."

"There's nothin' we can do about the team's image," Trina said. "Alexis was talkin' out the side of her mouth sayin' the wives need to dress more conservatively, tone down their makeup, and be at every home game on time ready to participate in courtside interviews if necessary," Trina said, shaking her head.

"Tone down our makeup?" Dawn incredulously asked.

"Uh-huh," Trina began, staring hard at Dawn. "And I can tell you right now she'd say somethin' about that gray stuff you got sittin' on your lips. What is that anyway?"

"It's Blade, by Mac," Dawn said, suddenly looking slightly self-conscious. "You don't like it?"

"Is that what she said, Casey?" Lorraine quickly interrupted. "She told everyone how to dress? That's extreme, even for Alexis. I mean, she's always talked about us being punctual for the games and I've always recognized that she sizes me up every time she sees me, but trying to tell us how to wear our makeup and how to dress, that's a bit much."

"But wait, it gets better. She even went so far as to tell us not to bother our men with any domestic squabbles until the play-offs are over," Trina said smugly.

"So she's suggesting that we ignore any problems we might have with the guys until after the play-offs? She can't be serious," Dawn said, peering into a small compact mirror. After a quick glance she clamped it shut, as if dismissing, Casey thought, anyone's petty concerns with her appearance.

Casey looked up at Remy, who appeared slightly amused. It was like a three-ring circus. Alexis was going overboard, but the team being sold was a real threat, and it was probably inevitable if the Flyers didn't win the championship this year. Casey doubted many of the other women even knew about the potential sale, and if they did, she was sure their men had a gag order on them too. No one was supposed to know. Collin had not even told Remy.

Truthfully, the guys didn't need any distractions right now, but how could she tell these women to change their style of dress and put their personal-relationship issues on the back burner until after the season? Hell, Casey didn't know if that was something she could do herself. She'd had to physically bite her tongue about a hundred times since she'd found out that Brent had been seeing his illegitimate daughter behind her back. She didn't even know if *she* could last until the end of the season, but she was willing to give it a try.

"You all are right," Casey said. "It does sound crazy but—"

"Sounds crazy? Casey, it is crazy. That woman is nothin' but crazy."

"Come on, Trina. Don't be nasty. She's not crazy; maybe a little pretentious and misguided, but she's not crazy," Lorraine said.

"Listen, Trina," Casey said soothingly. "I know you've been supporting Rick's career for years, but can't you just look at this as another way of supporting your man? I know this is a new team for you all, but in New York . . . well, things are done a little differently up . . ." Casey realized her mistake too late.

"Oh yeah, different than how us country folks down in North Carolina do things. That's right, things are more sophisticated up here, Miss Casey. I've supported Rick in every way imaginable, but this is ridiculous."

Trina could be so impossible at times.

"Trina, that's not what she meant," Remy finally interjected. "I hate to tell you this, but it *is* different for the guys playing basketball in the number one market in the country—just like it is for any entertainer working in New York City. They're under much more intense scrutiny than any other place in the United States. The critics are tougher, the fans are tougher, the pressures are more abundant. It's endless. And you know who else is included in that invasion? Us. The women behind the bench. I know you all aren't public figures in your own right, but the media considers you fair game whether you like it or not, even those of us who aren't even married to the guys," Remy said, walking toward Trina.

Casey gave Remy a silent smile of thanks for coming to her rescue. Remy was her girl. Casey had begun to feel as if she was in over her head, and she was glad to have an ally.

"Look," Casey said, "I know it may seem stupid on the surface, but think about it. How many times have any one of you gotten into an argument with your man before a game and it ruined his concentration and he ended up having a bad game? I know that's happened to all of us at some point. And even if the argument was his fault, hell, we're women, after all. We know we're really stronger than men when it comes down to it. Is it going to hurt us to hold our tongues just until the play-offs are over? There's a lot riding on this season."

"Casey, that's a lot to ask someone. It's not like anyone plans to get into an argument with their man, but things happen, and when they do, who can hold back their feelings? I know it's almost impossible for me," Dawn said.

Dawn, the young fiancée of the hot rookie Michael Brown, had a bewildered expression on her face. As Casey looked at her, she knew how bright Dawn was and she was also certain that Dawn admired and trusted her. Since the season had begun, Casey had, in a sense, taken Dawn under her wing. But Casey realized that a few of the wives resented Dawn because she was white and Michael was black. For some, that alone was enough to dislike Dawn. They blamed her for stealing one of their good black men, especially a wealthy one. And as much as Dawn respected Casey, she did not want to misuse this trust by manipulating her. Yet this was for the greater good of the team, wasn't it?

"Think of it like this, Dawn. I know you're doing a psychiatry residency, but you're gonna have to do a surgery rotation too, right? If you had a big operation scheduled and Michael started an argument with you the night before this surgery, there'd be two ways to look at it. True, he may have had something on his chest that he couldn't wait to get off, so he decided to tell you exactly how he felt and he goes off on you like there's no tomorrow, and sure, he has that right. But him cursing you out might also be considered selfish as far as your work is concerned. Sometimes, when you truly love someone and want what's best for them . . . it's not always about being right and getting the winning point across . . . it's about being selfless, too, for the greater good of the relationship, not the quick-fix, self-indulgent point you might be trying to prove for the sake of your own ego. You follow me?"

"Makes sense," Lorraine said, nodding her head in agreement.

Casey looked at Trina lying back in her chair; she had her eyes and lips turned up to the intricately plastered ceiling in an "I'm not buying it" expression.

"So all I'm saying is, maybe we can be a little less selfish during this time and realize how important the play-offs are for the Flyers. Let them have their full sense of concentration. If you wanna curse them out the entire off-season, that's your prerogative, but in the meantime we really could help them keep their minds on the game."

Dawn seemed to be digesting everything Casey was saying to them all.

"I hear what you're saying, Casey, and I understand not needing to stress out our men," Lorraine said, sitting forward and snatching up another one of Trina's miniature cakes. "But Alexis wants us to be at all of these games on time. She knows some of us work. I know my job at the hospital is unpredictable sometimes, especially when I get a critical patient in ten minutes before my shift is supposed to be over. She's gonna have to cut us some slack there. I mean, I'm not about to start missing work, play-offs or not."

"Me neither," Dawn chimed in.

"Well, neither am I, and I think even Alexis understands that, and if she doesn't, that's her problem," Casey started. "But when we do go to the games, we can at least arrive on time."

"Unless we're running late and we're coming from work," Lorraine said with a satisfied smirk.

"Well, whatever the reason, just make sure you get your butt there whenever you can," Casey said, glad that the mood had turned lighter even though she knew she had not gotten through to Trina, at least on the conservative-clothing part. As far as the games were concerned, Trina rarely missed them and was always early.

"I'll be there like I always am, but I'm gonna be comfortable, that's for sure."

"All right, Trina, but—"

"Excuse me, ladies." Martha, Casey's live-in housekeeper, interrupted Trina. "The doorman just telephoned up and there's a Kelly Tucker downstairs to see you, Casey."

"Kelly?" Casey questioned, turning toward Martha.

"Yes."

"Okay, thanks."

How did Kelly know she was having some of the women over?

"Do you want me to have the doorman send her up?" Martha asked, standing in the library's doorway.

"No, thanks. Tell him that I'll be right down."

"Sure."

Martha hurried out as Casey stood up and looked around the room suspiciously.

"Did anyone mention to Kelly that we were getting together?"

Casey watched as everyone shook their heads no and looked around, staring at one another, confused. All of the women had witnessed Kelly in action at one time or another and they knew what a loose cannon she could be.

"What's up with the 'Tucker' last name?" Trina demanded. "When's that girl gonna learn? Didn't Steve have his new girlfriend at Alexis's house for the breakfast?"

"Yeah," Casey answered. "Her name's Stephanie. I'll be right back." Something had to be up for Kelly to crash in on her like this.

Riding down in the elevator, Casey hoped Kelly didn't come over to confront her about being snubbed today. Casey knew that Alexis had not included her in the breakfast at Steve's request, but Kelly considered Casey her friend. How could she explain not inviting Kelly to her own home?

As soon as Casey arrived in the lobby, she noticed Kelly and Diamond sitting on one of the guest chairs. Kelly looked uncharacteristically demure as she held her adorable twenty-month-old daughter in her lap.

"Hey, Kelly."

"Hi, Casey! I'm so glad to see you, girl," Kelly excitedly said, standing up to greet Casey as if she were her long-lost sister.

"Were you just in the neighborhood or something?" Casey asked after a long, tense silence.

Casey watched as Kelly cast down her eyes and then quickly looked back up and rubbed Diamond's small back.

"Is it possible for us to go upstairs and talk?"

"Kelly, it's not really a good time and—"

"I understand, I understand," Kelly quickly said. "And I'm really sorry for just coming over like this, but I need to ask you a favor."

"Well, you can ask me right here. Let's sit down."

Kelly followed Casey's lead and took a seat on the lobby chair across from her and started to speak. She stopped several times before finally uttering a sound other than a sigh.

"Casey, I know that you know that me and Steve have been having some problems lately."

Truthfully, she didn't think they were still together as a couple to even have any problems. Casey, like everybody else, knew they had a child together, but Steve behaved as if he and Kelly were history.

"I suppose I've heard that." Casey hesitated.

"Yeah, we've been having some difficulties, but I think we're gonna be able to work everything out real soon," Kelly said, playing with one of Diamond's short braids.

What was she getting at?

"I . . . we, me and Diamond haven't seen too much of him lately, and I know all we need is to have a little more family time with him. Then we'll be able to get things back on track. You know what I mean, Casey? Like when you tryin' to work things out with your man?"

"Yeah," Casey said defensively. She wondered just how much Kelly knew about her issues with Brent.

"Well, that's what I'm tryin' to do with Steve. I want us to be a family again. I mean, I am still his fiancée, after all." The real Kelly peeked out, flamboyantly waving the rock Steve had given her in Casey's face.

Casey had no idea what was really going on between the two of them, but she had no interest in playing mediator. All she knew was that Steve had asked Alexis to invite another girl to the breakfast. Someone who was a polar opposite of Kelly.

"I see," Casey said, afraid to find out the favor Kelly wanted from her, but her guests were still upstairs and she was anxious for Kelly to get to the point. "Well, what do you want me to do?"

"You know Diamond is finally old enough to understand what her daddy is doing out there on the basketball court."

Casey looked at the little girl, who was under two years old, and very much doubted that she knew what her daddy was doing running up and down the court.

"And with the way things have been between me and Steve, I don't know if he's even gonna invite me to the first play-off game," Kelly said as she began to sniffle. "This might be Diamond's only chance to see her daddy in the play-offs."

The truth finally came out. Kelly wanted a ticket to the first play-off game, and the closer the seat was to the court, the better. Of course, Casey's seats were better than any of the other wives' as Brent was the franchise player for the New York Flyers. Not that any of the other women would have even considered letting Kelly sit with them at the

Mecca Arena. They'd all seen her act out on numerous occasions. Casey was certain none of them wanted to be bothered and she had to admit to herself, neither did she under the circumstances.

"So . . . I was wondering if we could maybe use your tickets."

"I'm not sure if Brent is going to need them yet."

"I'd only need one, Casey. Diamond could sit on my lap . . . or yours," Kelly said as she coyly giggled, completely out of character. "And you know how she loves to be up under you, Casey."

Yeah, right. Flattery was obviously Kelly's tactic for the day.

"I'll have to check with Brent," Casey lied. The seats were really hers to do with as she pleased.

"Come on, Casey. Doesn't he get other tickets? Diamond and me will only need one, right next to you. Please, come on, Casey. For the baby's sake. I just want her to see her daddy play."

Casey didn't know what to do. She knew how resourceful Kelly could be, and she would probably get into the game whether Casey gave her tickets or not. But she'd probably make a scene in the process, while trying to sneak in. At least if Casey let Kelly sit with her, she could monitor her behavior and prevent anything embarrassing for the team from happening. Especially if Kelly came into contact with Stephanie, Steve's girlfriend.

"Dada. Daddy," Diamond suddenly said, with a huge smile on her cute face.

"No, Daddy's not here right now, baby. Maybe you'll see him tomorrow. Hopefully," Kelly said, hugging Diamond tightly against her silicone-enhanced, protruding bosom.

Kelly looked at Casey pleadingly with a pathetic expression on her face.

Casey hoped she didn't regret what she was about to agree to. "I'll probably be able to get you one ticket, Kelly, but that's it."

"Ooohh, thank you, Casey! Thank you so much! Diamond, can you say thank you to Auntie Casey?" Kelly said, beaming at her daughter.

Oh, so free Flyers tickets are the going price for being named an auntie these days?

"I need to get back upstairs, Kelly." Casey began thinking once again about her guests. "I'll see you tomorrow night."

"All right, Casey! Thank you so much, girl. I really appreciate it, and so does Diamond," Kelly said, jumping up and snatching her Moschino purse over her shoulders. She hitched Diamond up on her hip. "I'll see you tomorrow, girl. Go, Flyers!"

Casey shook her head in disbelief as Kelly scurried out of her building. She watched as Kelly virtually tossed Diamond into the backseat of the white Mercedes-Benz double-parked in front of her building on Central Park South.

What have I gotten myself into this time?

"Boy, you can't check me." Paul, the Flyers' starting point guard, taunted his teammate Collin as he dashed past him, making an easy layup.

"Yeah, that's not gonna be what you sayin' when Tim Hardaway throws up those three-pointers over your short ass." Collin laughed as he walked off the court toward the bleachers to grab a towel. Even at small forward, Collin was one of the taller guys on the court, standing six feet eight inches. Paul, at five eleven, was considered short, at least in basketball terms. Collin was not a great ball handler like Paul. It wasn't really required in his position, but he could shoot the ball well and defend even better. Paul was a great defender, too, and he distributed the ball as well as any point guard in the NBA. But a great shooter, Paul was not.

"Hardaway ain't got nothin' on me. You had enough ass-whippin' for one day?" Paul said, running out past the three-point arc and sinking a shot. "Nothing but net, boy!"

"Let me see that when it counts," Collin said as he wiped the sweat off his face with the soft white cotton towel.

"Skills, baby, nothing but skills. I'll do that with one second left in the final championship game."

"The proof is in the pudding—plus we got to make it there first. But I guess we'll be on our way tonight." Collin wrapped the towel around his neck and began walking toward the locker room. They were the last two players at practice.

"Oh, so you've had enough? You gonna wimp out on me again?" Paul said, throwing the ball directly at Collin.

Collin reflexively caught the brown leather sphere that had been so good to him and began tossing it back and forth between his large hands. He felt slightly torn looking at Paul's expectant face. They'd only been out on the court for fifteen minutes. Normally they'd play one-on-one for at least an hour after practice, and then go to Zinger-man's Deli and talk trash or politics, depending on their mood. At least that used to be their routine.

"Man, I've got some work to catch up on."

"You cuttin' out on me again?" Paul said as he snatched one of the folded towels resting on the courtside cart.

"Yeah, you know, business calls," Collin lied.

"Sure, man, you just wore out, you know how you old men are." Paul slapped Collin on the butt as they entered the locker room together.

Collin and Paul headed straight to the shower. Collin felt terrible being dishonest with his friend, but he didn't know how else to handle his situation. What was he supposed to tell Paul? At this point it was more than Collin's ego that was hurt by Flyers management. His pride was deeply wounded. He was going to be a free agent at the end of the season, and management had not even approached his agent. He was a three-time All-Star and they had so little respect for him that they were making him play out his contract. Collin used to think he was the man. Management's nonchalant treatment was a rude awakening.

Collin jumped in the steaming hot shower in a whirl of confusion. The stinging streams of water temporarily cleared his mind. He knew he couldn't go on like this forever. Something had to give. There was no telling what was in store for him after the play-offs were over. Truthfully, Collin could be seriously injured playing his ass off during the play-offs and his career would be over. One torn ligament and his basketball days might come to an abrupt end. And Collin still hadn't gotten that superlarge NBA contract like Paul, Steve, and most of all, Brent.

"Yo! Yo! Collin!" Paul shouted as he slapped Collin with his wet twisted washcloth.

"What's up, man?" Collin said, snapping out of his reverie.

"You coming to Zingerman's at least?"

Collin felt the stinging in his chest where the washcloth had just struck. He hesitated before answering.

"Uhh, not today, man." He was beginning to feel worse. Collin could not help but notice the look of disappointment on Paul's face. It had been almost a month since Collin accompanied Paul to the deli. He was beginning to run out of excuses.

How could Collin explain to his friend the range of emotions he was feeling? Anger. Confusion. He felt jealousy too. He was feeling resentment that Paul's life was packaged up so neatly. Everything was settled for him and his wife, Lorraine. Paul was set for life. He had a wife he adored and a strong spiritual base. Things were definitely not so perfect with Collin's life. Even if he did sign a multimillion-dollar deal, it wouldn't resolve the other issues.

Collin turned off the shower faucet and slipped past Paul to his locker. As Collin began to dry off, he sensed a presence behind him.

"Is everything okay, Collin?"

Collin feigned laughter as he turned around to face Paul. "Yeah, man, everything's fine. Just a hectic time for me, ya know? Between Remy's schedule, the play-offs, my work, free agency . . . there's a lot going on," Collin said, purposefully leaving free agency last as he nonchalantly sprayed on deodorant. Sometimes guys in the league looked at free agents who weren't signed by their teams as scrubs, or even worse, pitied them.

"Oh yeah. Free agency, it's a pain, especially since we don't know what's happening with the team. I understand, man. I guess your agent has you in and out of strategic meetings with management," Paul said, nodding his head.

"Exactly, I'm up to my ears," Collin lied again.

"Cool, but when you get some real time, I'm regaining my title." Paul smirked.

Collin laughed as he watched Paul go to his own locker, thinking about Paul "regaining his title." He and Paul had an ongoing competition of one-on-one, and Collin was ahead of him by two games for the year.

Collin pulled his sweater over his head and sat down on the pine bench next to his locker. Pulling up his faded Levi's, he knew he was going to have to level with Paul sooner or later. He was tired of lying. Collin needed to confide in a true friend about a lot of things. If he didn't, he was going to burst keeping everything bottled up inside.

Dawn wrapped herself in a long, fluffy white Calvin Klein bathrobe and headed toward the bed where her fiancé, Michael, was resting. She had just received the robe that morning amidst boxes of clothing from the vice president of Calvin Klein Underwear. One of the perks of being engaged to a Flyer was that a lot of top designers invited the players and their significant others to their New York offices and sample rooms to sift through the latest collections, allowing them to select all of the clothing they desired.

Dawn realized quickly in the beginning of her relationship with Michael that the more celebrities had, the more people gave them. Of course, she suspected these same generous people would not remember Michael Brown when his playing days were over. She and Michael had taken advantage of the offers just the same. Neither turned down free goods from Karl Kani, DKNY, Tommy Hilfiger, Perry Ellis, Hugo Boss, or Calvin Klein.

Dawn lay down on the bed and cuddled up to Michael. She could have stayed there with him forever. She cherished moments like these when she had Michael all to herself. Sometimes she felt as if there wasn't enough of him to go around. He had people tugging at him from every direction. She had begun to feel as if even she was demanding too much of his time and attention. Dawn knew that Michael loved her, but he was so focused on winning the Rookie of the Year award, bringing home an NBA championship, and being the official spokesman for every company seeking his endorsement that she felt like an afterthought. She needed an appointment just to see a movie with him, and she was afraid to broach the subject of their wedding date for fear of making him angry. She knew he would only think of an excuse to quiet her for the moment.

Dawn pressed herself closer to him, not wanting him to leave. She wanted to stay spooned together with him all day and night. She moaned softly as he rubbed his hand over her bottom. Dawn knew she had different ideas about the touch than Michael. For him, it was an obligatory caress before he left for the arena. She could sense his nervous energy. He was bucking to get out of bed and head to the Mecca as if he had something to prove to the world.

She wished it could be as it was when they were in college. It had been etched in stone at Stanford that he was already the big man on campus. He had had nothing to prove on the collegiate level anymore. The only thing he'd been interested in proving back then was how he wanted to spend the rest of his life making Dawn happy.

Dawn held tight to Michael's midsection as he tried to inch his way out of bed. She looked at the clock and knew he did not have to be at the Mecca for game one of the play-offs versus the Philadelphia 76ers for another three hours.

"Where do you think you're going, Mr. Brown?" Dawn said, forcing a smile in her voice, trying to keep in mind what Casey had said at her apartment yesterday morning.

"I have to watch some extra films before the game."

"Do you have enough time to roll around in the bed with me before you go?" Dawn said, trying to tickle him.

"Come on, Dawn, relax. You know how important the first round of the play-offs is. If we can sweep them, we'll have a few more days of rest and practice than whatever team we're gonna have to play in the second round," Michael said, sitting on the edge of the bed.

Dawn felt a lump in her throat, but she once again remembered Alexis's edict via Casey and promised herself she would not pressure him about anything right now. She also reminded herself about the disturbing news Brent had passed on to Michael about the future of the Flyers.

"I understand. I just didn't know you had to get there so early."

"Things have been hectic since Brent told all the guys about the team possibly being sold. Some of the fellas are acting like we should be packing our bags for Albany, like the deal is as good as done. It's making everybody talk and act crazy."

"I hear Albany is pretty nice in the winter," she said with a smile.

Michael scrunched up his face as if he were eating a sour grape. "Do you know how much endorsement money I would lose if the Flyers moved to Albany? That would be the worst thing for my career," Michael spat out.

"That would be the worst thing?" Dawn said, barely able to contain her disgust. "Michael, I know you've heard what kind of a man Leonard Hightower is. How about the fact that you'd be working for a racist jerk who would probably fire you if he knew you planned on marrying a white woman," Dawn said, scarcely believing that Michael only seemed concerned with his image and endorsement money.

Dawn was of Italian-Irish descent, with the violet eyes of Elizabeth Taylor and the cheekbones and full, pouty lips of Sophia Loren. Her thick, honey/blond hair was trimmed to all one length resting on her shoulders. The two of them made a handsome couple, with Michael's flawless mocha complexion covering his lean yet muscular six-foot-five-inch frame. With his large, expressive brown eyes and killer smile, if basketball didn't work out for him, then modeling could certainly be an alternative career. But basketball was his game, and Michael was quickly proving to be among the best.

"Don't get paranoid. Nobody's thinking about whether or not we get married but you."

"So I see," Dawn said, jumping out of bed and hurrying into the bathroom.

Michael quickly followed behind her. "Why does everything have to come back to us getting married?" Michael said, exasperated.

Dawn sat down on the edge of the bathtub and tried to calm herself. She did not want to say something she would regret later, especially on the first night of the play-offs. She never wanted him to walk away angry.

"Listen, Michael, let's not fight about this. My point was not to bring up the topic of marriage. I was just expressing my concern about the possibility of you having to work for a bigot. I was worried about your future working conditions. Okay, sweetheart?" Dawn took a deep breath and stood up on her tiptoes to kiss Michael on his chin. "Now, get on out of here and kick some ass tonight. Do you want me to make you a sandwich to eat on the way?"

"No, I'll grab something at the arena. I'm sorry, Dawn, I don't want us to fight either. It's just a stressful time, but I promise as soon as the season is over . . . it'll get better." Michael reached down and embraced Dawn.

Dawn quickly closed and locked the bathroom door after Michael left, as if he were there to see the steady flow of tears. Dawn stared at her clear eyes in the mirror and wondered if Michael had seen through her charade. He was right; for her, everything did come back to when they were going to get married. She wanted to share the rest of her life with Michael and she was tired of waiting around for him to decide that he wanted to make that commitment. When he'd told her that things would get better once the season was over, she'd been hoping he would follow that up by saying they could start planning their wedding. It seemed as if he had one foot in the door of their relationship and one foot out.

They had dated for three years at Stanford, and right before he graduated and was drafted, he had proposed to her. That was over a year ago. He'd promised that they'd get married before the season was over. Somehow, right before training camp began last October, Michael had managed to give Dawn a lame excuse about Coach not thinking it was a good time to plan a wedding. Since that time, Dawn had gotten an assortment of reasons why they had not gotten married: from Michael and his procrastinating, to his sports agent, Jake Schneider, who never thought marriage should be on any of his client's list of priorities, to the groupies sitting in the stands at the Mecca Arena who said that rookies never got married during their first year in the NBA. She surmised that Michael's real reason for not having married her was a combination of everything.

Dawn hated that she was feeling so needy. Before Michael, she never questioned her complete independence and relied on no one. Now she wondered if loving someone as much as she loved Michael brought out her insecurities. Her father had run off and married his twenty-two-year-old secretary the day before Dawn's third birthday.

Dawn was not interested in history repeating itself in her relationship. She saw the debilitating effect her father's walking out on them had on her mother. After he left, Dawn's mother was never the same person. Feelings of failure and inadequacy tainted the rest of her stressful life. Watching her mother year after year in such a self-pitying state made Dawn determined not to go down that same path. Ironically, it made Dawn fiercely independent yet so needy at the same time.

Two years ago, her mother had died of breast cancer. Dawn was left financially independent. Her mother would have been proud of the strong, self-contained young woman she'd become. In seven years Dawn had completed Stanford's accelerated joint degree program and received a bachelor of science degree in biology and her doctorate of medicine. Her life was almost complete.

Now Dawn was prepared to do just about anything to ensure that her relationship with Michael worked out. She was even willing to put aside pressuring him about marriage so that he could concentrate. He was, after all, a twenty-two-year-old multimillionaire with a mission to win an NBA championship and Rookie of the Year award. She knew the last thing he needed right now was her nagging him about marriage, or anything else for that matter. What he needed was her unconditional love and support. She thought again of Alexis's edict. Yes, Dawn decided, she'd just have to put her selfish interests on hold for a while.

Trina Belleville smoothed her graying hair self-consciously as she sat at a corner table in the Mecca's Family Lounge. She was waiting to see a welcoming or even familiar face, but thus far, no luck. Looking down sourly at her second empty plate, she used her plastic fork to fiddle with the remains of shrimp tails. She fanta- sized about getting up and walking around the busy room, going from table to table, holding court, as she used to do when Rick played for the Char- lotte Hornets. That was North Carolina, with different people and a different set of circum- stances. Here she was worried that everyone might stare at her wide bottom and protruding stomach. She had to force herself into the largest pair of slacks in her closet: size sixteen.

One of the fringe benefits enjoyed by the wives of the Flyers was the VIP Family Lounge. This was where all of the family members of the players would convene before, sometimes during, and certainly after the games. Trina had always loved it because of its vast array of delicacies, ranging from several types of salads to five or six entrées, seven to ten side dishes, and a separate dessert table. This was the arena's unofficial meeting room, and more drama occurred here than on Broadway. It was where the players' wives kept tabs on one another, the place to keep abreast of who's new, who's out, who should be out, and who's in. And of course, who's pregnant. Here the women were expected and encouraged to be natural extensions of their mates. As Trina watched some of the wives and girlfriends trickle in, she contemplated, rather morosely, the irony of this: how she was an extension of her husband not only here, but everywhere she went.

Even though Trina and Rick had spent a whole season in New York, she was still having a difficult time adjusting. Staring around the bustling Family Lounge, she felt overwhelmed. For the past fourteen years, she had followed Rick to five different NBA cities, and none of them was anything like New York. Almost since the day Trina had arrived in the city, she'd felt as if she was a few steps behind all of the other wives and girlfriends, always trying to catch up but never quite knowing how.

Looking at the fashionable, trim, fit women, some even mothers of the players, Trina felt way out of her league. She and Rick had attended and graduated from Tennessee State together. Of course, she'd never put her degree in sociology to use, at least not in a job that paid. Yes, she received an allowance from Rick, and she certainly deserved every cent. But somehow Trina imagined it wasn't quite the same as making her own way in the world, something she'd been giving more and more consideration to: making her own money. Looking at the people around her and even a few of the other Flyers wives and girlfriends, she saw they really seemed to have their acts together—careerwise and physically. She must stick out like a sore thumb.

When Rick had been playing for the Hornets, the games didn't seem like fashion shows the way they were here in New York. At the Mecca, Trina felt like an outcast because her clothes didn't have a MADE IN ITALY tag and her body wasn't made by Jake—hardly.

Trina jumped as one of the players' daughters rammed into the back of her chair while chasing the assistant coach's son.

"Watch it, little lady, you're gonna hurt somebody!" Trina said, rubbing her back.

"You're not my mama," the sassy little girl retorted as she continued to run around the room in her black and red Moschino jeans.

"I know, 'cause if I were your mama, you wouldn't be running around this room like you didn't have any sense," Trina said under her breath, rolling her eyes as the little terror ran off.

She felt she had excuses: she had two small children and a demanding husband who left her no time for herself. But Trina knew that even if she did have any free time, the last thing she'd want to do would be to go huff and puff herself into exhaustion at some gym. She would much rather stay at home and snack on the various culinary delights she loved to prepare for her family, friends, and neighbors. Recently a neighbor friend of hers whose husband owned the local Safeway grocery store convinced Trina to start supplying their bakery with homemade treats.

Even though Trina had ballooned up to nearly two hundred pounds, she was an attractive woman with rich, ebony-colored skin. She rarely made attempts to enhance her looks, though. Trina was prematurely graying and her usual hairstyle was a snatch-back feathered concoction reminiscent of the early eighties. She also never bothered with much makeup . . . and had no intention of wearing it despite Alexis's orders. Trina had ignored her and then Casey on that count.

Trina swiveled her chair around and caught a glimpse of Remy entering the lounge. Just about everyone in the room turned and gazed at the star as she headed toward the fully stocked bar. Three little girls and boys rallied around Remy, clinging to her pantsuit, which Trina noted was uncharacteristically conservative. Trina chuckled under her breath thinking about how Remy had obviously been influenced by Casey, who, as far as Trina was concerned, was behaving like Alexis's puppet.

Casey, along with Lorraine, had been the most welcoming of the wives from the start. But Trina was an old-fashioned woman at heart. She liked her family and personal affairs to be handled at home behind closed doors. Rick took care of the business of basketball. Trina attended every home game and genuinely supported her husband and his career, both on and off the court. Although Rick had not mentioned it to Trina himself, she had overheard a conversation he'd had with his agent about the team possibly being sold and moved if the Flyers didn't win the championship this year. Apparently the prospect had everyone up in arms. She knew not to ask Rick about anything that related to his work for fear of him accusing her of meddling. Besides, what was happening with the Flyers and the powers that be was out of her control. She was not about to let Alexis or Casey get her tangled up in her husband's business affairs.

For one thing, Trina did not oppose the prospect of the team being sold and relocated to Albany. Rick would not be hurt by the loss of any endorsement opportunities. He was at the end of his career anyway. No corporations were banging down his door to advertise their products. There were younger, more athletic, more marketable players taking his place all the time.

As Trina watched Alexis glide into the Family Lounge with her prep-school-poster daughters in tow, she was reminded of the cover of a *Town & Country* magazine. Maybe Albany would not be that bad. Trina welcomed a change of scenery. She wasn't even sure she could handle one more glittery season with the frantic, chaotic pace of the Mecca.

She and the kids went where Rick's career took them, and the final destination did not matter. So long as they were together as a family, they all eventually learned to adjust. Certainly it was a hassle packing up and moving an entire household time after time, and school placement for the kids was a chore in and of itself. Still, it was part of the life of a professional athlete. The summers were still theirs and they had a home in Florida where the kids had plenty of cousins their ages and a slew of friends to give them a sense of stability. Trina had never had complaints about the transient nature of their life until they hit the fast pace of New York.

New York, the Flyers, and everything that accompanied them deified the position of a professional basketball player in this town. And it had brought out the worst in Rick. The accessibility of a boundless nightlife clearly was a disaster.

Just then Casey arrived in the room and hugged Paul Thomas's brother and sister. Trina waved her hand to get Casey's attention as she worked the crowd.

Alexis stopped Casey in her tracks before she had a chance to weave her way to Trina's corner table. Mrs. Coach, as Trina thought of her, looked like she was having a secret conference with Casey right in the middle of the Family Lounge. Her two daughters were obediently sitting on the brown leather sofas with their ankles crossed, reading books. Alexis had obviously not spared her daughters from etiquette lessons.

When Casey finally approached Trina's table, Remy was by her side.

"Well, hello, ladies. You two on your way to a meeting on Wall Street or something?" Trina said in a kidding tone.

"Hey, girl, we do look a little uptight, huh?" Remy said, running her hands over her suit.

"A little?" Trina laughed, thinking how Remy rarely spoke to her unless she was with Casey.

Trina sometimes felt like Casey's charity case. Casey was so sophisticated and seemed revered by everyone associated with the Flyers.

"Ladies, it *is* the play-offs," Casey reminded gently.

"I know. Casey, you have me dressing like I'm Murphy Brown," Remy said, playfully shoving Casey on the shoulders.

"And I'm sorry for stepping out of line, Miss Alexis." Trina motioned to her own casual sweater smock.

"Well, Alexis just wanted us to look really professional for the play-offs since there's going to be a lot more media coverage on us during this time."

Trina pointed to Alexis, who seemed to have Lorraine cornered at the bar. "Looks like she's debriefing her."

"And I'm sure you weren't exaggerating about *Mrs. Mitchell's* directive." Remy laughed.

"So kill me, I'm only the messenger delivering the bad news . . . Hey, simmer down, Sarah." Casey chided the same little girl who had bumped into Trina's chair moments before.

"I'm sorry, Casey," Sarah coyly said as she slowly walked away from them, checking back over her shoulder to see if Casey was looking at her.

Even the kids knew who had power—and who didn't, Trina thought.

"You ready to go down now?" Remy asked Casey.

"I guess so."

"You're going now?" Trina asked, feeling a bit left out.

"I don't know about you, girl, but I want to see Collin stretch and warm up. That's my favorite part," Remy said, clasping her arm around Casey's.

"Trina, want to come with us?"

"Naw, I'll see you girls at halftime or after the game. I'm gonna grab a little dessert. Hopefully we can get a win tonight."

Watching the two of them walk toward the exit, Trina thought they looked like they could be two prima donna models on the cover of *Essence* magazine. As they headed out, it looked like the parting of the Red Sea the way everyone in the lounge scurried around them, wishing *them* luck for tonight's game. They always had to be on their best behavior. Trina was glad she didn't have that problem. She just wanted to have a few chocolate chip cookies and enjoy the game. She didn't have to keep up appearances for anyone.

Michael rushed to the elevator in the basement garage below the Mecca Arena. He was angry with himself for getting drawn into an argument with Dawn. She had a way of making him feel guilty all the time just because he had a busy schedule. And her obsession with get-ting married was the last thing he needed to deal with right now. When he had left her in their Fort Lee, New Jersey, condo earlier, she had looked so devastated and pitiful, he ended up turning his car around and going back to check on her. He found her there alone, locked in the bathroom. One thing had led to another, and now he was going to be late for the first game of the play-offs—fined a shitload of money for sure and maybe worse, depending on Coach's mood.

"Damn! How do I get myself in these situations?" Michael said to himself as he reached the elevator that would drop him off down the hall from the Flyers' locker room. Thank God I missed the hordes, thought Michael, relieved that he had been given clearance to park beneath the structure along with the other starting players rather than in the more public part of the garage. It gave him a few more minutes to spare when he was running late. Although the parking priority seemed like unfair star treatment, there was actually a rationale behind it. Space inside the Mecca was limited, and management had to draw the line somewhere in determining the allocation of the few remaining parking spaces. The logic was that since the easily recognizable starting players were more likely to be mobbed by the fans before and after a game, they were allowed to use the basement garage with its guarded entrance.

Most of his nonstarting teammates did not mind their parking situation since it allowed the fans access to them after the home games. Signing autographs seemed to make most of the players feel like celebrities, especially if they had just spent most of the game keeping the bench warm.

While Michael enjoyed the attention he got as a result of his various local commercials, he had grown tired of the mobs of fans who accosted him constantly. After a while it had become intrusive, particularly when he was out trying to have nice quiet dinners with Dawn. The young female autograph-seekers tended to be more aggressive than the males or even the kids. He knew fans like those made Dawn uncomfortable. But he planned on staying in New York— maybe for longer than his basketball career, and she'd have to learn to accept his life.

He had dreams of acting once his basketball career was over. Michael wondered how Dawn would react if he ever had to do a love scene in a movie. She would probably trip out just as she had today. No time to think about that. Michael darted out of the elevator. He was going to be fined another $750 for arriving late.

He'd already been fined once during the regular season. He had walked out onto the floor four and a half minutes late and tried to explain to Coach about the traffic he'd run into coming down the West Side Highway. Coach had not wanted to hear any excuses. He had cut Michael off in midsentence with a wave of his perfectly manicured hand and a terse reply of "Not on my team."

Michael had not given the incident a second thought until he'd received his next pay stub and noticed the deduction under "Team Fines": a figure almost as bad as the New York state and city taxes routinely deducted. Fines seemed to be handed down so arbitrarily. Michael began to hear of deductions for fines for anything, from one of his teammates speaking to the media without prior permission from management to one of the guys' pager going off during a meeting. Mitchell was tough—sometimes too tough, thought the young rookie. But Michael had to admit to himself, Mitchell sure kept his guys in line, not an easy task.

As Michael reached the entrance to the locker room, he looked at his watch one last time. He was a full hour late. Forget fines. Coach might punish him in other ways, such as benching him during tonight's game, which was scheduled to start in thirty minutes. Tentatively opening the locker-room door, Michael promised himself that from this day forward, no one was going to come between him and his goals as a basketball player or an international celebrity. The world was his, and he did not have time for anyone obstructing his path—even Dawn.

"Do you know who I am? Excuse me, but do you know who I am?" Kelly angrily asked the security guard at the entrance to the Family Lounge while she struggled under the weight of her daughter. Diamond sat on her hip with a bewildered expression on her face.

"I'm sorry, ma'am, don't know who you your name isn't on guard patiently ex-

"Well, there's obvi- My fiancé is Steve here is our daughter, and if ter let me in that room now!" Kelly shouted as Diamond began to cry.

but I'm new here and I are, but unfortunately the list," the security plained.

ously been a mistake. Tucker and this little girl you value your job, you bet-

"I'm sorry, ma'am, but if you just give me a moment, I'll go in and check," the guard said.

Just then, Casey and Remy walked up behind the security guard on their way down to Casey's seats. Catching her eye, Casey realized that she had assumed Kelly would be able to enter the Family Lounge and retrieve her ticket as she did when Steve left her tickets. Casey hadn't taken the beefed-up security measures for the play-offs into consideration. She should have remembered to leave Kelly's name at the Family Lounge door.

"Sir, I'm Casey Rogers, and this woman's name is supposed to be on the list. Now, please let her in," Casey interrupted the security guard. The guard immediately stepped aside, sputtering his apologies.

Casey led Kelly and Diamond to the foyer area of the lounge.

"Was that guard tripping or what? He needs to learn some manners," Kelly snapped.

"Just chill out for a minute, Kelly; you know how tight they get with security during the play-offs. I should have remembered to leave him your name myself."

"He didn't have to disrespect me like that. I don't know who he thought he was, talking to me any kind of way." Kelly shook her free hand, making her bangle bracelets clatter loudly.

"Relax, don't start making a scene," Casey began.

"A scene? I've been coming in here all year long and now they're gonna act like I don't belong."

Casey took a deep breath. "Listen, Kelly, lower your voice; you don't want everyone in your business."

"I wouldn't have to be going through this if Steve hadn't taken my name off the permanent list. I know what he's up to. He was hoping I wouldn't show up tonight. I can't wait to see his sneaky ass after the game," Kelly said, sounding more incensed with each word.

Casey looked over Kelly and Diamond's shoulders at Alexis, who was quickly approaching them in the alcove.

"Look, Kelly, let's just try and enjoy the game, okay?" Casey said quietly.

"Right! I'm gonna enjoy it all right, especially from where I'll be sitting," Kelly said.

Unfortunately, Casey knew exactly why Kelly was going to enjoy her view. From her seats, Kelly could keep track of whoever was occupying Steve's complimentary seats across the court—and if Casey figured correctly, it would probably be his new girlfriend, Stephanie.

Kelly, holding Diamond, practically sprinted to the seats in front of Casey and Remy; Remy began to shake her head. Casey knew that Remy was pissed that she'd invited Kelly to sit with them, but Kelly had caught Casey off guard when she'd just shown up at her apartment begging for the coveted ticket. Worse, Kelly was getting more riled, and Casey was afraid she'd pull one of her infamous scenes in front of Alexis.

The tension worked its way up and down Casey's spine as she berated herself for getting in the middle here. The last thing she needed was to take on someone else's problems. She had enough personal issues to last her a lifetime. True to her foolish promise to Alexis, she had not brought up any subjects that might disturb Brent's concentration. Unfortunately, what Casey was aching to talk to Brent about was more than a mere topic of discussion that could dangle between them until the play-offs were over. Brent was deceiving her, again. She felt as if she were going to burst from holding it inside. At least she hadn't been forced to be in his company much while he was preparing for the play-offs. Between watching game films of the 76ers, participating in interviews, practice, physical therapy, and extended naps, it wasn't difficult staying out of his path. Ironically, even though she persuaded the other women to hold their tongues with their men, Casey didn't know if she could do it much longer.

"Casey! Casey! Earth calling Casey!" a deep male voice said, interrupting her reverie.

Casey looked up, scarcely realizing that she had entered the folds of the sold-out Mecca Arena with its twenty thousand–plus anxious fans in the stands waiting for the main event. She felt surreal in her surroundings as Phil Jones, the Mecca's Flyers correspondent, grasped her arm and shoved a microphone in her face.

The blaring music began pounding in her ears, and the neon lights circling the arena caused Casey to involuntarily squint. She might as well have been waking from a deep sleep.

"How about a pregame interview from my favorite Flyers wife?" Phil said, motioning for his cameraman to assume the position.

"Gosh, Phil, you caught me off guard," Casey said, feeling flustered.

"So I see; nervous about the game, huh?" he said with a grin before turning toward Remy and Kelly. "Pardon me, ladies, how are you all doing this evening? Nervous for your men as well?"

"Me, nervous? Never. Hey, Casey, go on and do your interview; I want to catch Collin warming up," Remy answered, heading down to the court trying to spot her man. The renowned Mecca correspondent hardly noted her departure and immediately pounced back on Casey.

"I'm coming with you," Kelly yelled at Remy's back. "Can I have my ticket, Casey?" she asked, holding out her greedy hand for the cherished courtside seat.

Casey looked longingly after Kelly and Remy as they wove their way through the bustling arena, wishing she could escape Phil's probing questions. The aisles and seats were filled with crowds of people in business suits, designer clothes, blue jeans, miniskirts, and New York Flyers paraphernalia. Little kids wore jerseys with Brent's number 51 on the back, and attractive women of all ages boasted T-shirts with Michael Brown's picture on the front. Strobe lights flashed back and forth over the hordes of people in the arena fighting to get a view of the players warming up on the court. Up in the higher seats, fans with high-tech binoculars studied the players and the variety of stars, ranging from Will Smith to Cindy Crawford to John F. Kennedy, Jr., who were sprinkled throughout the Mecca. Purple and black, the Flyers' colors, were waved wildly on towels, banners, and assorted souvenirs throughout the stands.

"Surely you can find someone more interesting than me to interview tonight," Casey said. "There're all those celebrities here for the play-offs. How about Woody Allen?" Casey pointed across the court.

"Still too controversial," Phil said with a wave of the hand.

"Well, there's Ivana Trump sitting in Star Row."

"She's too chichi."

"What about Ed Bradley? His seats are right near mine," Casey offered.

"He's out of my league," he said, "too intellectual."

"What about Remy?" Casey said with a smirk, knowing Remy

would be annoyed. She liked tweaking her friend about her star status.

"Remy's too much of a diva for me." He hesitated. "Besides who else could be more interesting than the wife of the legendary star of the Flyers, who I might add is a gorgeous personality in her own right? No, you're not getting off that easy, Casey. I want the scoop. How was Brent feeling before he left for the game? Does he think they can sweep the Seventy-sixers? I want to hear it all."

"Coming through! Beep! Beep!" The cotton-candy man shoved past the two of them heading toward a frantic baseball-cap-clad father motioning to him above the squeals of his young boys.

"It's a circus in here tonight," Casey said after almost being knocked down by the overzealous salesman. She knew the food vendors depended on quantity sold to make their commissions.

The smell of peanuts, onions, popcorn, pretzels, and hot dogs floated through the air. Casey looked at the hundreds of cameramen jockeying for position at each end of the basketball court. She began to feel warm from the intense overhead lights, and she could have sworn that her whole body was vibrating from the Dolby sounds of "We Are the Champions."

Throughout the stands, purple-and-black-uniformed waiters dodged teenagers holding cumbersome signs with catchy phrases created in hopes of being televised on ESPN or NBC. WE LOVE THIS GAME banners were hung and MR. ROGERS'S NEIGHBORHOOD signs were waved throughout, referring to the Mecca belonging to Brent.

"So, Casey, can the Flyers do it this year? Can they break the championshipless drought?"

"One game at a time, one game at a time," Casey said diplomatically.

"Come on, how about a prediction," Phil pressed.

"I never make predictions . . . and I think I better get to my seat," Casey said, motioning to the Flyers dancers being lowered from the ceiling by purple ropes onto the court. Casey knew this was the favorite part for many of the audience members since they were afforded an unobstructed view of the taut rear ends of the dancers in their purple velour Daisy Duke shorts. Landing on the court, the dancers eased into backbends, much to the crowd's delight, generously exposing their other assets.

"I'll find you after the game, Casey," Phil said rather cattily as the lights were dimmed.

Fat chance, Casey thought as she quickly continued down the stairs to her seats.

As one unit, it seemed, the crowd was on its feet roaring at the top of its lungs as a multicolored laser light show began. The traffic in the stands was so thick, Casey found herself saying, "Excuse me" to a different person every couple of feet. When she finally reached her seat, Diamond was barely steadying herself as she stood in Casey's chair while Kelly and Remy were on their feet clapping. Diamond looked like she was seconds away from slipping down and being trapped in between the collapsible seat.

Casey covered her ears as she tried to adjust to the thunderous noise throughout the arena. Her mood did not match her festive surroundings. She was having a difficult time joining the excitement. Picking Diamond off her seat, Casey sat down and tenderly placed the little girl on her lap. She began to absentmindedly stroke her back, feeling sorry for the confusion Kelly put her innocent little girl through. Kelly barely noticed that she had moved the child. Casey felt like a small child herself, vulnerable, scared, and needy as the din roared around her.

"Get up, girl," Remy said, leaning down and shouting into Casey's ears. "They're about to introduce your man; just cheer for the jerk since you're here. Come on, Casey!"

Placing Diamond on her hip as she stood, Casey felt light-headed. She was standing there pretending to cheer on the outside, and inside feeling torn apart.

Casey gazed at Brent across the court as he jumped up and down in excited anticipation. She watched him in the shiny purple and black sweats that clung like glue to his rock-solid body. Everything about Brent looked completely manly to her. Even though she was angry with him, she still saw him as looking divine with his clean-shaven head and gorgeous body. In honor of the play-offs, most of the guys on the team had shaved their heads in a symbolic act of camaraderie.

Sensing her staring at him, Brent looked at her across the court and blew a kiss. Casey obligatorily nodded her head and gave him the thumbs-up as the Flyers spotlight landed on a huddle of the guys.

Although Casey would have thought it impossible, the music was turned up another notch as the Flyers veteran announcer, Bud Zanny, prepared to introduce New York City's beloved team. Even Diamond knew the routine and started to shout, "Go Flyers Go!"

"Introducing your starting lineup!" Bud's trademark animated voice bellowed above the roar of the crowd.

"At point guard, in his fourth season out of Howard University . . . your cocaptain . . . *Paaauuul Thooommas!* At shooting guard, in his rookie year out of Stanford . . . *Michaaaeeel Brooooown!*"

Casey covered her ears, the screams were so loud for Michael, the lady-killer. He got as many cheers as Brent and he was only a rookie. The joke was that all of the little girls, teenyboppers, and college ladies came to see him and that all of the women came to watch Collin DuMott, the smooth operator.

"At center, in his fifth season, out of Georgia Tech . . . *Steeeeve Tuuucker!* And at small forward, in his eighth season in the NBA, out of Arkansas State . . . *Cooolliiin DuuuuuuuuMott!*"

Casey watched as the starting players ran through the area cleared by the nonstarting players. They gave each other high fives and they bumped chests in their "man's man" ritual. Even though the game had not yet begun, sweat flew from the players onto the hungry front-row fans.

Casey listened to the drum roll that always embarrassed Brent. It was the precursor to the team's All-Star Olympian being introduced, and it never failed to make the crowd go absolutely wild.

"Last but definitely not least, at power forward, your team captain, in his ninth year out of Duke University with the New York Flyers . . . *Brent Roooooooogers!*"

Casey watched as Brent ran through the line, both arms up in the air and the NUMBER ONE sign on each hand extended to the sky. If the energy in the arena was intense before his introduction, it was flat-out electric as all of the Flyers formed a huddle around Brent. All of their naked heads were bent forward, pressing against each other as if in prayer.

Casey sat back down and let the game begin. For her, it was already in progress.

Dawn Simpson stared vacantly out the backseat window of the chauffeur-driven sedan en route to the Mecca. She desperately hoped the puffiness around her eyes from her crying earlier had gone down. She scarcely noticed the spectacular New York City skyline as the car smoothly traversed the George Washington Bridge. She was running late and was surprised that she had even mustered the energy to attend the game after her tumultuous day with Michael. If she was lucky, she would make it to the arena by the end of the second quarter.

As Dawn ran her fingers through her hair, it seemed that nothing was going right for her except her work at Good Samaritan Hospital, where she was a first-year resident in psychiatry. This was one of the most sought-after residencies in medicine. Of course, Michael's schedule had played a part in her choice since once she completed her residency, she would have normal hours and not be on call in the traditional sense. This way she would have more time for Michael. Sometimes Dawn wondered if she'd made the right decision.

She could still feel the frustration coursing through her from their earlier run-in. Recently it seemed as if every comment she made to him resulted in an argument. Dawn shook her head thinking how different things had become between them since he'd been drafted by the Flyers and they'd experienced all that accompanied it. Again she thought of marriage. Then she remembered a disconcerting conversation from the previous summer.

It was during the Flyers' postseason annual trip to the Bahamas— sort of a bonus from Hirshfield, even though they hadn't won the championship. This had been Dawn's first opportunity to spend time with Casey, Lorraine, Remy, Trina, and Kelly. The women had all been sunbathing on the white-sand beach at the Ocean Club on Paradise Island when the subject of marriage among the NBA couples came up. Michael had just proposed to her the month before, and Dawn was still floating.

Now Dawn remembered Kelly's drunken laughter between gulps of strawberry daiquiris.

"Girl, guys in the NBA only get engaged to put off marriage. Sometimes they even break down and let their fiancées live with them. Of course, if they allow this, it tacks on another two years to the running engagement. And if the player is a rookie and he gets engaged, forget about it. Rookies don't ever get married during their first year," Kelly had cackled before finishing off her drink.

"I hate to admit it, but you're right about the rookies," Casey had interjected, addressing Dawn directly. "The young guys, especially those on a hot team, seem to only have time for basketball and endorsements. And, of course, nightclubs on the road and signing autographs anywhere and everywhere."

"Yeah, but can you really blame them?" Remy had said, sitting up on her towel and lifting up her Jean Paul Gaultier sunglasses. "They're young kids with the world at their feet. It's a heady position to be in. I know when I had my first hit with Atlantic Records, nobody could tell me anything. I just knew I was all that and then some. They just have to get it out of their system and have some fun with their new status. Believe me, for most of them it will pass and they'll find out that all the hype and glamour in the world can't replace a meaningful relationship."

"Unfortunately, sometimes it takes too long for them to realize this, and by then they've lost the one person who genuinely cared about them," Casey had said, turning over onto her stomach.

At the time, Dawn had been certain that Michael was different from the rest of the guys. She believed their relationship was special, above the problems that these other troubled couples might experience.

Love had always been so real between Dawn and Michael. They were in complete sync with one another. Dawn had been in her sixth year of Inteflex, an accelerated program compressing undergrad and medical school into seven years. She had just begun her "shadowing" of doctors during their rotations, and at the time, Michael had been a patient suffering from a severe bacterial sinus infection.

Dawn softly chuckled thinking about Michael that autumn afternoon one week after she first met him, swearing he was dying from an ingrown fingernail.

"Doc, I've got something I need your help with," Michael had said, holding his right forefinger as if he were in excruciating pain.

Dawn had not realized that he was asking for her assistance until one of her classmates eating with her in the cafeteria nudged Dawn's arm. They had all begun to feel like real doctors wearing their white coats.

"What can I do for you?" Dawn had asked him, slightly confused.

"You're really going to make this hard for me, aren't you?" Michael had said, looking flustered.

"Make what hard for you?" Dawn had answered, still confused.

"I've been trying to track you down all week, ever since I first came into the emergency room," Michael had said, inching closer to the table.

Dawn had realized that the finger was a ruse—he wanted to ask her for a date. Although she was not opposed to interracial dating, it would be a new experience for her. She was mostly shocked that Stanford's star basketball player would be interested in her. As far as she could tell, they were total opposites, from their social circles to their career paths to the color of their skin.

None of these differences had seemed to matter to Michael. He had pursued her relentlessly, showing up at the hospital on various excuses for six weeks straight until she finally relented and went out with him. In reality, the numerous lunches they'd shared in the hospital cafeteria were more than enough to convince Dawn that she was thoroughly moved by Michael Brown.

Michael had been majoring in biology and he displayed a sincere interest in Dawn's work and her personal life. They had become friends, and the potential to become lovers had hovered over their every conversation and debate.

She had felt an immediate and unexpected attraction toward Michael. Dawn thought him incredibly handsome. He'd reminded her of a younger, taller version of Denzel Washington.

Dawn thought back fondly to how their interactions at Stanford had been charged with an undercurrent of sexual energy, mutual respect, and mutual desire to be together. Wow, how times have changed, Dawn thought as the sedan slowed down.

"Right by the purple awning will be fine," Dawn said to the driver, leaning forward, directing him to the VIP entrance of the Mecca.

"You're kind of late for the game, aren't you, miss?" the driver asked as she pulled the door handle to exit the vehicle.

"Am I?" Dawn said over her shoulder as she headed toward the entrance.

There was definitely a change in Michael's behavior of late; Dawn could not lie to herself about it. She knew he was under a tremendous amount of pressure right now and she should cut him some slack, but there was a strain in their relationship. She wanted to believe he was still trying. Dawn thought about earlier that day when he'd left the apartment in a huff and had come back to kiss and make up. Even though they had fooled around and cuddled for a couple of hours, still it felt vacant to her, as if he were doing her a favor or paying penance by giving her a few extra moments of his precious time.

Or was she being too harsh? It was all so confusing, Dawn's head felt as if it were about to explode. Maybe she needed to just relax and stop obsessing over it. Michael was her man and one day they were going to get married. Period.

Dawn reminded herself that she had a couple of days off from work coming up in the next few weeks. Maybe she'd join him on a road trip; it might be just what she and Michael needed, some quality time alone together. Dawn envisioned them in a hotel together relaxing, no phones ringing. She would make the suggestion to him after the game, hopefully over a victory dinner.

As Dawn entered the empty Family Lounge, she glanced at one of the numerous television monitors that broadcast the game and noticed that the first half of the game had just ended. The score flashed on the screen. The Flyers were blowing Philadelphia away by twenty points. She knew this would make Michael happy.

Dawn was starving. She prepared herself a plate and then found a seat before the hordes of people returned to the room for halftime. Although she had become friendly with some of the wives—and of course, Casey Rogers and Lorraine Thomas had been by far the kindest—the other mates were standoffish, even accounting for her erratic work schedule. She admitted to herself she could try a bit harder to fit in.

She knew that some of them resented her because she was white. She had overheard on more than one occasion whispered conversations not meant for her. "I get tired of all our professional single brothers getting snatched up by white chicks, gettin' our men to slave away for them." Of course, the offending party would qualify the statement: "Dawn, you know we're not talking about you; you're different. We know you really love Michael and you got your own thang goin' on." Dawn often wondered how they could know anything about her. When she mentioned the incidents to Michael, he dismissed them as gossip.

Seated at one of the round tables, Dawn began stuffing herself with skewers of broiled shrimp and fusilli tossed with vegetables. Soon the room began to fill around her. Flyers family members and friends began to convene around the bar for refills in anticipation of a victory. Dawn only recognized a few of the faces. She knew that a lot of the players' relatives flew in for the play-offs. Michael's parents planned on coming to town if the team advanced to the next round.

Robin Stillman, the assistant coach's wife, with her stiffly sprayed hair, approached the table where Dawn was sitting and flopped down next to her, making the air escape from her chair cushion. Her hair did not budge.

"Hey, Robin. How's it going?" Dawn asked, realizing her mistake too late.

Robin Stillman was the official Flyers gossip queen; worse, she was like Alexis's lapdog. She kept abreast of everyone's business on the team and sometimes created business when none was there. Robin was more concerned with other people's affairs than her own.

"Giiiirrrl, I didn't see you in your seats. You know Alexis is going to have something to say about you being late."

"Well, I'm going to try to make it up and catch a couple of the away games, maybe in the next round—when they make it. I have some days off from work coming up."

The woman positively stared at her. "Dawn, I realize that this is only your first year here, but you can't be serious about going to an away game, especially during the play-offs. You should know by now that it's against team policy for the wives to go on the road, unless, of course, we make it to the finals. You're just asking for trouble."

"Michael and I make our own policies."

"You'll learn," Robin said, patting Dawn's hand. "Well, anyway, you sure did miss a good first half." Robin scooted closer to Dawn.

"I know, they're killing Philadelphia," Dawn said, taking a forkful of her pasta, trying not to let Robin's comments affect her.

"That's not what I'm talking about! You missed Kelly. She's sitting in Casey's seats, drunk as a skunk. I hate to see what she's going to be like after halftime. I don't even know why she bothered to show up. Everybody knows that Steve is finished with her. He even has a new woman, Stephanie. Real class. She was great at Alexis's breakfast," Robin said, raising her eyebrows expectantly as she looked at Dawn.

Before Dawn realized what was happening, Robin snatched her left hand and pulled it within six inches of her face.

"When did Michael give you this?" Robin panted after Dawn's perfect five-carat, pear-shaped, blue-shadowed diamond ring.

Dawn slid her hand away as tactfully as possible. She rarely wore the ring because she had to take it off so much at the hospital; she did not want to risk losing it.

"When did you and Michael officially get engaged?"

"I'm sure you must have heard," Dawn said quietly.

"Well, Michael sure hasn't discussed it with anyone," Robin said, a smug look on her face.

"What's that supposed to mean?" Dawn said, hating herself for taking the bait.

"You haven't seen the latest edition of *Flyer Life*, huh?" Robin rolled her chair to an adjacent table, snatching up an issue of the publication. "Michael was spotlighted in this month's issue. They have an eight-page article on him, big photo spread and all. When they ask him his relationship status, he says that he's unmarried," Robin continued, leafing through the magazine to find the exact quote.

"Well, we're not married yet," Dawn said, feeling her solar plexus thrum. Michael had not even mentioned the showcase in the magazine. Why hadn't he told her?

"See, right here; he sure doesn't mention he's engaged either." Robin shoved the magazine inches from Dawn's face.

Against her better judgment, Dawn grabbed it and began feverishly scanning the article. Her eyes couldn't absorb the words fast enough. The nerve of him!

"But you know how rookies are, Dawn; they're so wrapped up in what's going on with them, they don't have time to think about anyone else except themselves and maybe their mothers. The girlfriends just get pushed to the side. Don't take it personally. You're lucky with Michael. He seems like he's basically a good kid."

Dawn finished reading the article and looked at the photo layout of Michael, which included a shot of him as a child as well as a picture of him with his parents. Where was *her* picture with Michael?

Suddenly Dawn almost jumped out of her seat, feeling hands on her shoulders.

"Play-off jitters, huh? I missed you during the first half," Lorraine Thomas said, leaning down and kissing Dawn on the cheek.

"Yeah," Dawn managed to utter, her heart too hurt to say much more.

"Hello, Lorraine. I guess I'll leave you two ladies, the half is just about over. Dawn, don't let that article bother you. You know how these guys can be," Robin triumphantly said, rising from the table.

"What's wrong, Dawn?" Lorraine asked.

"This," Dawn said, pushing the article toward Lorraine.

"This? I read this article already. It was very flattering to Michael. What's the matter?"

"Do you always have to be so diplomatic? My point is, he didn't mention my name or the fact that I even exist."

"And I suppose Robin brought that to your attention, huh?" Lorraine said, turning up her lips.

"Well, yes."

"Dawn, look at the source. That woman's life goal other than being Miss Runner to Alexis is to get under our skins. Don't give her the satisfaction. She knows nothing about and has nothing to do with your and Michael's relationship. That's y'all's business and don't you forget it."

"Yeah, but that still doesn't explain why Michael didn't even mention that he has a fiancée in the article."

"Dawn, let me tell you something that I learned by being married into this profession a long time ago. When those reporters go to interview our men, they've already made up their minds of what they want to print. For all you know, Michael did tell them about you and they chose not to print it. You see the title of the article: 'Hotter than Fire.' And look, it was a female reporter. Maybe she wanted to depict him as a young hot stud. You don't know what her angle was. All you need to know is that Michael is your man. If you all have problems, don't let it be because of anyone else. You know what I mean?" Lorraine said, rubbing Dawn's back.

"I guess so," Dawn said, unconvinced.

"Michael is crazy about you. Anybody that's around you two can see that. Come on, let's go down and catch the second half of the game," Lorraine said, standing up.

Dawn reluctantly stood up and threw away her plate and empty soda can. She knew Lorraine was only trying to help, but her words offered little consolation. Even if what she said was true about the reporter's angle, it was still unlike Michael not to tell her about the interview. Why did he hold back? For the first time, Dawn was really scared that she might lose him. She felt as if he was slipping right through her fingers.

The crowd at the Mecca grew so boisterous after the win, Casey wondered if the arena would ever clear out. Fortunately, Kelly had been sedate throughout the second half, albeit in a drunken stupor. She had kept her outbursts to a minimum even though Stephanie had been perched in Steve's seats. The fans lingered in hopes of catching one of the players—any one—doing a courtside interview. Casey was curious how long Kelly would linger to catch Steve.

With the exception of Rick Belleville's blowup at the head referee in the third quarter, costing the team time and points, the Flyers had effortlessly demolished Philadelphia 110 to 80. If this first game was any indication of what the series would look like, Casey knew it was going to be a three-game sweep. The Flyers had played as if the 76ers were no more than a Division III college team. What she saw tonight amounted to an exhibition showcasing the Flyers' superior talent over their opposition.

Usually Casey took pride in Brent having a good game, but tonight was different. She didn't feel much of anything. He had performed like the All-Star he was, but she had far too many distracting thoughts to enjoy it. Between Brent's latest deception, Alexis's demands, and baby-sitting for an intoxicated Kelly, Casey had her fill of drama. She felt like losing it herself.

Looking now at Kelly, her eyes glazed, Casey wondered how to get her home safely. Kelly had ordered one gin and tonic after another throughout the entire game; meanwhile Steve never once looked in her direction. Casey felt for Kelly and knew she must be devastated. Luckily, Diamond was probably still too young to have noticed anything peculiar about her mother's behavior. Still, Casey was relieved that the sweet little girl had fallen asleep on her lap. It was so unfair that this innocent child had to be in the middle of her parents' feud.

"You two ladies plan on sitting here all evening? Because I'm about ready to head back to the locker room," Remy said as she freshened her bronze lipstick.

"Oh, would you mind if I slipped back there with you, Remy?" Kelly said, coming out of her haze for the first time since noticing Stephanie in Steve's seats.

"Kelly, you think maybe you ought to get Diamond home? She seems exhausted," Casey suggested as gently as possible.

"She's all right, she's getting some rest right now. I need to talk with Steve before I go anywhere." Kelly glanced at her sleeping daughter. "And I want her daddy to see her before I take her home."

Casey watched as Kelly rose unsteadily to her feet. She then looked quickly across the court through the crowd to get a glimpse of Steve's seats. She hoped Kelly didn't follow her line of vision. Casey watched as Stephanie walked toward the locker-room waiting area, obviously to meet up with Steve.

"Kelly, you know the reporters are going to be hounding Steve after the awesome game he had. He's probably not going to be out for at least another hour."

"I don't mind waiting," Kelly said, crossing her arms over her volup-tuous chest.

"Well, I mind waiting out here," Remy said. "Casey, you know how quickly Collin gets changed. I want to catch him and firm up our plans," Remy said, dabbing some powder on her face from her silver compact.

"I'm right behind you, Remy," Kelly added, her words slurred. "Casey, you can give Diamond to me." She wobbled toward Casey.

Casey held tight to Diamond, her mind racing, echoing Alexis's words. She had to come up with a way to keep Kelly from going back to the locker room.

"Why are you so anxious, Remy?" Casey asked. "You and Collin have something special planned?"

"We're supposed to have a nice, quiet, romantic dinner followed by . . ." Remy started with a wicked grin on her face. "Well, let's just put it this way; it's been a looong time since I've had a memorable evening with my man."

"You're not alone; it's been a long time for me too," Kelly said, clutching Remy's arm. "Longer than I care to mention. Come on, Remy, let's go get our men."

Casey stood fixed in her spot as Remy and Kelly walked across the basketball court toward the locker-room entrance. She realized there was no stopping Kelly. So she gathered up her purse, certain that it was soiled with beer, soda, mustard, confetti, and layers of dirt from the filthy Mecca floor.

Careful not to awaken Diamond in the process, she looked across the court at Kelly and Remy as she pulled her purse strap over her shoulder. They were just about to enter the waiting area outside the locker room. She swallowed hard noticing the photographers and reporters. Casey shuddered to think about what type of scene Kelly was going to make when she finally caught up with Steve. What would happen if Alexis witnessed the outburst? Or, worse, if Coach did? Casey felt as if she were on her way to the front lines to witness battle.

The waiting area outside the locker room was a buzz of activity filled with cameras and flashing bulbs, reporters and groupies all lining the walls next to Nike, Gatorade, and other product reps bumping against agents, attorneys, and a host of other people hoping to assist or, more accurately, kiss up to the players in some fashion. Casey unsuccessfully scanned the crowd, looking for Kelly. Her drunk friend had disappeared quickly. Casey saw Lorraine Thomas across the room deep in conversation with Dawn and then noticed Remy talking to Collin. Still Kelly was nowhere in sight. Casey only hoped she had not passed out in some remote corner of the Mecca.

"Mama. Where Mama?" Diamond said, awaking from her slumber.

"Mommy will be back, sweetie," Casey said as she rocked Diamond back and forth.

"You look like a natural at that. How's my favorite wife?" Jake Schneider said, and gave Casey a wet kiss dangerously close to her mouth.

"I'm fine, Jake, and yourself?" Casey said stiffly, staring at his toupee, which was a good three inches below Casey's nose.

Jake Schneider was one of the best and certainly the slimiest of sports agents. No Jerry McGuire was he! Much to Casey's dismay, Brent was one of Jake's clients, and had been since he'd graduated from Duke. Jake represented the majority of top players in the NBA, and instead of treating them like CEOs of million-dollar corporations, he acted as if they were little boys with second-grade educations. His behavior toward their wives was even worse. Casey was almost certain Jake treated the mistresses better. That would be his style.

"Things are going well for me," Jake said. "I'm just waiting for my guy to get out of the shower so we can make our reservation at Le Cirque. Not that they wouldn't hold the table all night for Brent Rogers. But you know better than anybody how long he can take to get dressed. I bet the big fella stays in the mirror longer than you, Casey." Jake laughed as he removed his tortoiseshell glasses and wiped his eyes and forehead with a white silk handkerchief, as if such a fragile piece of fabric could remove the slime oozing from his every pore.

Casey was surprised. "You and Brent are going to dinner?"

"He didn't bother to tell you, huh?"

"Not yet."

"Don't take it personally. You know these guys. The only person they remember to tell important things to is their agent. Sometimes I feel like a wife."

Casey had to stop herself from rolling her eyes into the back of her head. She was determined not to let this man get under her skin—but it was difficult. He always wanted to be one up on the wives and girl-friends when it came to *his* athletes. Jake had to have complete control over all his clients by any means necessary.

"Hey, I have a new one for you, Casey. Did you hear about the vet-eran ball player and the rookie? Well, the rookie player says to the vet-eran player, —'So, are you married man?' And the veteran player says, —'Yeah, I am at home games.' Get it? He's only married at home games." Jake laughed hysterically.

"Good one, Jake. You're in rare form this evening. Enjoy your din-ner with your number one hero. And would you tell my husband I said good night? I have to help get this little one off to bed." Casey turned and spotted Remy and Collin across the crowded room. They would give her a good escape from the slime bag.

"Oh, is this the little girl?" Jake said, grasping Casey's shoulder before she could walk away. "I didn't know that you'd finally agreed to let her come and visit the two of you."

Casey could not believe that she heard him correctly. It amazed her how someone without an ounce of decency or diplomacy man-aged to rake in new clients. She knew he was one of the best at con-tract negotiations, but when it came to emotional intelligence, he had none.

"I don't believe I heard you correctly, Jake. What did you just say to me?"

"Isn't this Nikki?"

Casey was stunned into silence. She knew that Jake was a tactless control freak whose motto was "Divide and conquer," but this was by far the lowest he had ever sunk. And it was such a deliberate attack. Jake knew very well that the little two-year-old girl she was holding was too young to be Brent's daughter. What the hell had gotten into him? He seemed to really be getting off on attacking her. What's more, there was nothing that could be done about it. Even if Brent were to fire Jake, he would still collect 4 percent of Brent's salary for the next six years, and 15 percent of several multimillion-dollar endorsements. There was not a thing she could do about his presence in their lives.

"Good-bye, Jake," Casey managed before she walked in the direction of Remy.

"Wait, Casey," Jake began. "Why don't you join us for dinner?"

She could almost see Jake triumphantly sneering behind her.

Ignoring him, she worked her way through the crowd and plastered a fake smile on her face as she played the part of Mrs. Brent Rogers. She spotted Collin hurrying away from Remy. Casey figured he had probably forgotten something in the locker room.

"Have you seen Kelly?" Casey asked Remy as she approached her.

"No," Remy said curtly.

"I wish she would bring her butt back here. Diamond needs to be in bed, and the way I feel now, so do I. Brent's going out to dinner with Jake, and he didn't even tell me anything about it. Once again, I'm going home alone," Casey said, continuing to search the room for any sign of Kelly, watching enviously as Paul and Lorraine Thomas hugged each other, laughing at some private joke. Why couldn't that be her and Brent right now?

"I can't believe him," Remy said, shaking her head, looking past Casey.

"Isn't he a jerk? He used to represent Collin, didn't he? Collin was smart to give him the boot. Jake has no respect for the players or their wives. I can't stand him. You wouldn't believe what he just said to me."

"Casey, I'm not talking about Jake. I'm talking about my inconsiderate-ass boyfriend. He just stood me up!" Remy said.

"What happened?" Casey said, realizing for the first time that Remy was upset too.

"He just told me that he had some extra work to do."

"He didn't stand you up, Remy. He has work to do. At least he told you himself."

"Casey, you know that it's been weeks since we've had a quiet evening alone together. The least he could do is make some time for me. He could have told me before the game that he had plans. I wouldn't have even come to this stupid blowout of a game if I wasn't going to be able to see him afterwards."

"Listen. Just relax. Both of you have hectic schedules. There've been a lot of times when you've been too busy to see him because of your work. He's not inconsiderate. Now, I know inconsiderate first-hand, and Collin is not like that. He's different."

"Yeah, real different. Asshole, standing me up."

"He didn't stand you up—standing you up would've been to just leave and not say anything at all. At least he—"

"I know what a stand-up is," Remy interrupted. "I'm just pissed. I'd been looking forward to this evening for a while."

Casey genuinely felt bad for her friend. It was not like Remy to show her disappointment. But Casey was fresh out of solutions for herself; how could she make Remy feel any better?

"Look at it this way, Remy; it's his loss. If he doesn't want any ass tonight from his beautiful woman, then that's his problem."

Casey noticed the tense look leaving Remy's face.

"Yeah, yeah, that's right. It's his loss. Maybe I'll get some from somebody else."

"That's the spirit." Casey laughed. "Even though you and I both know Collin is crazy about you. Don't hurt that poor boy like that."

"Well, maybe next time he'll think twice before canceling on me," Remy petulantly said.

"Come on, Remy. We both know he's not that bad. Collin's ten times better than most of the guys on the team," Casey said. She understood Remy's disappointment all too well, but still, Collin was a prize. He was sensitive and very mature. Other than Paul Thomas, Collin was the only other player whom Casey had never heard any gossip about. "Girl, you have a good man, stop complaining," she chided Remy. But Casey knew that none of that mattered to a woman when she felt that she was being scorned. Staring at Remy, Casey realized there was probably only one way to lift Remy's spirits.

"Stop it, Casey," Remy began as she crossed her arms over her chest. "Why are you looking at me like that?"

"You look frustrated and sad and . . . I think under these circumstances, you and I owe it to ourselves to have some fun tonight—even if it is without our men."

A conspiratorial look spread across Remy's face. They both enjoyed a fun evening out on the town every now and then. It was their ladies'-night thing. Of course, neither of them was a big drinker, and Casey had a difficult time holding her liquor, but that never stopped them from having a good time.

"So where should we start?" Casey asked. "Jet Lounge for drinks?"

"Then on to Panthers for dancing and young studs."

"Sounds like a plan, but I have to find Kelly first," Casey said, slightly regretting making plans as she was exhausted, mentally and physically.

"Mind if I wait in your car?" Remy began. "I need a change of scenery."

"Nope, just open up my purse and grab my keys. I'll see you in a few minutes."

The crowd slowly began to thin out around her, yet she still could not find Kelly. Casey began to pace the waiting area hoping that she would return. Maybe she was just in the ladies' room freshening up in preparation to see Steve.

"Oh my God, Casey! Do you see him? Just standing over there. He's awfully bold if you ask me," the Flyers Gossip Queen said, appearing from around the corner.

"Who?"

Robin leaned into Casey, lowered her voice, and pointed. "Leonard Hightower. He has some nerve showing his face around here. Look at him. See him over there?"

Casey looked through the thinning crowd but did not notice him. She wondered how Robin Stillman knew anything about Leonard Hightower. Apparently it wasn't as big a secret as Alexis had led her to believe.

"See Jake Schneider?" Robin panted.

Casey nodded seeing Jake saddled up next to Coach Mitchell, who looked like he was ready to grace the cover of GQ, once again. Jake Schneider looked like the troll he was standing next to Coach.

"Now see the guy with the bright red hair who looks like he's surveying the room?"

Casey saw the beefy guy with the fire red hair; no one could miss him. In fact, she remembered seeing him earlier in the evening.

"Hightower is directly to his right; he has the thick salt-and-pepper hair. Doesn't he look pompous?"

"Actually . . . yeah, he does," Casey said, agreeing with Robin Stillman, probably for the first time in their entire acquaintance.

He also looks a lot younger than any of the photos I've seen of him, Casey thought. But he looked unmistakably slick, as if he was three steps ahead of everyone else. He had a Jack Nicholson quality to him, except he was more polished, almost painfully. Magnetism surrounded him, so much so that reporters were continually approaching him trying to get his attention—though the burly redheaded man promptly intervened on Hightower's behalf every time they got within a five-foot radius.

"And did you see him prance in like he owned the world at the beginning of the third quarter, having that redheaded guy oust some young actors from Star Row?"

Actually, Casey had seen him arrive after halftime with the redheaded man in tow, but she hadn't realized that he was Leonard Hightower of Hightower Enterprises. It looked like he'd had plastic surgery performed on his face, and Casey could have sworn that his hair used to be completely white.

"He acts like he owns the Flyers already. Heck, he was acting like he owned the Mecca Arena," Robin disgustedly said.

For the impending sale to be such a secret, Robin was certainly talking about it freely, but Casey had to remind herself of what a gossip Robin was. Why would she behave any differently now? In reality it probably really didn't matter to Robin whether the Flyers were sold as long as she still had a forum in which she could dish dirt. Robin's husband, Bob Stillman, the assistant coach, had probably sworn her to secrecy about Leonard Hightower trying to buy the team. It was a shame she couldn't even keep her word to her own husband.

Whatever the situation, Casey did not have time to think about it now. Remy was in the car waiting for her, Diamond was getting antsy and heavy in her arms, and Casey was getting more tired with each passing second.

"Robin, have you seen Kelly around?"

Robin's eyebrows immediately raised another notch, as if she had sniffed out a fresh scandal.

"As a matter of fact, I have. I spotted her around the corner at the front of the locker-room door. She's obviously drunk and it looks like she's set up a vigil waiting for Steve," Robin said, quickly forgetting about Hightower. "Are they even together anymore? You know Steve's eccentric new girlfriend Stephanie was at Alexis's breakfast. Speaking of which, if I were you, I'd go and get Kelly before Alexis spots her. You know we want to keep up appearances, especially with all that's going on around here." Robin earnestly nodded her head toward Hightower once more. One would have thought that the future of the universe depended on Kelly's behavior.

"Thanks for the tip, Robin," Casey said as she made a beeline to the locker-room entrance.

Kelly looked pathetic standing at the front of the locker room peeking in the players' dressing area each time the door opened to see if Steve was the next player coming out. Why was Kelly subjecting herself and Diamond to such public disrespect?

"Kelly, you really need to get Diamond home," Casey said, cutting to the chase as she approached Kelly.

"I'm coming in a minute. I just saw Steve. He's about to come out now," Kelly said, expectantly staring at the double doors.

Steve was barely out of the locker room before Kelly pounced on him like a cat awaiting its prey. "Who was that in your seats, Steve?"

Steve ignored her, leaned down and greeted Casey with a kiss, and relieved her of Diamond.

"Hello, sweetheart. How's my little angel?" Steve said as he held tight to Diamond.

"Oh, now you're not even gonna speak to me?" Kelly irately asked, placing one hand on her hip.

Casey noticed that even drunk and angry, Kelly oozed sexuality with her bare cleavage heaving up and down.

"What are you doing here, Kelly?" Steve said calmly.

"Excuse me? What do you mean what am I doing here? 'Cause I have a right to be here. That's why."

"Kelly, you've had too much to drink, and I suggest you get yo'self home before you do anything else embarrassing."

"Embarrassing? Embarrassing? I'll tell you what's embarrassing: you having that girl up in my seats, me being treated like a common criminal when I tried to get in the Family Lounge. That's wrong," Kelly said, getting louder with each word.

"What's wrong is you showing up here when you weren't invited," Steve spat out.

"I don't need an invitation. I'm your fiancée, damn it."

"*Were* my fiancée, past tense. Now, go home and get Diamond to bed. You're testing my patience."

"Are you crazy, boy? What do you mean I'm testing your patience? You better get your priorities straight. Me and Diamond are your family. We're the ones who are going to be here when all the groupies are gone," Kelly shouted as she shoved Steve against the wall. Diamond started to wail. Steve looked to Casey helplessly.

"Stephanie is no groupie and you better watch yourself. Shit, you're one to talk," Steve said, looking flustered.

Just then, Alexis rounded the corner and stared at the two of them disapprovingly. "Is everything all right here?" she said, looking over the situation. She glared at Casey accusingly as if she had somehow disappointed her.

Knowing that she would not be in the mood to hear Alexis's mouth later, Casey took her cue and intervened. "Look, you two, why don't you settle this at home, in a less public forum. And Diamond doesn't need to see this."

"I think that's the best way to handle your domestic squabbles, behind closed doors instead of making a scene. And, Steve, I'm shocked that you would allow someone like her to draw you into this . . . this type of exchange," Alexis said distastefully.

"You want to know what I think, Alexis—" Kelly began before Steve covered her mouth with his hands.

"I'm going to take her home and get her to bed, Alexis. Pardon her behavior, she's had a bit too much to drink."

"So I see. Let's make absolutely certain that it doesn't happen again in the future. Do you follow me? I'm counting on you, Steve," Alexis said before she sauntered away from them, leaving the unmistakable scent of Chanel No. 5.

Casey noticed Steve's about-face dealing with Kelly in the presence of Alexis—apparently she had that effect on everyone.

"Ouch! Stop biting me, Kelly. What the hell is the matter with you?" Steve said, snatching his hand from her mouth.

"You used to like it when I bit you," Kelly sneered. The only word Casey could think of to describe Kelly's laugh was *maniacal*.

"Casey." Steve dropped his voice. "You know my friend Stephanie?"

Casey nodded her head.

"Would you do me a favor and tell her that I had some family matters to attend to?"

"All right, Steve, but get them home safely."

Casey walked back out to the waiting area, annoyed that she was further drawn into this web. She easily found Stephanie, a tall, graceful girl with her hair worn in short, twisted dreadlocks that Robin Stillman *would* consider eccentric. She was a regal beauty with striking features, and Casey could almost feel the dignity and class with which she carried herself, like an African princess. She and Kelly were opposites in their dispositions—Stephanie the gazelle and Kelly the jackal. Casey passed on Steve's message, and felt guilty when Stephanie calmly said, "Thanks Casey. I appreciate it girl." They left the arena together and walked out to the parking lot, exchanging uncomfortable stiff smiles, neither knowing what else to say under the strained circumstances. Ironically, had they met in a different situation, they would probably be friends.

Casey breathed a sigh of relief as she reached her car. "So much for the first play-off game," she said as she opened the door to her Jaguar, wearily sat down in the soft leather seat, and leaned her head back.

"Don't look so tired on me, girl," Remy said, looking at Casey.

"I feel like I just got gang-banged by half the Mecca Arena."

"Does this mean you're backing out on me?"

"Would you be upset?" Casey said, feeling slightly guilty for disappointing her friend.

"Well," Remy began before letting out a long yawn, "I'm pretty beat myself and I know you have to work in the morning. I'll settle for a lift home and a rain check."

"You got it—on both counts."

As Casey started the car, she hoped this first game was not an indication of what lay before her during the rest of the play-offs. Yeah, the Flyers had won, but the personal scores seemed much too high a price to pay.

Steve Tucker's temples throbbed as he cruised along the Henry Hudson Highway. He checked his rearview mirror and saw Kelly passed out in the backseat. Diamond was stretched out next to her mother, soundly sleeping. It pained Steve and pissed him off at the same time to see how Kelly had fallen apart after their breakup. He understood that she was having a difficult time accepting his decision, and he was trying to be patient with her for the sake of Diamond. But it was never easy with Kelly, and he was nearing the end of his rope dealing with her bullshit. She was a passionate, compulsive woman, and ever since their problems began a couple of years ago, she'd become unbearably possessive. She was definitely in serious denial about their relationship. And lately she'd taken out her frustrations by drinking, which had really begun to worry Steve. He wanted to help her, but she was so high-maintenance. In fact, she said she'd get help, but only by going to couples counseling rather than rehab.

Steve listened to Kelly's breathing become heavier as she changed position. There was no doubt about it, she was a beautiful woman. It was a shame to see her turning into someone nasty, angry, and ugly. Well, nastier than she had been if that was possible. Kelly refused to take responsibility for her own actions. She blamed everyone else for her problems. She claimed that other women had interfered with their engagement, that Steve was the reason she constantly drank, and it wasn't her fault that Diamond was frightened all the time by her mother's erratic behavior. Her will was relentless, but it was concentrated on the wrong things. Steve shook his head in bewilderment.

Looking at the city skyline as he drove across the George Washington Bridge, Steve felt a pang of regret that he had sent Stephanie home. He wanted her with him right now. Sometimes he felt as if he was never going to be able to move on with his life. Kelly was like gum on the bottom of his shoe.

Although he had broken off their engagement over a year ago, he still allowed her to live in his mansion, while he had relocated to a small apartment in Manhattan. Occasionally he did have a slipup and would sleep with her. He was powerless against a certain access code she had to him sexually, and in moments when they clicked, it was impossible to turn her down. Because he felt guilty over this and sorry, he had even continued giving her tickets to the games until last month. But her behavior at the games was becoming so inappropriate that Coach had warned Steve and had firmly suggested that she not come to any more games. It was apparent to Steve that he wasn't doing Kelly any favors; he was playing a role in her fatal attraction. And the poor child sleeping so sweetly in the backseat, content to be snuggled up with her mom—it felt like a maze he couldn't find his way out of. Then there was the issue of Stephanie.

Steve had met Stephanie at a party in downtown Manhattan. She was beautiful and smart. Steve was relieved to learn that she was divorced; to him, it meant she was realistic about relationships. She would know if it wasn't meant to be. For the past month since they'd been seeing each other, Steve had been trying to convince Stephanie to come see him play, but she had gently declined until he straightened out his business with Kelly. Steve had assured Stephanie that Kelly no longer received any tickets, and ironically, tonight had been the first time Stephanie had finally agreed to come to the Mecca.

Steve pulled up the long driveway to the massive contemporary house Kelly had chosen in Englewood, New Jersey. He reached for the garage opener that he used to keep attached to his sun visor but did not feel it there.

"Kelly . . . Kelly . . ." Steve said leaning over the seat.

Kelly did not stir. Steve got out of the car and walked to the rear passenger door and lightly shook her shoulders. She began to move a bit before slowly opening her eyes.

"Hey, baby. Where are we?" Kelly said in between yawns.

"You're home. Can you make it out of the car all right? I'll get Diamond if you open the garage," Steve said as he leaned across Kelly to pick up Diamond.

"Is Daddy going to spend the night with us?" Kelly said, stumbling out the backseat onto the redbrick driveway.

"No. Daddy is not going to spend the night. I just want to make sure you and Diamond get to bed safely. Now, will you open the garage?"

Kelly opened the garage and wobbled inside. Steve carried Diamond, careful not to awaken her. The house had never felt like home. It was a showplace for all that Kelly coveted. At the time, he had readily agreed. He had been so ecstatic about her pregnancy with Diamond.

Steve effortlessly strode up the wide spiral stairway that was closest to Diamond's room. It smelled sweet, like Baby Magic lotion. It reminded him of the good that came out of his relationship with Kelly. Diamond was such a gorgeous little girl, just like her mother. It was sad that he and Kelly had grown apart. Rather, Steve had grown up and Kelly had remained the same high-strung teenage girl he'd met years ago back in Atlanta.

Kelly had been the first woman he had ever slept with, and to date, the very best. But the sex had not been enough to sustain a meaningful relationship. Emotionally, mentally, and culturally, Steve had grown to a different plane than Kelly, and over the past three years, their lives had taken separate directions. It was no one's fault, it was just a fact that Steve was unable to overlook anymore—even for the sake of Diamond.

Steve removed Diamond's clothes and changed her wet pull-up diaper. She was just reaching the age when the cute baby fat on her legs was becoming lean. He pulled her Winnie the Pooh nightgown over her head and laid her down in her new toddler bed. Steve kissed her on the forehead and, not being able to resist himself, nuzzled both of her chubby cheeks. He watched her slow, even breathing for a few moments before he tore himself away.

"Good night, sweetheart," Steve said as he left her nursery and headed to the double case stairway.

"You're not leaving now, are you, Daddy?" Kelly slurred at the top of the staircase in a black lace negligee.

"Kelly, you should really get some rest," Steve said, pushing past her down the stairs. He was anxious to hurry and leave before he did anything he might regret later.

He picked up his pace as he heard Kelly clamoring after him.

"But you just got here. Don't you want to have a nightcap or something with me?" Kelly whined.

"Kelly, you've had enough to drink for one evening. Why don't you just get some sleep?" Steve said, continuing toward the garage door.

"You're not leaving, Steve. This is your home here with me and Diamond," Kelly said, running up behind him.

"Good night, Kelly," Steve said as he opened the door leading to the garage.

"How do you think you're going to get home without these?" Kelly said, dangling his car keys so they made a menacing clanking sound.

Stopping in his tracks, Steve turned around to face Kelly. "Kelly, give me those keys. I'm not playing with you."

"If you can catch me, I'll give them to you, but only after you play with me first." Kelly began to run toward the first-floor master bedroom.

"Kelly, stop this. You're behaving like a child."

Steve began to take long strides toward Kelly but he refused to chase after her.

"Come and get me, Steve!" Kelly said as she reached her bedroom.

When Steve caught up with Kelly, she was stretched out on the bed with her hands behind her head underneath a tan silk pillow. Steve stood at the foot of the bed and forced himself to keep that access button turned off. Remember, she's more trouble than the sex is worth, he told himself.

"Kelly, stop acting stupid and give me the damn keys."

"Come and get them. They're just behind my head; you know where that is, don't you?" Kelly teased.

The bell went off in those parts of his body and mind he could not control. He felt himself begin to perspire, always a bad sign when he was in Kelly's presence. He knew if he wanted to get out of there with his pants on, he would have to move—now.

Before Kelly had a chance to react, Steve quickly reached under the pillow, snatched the keys out of her grip, and literally ran out of her bedroom through the foyer and the kitchen, out the garage and into his car.

Starting his midnight blue 600 SEL Mercedes, he sighed with relief. Getting away from her tonight seemed as important as escaping a raging tigress. Steve was determined. Stephanie was his woman now, and he had no intention of destroying that relationship.

It was far too precious and genuine.

"Come on, Tony, it was a good take!" Remy impatiently hollered to her favorite video director. Well, sometimes favorite, except on days like this when he insisted on doing twenty takes of every scene. It wasn't as if her video was going to be up for an Oscar.

"No, Remy, not even a little bit. It sucked; you weren't even with me."

"Tony, cut me some slack," Remy said, squinting her eyes to catch a glimpse of the red glowing digital numbers above the camera. It seemed as if she had been at the studio forever.

"Remy, it's three minutes later than the last time you checked the clock." Pam, the costume designer, looked at Remy and rolled her eyes.

"For God's sake, I'm squeezed into this thing like a damn sardine! I can hardly breathe," Remy said, trying to adjust the snug suede vest whose straps crisscrossed at least a hundred times over her back. "I need some air," Remy said, clenching the garment's neck.

"Stop acting like such a goddamn diva! You've been missing in action all day, girl. What the hell is wrong with you?" It was obvious Tony was furious, but Remy couldn't help herself. She couldn't take one more minute in the outfit. She wanted to get out of there.

"Listen, no one is going to believe me when I sing 'Happiness Is Divine' when I look like I'm choking to death," Remy said, loosening the leather straps, really thinking no one was going to believe her because she was so unhappy.

She stepped down off the set, which was designed to look like a fifties retro lounge. Remy inched toward Tony with a pathetic expression on her face, hoping he'd call a wrap. Tony had directed her in three of her most popular music videos. He was known for pushing everyone—cast and crew—like workhorses, especially Remy. He expected a lot from her, and she knew she shouldn't test his patience for fear that he would not work with her anymore. But she was playing a role today that she wasn't capable of handling.

It was already five o'clock and she knew Tony could shoot and reshoot all night. She always operated at a high energy, but he managed to surpass even that limit. On most occasions. Today her thoughts were far too preoccupied with Collin to give any of herself to Tony, the camera, or her fans.

"Get on out of here, Remy. I know you want to see your man play at the Mecca tonight," Tony said dismissively.

Naturally Tony and everyone else on the set would assume that was the reason she was so anxious to leave. Why wouldn't they? Weren't she and Collin supposed to be the "hot" couple of New York City? How could she explain to them that her relationship was crumbling because her boyfriend was under too much pressure to confide in her? Collin had too much pride to turn to her for strength or for anything else these days.

"Tony, you're a doll. Thanks. I'll make it up to you, I swear, " Remy said, keeping up the front as she threw her stuff into a Ferragamo carryall bag and headed for the door.

"Can you blame her? I'd be hurrying over to the Mecca, too, if I had a chance to check out that fine ass rookie Michael Brown in shorts," Pam said.

"Shoot, if I had Collin DuMott waiting for me, I'd be rushing too. And the play-offs? Who can blame you, girl? I'd split for there just to see who was in the audience." Remy's hairdresser gave Pam a high five.

"Try to get some sleep tonight," Tony barked after Remy. "We start at seven sharp tomorrow morning. I want to get to the Brooklyn Bridge scene by early afternoon."

"Sure, sure, Tony, see you tomorrow," Remy said, letting the door of the studio slam behind her.

Once in the limousine heading uptown, Remy thought about everyone's fascination with celebrities—especially when two of them dated. It sometimes bothered her that people thought her relationship with Collin was public property since she and Collin were both public figures. Even her own staff sometimes overstepped the line. Remy had a huge, possessive fan base. One of the major appeals of her music was its "mood-shaping" effect. Remy's music was uplifting, inspirational, and soulful. Her music and lyrics were often said to make one feel like a bird taking off on a fantastic voyage.

Now that she and Collin were "public," these fans, as well as a number of her friends, frequently assumed that any mood fluctuations she experienced were directly attributable to Collin. When she made live appearances, if the mood she projected was sexy, it was often perceived as insight into their love affair. Her public thought that by following Collin's statistics, they could evaluate the status of their relationship.

At home in her SoHo loft with its soaring ceilings, she realized it was only one hour until tip-off. She had been teetering all day about whether to attend the game. Last night Collin had left what amounted to an obligatory message on her machine about leaving her tickets for the second game against Philadelphia. His tone had been noncommittal as far as any plans after the game were concerned. Sitting down on her vanity chair, Remy peeled the skintight buckskin skirt off her toned thighs. She looked at herself in the mirror before removing the charcoal makeup from around her delicately slanted eyes, which she had inherited along with her straight jet black hair from her Japanese father. But her tan complexion and full lips came directly from her Haitian mother.

Remy used a Q-tip to wipe away the mess beneath her eyes. She stared at her reflection, contemplative.

What are you doing?

Remy had consciously turned her thoughts off during the video shoot, at least for a while. But now she wrapped herself up in thoughts about Collin. She had never allowed a relationship with a man to affect her work. It was bothering her that she was doing it now. Remy cared deeply about Collin and they had enjoyed a fulfilling relationship for the past three years. Part of what had kept their connection fresh was their mutual respect for one another's need for space.

Remy had always preferred being free, and she knew Collin shared this attitude with her. She was not a woman who felt she had to have a man to be complete. She hadn't had an exclusive boyfriend until she was twenty-two years old. That was really the first time she felt relaxed enough about her career to listen to the deeper rumblings of her heart. Since then, she'd dated plenty, but never had the desire to settle down. She always wondered where the term "settle down" originated. Remy had never wanted to "settle" for anyone.

She thought of her hit single, "Happiness Is Divine." Indeed, Remy considered herself to be happy for two reasons: her parents and Collin. Her mother and father had instilled in her that happiness comes from within first and that no material item would ever bring her lasting contentment. That spiritual valve helped keep her grounded in the unreal world of a star. And then there was the love she had for Collin. The sense of peace she felt in his company brought her a joy she was unable to duplicate in his absence, a feeling she wanted to last forever. But recently he'd been unavailable to even share her company.

Yet they were only boyfriend and girlfriend. There was no rule stating they had to spend "X" number of days together. Neither of them had ever broached the topic of marriage except to say that they saw no need for it. Why was she allowing love for a man to change her? Her relationship with Collin was fine the way it was right now—or the way it used to be. They spent time together whenever they could, they shared wonderful vacations to exotic destinations, and they had deep passion. Their connection needed no more definition. But didn't it need time and nourishment?

Remy reprimanded herself for not leaving well enough alone as she jumped up from her vanity and headed into the living room. Everything was perfect the way it was now. Wasn't it? Why was she entertaining ridiculous thoughts of lifetime commitments? She was a free spirit. That was her commitment. Yet she felt so jumbled inside. And now here she was, making a conscious decision to ignore his invitation to the game. Why was she pulling back now? Did she want Collin to chase after her, to beg her? That wasn't his style or hers—to play games just to get more attention.

Walking toward one of the ten-foot windows in her loft, Remy lowered the blinds. The eight huge windows in her corner loft were ideal for taking in the sights of SoHo and capturing the sun on the whitewashed pine floors, but she knew from experience not to leave an unobstructed view into her apartment after dark. The last time she left her shades open in the evening, the paparazzi caught her clothed in an old terry cloth robe and a mud mask on her face. Naturally the photographs found their way into the *National Enquirer*'s "Would You Be Caught Dead in This Outfit?" section.

Sure, Collin had invited her to see him play, but she couldn't shake the feeling that he would be too busy, once again, to meet her afterward. She was tired of him pushing her away, and more important, she did not want to risk his rejection. Remy fell back on her goose-down sofa and snatched up the television remote control, determined not to chase him anymore. If Collin wanted to see her, he would have to call her and make an official date. After all, she had her pride too. Flicking through the channels, Remy hoped that he'd call her after the game to find out why she hadn't come. That would make him realize he couldn't take her for granted. In fact, tonight would be a perfect time for her to catch up on some phone calls.

Collin DuMott was out of her thoughts.

"You played a great game tonight, Mr. Thomas. Could I get your autograph too?" the pretty young woman asked as she pushed the piece of paper from under his teammate's hand toward Paul.

Paul felt a quick smile start to pull at his face when he saw his team-mate grin at his reac-tion to the woman's suggestive stance. She was leaning over their table, exposing her plump protrusions from every angle. Paul quickly averted his eyes and glanced down at the torn, lipstick-stained tissue in front of him. He signed his name and playing number 2 with a flourish and handed it to the woman.

"Thanks, guys. If you ever need a return favor, call me." With a seductive wink and a toss of her hair, she placed a business card on the table and slowly sashayed away.

"Yeah, sure thing," Paul said, looking at his teammate and shaking his head. "It never ends, does it?"

"Nope," he responded. "And it's not supposed to, at least not while we're still playing."

"You've got a point there," Paul agreed, looking around the crowded restaurant.

No matter how many people showed up at Jezebel's Restaurant, the Flyers were always given priority seating at the very best tables. On game nights in particular, masses of people tried to get reservations at the popular eatery, hoping to get a glimpse of one of their favorite players. Even the guys from the opposing teams frequented the restaurant, with many game nights ending in a spirit of forced camaraderie among the competitors that only a good meal and funny league anecdotes could provide.

"Listen, I didn't bring you here so the groupies could get their fill of Paul Thomas," he said jokingly.

"Aw, and I thought you were tryin' to hook me up." Paul laughed and sat back in his chair.

Paul was curious why his teammate had rushed over to him as soon as they entered the locker room after their second win over Philadelphia. The two men were good friends, but they rarely had dinner unless they were on the road. Now he had asked Paul to grab a bite to eat out of the blue. Paul hadn't really felt like joining him because he wanted to hurry home to Lorraine, but the way his teammate had approached him was more of a friend's plea than a mere request to grub on some soul food.

Seated at the discreet plush corner booth, he began speaking as soon as their orders were taken. "Paul . . ." He hesitated. "You're my boy, right? Always there for me . . ."

"Through thick and thin, man."

"And I can trust you, right?" he continued.

"Always, man. Whatever you say to me, the buck stops here."

Before he could continue, the waitress returned with their drinks, hovering over their table to the dismay of the other customers. Paul's teammate took a long swig of his Amstel Light and roughly cleared his throat.

"We're fine, thanks," he said, looking up at the waitress's expectant face.

Finally she left them alone when she realized that neither of them was interested.

"Do you remember the last Bible study you held for the guys right before the play-offs started? You ended the session by asking if any of us had any other things we wanted to discuss. Well, I wanted to say something then, but I didn't know how, and I'm still not sure how to say what I need to tell you . . . but . . ." He seemed unable to go any further. He clasped his hands together and looked down at the table.

"What's up man? Talk to me," Paul said, bothered by his teammate's obvious discomfort.

The two of them had always been open and honest with one another about issues both on and off the basketball court. Paul wondered just what kind of burden could cause his boy to act so tentative with him.

An awkward silence hung over their table.

"Is it your woman? The two of you havin' problems or somethin'?"

"No, no, it doesn't have anything to do with her; well, at least not directly. She doesn't know anything about this; that's part of the problem," he slowly responded.

"Are you sick? You don't have AIDS, do you?" Paul worriedly asked, taking a second look at his teammate.

"Naw, man! I'm not sick. It's nothing like that. I . . . I . . ." he said, clearly flustered. "I'm going through a tough time right now."

"Well, what's up? Talk to me. You worried about the team being sold?"

"No, Paul, it's not that. I'm . . . I . . . I think I'm gay," he said, blurting out his last few words.

Paul quickly reached for his water glass and knocked it over as he blindly groped his hand across the table. "Shit!" Paul said as he reached for the toppled glass. He placed his cloth napkin over the wet areas and began dabbing frantically at the soaked linen covering.

"Shocked?"

"Honestly?" Paul asked.

"The look on your face says it all."

"This is coming out of left field. I mean . . . I . . . you . . . you've been involved with a woman, with women, period, for as long as I've known you. I assumed you liked women."

"I do like women and I truly love the one I'm with, but just not in that way. I guess I've known for . . . a while," he said, casting his eyes downward.

"How long have you felt this way?" Paul said, regretting not being able to hide his astonishment.

"I don't know exactly, probably since the time I was *supposed* to start liking girls. I'd hear all my friends in junior high talking about the little honeys they were crazy about. I never really felt that out-of-control passion. I put so much into basketball and homework, I kind of told myself that was the reason I had no interest in them."

"But you still had girlfriends?" Paul asked, confused.

"Yeah, a few, over the years. Nothing really serious, until my woman now. But then, I was just going along with society's program for a jock like me. You know, I had to have a woman on my arm, and the finer, the better. But my lady is more to me than that, she's still my friend. But I can't pretend anymore. I've never felt complete with a woman. It always seemed like something was missing, but I was never able to pinpoint it until . . . until . . ." He trailed off.

Paul knew where he was going with the conversation and really didn't want to join him there. He wasn't prepared to hear the gory details. Paul watched his teammate's face play out his contradictory inner struggle: confusion, agony, and certainty.

"Hey, man, you don't have to go on if . . ." Paul started.

"I know, I know, but I want to, I really want to. I've just discovered that something major was missing in my life. He . . ." He checked out Paul's face. "It's given me peace and contentment that I didn't know was possible." He stumbled through the sentence as if he could not believe what he was saying himself.

"And it's also made me more confused, angry, and frustrated. Hell, I don't know." His turmoil was obvious. "I just had to tell somebody, and you're always there for all of us. I had to let it out, get it off my chest. I mean, it's a big part of who I am . . . what I am."

Paul downed the last bit of Merlot in his wineglass. He did not know what his friend needed or expected of him. Paul also didn't know why he suddenly felt so uncomfortable. He was more anxious than ever to get home to his own woman. Gently shrugging his shoulders and looking him directly in the eye, he said, "To each his own my friend . . . to each his own. And you'll always be my boy." Paul tried to convince himself of that statement as much as his teammate.

He genuinely felt for his friend, but there was a part of Paul that believed being gay was unnatural and counter to the teachings of the Bible. After all, God did make Adam and Eve, not Adam and Steve. On the drive home and entering the warmth of his home, he could not stop thinking about his teammate's confession.

Paul switched off his kitchen television set with disgust. Sometimes he wondered why he even bothered to turn it on. Tonight he had been unable to stop himself. Seeing how he stacked up against Allen Iverson would be a good distraction for him. Paul made it a practice to catch the midnight replay broadcast of the Flyers' home games. Lorraine had not come to the second game against Philadelphia and she had been in a deep slumber when Paul arrived home. He could not stop thinking about the revealing news. Not that it was news. It was more like an unsettling jolt. Paul wasn't quite ready to discuss it, not even with Lorraine. He had needed something to distract him from what his boy had told him. Not that the New York news channels took his mind off anything, except by reminding him of all the bad things in the world. Even when there was a potentially positive story, the media put a negative spin on it.

Normally Paul would have read a few passages from his Bible, but when he had tried to pick up the Book, he just as quickly replaced it before even opening it. His head was too scattered. The news media had not offered much solace either.

The Flyers had blown out the Philadelphia 76ers for the second time in three nights, and this was still not enough to satisfy the New York sports reporters. The New York press was determined to trash every accomplishment the Flyers made. They claimed it was meaningless that the Flyers defeated Philadelphia since they were never going to beat the Chicago Bulls to get to the championship series anyway. The fact that the Flyers had a better record than the Bulls and actually had the best record in the entire NBA was discredited as well. The media attributed their winning record to an easy schedule during the regular season, no back-to-back games like most other teams, and finally, sheer luck.

Paul shook his head as he rose from the kitchen stool. He reached into the bleached pine cabinet closest to the refrigerator, which contained more painkillers and anti-inflammatory pills than most pharmacies. The eighty-two-game season had taken its toll on his knees, along with the first two play-off games, and they were inflamed and throbbing. Paul swallowed two long yellow tablets in hopes of them performing a miracle on his banged-up legs. He seriously did not know how much longer his body could take this constant abuse. Paul was the smallest guy on his team, and in his position of point guard he was knocked around in the course of the game more than anyone else on the court except the opposing point guard.

Even though Paul felt physically exhausted, his mind was racing with too many thoughts to sleep. The prospect of the team being sold and relocated to Albany if they did not win the championship hung over every game like the stench of a cigar. And Leonard Hightower, lurking around the first two games as if he was checking out his new inventory, didn't help matters. Paul knew the Flyers had the talent to go all the way this year, but he did not know if they had what it took mentally. The team needed to pull together and start behaving like adults instead of a group of freshmen in high school.

It was not only his teammates' immaturity that bothered him. Their blatant lack of morals and complete self-centeredness were a constant source of trouble for the team. Arguing with the referees, picking fights on and off the court, disrespecting women and themselves had all made it increasingly difficult for Paul to tolerate the selfish attitudes of most of his teammates, who were only concerned with their next contracts or how many individual statistics they could rack up instead of focusing on winning for the team. Paul also detested the hypocrisy and the lies. He had yet to figure out why most of his teammates even bothered to get married or engaged when all they did was cheat on their women as soon as the team went on a road trip—if they waited that long. And now with his boy talking about being gay, Paul shuddered to think where the team was headed.

Paul finished turning off all the first-floor lights that Lorraine insisted upon keeping lit when he was not at home and limped toward their bedroom. As he reached the base of the stairs, he began replaying his teammate's admission. It *was* shocking. As much as Paul hated to admit it to himself, he held certain stereotypes about gay men. His boy did not fit the image. Paul was also reluctant to think about what the Bible said about his friend's choice of lifestyle.

On one hand, Paul was flattered that he trusted him enough to confide in him, but he also felt burdened by such a heavy weight. It was a volatile piece of information that Paul would never disclose to anyone else, especially now that his friend's secret was his as well. If the other guys on the team ever found out, they would never let him live it down. Some of them were so infantile, they probably would not even want to take a shower with him anymore. Paul shuddered to think what Coach Mitchell would have to say, especially with the impending sale of the team and the efforts at revamping its image. Paul knew enough about Leonard Hightower to realize that if he was as big a racist as everyone asserted, he would be doubly hostile toward a gay African-American basketball player.

Paul could not help but wonder why he had told him. Still Paul had listened and tried to be a friend as he spilled his guts. Somehow, congratulating him did not seem like the appropriate reaction under the circumstances.

In retrospect, Paul realized he'd done the only thing he knew how to do: be a friend. He'd been there for him when he needed to talk and he had not judged him. At least not to his face. Privately, Paul thought homosexuality was anti-Christian and against the teachings of Jesus.

Paul attempted to shut out all negative thoughts before entering the bedroom. He needed his rest and he wanted to give all of himself to Lorraine. Although he had wanted her to come to the game tonight, he knew that she had agreed to work a double shift the night before. It would have been impossible for her to stay awake. As Paul turned the glass knob on their bedroom door, he took a small measure of comfort in the fact that she was safely in bed right now. It was one less night that he had to worry about her driving home late from Harlem.

Paul quickly tore off his shirt and eased down his pants before he slid in next to his wife. Moving next to Lorraine's warm body, Paul lifted up her hair and gently kissed the back of her neck.

"Stop it! Leave me alone!" Lorraine said, twisting away from him.

"What? What did you say?" Paul said, sitting up in bed, completely bewildered.

"I didn't do it! I didn't do it!" Lorraine said, panicked.

"Honey, what's wrong?" Paul said as he turned on the bedside lamp.

"Leave me alone! Go away! Go away!"

Paul turned his wife toward him and saw that her eyes were tightly shut and her eyeballs were frantically twitching beneath the closed lids.

"Lorraine, wake up, honey, you're dreaming. Wake up, baby," Paul said, slowly pulling Lorraine to a sitting position as she fought him in the process.

"Leave me alone! Leave me alone!" Lorraine continued to holler as her head rolled back like a rag doll's.

Paul shook Lorraine gently to wake her. Her breath came in quick, short gasps and her lips were cracked dry. Slowly she pried her eyes open and looked at Paul as if he were a stranger. Her gaze began to dart around the expansive room.

"Are you okay? You were having a nightmare," Paul said, pulling Lorraine's limp body into his.

Lorraine did not respond to Paul except to move away from him and stare into the distance with large, vacant eyes. It scared Paul, the way she was looking. Tears began to stream down her face before she covered it with her hands and began to shake her head.

"This can't be happening to me. I can't take this, Paul."

"What? You can't take what, honey?" As Paul reached for Lorraine, he watched her whole body stiffen. "Baby, what's wrong? You're beginning to frighten me," Paul said, reaching for her hand.

"Would you get me some water?"

"Will you please tell me what's wrong?" Grabbing some tissues from the nightstand, Paul leaned forward and wiped Lorraine's tear-streaked face. He looked at her questioningly.

"Well?" Paul refused to let up.

"It was just a nightmare," Lorraine quickly said.

"Some bad dream. You want to tell me about it?"

"I don't really remember. It was just scary, that's all . . . I'm fine . . . My throat is just dry right now . . . I'll get the water myself," Lorraine said as she started to get out of bed.

"No, no, let me get it. You just relax. Do you want anything else?" Paul said, standing up.

"Just some aspirin."

"No problem," Paul said, heading toward the door.

"Paul?"

"Yeah, baby."

"Thank you."

"You don't have to thank me," Paul sincerely said to his wife as he left their room.

He was not convinced that everything was all right. Lorraine had been more than scared. She had been terrified.

"If I have to tell you kids to be quiet one more time, I'm not taking you to Discovery Zone tomorrow!" Trina firmly told her six-year-old daughter, Monica, and her ten-year-old son, Marcus.

"Why do we have to be quiet, Mommy? I ate all of my pancakes. That was Marcus screaming," Monica said in her high-pitched voice.

"That wasn't me, Mom. Monica kept putting her feet on me under the table so you couldn't see her," Marcus said.

"I did not! I didn't touch him at all!" Monica screamed as she kicked Marcus under the table one more time.

"Look, I've had about enough of both of you. I told you to lower your voices while Daddy is sleeping. You know he had a hard game last night and he has to leave town today."

"Why does Daddy have to leave again? He's never home," Monica whined.

"So they can beat Philadelphia and win the series," Trina explained.

113

"Yeah, wouldn't it be cool, Mom, if they could sweep the Seventy-Sixers?" Marcus said excitedly.

"Sweep them? Why would they sweep them?" Monica asked, confused.

"Don't you know anything, dork?" Marcus said to his sister.

"I know a lot and I'm not a dork," Monica said.

"Well, how come you don't know what sweep means?"

"I do know."

"No, you don't. You just said you didn't know five seconds ago."

"I do know!" Monica hollered.

"Lower your voices, now! And, Monica, stop kicking Marcus. I saw you do it, young lady; you're not that slick," Trina said, grinning to herself.

Every time she looked at her little girl, she could not help but smile. She had almost lost Monica when she was born two and a half months early, weighing in at a little over three pounds. Monica was her miracle child, and she kept her laughing even through all of her mischief.

"I sure am glad Daddy doesn't have to guard Allen Iverson, 'cause it wouldn't matter how much rest he got. He made Paul Thomas look like an old man. He runs circles around everybody."

"Who would run circles around me?" Rick Belleville said groggily, his six feet eleven inches nearly filling the doorway of the kitchen.

"Allen Iverson, he's the fastest!" Marcus said.

"I schooled that little boy," Rick said as he headed straight to the refrigerator, grabbed a gallon jug of Tropicana orange juice, and began sucking it down in large gulps.

"Sure you did, Dad," Marcus snickered.

"How'd you sleep?" Trina asked Rick.

"I could hardly sleep with all the noise y'all were making down here."

"I was quiet, Daddy, because I want you to play good," Monica told her father.

"I know you were, sweetie. I wish everybody else was too," Rick said, giving Trina the evil eye.

"Sorry," Trina said quietly.

"Sorry. You're always sorry, everybody's always sorry."

"Do you want some breakfast?" Trina asked.

"After I shower, but just some plain pancakes and eggs. None of that fancy stuff you be experimenting with."

"Fine, Rick."

"I'm serious, Trina. I don't want no scallions or garlic or nothing crazy in my eggs."

"Okay, Rick, give me a break," Trina said, looking to see if the kids were watching them.

"Give you a break? You're kidding me, right? All you ever get is breaks. I don't ask much of you except to keep the house quiet while I'm sleeping. It's the play-offs. You been around long enough to know how important this time is for me, especially on a new team. Damn! It's not like you have a real job. The only thing you have to do is cook me my meals. All I wanted was to have a decent night's sleep." Rick slammed the orange juice jug on the Corian countertop.

"You would have had a good night's sleep if you hadn't come home at four-thirty this morning," Trina said under her breath as Rick stormed out of the kitchen.

After all these years, Trina should have been used to Rick's outbursts, but it still stung each time he disrespected and belittled her, especially in front of the children. She was so tired of him blaming her for everything that went wrong in their lives. He was the one who had been running the streets doing God only knew what until the wee hours of the morning. And he had the audacity to be angry because his family was disturbing him. He should have been awake hours ago.

Trina fought off a wave of nausea as she walked to the refrigerator to get the eggs for Rick's plain breakfast. Times had changed for them. The changes had been gradual, but they were changes just the same. And judging by how testy he had been since the end of the regular season, it did not seem as if his mood was going to improve any time soon. Rick's outbursts on the basketball court had become more frequent despite the fact that the Flyers had decisively won the first two games of their series against the 76ers. Rick had been prone to blowups on the court for years, but usually he had a reason for exploding. Now he seemed to be lashing out for no apparent cause.

Trina recognized that Rick was under a great deal of pressure, but it troubled her that she was always the target of his frustrations. She had to remind herself that she was the only person at whom he could vent without fear of any repercussions. She never stood up to Rick. She let everything slide and played the part of a dutiful wife. She used to relish her role. These days she just felt as if she was going through the motions.

Trina forced herself not to get worked up over Rick's antics. She had other, more pressing issues with which to concern herself. Judging from the way she was beginning to bust out of all of her clothes, one of them was not going to wait much longer. She already knew how he felt about the topic of pregnancy, and she had no idea how she was ever going to break it to him. Maybe she could avoid it until the season was over, but truthfully, she did not think it could wait that long.

She also had a financial matter to discuss with him, which was always a sore subject. During their thirteen years of marriage, she'd rarely asked him for more than her monthly allowance, and each time she had, he had been reluctant to give her more than her allotment. Rick even complained when their small joint household account ran short of funds. He deliberately kept the majority of their liquid cash in his own private account, ensuring that Trina was financially dependent upon him. Rick had always firmly believed that the money he earned on the court was his and his alone. He constantly reminded Trina that her monthly stipend was more than she deserved. This time she was determined not to back down. Trina was prepared to secure a loan if necessary.

"My breakfast ready yet?" Rick said as he bounded back into the kitchen, freshly showered, smelling of Coast soap.

"I'm just flipping the last two pancakes," Trina said, turning over the fluffy, golden brown hotcakes.

"You didn't do anything fancy to my eggs, did you?" Rick said, greedily looking at his breakfast plate on the counter.

"No, Rick. Where do you want to eat?" Trina said, emptying the eggs out of the skillet.

"I'll take it in my office. Did you remember to make coffee?" Rick said as he strode toward his office.

"Do I ever forget?" Trina said, placing the utensils and napkin on his tray.

"It's not flavored coffee, is it?"

"It's plain, Rick."

"Good. I don't need anything messing with my stomach today. I have a meeting with Coach Mitchell and I need all my faculties in tip-top condition," he said as he left the room.

Trina finished setting a lap tray, what had become the equivalent of Rick's dining room table, and carried it into his office where he was hunched over going through some files. Trina carefully placed the heavy tray on his desk and sat down in the chair across from him. When he finished rummaging through his papers, he looked up at her expectantly.

"Did you forget something?" Rick said, pouring the heated syrup over his pancakes.

"Rick, I need to . . . ask a . . . a favor of you," Trina stammered.

"How much do you need this time?" Rick said, ferociously cutting his pancakes into perfect squares and triangles.

"If you could maybe just give me an advance on my allowance, that should be enough."

"You act like money grows on trees. Don't you get more than enough as it stands?" He reminded her of her father, God rest his soul.

"It won't cover what I need," Trina said, looking down at her hands while nervously wringing them together.

"What could you possibly need that you don't have right now? Somebody, please tell me."

"I need some start-up money for my baking business," Trina said hopefully.

"For your what?" Rick laughed hysterically. "Come on, you're gonna make me choke on my food, girl. You've got to be kidding. Is this some kind of joke?" Rick snickered.

"I'm serious." Trina stared at Rick as he cracked up, sputtering bits of his food over his desk.

"Just forget it, Rick. I'll get a loan. You won't have to be involved at all. Forget I ever asked you."

"I will forget it, but if you start a cooking business, you're gonna need a hell of a lot more money than an advance on your allowance. You're gonna need a small fortune for legal fees after all your customers need their stomachs pumped from the concoctions you be whipping up."

"Forget I ever mentioned it, Rick," Trina said as she swiftly stood up and turned on her heel toward the door.

"Oh . . . Trina, one more thing," Rick said, still giggling.

"What!" Trina said with her back to him.

"Don't forget to pack my gray Calvin Klein suit. Whew, girl, what you need is to take yourself down to Laugh Factory and try out your act on their open-mike night."

Trina could still hear Rick chuckling as she returned to the kitchen. If she had more nerve, she would have called him an asshole to his face. He constantly humiliated her. This time it was going to be different, though. He had no way of stopping her from getting a small-business loan. At least she had the credit to do that on her own. Even though she didn't have the guts to tell him she was pregnant.

Rick was getting antsy sitting in Mike Mitchell's posh office. The space was more suited for a highbrow corporate boardroom than the office of an NBA coach. Rick had been a member of five different NBA teams over a fourteen-year career, but he had never played for a coach who had as much style and panache as Mike Mitchell. Rick had also never come across a coach with an ego as big as Mitchell's. He watched Coach calmly dictate several orders into the phone as if he were reciting a grocery list.

As Rick looked at the expensive walnut paneling, he braced himself for the reprimand he knew was forthcoming. It wasn't enough that the league fined him one thousand dollars for each technical foul he received as a result of his blowups during the games. Now he was forced to sit through his coach's one-on-one rebukes. He had been dealing with scoldings from coaches about his outbursts since he'd started playing basketball in junior high, and he had no intention of behaving differently now. Rick had accepted long ago that he was a passionate player, and it was far too late in his career for him to change. It was unusual, though, that Coach Mitchell planned this private meeting. Coach would sometimes curse him in the heat of a game, but overall, Rick had always gotten the impression that Coach welcomed his spirited and sometimes overzealous style of play. Maybe Rick had become too aggressive on the court lately even for Coach's liking.

"Rick Belleville," Coach Mitchell said as he hung up the phone and leaned back in his forest green leather wing chair.

"That would be me," Rick said, leaning back in his seat as well.

Rick and Coach locked eyes, and neither spoke for what seemed like several minutes. If Coach wanted a game of stare-down, Rick was as formidable a competitor as Coach could hope to encounter. One thing that Rick did not do with anyone was back down, even for "Coach of the Decade," as *Sports Illustrated* had labeled him. Rick had seen younger, easily intimidated players frequently slink out of Coach's office after he'd had a "talking to" with them. Coach may have been one of the most feared and respected men affiliated with the NBA, not to mention one of the most handsome and classiest, but Rick was unfazed—well, almost. Mitchell had more control than any other coach in the NBA. He probably had more power than most team general managers.

"Why do you think I called you in here today?" Coach said, locking his hands behind his head.

Rick followed suit and locked his hands behind his head as well and looked his coach directly in the eyes. "Hmmm, could it be my attitude on the court?" he sarcastically said. Those were the famous last lines of his ex-coaches and ex-general managers, "great player but poor attitude on the court."

"Somehow I thought you might think that," Coach began as he leaned forward and opened the top drawer of his desk, pulling out several envelopes.

"That's not what this meeting is about?" Rick asked, slightly leaning forward.

"Rick, although you do have a tendency to go off the deep end at times, that's the least of your problems," Coach said as he pushed the envelopes toward Rick.

Rick knew what they were as soon as he saw them. He recognized the Caesar's Palace, Taj Mahal, and MGM Grand hotel and casino emblems all too well. He had been throwing away the notices that were sent to his post office box for the past several months.

"And how did you get these?" Rick asked.

"How long did you think you could ignore almost a million dollars worth of debt before they tracked you down at your very public place of employment?" Coach said, ignoring his question.

Rick picked up the envelopes and looked at the name typed on the front of them.

"If I'm not mistaken, these are addressed to Rick Belleville. You had no business opening them."

"And you have no business jeopardizing the reputation of this team!"

"What I do when I'm not working is my business, not yours or this team's," Rick said, grabbing the envelopes and stuffing them into his sweat-suit pocket.

"In case you've been too busy gambling to notice, this team is on the verge of being sold. I, for one, don't want that to happen, and I'm pretty sure your teammates don't want that either."

"I don't want that to happen either, but that has nothing to do with what I do in my spare time. I'm a grown man," Rick indignantly said.

"Well then, act like it and take responsibility for your debts. The last thing this team needs right now is a *New York Post* headline claiming that you're dodging loan sharks."

"They're not loan sharks, they're reputable casinos," Rick shot back.

"Who's being naive here? Who do you think runs these casinos, and who do you think they're going to send out to muscle you into giving them their money?"

"Like I said, Coach, this is my—" Rick started.

"No, like I said, you set up whatever payment plan you need to get them off your back immediately. And from this point on, all casinos are off-limits to you. I don't want to take a chance of you even being seen inside of one."

"Do I look like my name is Michael Brown? You think you my daddy now too?" Rick said, feigning laughter.

"Not even close. But I don't want the *team* hurt, and I'll do whatever is necessary to make sure that doesn't happen."

"Is that it?" Rick said, standing up.

"Sit down. I'm not finished talking to you."

"I'm fine standing."

"Have it your way. Handle your affairs and do it expediently and quietly. I don't want this in the papers."

"Finished?" Rick said, turning toward the door.

"One more thing. When you embarrass this team, you embarrass me . . . and *that* is something I will never tolerate. Now I'm finished. Close the door on your way out."

Rick was wrong about Mitchell. He did have the ability to intimidate him. Rick was fuming as he closed the door and walked down the hall toward his locker, thinking about what a self-centered bastard Coach was. Their entire conversation had nothing to do with the team. Mitchell was concerned about his own ass. He did not want to appear less than perfect to the public. Ultimately Coach was not concerned about how the Flyers looked or Rick's gambling. He only cared about his pristine reputation and the next magazine cover he would adorn.

Despite her somber mood, Casey could not suppress a grin watching Brent gyrate his shoulders while driving his Bentley. He was grooving to Puff Daddy's song "Let's Dance." Brent may have been a world-class ath- lete, but a dancer, he was not. Casey and Brent headed north along the Palisades Parkway toward the DuMichelle Antique House for its monthly auction. The trip on this highway was a monthly outing for them that they had missed for the last couple of months. They 18 used to take lunches with them when the weather permitted and stop at one of the scenic pic- nic areas to eat, but as if by mutual, unstated agreement, they skipped that ritual this time.

Casey realized that there was no reason for her to feel guilty, but that awful culprit was creeping up on her as she contemplated broaching the topic of Brent's daughter with him. He was in such high spirits and the day was so beautiful, she didn't want to ruin it even though she had every right in the world to be angry with him. She also thought about Alexis's admonitions about letting the guys have their concentration. But ever since the play-offs had begun, it had become increasingly difficult for Casey to hold her tongue.

"Baby, I really think we have a chance to do it this year." Brent beamed as he caressed Casey's thigh through her blue jeans.

"Really?" Casey unenthusiastically said.

"Yeah. One round down and three to go. It's gonna be tough, but when we get by Chicago, that championship ring is as good as ours!"

"I hope you guys do it this year," Casey said, watching the insects smash against the windshield.

"I know you do, baby. You've always been so supportive, even when your schedule has been hectic. I appreciate that, more than you'll ever know," Brent said, grasping Casey's hand and bringing it to his lips.

Now he was making it extra hard on her. Why did he have to be so sweet to her when she wanted to curse him out? Casey kept quiet and continued looking straight ahead.

During these outings in Brent's automobile with its tinted windows, they had their rare opportunities to speak to one another undisturbed by fans, phones, or television noise. This was the place they conducted most of the family and household "business."

"Oh, I forgot to tell you, Brent Junior called before you got back from Philadelphia," Casey said.

"What was he talking about?"

"Nothing much. He had just finished watching the game and he was excited that you all were going to advance to the next round."

"Oh, he probably wants to come to town when the Heat series begins. I think that boy likes to see Alonzo Mourning play more than his own father. Well, I guess that means we need to check on some flights for him." Brent laughed as he sped along.

"You mean you want me to check on some flights?"

"Would you mind, baby?" Brent said, squeezing Casey's thigh.

"No, I wouldn't mind, but are you going to be able to spend any time with him when he comes?"

"What's that supposed to mean? I always spend time with him," Brent said.

"When you're not at practice or at a meeting with Jake or Nike or at a game or out to dinner with a sponsor or taking a pregame nap," Casey said, exasperated.

"Where's all this coming from? I thought we were going to have a nice pleasant afternoon together."

"Oh, I guess it's not pleasant when I bring up your parental responsibilities. You're going to expect me to change my schedule to accommodate Brent Junior when he comes to town."

"No, I'm not. It's been a long time since I asked you to rearrange your schedule for him or me. Casey, you know that's an old issue that we resolved. What's this really about?"

"Well, it doesn't seem like that long ago to me," Casey said, crossing her arms.

"I'll tell you how long ago it was. It was at least three years ago, but now that we're on the subject, what's so damn wrong with compromising? You're so stubborn sometimes, you forget that compromise is what marriage is about."

Casey spun her head around so fast to look at Brent, she thought she was going to get a crook in her neck.

"Don't you dare tell me what marriage is all about. You don't have that right and you don't have the slightest idea what marriage is about," Casey spat out.

"Is this discussion about Brent Junior or our marriage?" Brent said seriously as he turned down the car stereo.

"Well, now that you mention it, how about trust in a marriage? It's obviously lacking in ours."

"Casey, what are you talking about now? Why are you bringing up old issues? It's counterproductive. I thought we had moved beyond that."

"Don't talk to me in that condescending, holier-than-thou tone! Obviously it doesn't seem to be so past to me," Casey said.

"Look, I've tried to be patient with you, but you won't let the past go and—" Brent started.

"No, I think it's you who can't let the past go."

"What's that supposed to mean? I . . . I've been faithful to you since all that stuff happened."

"You haven't been honest with me."

"Casey, what have I done now?" Brent pleaded.

"You tell me," Casey icily said.

"What is this, some sort of trick question women use to get their husbands to admit their sins?"

"If they have something to admit, yes," Casey countered.

"Well, try again, because my slate is clean."

"Brent, I'm going to give you a chance to come clean with me. Are you being honest with me about every single thing in our relationship? Don't lie to me, Brent. I mean it."

Silence. The car was in complete silence. It stung Casey's ears. The only noise came from the wind whipping against the vehicle as they turned onto 87 north. A part of her wondered if she wasn't ready to hear what he had to say, but still, she had to know the truth.

"Casey, why do we have to go through this? Can't we just—"

"Brent, I'm going to ask you one more time, and if you lie to me, I'm finished. This marriage cannot take the strain of one more filthy fucking lie. Now, talk to me, and I want nothing but truth coming out of your lips," Casey said as her eyes welled up with unshed tears.

Brent pulled the car into one of the rest stops along the highway. The heat of the sun was beating down on Casey through the front window. Parking the car, he took a deep breath and turned toward Casey.

"It's so bad you had to pull off the road, huh?" Casey said, shaking her head in disbelief.

Brent reached for Casey's hands, but she pulled away, her back smashed against the door and her head rubbing against the passenger window. Casey shook her head as she looked at Brent.

"Casey, I've been corresponding with my daughter."

"Define 'corresponding.' "

"I've spoken with Nikki and I've arranged for her and Brent Junior to meet and . . ." He faltered.

"And what, Brent? What else did you arrange? Don't get silent on me, damn it!"

"I arranged to visit with Nikki."

"Where? How many times?"

"On the road. On a few occasions."

"Oh, on a few occasions that you forgot to mention to me. Kind of like when you hooked up with her mother in the first place. And did Nikki's mama bring her to meet you?" Casey said, barely able to process that she was going through this with Brent again.

"Yes, she did."

"Oh, I see, and I suppose the two of you had a lovely little reunion. How cozy. Did you ever plan on telling me about your relationship with your daughter and your renewed relationship with her mother?"

"There's no relationship with me and Nikki's mother. I was going to tell you eventually, but . . ."

"But what? Do you have any idea how humiliating it was to have to hear about this from your coach's wife? I must look like a damn fool to them. How many other people know?"

"Casey, I'm sorry you had to find out like this!"

"I didn't *have* to find out like this; you're the one who chose not to tell me."

"The reason I didn't tell you is because I knew how you'd react, unreasonable, just like you're acting now."

"Tell me something, Brent. How am I supposed to react? Pardon me for not exercising the proper etiquette. What was I thinking? Silly me. 'Oh, congratulations on the birth of your daughter! Isn't parenthood wonderful! I'm so glad that the two of you are getting an opportunity to spend time together. How's your wife holding up after the birth? Oops. I mean your mistress. I forgot, your wife had a miscarriage just about the time that silly paternity suit came about. I'm sorry, but I offer my congratulations just the same. And I'm so happy that you're bonding with your child.'" Casey screamed, banging the dashboard with her fist. "Is that a more appropriate reaction, Brent?"

"Casey, you're blowing this way out of proportion. Would you please calm down and give me a moment to speak?"

"I'm blowing this out of proportion?" she yelled, outraged.

"Actually, I think you are. You're being selfish about it. Whether you like it or not, Nikki is my child. There's nothing I can do about that now."

"I think I have a right to be selfish about my husband when it comes to who he's sleeping with."

"I'm not sleeping with anybody but you."

"Now. Maybe," Casey said, turning away from him.

Brent reached for Casey's chin and turned her face toward him. Casey was in no mood to speak to Brent, much less look at him.

"You have every reason to be upset with me, and I can't fault you for it one bit. You have the complete right to be angry with me. I remember what the counselor said about it being healthy to be angry—"

"Fuck the counselor and fuck you too," Casey interjected.

"Casey, you don't mean that—can't you just please try and see the situation from my perspective? I know what I did was wrong. I know that. But is it wrong for me to want to see my daughter, to have a relationship with her? She's my flesh and blood, Casey. Can you try and understand that? I know I should have said something to you about it, but I was afraid of getting you upset again. I can't just turn my back on my own child. I would be as bad as all those other men that we read about in the newspapers and see on the TV who make thousands of babies and never take care of them," Brent implored.

"Isn't her mother getting enough money? Why can't they just cash their monthly checks and disappear and let us live our lives? I feel like we're going to be haunted by them forever," Casey cried.

"It's not that easy. I wish it was. And, baby, I don't want anything to do with Nikki's mother. I just want to know my little girl and I don't want her growing up thinking that she had one of those fathers who deserted her. It's only right. Nikki didn't ask to be brought here. Because of my irresponsible behavior, she was conceived. I know you, Casey; you wouldn't respect any man who didn't take care of his own child. How can you expect any less of me?"

"I don't think my expectations of you can be lessened any more than they already are," Casey said, covering her face with her hands.

"Come on, Casey. Don't be like that. Can you please try and understand? It doesn't have to be such a bad thing. We can make it through this together. Can I count on you to be by my side in this? Come on, baby, for better or for worse. And, honey, I promise you, the worst is over. We're partners, we're a family. I need to know that you're going to be by my side," Brent said, gazing into Casey's eyes.

"Brent, I just don't know. You're constantly lying to me. There's no way for me to defend myself against a lie. I'm tired of being hurt."

"Casey, I promise—"

"Brent, please don't promise me anything right now," Casey interrupted. "You're in no position."

"Don't give up on me, Casey."

"Let's get out of here. Please, I'm ready to go."

"Can I take that as a yes, that you're with me?" Brent asked.

"Let's just go, Brent. I can't really plan beyond today."

"Fair enough," Brent said, starting up the car and putting it in gear.

What was Kelly up to now? Steve thought as he paced back and forth in front of the fourteen-foot etched-glass door. She had called him frantically, claiming that Diamond had a fever. Steve was so accustomed to Kelly conjuring up hare-brained schemes that he had been reluctant to respond to her emer-gency message. God, he hoped that Kelly was not pathetic enough to lie about her own daughter's health; then again, lately nothing seemed beyond Kelly.

Steve refused to use the key to the door as he stood outside the home that was technically his. He was hoping it would sell soon and was seriously considering lowering the asking price by two hundred thousand dollars so it would go faster. It was time to close this chapter of his life. He no longer wanted Kelly in his life, and certainly not living in a place for which he was paying the mortgage.

That was another reason he had consented to see Kelly today. Over a month ago, Steve had received the legal document that would put into action Kelly's eviction. Steve had been procrastinating serving her the papers since he had told her she had until the end of the year to leave. But he could no longer put it off—it was only the beginning of May now. He wanted to have a life of his own again—not one dictated by Kelly's deceit. Although he was concerned for Diamond's welfare, he felt in the long run it was better for the child not to be torn between him and Kelly.

The way he saw it, he had been overly generous and patient with Kelly despite her lies and manipulation. He even still provided her with a hefty monthly living allowance that supported her lavish lifestyle. Steve reminded himself not to be seduced by her, a feat that was nearly impossible, as he had learned the hard way. She had almost broken him. He thought back to the first time he realized Kelly's ability to deceive in order to get what she wanted. It had been the end of his fourth season playing for the Flyers, and they had just moved into their new house.

"Diamond! Diamond! Daddy's home. Where's my little girl?" Steve had bellowed out, walking into the kitchen.

He had come back to New Jersey two days early from a road trip because he had to see the Flyers' orthopedic surgeon about an injury to his wrist.

"Kelly! Diamond! Where's everybody?" Steve said, looking around the family room.

Steve ran upstairs to Diamond's room, thinking she might be napping. He always missed her when he went on road trips and was anxious to see his little girl.

As Steve made it to the top of the stairs, he tiptoed to Diamond's room, not wanting to awaken her if she was sleeping. He just wanted to look at her tiny face. When he reached the door to her bedroom, it was completely shut, which was unusual. If Diamond was napping, Kelly normally kept the door slightly ajar.

Steve grasped the doorknob and began to turn it slowly, when he heard a man's laughter in the nursery. Steve stopped in his tracks and wondered what was going on. He leaned his ear so it was pressing against the door and listened. He heard Kelly tell Diamond to show "Daddy" her new tooth. With that, Steve stormed in, confused.

The sight Steve took in momentarily calmed him.

"Daryl. What's up, man? I didn't know you were coming to town," Steve said, puzzled as to why his childhood buddy was in his house when Steve wasn't due home for another two days.

The instant Steve asked the question, he knew something strange was going on. The three of them were sitting on the floor together, the picture of family harmony with the exception of the expressions on the faces of the adults. Kelly froze, and Daryl became jittery at first and then defensive-looking. Diamond was the only one in the group who continued to innocently coo.

At first Steve just knew that Kelly and his boy were having an affair and he had busted in on them.

"So is somebody going to tell me what's going on here?"

"Steve, it's nothing. Daryl was just in town visiting," Kelly stammered.

"Just visiting, huh? I had no idea you and Daryl were on visiting terms."

Steve watched Kelly nervously stand up and straighten out her clingy T-shirt dress.

"Look, Steve, Daryl had some business up here and—" Kelly began.

"So now you up in Daryl's business?" Steve said, looking at his boy with eyes of stone. Steve could feel his nostrils begin to flair against his will.

"I just have one question. Wouldn't a motel have been a better place to meet than in my daughter's nursery? Don't I give you enough money to get a baby-sitter, Kelly?" Steve contemptuously said as he leaned down and picked up Diamond.

"Hold up, Steve, I have a right to—" Daryl began as he stood up, eyeing Steve.

"Shut up, Daryl! Listen, Steve, why don't we go downstairs and—"

"No! I'm tired of shutting up, Kelly, and I'm tired of hiding this," said Daryl indignantly.

"Look, you can do whatever you want to do, just not in my house in front of my daughter. Now you both can get to steppin'."

"Steve, me and Daryl ain't having no affair!" Kelly pleaded.

"Anymore," Daryl added.

"I'm not interested in hearing about your love squabbles. Why don't you two go check into the Howard Johnson down the street," Steve said in disgust.

"I told you, I'm not sleeping with Daryl."

"Then what the hell is he doing here all cozied up with you and Diamond?"

"Because I have a right to visit my daughter, that's why," Daryl said, taking a few bold steps toward Steve.

"Daryl! What the hell is your problem?" Kelly hollered.

"What did you just say?" Steve said, shocked.

"Don't listen to him, Steve, he's crazy. He must be on drugs or something," Kelly said.

"I'm not crazy and I'm not on drugs. Diamond is my daughter and I'm tired of having to hide it. I have a right to see her when I want. Just 'cause you're Mr. Big-shot Basketball Player with loads of loot don't mean that I got to give you my daughter," Daryl spat out.

Steve had never fainted before, but he felt as if he was going to go down at any moment. The room seemed to spin around him and he was short of breath. It was as if someone had shut off the air supply.

"Steve, Steve, are you all right?" Kelly worriedly asked as she inched toward him.

"I'm sorry, Kelly, and, Steve, I'm sorry for you, too, but right is right. Diamond is my daughter," Daryl said.

Steve could not force any words to escape his mouth. This was not happening. He didn't want to believe it, but as much as he hated to admit it to himself, it rang true. He remembered the month before Kelly told him she was pregnant. She had just returned from a three-week stay in Atlanta where they had both grown up. The night she had returned from her trip, Steve was sick in bed with the flu and in a deep sleep. He recalled her virtually forcing him to have sex with her even though he was exhausted and felt terrible. Thinking about it now, it was as if she was covering her tracks, just in case she turned up pregnant. She could point to that night so the timing would be right. In actuality, she must have fooled around with Daryl while she was visiting Atlanta.

"Steve. Say something, Steve. You look sick," Kelly said, walking up to him.

"Is . . . is it true, Kelly?" Steve said, staring off into space while still holding Diamond.

"Steve, Diamond loves you like you're her daddy," Kelly said lamely.

"Kelly, I think I at least deserve the truth about this," Steve said, choking on his words.

"Come on, Steve; me, you, and Diamond, we're a family."

"Damn it, Kelly! Stop bullshitting me! Just admit it!"

"Please, Steve," Kelly cried.

"It's true, man; I got the blood tests to prove it," Daryl said triumphantly.

"Steve, I'm sorry," Kelly said, trying to put her arm around him.

"Just . . . just don't come near me." Steve had handed Diamond to Kelly and begun backing out of the room.

Steve had been shattered. He'd felt as if his life had just come to an end.

Now, as he rang the doorbell for the fifth time, Steve said, "Kelly, stop playing games and open up this door."

It sure as hell was time to move on, and his first move would be his date with Stephanie in exactly three hours. They were going to try Casa La Femme, a Moroccan restaurant Stephanie had read about in *Taste Makers New York*, and he did not want to be late. Ever since the Kelly incident at the Mecca, Stephanie had put a hold on the sexual part of their relationship. She wanted to be absolutely certain that Kelly was out of Steve's life for good.

Steve was almost ready to leave, but the possibility of Diamond truly being ill kept him waiting. Finally Kelly came to the door. Regardless of the little girl's parentage, he still loved her and would always hold a special place for her in his heart.

"Where's Diamond?" Steve said as Kelly flung the door open.

"Why didn't you just use your key?" Kelly said, closing the door after him.

Steve looked around the room suspiciously. Kelly had something up her sleeve. All of the downstairs blinds were shut and the lights were dimmed, making it seem much later than four o'clock in the afternoon.

"Is Diamond in her room?" Steve said, rushing toward the stairs, trying to ignore Kelly in her tight, ankle-length skirt.

"She finally got to sleep. Her temperature dropped back almost to normal. I think she's gonna be all right. How about you? Are you all right?" Kelly said, leaning against the vestibule wall, revealing a generous slit in the front of her skirt.

"Kelly, no more games. Diamond wasn't even sick, was she? This needs to stop." Steve was actually talking to himself. He felt flushed just looking at the long, long, perfect legs.

Kelly slowly moved away from the wall and sashayed into the living room. He caught himself staring at her taut rear end through the clingy material. No matter how many beautiful women Steve encountered in his travels, no one could push his buttons like Kelly, not even Stephanie. He had learned that the passion wasn't healthy—that it was more like a drug than an expression of affection. Still, he was aroused just looking at her.

When Kelly reached the white baby grand piano, she hesitated, keeping her back to Steve.

"You used to like my games, Steve," Kelly said, placing both of her hands on the piano.

"Yeah, well, that's just it. I'm tired of playing them."

"Ahh. I don't know about that. I think we can get things back on track."

How could he break her hold on him? She was even more dangerous when she was sober.

"Look, Kelly . . ." Steve began.

"Wouldn't you rather do the looking?" Kelly said, unzipping her skirt and peeling it to the plush cream carpeting.

Steve's eyes were glued to Kelly as she leaned over to step out of her skirt.

"Kelly, put your skirt back on. That's the last reason why I'm here," Steve stammered as he neared her as if she were a magnet and he a flimsy paper clip—his worst fear.

"Then why can't you talk straight, Steve?" Kelly said as she faced him and removed her black silk blouse, revealing full, overflowing breasts resting in a black silk push-up bra.

"Kelly, this is foolish; you know it's over between us," Steve said, wiping his sweating brow.

"Don't you know by now? It's never going to be over with us. You were my first love and I was yours. Now, it's been much too long since we've been together. Why don't you just come over here and fuck the shit out of me like I know you want to do."

Kelly began rubbing herself between her legs under her G-string underwear. Steve hated the fact that she knew all of his weaknesses.

"Kelly, you're way out of line. How can you be like this when your baby is right upstairs? Now that I see Diamond isn't really sick, I want to tell you . . . I want you out of my house. I'm giving you a month to get your things together and leave."

" 'Kelly, you're way out of line. I want you out of here right away,' " Kelly said, mocking him as she turned her back to him once again and unfastened her bra.

Damn. Her voluptuous ass always seemed to be perked to attention, Steve thought. Kelly then bent over, touched her toes, and tauntingly looked at Steve upside down between her legs.

"You're making a fool of yourself, Kelly. I don't want . . . any part . . . of you. Not now, not ever," Steve said, not breaking his gaze from her body. He realized that he was completely hard and gingerly shifted his weight, so Kelly wouldn't notice.

Suddenly Kelly spread her legs and dropped into the splits, a move that always brought Steve to his knees. She had worked briefly as a dancer in a little club back home, and the graceful moves of an animal untouched by civilization remained in her sexual repertoire. Steve felt all control leave his body as he dropped down on the floor, rock-hard and horny. Even as he beckoned to her, a victim of his own raw desire, his mind was fighting, telling him any second the need would pass. But his intellect lost. How could it not? He spread his legs almost involuntarily as Kelly slithered toward him on all fours, licking her lips as she glided closer to him.

By the time Kelly reached him, his desire to release was overwhelming. She grabbed Steve's thighs and dove her head in between his legs, taking small bites at his bulk through his slacks. He was so hard, her bites sent tiny quivers up his spine. Steve could not stop himself from groaning as Kelly removed his dick from his pants and placed it all in her mouth in one slow, deliberate swallowing motion. Just as Steve felt himself about to climax, Kelly mounted him and rode him until he exploded into her.

Within seconds of coming, reality hit. Even as he was still panting and sweating, he quickly pulled his pants back up.

Immediately disgusted with himself, he felt instant regret. His body reeked of her scent and he felt dirty. The sexual power that she had over him was unsettling. It had been that way for years. It had to end. It was unhealthy for his relationship with Stephanie, for himself, for Kelly, and most of all, for Diamond.

"See, that wasn't so bad, was it, baby?" Kelly purred as she slipped on her blouse and pulled up her skirt.

Steve stood up and reached inside his jacket pocket.

"Kelly, that was the last time. I mean it," Steve said as he removed the papers from his coat.

"Was it now?" Kelly asked.

"Kelly, I've been asking you to leave and find your own place, but you obviously haven't taken me seriously," Steve said as he quickly tossed the Notice to Vacate document on the coffee table. "So you leave me no other choice."

"Steve, how can you say that after we just made love? That was beautiful and this is our home, remember?"

"Kelly, get it straight! We *fucked*. I think I've been more than fair with you. It's time for you to go. You've got one month." Steve began walking toward the door.

"Steve! Steve! What the hell is this?" Kelly said, running up behind him, waving the Notice to Vacate document in his face.

"Kelly, don't make this any more difficult than it has to be."

"Where are we supposed to go? I'll be damned if I'm going back to Atlanta with nothing but my baby and a suitcase!" Kelly said, throwing the papers at him.

"Kelly, I don't care where you go. It's not my responsibility. Call Daryl now."

"He's useless and you know that. You're Diamond's real father. You can't just throw us out like this! I'll take your ass to court!" Kelly shouted.

"Don't threaten me, Kelly. I don't take well to threats. Stop worrying, you'll figure it out. You always land on your feet," Steve said with a smirk as he continued trying to leave.

"I won't let you see Diamond, then."

Steve stopped in his path. She knew that was a sore subject between them.

"Kelly, I can only hope that you love your daughter enough not to hurt her that way. She'd be the one punished more than me."

"I love her enough to keep us together as a family."

"Kelly, you're only concerned about yourself. Just like you were when you lied to me about Diamond being my daughter in the first place. All you wanted was a baby by a baller. I could have been any number on any team. It wouldn't have mattered to you."

"What's so wrong with wanting to make sure my baby has a good life . . . a better life than I had?" Kelly cried.

"Kelly, save that act. It's getting real tired. I'm outta here," Steve said, shaking his head.

"Don't you walk out on me, boy! What the hell is wrong with you!" Kelly screeched. Steve heard Kelly's screaming as he turned around and flung open the front door, but he refused to look back as he headed toward his car.

Steve knew Kelly was outraged, but she had brought it on herself. He hadn't been too hard on her, had he? But he had just fucked her and then handed down her marching orders. He couldn't help having the feeling that he screwed her in more ways than one even though she had been manipulating him for years; not that he had behaved much better by just sleeping with her.

Swinging open the door to his Mercedes, Steve made a silent promise to himself that he would never succumb to Kelly again. He only hoped Stephanie didn't detect the look of guilt on his face. But he had accomplished one of the things he set out to do, he'd reminded himself. Kelly would be forced to vacate the home. Her free ride was over, and so was their relationship.

"What the hell?" Steve said, startled by a loud thud on his windshield.

Looking up, he saw Kelly running toward the car with a boot in her hand and bare feet. Before he knew what was happening, she threw her other high-heeled boot at his windshield. Steve flinched for a second time as it hit the glass with more force than the first boot. Kelly had a maniacal look on her face as she continued to charge toward his car. Had he gone too far by kicking her out or had she finally lost it?

Steve quickly shifted the car into reverse as she continued running toward him with her hands raised to the sky and fists tightly balled. Just as he put the car into drive, he felt a loud thud on the front of the car as Kelly hurled herself onto the hood, screaming bloody murder.

What the hell had gotten into her this time? Steve quickly lowered the window and leaned his head out. "Kelly, get the fuck off of my car. You're makin' a damn fool—"

Before he knew what hit him, Kelly reached into the car and slashed her long, jagged fingernails at him, narrowly missing his face but catching his hand. She had lost her mind! Steve fended her off with his wounded hand as she continued to claw at him.

"You can't kick me out, boy! This is my motherfuckin' house!" Kelly howled as she thrashed at Steve with one hand and held fast to the hood of the car with the other.

It was obvious to Steve that she was going for blood and the only way to get her off the front of his car was to speed up and hope that the momentum would throw her crazy ass to the ground. As he pressed his foot on the accelerator and simultaneously raised the window, Kelly snatched her hand from inside the car. She then held on to the hood with both hands as he began to pick up speed. But Kelly didn't budge. Switching tactics, Steve slammed on the brakes. She lost her grip and toppled onto the street. Steve continued moving forward but slowed down just long enough to see her stand up and brush herself off. She was all right. Thank God.

Speeding off, Steve knew he was finished with her—once and for all. They had both passed the point of no return.

*   *   *

"That bastard made me break my nail!" Kelly said as she ambled her way back to her front door, picking up her new boots off the driveway in the process. "Damn! He broke one of my heels too!"

Kelly held the tan stiletto boots up in the air and looked at the tire tracks on the leather. She felt like her boots, broken and run-down. Steve had a lot of fuckin' nerve thinking he could just drop her from his life like a bad habit. He couldn't brush her aside with a snap of the finger or with some legal document. She had stuck by him over the years. He'd still have yellow, crooked teeth if it weren't for her making him get them fixed so he could do some commercials. She and Diamond were not going to be living on the streets just because he got himself a new and improved hoochie.

Steve was trying to play hardball with her. He just didn't realize that he was way out of his league, Kelly thought as she entered the kitchen she had decorated. She would not go down without a fight. And she would be smart about it this time. Steve was going to get hit where it really hurt.

Kelly thought about the burly redheaded man who had approached her on three separate occasions over the past month. What was his name? Rock, Stone. Mr. Stone, that was it. He seemed to know an awful lot about the Flyers, Steve, and her. He'd done some research.

Spotting her purse on the desk in the kitchen, Kelly sat down and snatched it up. She remembered exactly where she'd put his business card—in a tiny compartment in her Louis Vuitton wallet. Finding the card, Kelly pulled it out. She'd even done some research of her own on the redhead's boss. Not that she had to delve too far. Leonard Hightower was on a different magazine cover every other week. She had discovered enough to realize that he was a real player.

Kelly dialed the number on the card, which read "Hightower Enterprises." Mr. Stone was the man she was looking for. He had told her that the two of them could enter into a mutually beneficial arrangement. Mr. Stone had told her to feel free to call when she was ready—the sooner the better, though, because the clock was ticking. She was ready now. Steve had left her no choice.

"Hightower Enterprises," the receptionist on the phone said into Kelly's ear.

"Mr. Stone, please."

Two can play at this game, Steve, but I'm better than you at it. I always have been.

"Where the hell could he be?" Casey asked, irritated as she clicked her cellular phone shut.

"Who?" Remy asked, peering at her image in the passenger-side overhead mirror. She puckered her lips and skillfully reapplied a layer of metallic Chanel lip gloss.

"My husband, that's who." Casey turned the volume down on the car radio and turned around to reach for her purse. She yanked it up from the floor behind the driver's seat and fished around inside her bag looking for her compact mirror. "I swear, Remy, sometimes I think Brent has the hotel put a 'Do not disturb' on his phone just to irritate me. He knows I hate that shit. It's not like we haven't talked about it before either."

Casey became more agitated with each passing second. "I'm his wife, damn it! I shouldn't have to listen to some hotel operator tell me my husband doesn't wish to be disturbed. I've asked him to at least leave my name with them so that my calls could go through, and this is what I get? For all I know, he could have some woman in his room," Casey said, swearing under her breath as she noticed a crack in her new purse-sized mirror.

"Damn, I just bought this thing," she said, disgusted.

Casey pushed the automatic button on the door panel, lowered the driver's-side window on her blue Jaguar, and tossed the compact out into the parking lot.

"Casey! Girl, stop tripping," Remy said, looking over at her friend. She squinted her eyes in the harsh glare from the rearview mirror light. "You know Brent isn't doing anything he shouldn't be doing. They have a game tomorrow night and he probably just didn't want people calling his room, disturbing him all night. You know how the fans and groupies are."

Remy placed her hand near one ear and pretended to have a phone conversation. "Hi, Brent Rogers, please. This is Babycakes, your number one fan. I'm down in the lobby and just wanted to know if I could come up to your room for an autograph or something."

Remy smiled as Casey started to giggle. "Come on, Casey. You know they've got to be bugging the hell out of the guys. It's the play-offs; what do you expect?"

"I know, but I still have a problem trusting him. His daughter, Nikki, is the result of your Miss Babycakes—a one-night stand with some groupie ho."

"And a very fertile one, I might add," Remy said, laughing.

"That shit is not funny, Remy," Casey said, irritated by her best friend's sense of humor. At the moment, Casey could not find anything funny about her husband and his three-year-old daughter.

"Besides, I don't think Brent would ever be that stupid again. Anyway, he probably has the 'Do not disturb' on because he's mad at me," Casey explained.

"Mad at you for what?" Remy asked. "Not about Nikki?" she said with disbelief.

When Casey had told Remy about Brent's undercover visits with his daughter, Remy, in true best-friend fashion, had reacted just as angrily as if it had been her own man being deceitful.

"He's upset because I won't let him walk away with an 'I'm sorry I made a mistake' type of explanation. I expect more from him and I let him know that. I don't know how he expects me to ever be able to trust him again when he keeps trying to hide things from me. It's a damn shame that I had to find out about him seeing Nikki from someone like Alexis, of all people."

Casey knew in her heart that from her husband's point of view, he was trying his best to make amends with her and keep their marriage intact. But she could not stop herself from continuing to blame him for his past mistakes, especially since he had just lied to her about having been in contact with his daughter all this time. Casey believed that with time she could probably forgive her husband for his infidelity, but she would never be able to put aside all of the lies and deceit.

"That's messed up. Alexis definitely didn't need to be in on that. She has enough fuel for her fire as it is," Remy responded. "Brent has a lot of nerve being angry with you because you're upset about all this stuff with Nikki. But you know how that goes too; you set the offense, he jumped on the defense. Men never seem to know when to humble themselves and just say, 'Baby, you're right. I'm sorry.' They like to turn stuff around and make themselves the victim time and time again. But you know what I've got to say about that?" Remy said with a smile.

"What?"

"Fuck 'em and feed 'em beans," Remy said, cracking up.

Casey joined in her friend's laughter and said, "Yeah, unless it's Collin we're talking about."

Casey immediately regretted her comment as she noticed a pained expression cast a fleeting shadow across her friend's face.

"Remy, I'm sorry. I didn't—"

"Humph," Remy said, cutting her off, "I'm not worrying about any Collin tonight. He's blown me off far too many times recently. Plus, they're in Miami tonight anyway. You know what they say about that, don't you?" Remy said as she playfully shoved her friend with her elbow.

"When the cat's away, the mice will play!" they both yelled in unison.

"Come on, girl," Casey said, pulling on her coat. "The party's inside and that's where we need to be."

"Let's go," Remy sang out as she swung open the car door. "I'm ready to party!"

"Good, me too. I'm glad you left your bodyguard at home tonight. We can have some real fun," Casey said, eyes gleaming. "Plus, Donnie will make sure the club's security guys watch over us."

Casey had known Donnie since she was five years old, having grown up with him in McClean, Virginia. They had been childhood friends, and now that he was one of New York's hottest club promoters, Casey always had access to the city's prime parties and underground happenings.

"He owns this place, right?" Remy questioned as they walked up to the club's entrance.

"Yep, and it's one of the hottest spots lately. He's really turned this place around," Casey said.

"Donnie and his fine self," Remy said, laughing. "What's he been up to lately besides running Panthers?" Remy asked.

"This keeps him pretty busy," Casey said as they peered at the club's drab exterior, a trend of most New York hot spots.

There was a long line of people in front of Panthers, hoping to get admitted into the club. Casey and Remy quickly walked to the front of the line where they were greeted by the club's tall, muscular bouncer.

"How're my favorite ladies tonight?" the bouncer yelled at them as they approached him.

"Hey, Bobby," Casey said as she reached up to hug him.

"Hi, Bobby, long time no see," Remy said. Bobby used to work as a security guard at the studio where she filmed most of her videos.

"If it ain't Casey and Remy together, in the flesh. Where're Brent and Collin? They must be on the road to let two fine-ass women like yourselves out alone," Bobby said, chuckling.

"We're solo tonight, just trying to get our groove on," Casey said with twinkling eyes and a devilish smile.

"Besides," Remy chimed in, "they're in Miami and there's no telling what they're up to right now."

"I'm sure they're getting themselves right for the next game and they don't need to be worrying about you ladies, so I'm gonna keep my eyes on you two tonight."

Bobby led them through the club's entryway and past the table where the young woman sat collecting money for the club's twenty-dollar cover charge.

"Thanks, Bobby, we'll see you later," Casey said as they reached the coat-check area.

"You two are straight?" Bobby said, hesitating by their sides.

"We'll be just fine," Remy reassured him quickly.

"Okay, holler at me if you need anything," Bobby said, winking at them as they walked away.

"Just what we don't need, a self-appointed bodyguard to scare all the fine guys away," Casey said, laughing.

Casey checked both their coats and straightened out her BCBG tight black fitted slacks. She unbuttoned her tan sweater so that her navel barely peeked out over the top of her pants and looked over at her friend. Remy was wearing a chocolate brown chic Versace jumpsuit. Placing one hand on her high, slim hip, she walked past Casey, only to quickly stop and strike a pose only a professional model could have emulated on the catwalk.

"Remy, what do you think? Would Alexis approve of our outfits tonight?" Both women started laughing as Casey grabbed Remy by her elbow. "Let's get out of this hallway before someone besides Miss Coat-check sees us."

As they walked out into the club's open atrium, Casey noticed people pointing and whispering at Remy. She knew how uncomfortable her friend could get when she was not onstage and people were watching her.

"Remy, I think the locals are getting a bit starstruck. Let's go downstairs to the VIP area. Donnie's probably down there anyway," Casey said, taking the lead.

"Good idea, I'm right behind you," Remy answered as she followed her friend down a narrow, curving stairway.

They entered a large, dark room where the music was loud and people stood around in clumps, holding drinks in one hand and cigarettes or cigars in the other. A huge Gothic bar lined one entire wall while plush couches and cocktail tables lined the other side.

Both the men and women who came to party and enjoy themselves were dressed to kill. People were drinking, talking, dancing, and laughing—the epitome of New York's nightclub scene. Sexual innuendo was in the air, and Casey and Remy were ready to partake of the night's festivities.

"Casey, isn't that the model Tyson over there by the bar?" Remy asked her friend, eyeing the tall, dark, and extremely handsome man across the room.

"Yeah, you should go ask him to be in your next video," Casey said, laughing. "He is fine, though. I wouldn't mind being in a video with him, and I don't mean a music video."

"You're crazy, Casey. Brent looks just as good if not better than Tyson. Tape your little stank videos at home." Remy was still laughing as Tyson caught her eye and acknowledged her with a familiar wave.

"Hey, there's Donnie," Casey said, waving at her friend. Donnie was sitting in a velvet-lined booth with three other guys.

All of them were staring at the two gorgeous women as they made their way across the dance floor. On their way, Casey and Remy passed two of the Wayans brothers, and Tyra Banks. Even with all of the celebrities there, Casey and Remy stood out and seemed oblivious as they radiated their own personal limelight.

"Tonight is a hot night," Remy said, as she glanced around the room.

"I know and it's going to get better. Look who's sitting with Donnie—Mr. Fine himself," Casey muttered under her breath.

"What's up, ladies?" Donnie exclaimed as he jumped up out of the booth and reached out to hug Casey. "It's about time you came out to play," he added with a mischievous grin.

"Donnie! It's good to see you. You remember Remy?" Casey asked as she stepped aside.

"How could a guy ever forget Remy?" Donnie responded as he took a step toward Remy. He looked her up and down, smiled, and shook his head. He reached for her hands and raised them both to his full lips. He softly kissed each hand and stepped back, glowing.

"Whew, Donnie, you sure know how to make a lady swoon," Remy said with a gracious smile.

Casey knew immediately as she watched her two friends that the chemistry between them was good. She was well aware of Remy's penchant for good-looking men, and Donnie could easily hang with the best of them in the looks department. He was about six feet three inches tall and built like a triathlete. He was a handsome brown-skinned brother with a Colgate smile and perfect cleft chin. His naturally wavy hair made him a prime candidate for the S Curl man, but it was his smooth, charismatic personality that made all the ladies fall for Donnie.

Work it, Donnie, Casey thought. Besides, Remy could use some male attention.

Over the years, Casey had become accustomed to the defensive shield Remy wielded to protect herself from her emotions. On occasion, whenever her armor was pierced, Remy would shut down and pretend to not have a care in the world. Casey knew that Remy was hurting inside right now, but like many celebrities, she had perfected her use of the shield and had it down to an art. Still, Casey was close enough to her friend to know that Remy could still be hurt by those she cared about, and right now, Collin DuMott was wreaking havoc with her friend's emotions.

Go 'head Donnie, Casey mused to herself. *Make my girl smile.*

"You ladies remember my partner, Mark, don't you?" Donnie asked, pointing at his business associate who was seated at the table. "And these two fellas here you may already know—Gregory Patrick and Kenny Young."

Casey and Remy greeted everyone at the table and sat down as each guy eagerly scooted over to make room for the women. Casey wondered if Remy recognized Gregory Patrick and Kenny Young. They were both starters for the New Jersey Nets basketball team. Gregory Patrick was known throughout the NBA as the finest player in the league, and Casey could easily see why. She was struck by how handsome he was. He could easily have been described as beautiful if one used the term loosely enough.

Gregory Patrick stood a full six feet six inches and was used to hovering over people. He was built, Casey thought, like a brick house. His honey-roasted skin was smooth as a baby's behind, and he had deep, penetrating eyes that were a dark, rich Hershey brown. His hands were enormous, and Casey smiled as she found herself wondering about his shoe size.

"I'm going to order another round of drinks. What are you two ladies drinking tonight?" Donnie asked, signaling one of the chic cocktail waitresses.

"Only the finest for the finest. Ladies, may I?" Kenny Young asked. "Let's get a bottle of Cristal and some chilled glasses for starters. How does that sound to you, Remy?" Kenny said, directing his full attention toward Remy, who was seated across the table from him.

"That's fine with me, thank you," Remy said as she tapped Donnie on his arm to ask him a question.

Champagne was perfect for Casey since she wasn't much of a drinker. She always had a problem holding it—a few sips was enough to get her blitzed, and with the confusion she was already feeling, getting a bit tipsy didn't seem like such a bad idea.

"So, Casey Rogers, what brings you out tonight? Shouldn't you be down in Miami helping your husband get ready for tomorrow's game against the Heat?" Gregory asked with a soft, seductive smile.

"Come on, Greg. You know Coach Mitchell doesn't allow wives on the road with his team. We're too much of a distraction, or so we've been told," Casey responded, unable to stop herself from staring at Gregory Patrick's handsome profile.

"Shoot, if you were my woman, I wouldn't let you out of my sight." Gregory looked at Casey as he spoke and she had to stop herself from letting her mouth drop open.

"Hmm, seems like I've heard that before somewhere," said Casey. She felt a soft nudge under the table and hid a smile as Remy tried to get her attention.

"Me too," chimed in Kenny Young. "Remy, if you were mine, you could forget about all that singing stuff. I'd have you up under me everywhere I went." He laughed out loud, obviously not realizing how obnoxious he sounded.

"That's . . . sweet of you, Kenny, but singing is my life and I wouldn't give it up for anyone, not even you," Remy said.

"Yeah, you say that now," Kenny said smugly. "I'd have you so turned out, the only thing you'd be singing would be my name when we were doing the do. 'Oh, Kenny, oh, Kenny, oh, oh, oh!' " He sang out as people began to stare at their table.

"Chill out, man, we've got ladies with us," Donnie interjected with a look of distaste plastered across his face.

"Yeah, relax, man. Remy's out of your league anyway." Gregory laughed.

Remy was quiet as she sat there looking obviously disgusted with Kenny.

"Whatever, she's practically married to that 'pretty boy DuMott' anyway, huh?" Kenny asked, looking at Remy.

Remy turned her head away as he stood up and put on his coat.

"Enjoy the champagne, ladies. I've gotta go." Kenny turned to his teammate and said, "You staying, man?"

"Yep," Gregory said, still looking at Casey. "I think I'll be here for a while."

"Peace out, everyone. Remy, if you ever want a real man when the Flyers move to Albany, call me." Kenny waved one hand high over his head and walked away.

"Would you guys excuse us for a moment? Remy, let's go to the ladies' room for a second. I need to freshen up." Casey stood up and waited for her friend to follow suit. She saw Donnie and Mark both lean in toward Gregory Patrick, probably to ask him what he knows about the Flyers moving to Albany, thought Casey.

The moment they entered the bathroom, Remy turned on Casey. "How do they know about the Flyers?!"

"Shh! One sec, I gotta do the check," Casey said, placing a long, slender finger over her lips before she walked by each toilet, kicking in the stall doors one by one. It reminded her of high-school days where the girls congregated in the bathrooms to gossip.

"I bet most of the players in the league know. You know how fast word travels in the NBA," Casey said solemnly. "I bet this whole threat to sell the team is part of the reason Collin's been acting so strange lately," Remy said thoughtfully. "That and his free agency blues." She stood with her hands on her hips and started tapping one high-heeled foot. She watched as Casey looked at her own reflection in the mirror, as if she would see explanations etched in the glass.

Casey looked up and caught Remy's eyes watching her in the mirror. "I don't know, Remy," she said, looking at her friend's reflection. "I don't know what to make of anything anymore," Casey made a face at the mirror. "But I'm not about to let it spoil our evening."

"Hey, me either," Remy responded lightly. "Let's get back out there; they're probably worried about us by now."

"I know. Donnie and Gregory probably have a ton of women surrounding the table drinking our champagne," Casey said.

"Oh, hell no!" Remy said, laughing as she grabbed Casey's arm and pulled her out of the ladies' room. "They're ours tonight."

"The champagne or the guys?" Casey asked playfully, casting a sideways glance at her partner in crime.

"Both!" Remy declared, facing her friend with a wide Cheshire cat grin on her beautiful face.

As Casey looked out onto the dance floor, she realized that she had lost track of how many glasses of champagne she'd had. Remy and Donnie were slow-dancing to an up-tempo song by Janet Jackson. Remy was laughing and leaning into Donnie at the same time Gregory touched Casey's hand.

"Would you like to dance?" Gregory asked as he held her hand.

Casey looked down at their hands, and something inside told her to say no thank you and walk away. But before she knew what was happening, he had intertwined his fingers with hers. She knew he had been flirting with her all night, she quickly rationalized, but she was just having a good time. What was the harm in being a little extra nice to Gregory Patrick?

I'm only having fun.

She did not have plans to go home with him or anything like that. Unlike her own husband, she fumed, who could choose to have a one-night stand with some stranger.

Casey quickly stood up, casting away resentful thoughts of Brent and her marriage. She was forced to grab Gregory by his arm to stop herself from toppling facedown on the table. Regaining her balance, Casey sheepishly looked at her companion.

"I'd love to dance with you," Casey replied enthusiastically. "Plus this is one of my favorite songs." Casey started snapping her fingers and moving her shoulders to the rhythm of the club's music.

"You sure you're okay?" Gregory asked her.

"Maybe a few too many glasses of bubbly, but I'll be fine," she said, laughing. "Come on."

Casey led Gregory out onto the dance floor and felt the music course through her body. She moved to the beat with a rhythm all her own, dancing the latest steps with a funky precision and grace.

"I didn't know you were such a good dancer," Gregory said, pulling Casey in closer to him so she could hear him over the music.

"You're not so bad yourself," Casey said, flattered.

"I try to get my groove on," he replied, bobbing his head to the music. "I bet you're good at everything you do."

Casey looked up at the hint of suggestion in his voice and was struck again by Gregory Patrick's handsome features. He placed one large hand on the small of her back, and Casey felt herself being pulled toward him until her breasts were flat against his hard, muscular chest. For a brief moment she wondered if anyone in the club was watching them. She prayed no one recognized her, because even through her drunken haze, Casey knew there would be hell to pay if it ever got back to Brent that she was out at a club slow-dragging with Gregory Patrick, of all people.

As Maxwell's "Whenever" started to play, Casey felt Gregory's hot, wet tongue slip into her ear. He started to whisper something, but Casey couldn't hear him over the noise and music in the club. She started to push him away and ask him to repeat whatever it was he was trying to tell her when she saw Donnie leading Remy off the dance floor. Casey watched as they walked through the EXIT door, which led to the club's private offices.

Just as Casey was about to yell at Gregory that he would have to shout for her to hear him, he put his arm around her waist and led her off the dance floor. Casey, drunk, giggled as she envisioned the two of them joining Remy and Donnie in the back for a private party.

Gregory pulled the dark, heavy curtains draping an enclosed booth and sat down, nearly pulling Casey into his lap. Casey saw another bottle of Cristal champagne chilling in an ice bucket and two flutes in the center of the table. She couldn't stop the smile that by now seemed plastered on her face.

The Nets player poured the glasses full of the bubbling golden liquid, turned to Casey, and said, "So, Mrs. Rogers, where were we?"

Before Casey had time to even think about responding, Gregory wrapped his athletic arms around her and started nuzzling her neck with soft, warm kisses. Casey's mind was like an electric panel that had short-circuited. Jumbled thoughts and emotions flew back and forth, and Casey could make no sense of her feelings as she let her head fall back onto her shoulders. She had never before cheated on Brent.

She felt herself succumb with an almost reckless abandon to Gregory's probing tongue and gentle hands. Casey realized the alcohol had taken its toll on her body and mind, and she seemed helpless to stop the attention being lavished upon her.

As much as Casey wanted to blame her husband and his infidelity for what was happening to her, she knew, even in her drunken stupor, that there was no excuse in the world that would explain the wonderful physical sensations coursing through her body at that moment.

Suddenly she felt Gregory place her hand in his lap to feel his rock-hard bulge. He rubbed her hand across it and leaned into her ear with his lips.

"Can Brent Rogers ball like this?" he asked softly.

"Can . . . can what?" she stuttered before realizing what was happening.

Casey was shocked. She looked up through her drunken haze and was disgusted when she saw Gregory Patrick's smirky, self-satisfied face smiling above her own.

"You asshole!" she yelled as she jumped up and grabbed her purse. "I can't believe you!" Casey was even more disgusted with herself.

"Wait a minute, Casey! Damn, I didn't mean . . ."

Casey ignored Gregory's pleas and pushed past the black curtains, trying to keep her balance. She glanced around and angrily swiped at her eyes, determined not to let the tears of shame and guilt fall.

She remembered seeing Donnie and Remy as they headed back to the offices, and rushed off in that direction, bumping into several people who yelled as she shoved her way past them. She saw Donnie's partner standing by the bar and asked him if he had seen her friends.

"Yeah, babe. They're in the office," Mark said, clearly concerned as he noticed the fresh tears welling up in Casey's eyes. "Want me to go get them for you?"

"Would you please? I have to go," Casey said, thankful that Mark did not ask her any questions.

Standing there, waiting for Remy, Casey wondered what the hell she had been thinking of. She was almost as bad as Brent had been.

What in the world got into me tonight, she thought. It seems like I'm trying to destroy my marriage and myself. She thought of all the drinks she'd consumed. She could not bring herself to think about how sick she would be in the morning.

Casey was relieved when she saw Remy standing beside her. She grabbed Remy's hand and pulled her friend along behind her. Looking over her shoulder, Casey saw Donnie staring at them as he stood in conversation with Mark.

"Thanks, Donnie," Casey yelled out behind her. "I'll call you later."

Remy stopped Casey outside the club and looked at her best friend. "What's wrong, Casey? What happened?" she asked, concerned.

"Come on," Casey said. "I'll tell you about it in the car. You're gonna have to drive. God, I wish tonight never happened."

"Damn! She has some nice titties," Kyle said, moving to the edge of his seat as the stripper maneuvered her body back and forth inches from his face.

"Yeah, and I bet they only cost her a few grand." Jake laughed as he slapped Paul on the back and winked at Brent across the table.

Paul watched his big teammate Kyle getting worked up as the dancer quickened her pace. Kyle looked like he was about to spontaneously combust. Paul could see the drops of sweat oozing down his face even through the dense cigar smoke hovering over the gentlemen-only nightclub in Miami. Paul never went with the guys to strip clubs, but Jake had called a meeting with him and Brent, and the agent had selected Miami's infamous Camelot Club. Paul was not surprised by Jake's choice. Strip clubs, racetracks, massage houses; hot spots in every NBA city were Jake's style.

"Easy, Kyle, maybe you ought to take your act back to the hotel," Brent said to his overzealous teammate.

Paul looked at Kyle becoming increasingly excited. He had his hands on the dancer's firm rear end now and he massaged her butt as his body swayed in rhythm to the music. Paul became worried watching Kyle go into overdrive and wondered if he should intervene. Even Paul knew, making physical contact with the strippers was strictly forbidden in these types of clubs. The last thing the team needed was a scandal to hit the papers the night before game number three against Miami. They had expected to arrive in Miami two games up on the Heat, but had split the two home games in New York and were now tied at one game apiece. The best of a seven-game championship series had just gotten longer.

"Looks like the two of you could use some lessons from your rookie. Michael's showing both of you up," Jake snickered as he lit up his huge Cohiba cigar and used it as a pointer to nod across the table.

Paul followed Jake's gaze and saw that Michael had two lap dancers at the same time. The young girls had each straddled one of Michael's legs and were gyrating their pelvises in circular motion. Paul couldn't help but smile at how well the women moved their bodies. If nothing else, they sure were talented dancers. It was too bad they were wasting their skills in a place like this.

"Hey, Michael, give her a fifty for me," Jake said, tossing the crisp bill across the table toward Michael.

"You got some of that for me, Jake?" Kyle hollered over the music.

"There'd be plenty more where that came from if you were my client, I guarantee you. You would have done much better with me."

"Yo! What'd you say, Jake?" Kyle asked.

"Don't pay him any mind, Kyle; he's just dangling carrots," Brent said.

"Carrots?" Kyle said with a dopey expression on his face.

Paul looked at Brent, and the two of them tried not to laugh in Kyle's face. Kyle may have been one of the fastest players in the NBA, but when it came to intellectual quickness, he was one of the slowest.

"I'd get him enrolled in an adult-education class too, maybe Conversation 101. Hell, I'd pay for it myself," Jake said, taking a long hit from his stogie.

"Well, considering how much of a commission you'd be making

off of him, I'd say that'd be awfully generous of you, Jake," said Brent.

"Hey, I only collected two percent on both of your last deals, and I don't agree to that low fee for all of my clients," Jake said defensively.

"Don't worry, Jake, nobody's trying to disparage your good name," Paul said, looking at Brent out of the corner of his eye.

"Excuse me, Mr. Rogers. I don't mean to bother you, but has anyone ever told you that you look like the Ralph Lauren model Tyson?" It was the petite platinum blond cocktail waitress.

Paul burst out laughing. No matter where they went together, it seemed as if every woman between the ages of fifteen and thirty-five told Brent that he resembled Tyson. Even Lorraine had told Brent that he had the same slanted bedroom eyes as Tyson. It never failed to embarrass Brent, especially since he had cleaned up his act. Brent rarely so much as looked in the direction of other women these days.

"Actually, a few people have mentioned that to me," Brent said politely.

"I mean your eyes and your deep, dark chocolate skin and your bald head. Jee, you're almost a dead ringer, and to think, you're a professional ball player too."

"Yeah, we're about to have a meeting right now, but it was nice talking to you too," Brent said as gracefully as possible.

"We could continue this conversation after your meeting. My shift is over in an hour," the waitress said, leaning into Brent.

"I don't think so. But thank you just the same."

Paul noticed the look of disappointment on the woman's face as she turned to walk away. She had the expression of someone who was just one number short of winning the lottery.

"All right, Jake. What's so important that you dragged us out tonight?" Paul asked, feeling antsy.

He wanted to call the hospital and check on Lorraine to make sure she wasn't volunteering to work any extra hours. She had been so exhausted lately. Maybe those terrible dreams would dissipate if she could get some uninterrupted sleep.

"Yeah, I feel beat down. My lower back is killing me," Brent said, stretching in his seat.

"I know a good masseuse. She could come to your hotel room," Jake offered.

"I'll pass. What gives, Jake?" Brent said.

Jake took a deep puff of his cigar and looked back and forth between the two men before speaking.

"I know I don't need to tell you guys this, but that was not good losing to the Heat in New York. It's one thing to lose down here, but the team can't really afford any home losses."

"We know that, but that's why we're gonna return the favor. We're heading back to New York to win game number five. No doubt about it," said Brent with conviction.

"How can you be so sure? Alonzo Mourning is eating Steve Tucker alive, and I don't see any signs of things getting any better. It's embarrassing."

"That's why we have the other guys to take up the slack," Paul began.

"You guys have got to deliver. I shouldn't tell you this, but Hirshfield is threatening to stop holding off Hightower Enterprises."

"Because of one loss . . . Thanks, Hal, we really appreciate the vote of confidence," Brent said, making a toasting gesture with his beer mug.

"No, not because of that exactly. Although the Flyers have been known to choke down the stretch. Leonard Hightower just keeps sweetening the deal. Word is, he may even try to pressure Hal into signing an agreement to sell before the end of the play-offs."

"How can he do that?" Paul asked.

"Because he's Leonard Hightower, and he's no fool. He wants the Flyers, and he usually gets what he wants. He knows that if the Flyers actually do win the championship this year, New York City is going to absorb the bulk of Hirshfield's costs to run the team. Hightower has no intention of taking a chance of that happening."

"I bet he's up under Hal like white on rice," Brent said in disgust.

"And then some," Jake added.

"Greedy bastard. He thinks he can just buy up anything or anyone that he wants," Paul said.

"So far he's had a damn near perfect track record," Jake said. "And from what I hear, Hightower's close to making Hal an offer he can't refuse. They're already offering thirty percent more than any other NBA team is valued."

"Jake, obviously you don't understand Hal. It's more than money to him. He wants to die owning this team. I just can't believe he'd give up on us during the championship. It doesn't ring true to me," Brent said, shaking his head.

"Brent, I've been around this league long enough to know that it's a business. It's not about family or sentiment or history—not any-more, and anybody that tries to convince you otherwise is lying to you," Jake said.

"You mean you don't love me like family, Jake?" Paul said, pre-tending to be crushed.

"Aww, that's different, Paul. We're on the same team. I'm always trying to do what's in your best interest. With both of you guys, with all of my clients," Jake said quickly.

"Really, Jake. I'm glad you cleared that up for us, 'cause my feelings were about to be hurt," said Brent.

"Listen, all I'm trying to get you guys to understand is that you're under the gun. And I don't know what you have to pull out of your arsenal to win, but whatever it is, you need to do it. Every game counts. You need to sweep every round of the play-offs to ensure that Hal doesn't sell the team."

Paul and Brent looked at each other. They had played together long enough to read each other well without words.

Coach was putting Jake on their asses just to crank them up some more—get the brain chemistry moving the body into overdrive. And it probably wasn't a bad idea, not for the agent and the coach, that is. But for the players, it was total stress-out time. Paul felt the pain in his knees signal an SOS just to remind him how much it could hurt play-ing his heart out on the court.

"Have either of you seen Blondie? I need a drink," Jake said, indi-cating the meeting had ended.

Paul looked around the room and saw the waitress standing by the bar. She caught his eye as he spotted her. "There she is," he said.

"Jake, on that note, I'm going back to the hotel to get some shut-eye. I wanna make sure we do sweep the rest of this series," Brent said, standing up. "How much do I owe?" He began to reach into his pocket.

"It's on me, but are you sure you don't want to join Michael and me for another round?"

"Hey, Jake, do you want us to win or you just trying to make us crazy?" Paul was confused at Jake's mixed signals.

"Nope, thanks anyway," was all Brent said as he leaned down to shake Jake's hand.

Paul stood and, not really feeling like shaking Jake's hand, patted Michael on the back. "Michael, save some for the game tomorrow."

"Aw, man, I'm getting out of here in a few minutes myself," Michael said, grinning from ear to ear.

"Yeah, I know, just one more lap dance. Peace out, man," Paul said as he followed Brent toward the exit through the crowd of the club.

As soon as Paul and Brent got in the back of the hotel courtesy sedan, Paul pulled out his cellular phone to call Lorraine. He wanted to make sure she was only going to work one shift, but more than anything, he was aching to hear her voice. But with each ring of the telephone, Paul became increasingly worried. Someone in her unit should have answered it already.

Over the last two weeks, she had experienced two more nightmares that he knew about. It troubled him that he couldn't figure out the source of her dreams. Nor would she talk about them.

"Paul . . . Paul?" Brent said, sitting up in the back of the car.

"What's up, man?'

"I don't get Jake sometimes. He talks out the side of his mouth," Brent said pensively.

"You're just now figuring that out?" Paul said.

"I know he's full of shit about that 'we are family' crap. That's not what I was talking about. Don't you think he'd want us back at the hotel getting our rest if we're trying to sweep the rest of the series?"

"Yeah, I was thinking the same thing. You would think that, but you know how Jake gets off on being seen out in public with his clients."

"Man, it just irks me that he talked to us about how important it is for us to win, then in the same breath invites—no, encourages us to keep on drinking all night."

"You know how Jake is. He thinks he's on the road with us, just like he's one of the players. He's trying to get his partying in before he goes back home to his wife."

"You just never know with Jake. Maybe his former clients don't call him 'Shaky Jake' for nothin'."

"Code blue! Emergency room! Code blue! Emergency room!" the loud robotic voice of Harlem Hospital's main operator roared through every speaker of the hospital's seventeen floors. This was followed by a screeching electronic wail that swept through the doors and walls on each ward.

Lorraine Thomas took a deep breath and sharply exhaled. She prayed for the patient being coded in the ER and hoped whoever it was would not be the hospital's latest mortality statistic. Lorraine was exhausted. She had forty-five minutes left in her twelve-hour graveyard shift, and she needed to go home and try to sleep. Maybe she'd even have a few minutes to talk to Paul on the phone. Lately that was all she had to spare him—a growing sore spot in their marriage. She knew it would be early to call him, but he insisted that she call him when she got home in the morning, no matter what time.

Paul had been putting more and more pressure on her to quit her job. He insisted she didn't need to work and recently had become increasingly annoying by constantly reminding her of the fact that he made over four million dollars a year playing for the New York Flyers. Lorraine was tired of explaining to her husband that her career meant more to her than finances.

Paul desperately wanted her to fit his perception of other NBA wives: always available. He would have been content for her to sit at home and do volunteer work for their church in between hair and manicure appointments along with shopping for the latest designer fashions. Paul expected her to plan her schedule around his practices and pregame naps and meals while regularly attending all of his home games.

But Lorraine could never relegate her life to being the trophy wife of a professional athlete. She absolutely thrived on being a nurse— even when she was dead tired. Sometimes she couldn't believe that Paul, who shared so many of her values, wasn't condoning her work at Harlem Receiving Hospital, considering what a difference it made to the people in the community where she'd grown up. This was something Paul did not fully comprehend, and she wondered if he ever would, having come from a small town in Alabama himself where the only community crisis was having to raise enough money to buy new uniforms for the high-school basketball team. Whenever they had an argument about her working, they both remained fiercely devoted to their positions. He incorrectly assumed her desire to give back to the community could be fulfilled by delivering food baskets to the sick and elderly, followed by being at home for dinner every night the Flyers happened to be in town—with a smile on her face, of course. She wanted more out of life, had to have more. Lorraine needed to save lives.

"Lorraine! Lorraine!" the head nurse on duty yelled at the top of her lungs.

She ran out of her patient's room and rushed over to the unit's charge station expectantly. "A new patient?"

"Yes," Francine answered. "And this one sounds like he's in really bad shape. They just coded him in ER, a nineteen-year-old Hispanic male suffering from gunshot wounds. It sounds like he's going to need plenty of blood just to get him stabilized, not to mention a new lung and half his face replaced. Then he'll be in perfect critical condition," she said sarcastically.

"Well, at least he's not in the morgue," Lorraine said, silently praying for strength.

"Lorraine," Francine said, glancing over at the unit's assignment board, "your shift's about over. Sign this admission over to the nurse coming on duty. Why don't you do yourself a favor and get your butt home; you look beat. The only thing that's gonna help him now anyway is prayer."

"I'm praying for him . . . praying that God gives me the strength to help him. What happened to the kid anyway?"

The charge nurse rolled her eyes before answering. "Typical drive-by shooting over in Spanish Harlem. Witnesses say this one took three bullets before he stopped staring at the commotion on the street and fell to the ground. What else?"

Lorraine cringed at Francine's callousness. She always had a flippant remark as if urban teenagers somehow deserved to be gunned down or clubbed to death. She knew she held higher standards than most of her co-workers, but the hollow look of utter despair in a mother's eyes after being told she would never see her child alive again gained one a sobering sense of reality.

Lorraine glanced at the scratched Swatch watch with the big, clear dial that she had worn throughout nursing school. She rarely found an occasion to wear the expensive watch Paul had given her for her twenty-fifth birthday. She felt it was too pretentious for the halls of the hospital, and her Swatch had served her well for years. She saw no reason to change now, though there had been many changes in her life.

She had grown up only ten blocks south of Harlem Receiving Hospital on Martin Luther King Boulevard. Her neighborhood had been plagued with gangs, drugs, and weapons. She understood firsthand that this violence had a very real effect on very real people.

By the time Lorraine was twelve, she had seen enough violence to last her several lifetimes. One day she witnessed the paperboy down the street being stabbed to death. Another day she saw the bag-check lady from Safeway fatally hit by a car. Lorraine knew only too well that these were real people with real families.

But even though she and Paul had money now, they weren't immune to problems. Paul had clearly been distraught right before the play-offs began over two weeks ago when he told Lorraine about the possibility of the team being sold and moved to Albany. Paul feared the politics of Leonard Hightower and Hightower Enterprises. Lorraine also was distraught, but for a different reason than Paul. She was not prepared to work as a nurse anyplace except Harlem, and the relocation of the Flyers could separate them. Although she had not told him she would not move, the question floated dangerously between them.

She loved Paul desperately, and if nursing was like breathing for her, Paul was the lifeline in their relationship. He was the rock and the stabilizer, with a strong spiritual base that held them together. Lorraine was willing to have a commuter marriage if Hal Hirshfield actually moved forward with the sale of the team. Unlike many of the other NBA wives and girlfriends, Lorraine did not have a problem trusting Paul when he was out of her sight. They enjoyed an honest, loving relationship. In fact, Lorraine suspected that Paul was far too traditional to ever agree to them living in two different cities, even if they were only a few hours drive from each other. That type of arrangement would be at odds with everything Paul represented. He was a man of honor and convention. She only prayed that it didn't come to that. She didn't want to be forced to choose.

Lorraine was oblivious to the sheets of rain beating down on her head. Her bangs were now plastered to her forehead as she stood before the old storefront. The front window of what used to be a Jamaican carry-out restaurant was replaced with layers of plywood, as if that thin shield could protect her from the memories that had begun to haunt her.

Lorraine worked only minutes away, had grown up a mere two blocks away, but this was the first time she had revisited the site in many years.

Her mind had been on automatic pilot when she left the hospital over an hour ago. Instead of heading uptown toward the George Washington Bridge, Lorraine had made a detour south. Now she stood before the scene that had recently returned in her mind along with the phone calls that tormented her.

She flinched at the sudden brightness of the lightning. She could have sworn moments before that a stream of blood oozed its way out the door onto the slick concrete. The puddles of water circled Lorraine's soaked loafers, which had taken on a deep burgundy color. Lorraine blinked her unreliable eyes and frantically wiped the rain away, certain that she was seeing things or going crazy. Grabbing the sides of her head as a shot of pain sliced through her right temple, she cursed as the images returned.

"Get up, Raino! We're gonna leave your sorry ass here if you don't get back in the car! You can't do shit about it now; come on!" Roy hollered out of the back window of the black low rider that the Disciples regularly used to cruise the neighborhood.

Lorraine's heart was beating like a jackhammer. The child on the ground before her could not have been more than eight years old. How had she gotten in the line of fire? Lorraine hadn't even known that Tommy and Roy planned on doing a drive-by. She knew they had beef with the local Jamaican gang, the Posse, but the plan to shoot up their hangout had been kept from the Disciples' girl members.

"Somebody call 911! Somebody has to call an ambulance!" Lorraine cried as she leaned over the young girl's limp body.

"Just get in the car, Raino; they gonna be here in a few minutes anyway," Roy shouted over the distant sound of sirens.

"Go! Just go! I'm not leaving her here. She's gonna bleed to death. We have to stop the bleeding," Lorraine said, taking off her coat to put under the child's head.

"Raino, get the fuck in the car!" yelled Tommy from the driver's seat. Tommy was the gang's leader.

"I'm not going anywhere . . . Can you hear me? You're going to be okay. What's your name?" Lorraine asked the wounded little girl.

"Raino, when the cops get here, you weren't with us and you don't know shit or you gonna find your ass bleeding on the concrete too . . . next to your mama! I promise you that," Tommy said before he skidded off down the street.

Lorraine grasped the girl's tiny hand. "What's your name? Can you hear me? If you can, squeeze my hand."

"Cri . . . Criss . . . Crissy," the little girl gasped.

Lorraine felt relief wash over her entire body as a sob caught in her throat.

"Ohh, good, honey. Oh, that's so good. Your name is Crissy? Oh, that's a pretty name."

"Mommy . . . Mommy calls me that," Crissy said as her eyes rolled back in her head.

"Crissy. Crissy! Talk to me. Squeeze my hand." Lorraine felt panic rise within her.

"I . . . I . . . want Mommy," Crissy quietly sobbed.

Lorraine watched helplessly as Crissy's eyes closed and her legs began to convulse.

"Come on, Crissy, come on! Please say something! Say something! Please, honey. You've got to speak to me," Lorraine cried, rocking back and forth as the tears streamed down her face.

When the police arrived, Lorraine was still hunched over the lifeless child in a state of utter despair.

"Ma'am. Ma'am?" a male voice said, interrupting Lorraine's thoughts.

"Yes? " Lorraine said, turning toward a young man in a neon green rain cover-up.

"Is that your car over there?" he said, pointing toward the red Range Rover.

"Yeah," Lorraine answered, still in a daze.

"I think it's about to be towed."

Lorraine glanced over in the direction of her car and saw the tow truck backing in for the steal.

"Oh, thank you, thank you so much."

"You're drenched. You're gonna catch your death out here." The young man stared at Lorraine. "Well, take care of yourself."

I think my death has already caught me, Lorraine thought as she ran through the thick rivulets of rain.

"Liza. Liza. You're not listening to me. How many times do I have to tell you, I'm not going? After my mini tour, try and reschedule it, or maybe I can do it when I perform in Chicago," Remy said in exasperation to Liza Anderson, her talent agent of seven years.

Sometimes Remy even bothered to Liza. Liza's only con- the biggest star in the whether that was a Liza's philosophy was to thing for success.

wondered why she explain anything to cern was Remy being Western Hemisphere, realistic goal or not. sacrifice anyone and any-

Remy pulled the phone away from her ear. She could not believe that Liza was complaining about the air play on "Happiness Is Divine." It was number two on the *Billboard* chart and number one according to the majority of other music industry polls.

"What about what I need? What about that? I'm tired. I just finished shooting three videos in less than two months. It'll be my one

day off in L.A. and I don't feel like crisscrossing the country just to do a talk show," said Remy adamantly.

Liza had a point, Remy knew. People didn't just turn down "Oprah."

"Liza, if I did the show, I'd have to fly back here for a two-hour concert, four hours after landing back in L.A. No, thanks."

"It's the perfect opportunity to plug the tour," Liza was saying, pleading in Remy's ear.

Remy did not respond. The few select shows she was doing had sold out months before. She was exhausted talking to Liza and she had more pressing issues to worry about than going on a television show, even if it was "Oprah."

"Look, maybe I'm just burnt-out Liza; I am human, you know," Remy said, walking with the telephone to the ten-foot window in her loft.

Remy knew Liza wouldn't buy it. Liza had known her too long and too well.

Liza hit Remy's hot button, saying, "If I told you the Flyers were going to be in Chicago, would it make a difference? You'd probably be gone in a flash."

"Collin has nothing to do with this," Remy said a little too defensively.

"You'd be on that plane in a hot second. You'd conjure up the energy to see him, but not for your career. Is that it now?"

Remy sat down on the ledge of her window feeling utterly defeated. Truthfully, if Collin had asked her to meet him someplace, she would have traveled the world to see him. But the fact of the matter was, every time she had asked Collin if something was wrong, he claimed that it was just a stressful time for him and that it had nothing to do with their relationship. He had promised Remy that his feelings for her had not changed. But what were those feelings?

"Liza, I'm not doing it. Now, please stop pressuring me about this," Remy said, fighting back the tears as she stared out her window, envying the anonymous pedestrians who could amble their way down Spring Street, families and loved ones having time and space for each other.

"All right, all right, don't worry about it," Liza was saying on the other end of the line. "I'll figure something out to tell them. We'll get you on 'Oprah' another time. You okay now, kiddo?"

"I'm fine," Remy said in a childlike voice.

"I just hope you don't regret it later," Liza said, and hung up the phone in Remy's ear.

Remy was used to Liza hanging up without saying good-bye. It was her trademark. She was one of the most aggressive, astute, and powerful agents at Talent Management International. Liza was also a big softy but she would die if she ever thought her cover as the toughest agent in town was blown.

The dial tone buzzing in Remy's ear pulled her out of her deep thoughts and she replaced the phone in its cradle. Remy walked toward the treadmill in the corner of her living room and jumped on it in hopes of clearing her mind. As she turned the mechanism on high incline, Remy's legs began to churn. Closing her eyes, she picked up speed and tried to pinpoint how and exactly when the distance had crept between her and Collin.

Running faster on the treadmill, Remy was determined to find a way to bridge the gap.

And she wondered about the link between Hightower and the team.

Even though Rick was in Miami in the middle of a game, Trina still found herself tiptoeing through his office. Unless Rick was sitting at his desk, the room was strictly off-limits to her and the kids. His word was so intimidating that it was not even necessary for him to put a lock on the door.

Trina felt a bit ashamed of herself as she sat down in his chair and opened the top drawer of his desk. Unlike most of the wives Trina knew, she did not regularly snoop into her husband's private matters, but she had been forced into action. The small-business loan Trina had applied for from their bank had been rejected. When she had received the letter in the mail, she had assumed there must have been a mistake. With Rick's annual income being over two million dollars, she should have been eligible for the paltry twenty-five thousand dollars she was applying for to back her venture.

The letter of rejection from the bank had not specified the reason the loan had been denied, so Trina had gone to the bank to investigate for herself. At first they'd been reluctant to divulge any information to her, but finally the private-accounts manager had advised her to check her TRW credit report.

"Yes! Yes!" Marcus screamed from the kitchen where he was watching the Flyers play the Heat.

Startled by Marcus's hollering, Trina banged her knee on Rick's desk.

"Damn, Marcus! What did I tell you about all that yelling, boy? You almost gave me a heart attack."

"But, Mama, the Flyers are about to win the game! They're gonna play the Bulls in the Eastern Conference finals! I get to see Michael Jordan!" Marcus hollered back from the kitchen.

"Just keep it down," Trina said as a wave of nausea washed over her. Even though she was well into her fourth month of pregnancy, she was still sick all day. She had also not told Rick yet. Somehow there never seemed to be a right time to break it to him, especially since she knew he was staunchly opposed to having more children.

Trina began pulling out the side drawers in hopes of finding some documentation of what Rick was spending all his money on. When Trina had received the TRW report, she had been completely baffled. There were five credit cards listed, which were all at the maximum limits, totaling over a half million dollars! Trina had also discovered that he had been bouncing checks for months, regularly dipping into the overdraft protection of their joint account and his personal account. Rick had always been so frugal when it came to spending money; this information was a signal that something serious was going on. Women. Drugs. She didn't know, but there was something. One thing she was certain of—if Rick was using drugs, her hands were tied. Coach wouldn't disrupt his team for anyone. Rick would be forced to play until the play-offs were over. Then the league would probably ship her husband off to rehab; a fine way to wind down a career, she thought.

Trina continued to search through all of Rick's files but was unable to find any receipts, canceled checks, credit-card notices, or anything that could shed some light on where all their money had gone.

Trina sat back in Rick's chair, feeling frustrated. How could he? During all the years of their marriage, he would get angry at her for spending too much money at the grocery store, and here they were almost bankrupt because of him.

She knew asking Rick where the money was going was pointless. In fact, he'd be angry at her for questioning him about it in the first place. She had to find out some other way. Trina and the children were dependent on Rick for their future financial well-being, especially with baby number three on its way. For all she knew, they may not have a cent.

Trina racked her brain as she pushed herself back from Rick's desk. There was no one in Rick's family she felt comfortable enough to call. She would never think of asking Coach Mitchell about this situation, and she didn't want to talk to any of the other players. Word would be out in a second.

Trina began pacing back and forth with her hands resting on her backside.

"Don Hammond!"

Of course! Rick's agent. He had always been a kind and fair man, unlike many of the sports agents Trina had heard about over the years.

Trina quickly ran back behind Rick's desk and began sifting through his business-card Rolodex, when one of the names on file caught her eye. Hightower Enterprises. That was strange. Why would Rick have a business card from someone at Leonard Hightower's company? From what Trina had overheard of Rick's conversation with his agent a few weeks ago, if she remembered correctly, it was Hightower Enterprises that was trying to buy the Flyers. She couldn't understand what Rick would be doing with this business card, but he kept so many secrets from her, especially concerning his business matters.

Well, this family's financial well-being is my business too, Trina told herself as she worked up the nerve to call Rick's agent.

When Trina heard Don's voice on the other end of the receiver, she almost hung up but stopped herself.

"Don?" Trina tentatively began. "This is Trina, Rick Belleville's—"

"How are you, young lady!" Don said in his usual good-natured manner.

"I hope I'm not disturbing you, but there's something I need to talk to you about."

"Of course you're not disturbing me. I'm just watching the game. The Flyers are seconds away from advancing to the Eastern Conference finals."

"Oh, they are?" Trina asked, feeling totally flat, not caring if they won or lost.

"Yes! And you must be so proud. Rick sure is having a great game. Don't tell me you're not watching it?"

"Ahh . . . no, not right now."

"You're missing the best part. Paul Thomas actually shut Tim Hardaway down in the fourth quarter, and they've swarmed Mourning with the defense; he's barely able to move," said Don excitedly.

"Oh, well, if I'm disturbing you, maybe I can—"

"Don't be silly, I always have time for my players and their lovely wives. Let me turn this TV off. The Flyers are up by nine anyway and there's only three seconds left in the game. What can I do for you, dear?"

She'd come this far; now, how to proceed? He was, after all, Rick's agent, and Trina assumed that Don's loyalties would be with his client. She wasn't very good at being cunning in these types of circumstances, and decided that the straightforward approach was her best option.

"Don, I don't want to put you in a funny position, but I don't know who else to ask about this." Trina took a deep breath before continuing. "A lot of our money seems to be missing, and I don't know where it's gone, and I thought you might know what's going on. I . . . I . . . ."

"Go on now," Don gently urged. "Take a deep breath."

"I feel so foolish bothering you about this, but I need to know what Rick is doing with all of our money and I'm afraid to ask him," Trina said nervously.

"I see."

"Like I said, I don't mean to put you in a funny position, but I didn't know who else I could turn to."

"Well, Trina, I have to tell you, this is rather awkward for me."

"I'm sorry, Don, but do you understand where I'm coming from? I've got Marcus's and Monica's futures to think about and . . ." She bit her lip before the news about the new baby could come tumbling out. "He hasn't told me anything."

"There are ethical implications for me to consider if I were to divulge certain private matters of Rick's," said Don.

"Certain what?"

"I have a fiduciary duty to Rick that does not allow me to discuss matters pertaining to him with outside parties."

"Well, I'm sorry I even bothered you, Don; have a good—"

"Hey, hey. Wait a second there. I said 'outside parties,' not his wife. I know how Rick can be just as well as you do. I just have to know this conversation doesn't go further than us. I don't want him going off the deep end if he finds out that I mentioned this to you. I had actually planned on calling you about this. I don't know how to say it, but I think Rick needs to seek professional help."

Trina's mind began to race.

"What kind of help? Please tell me it's not drugs."

"Trina, Rick has a gambling problem."

"A gambling problem? I know Rick plays some blackjack at the casinos every now and then, but a gambling problem, that's hard for me to believe."

"That's what he's been spending all of his money on. He owes quite a few casinos a sizable amount of money. It's definitely a problem."

"How much money are we talking about, Don?"

"A lot."

"What do you mean by a lot?" Trina worriedly asked.

"A whole lot. Over a million dollars."

Trina slumped down on the chair in front of Rick's desk, feeling as if the wind had been knocked out of her. Over a million dollars! And here, like a fool, she regularly made a point to cut out coupons when she went to the supermarket while he threw money away like yesterday's newspapers.

"Trina, you there?" Don asked, sounding concerned.

"Yeah, I'm still here."

"I take it you had no idea about this."

"None."

"I'm sorry I had to be the one to tell you. Is there anything I can do to help?" Don asked with obvious sincerity.

"I don't know," Trina said as she felt a bout of nausea catch in her throat.

"Well, if it's any consolation, you all are far from being broke. Everything is just tied up in mutual funds and stocks."

"Well then, why didn't he cash those in to pay the debt?"

"Good question—one I've asked him maybe a hundred times myself. It sure as hell isn't the penalty."

Trina wasn't educated, but she was smart. And she knew her husband. It took her about two seconds to figure out what was going on in Rick's mind.

"I'll tell you what I think," she said. "I think in the back of Rick's mind, so long as he had those funds, he wasn't broke—so he could tell himself it was okay to gamble. You see what I'm getting at?"

"Maybe. Anyway, Rick's been living paycheck to paycheck, spending most of the money gambling, trying to win back what he's lost. I think I may have finally made some headway with him. He seems to have cut back, but I think he's got to quit completely. And I don't think he can do it cold turkey. He has to get some professional help."

"I can't see Rick getting that kind of help from anybody. He has too much pride."

"Trina, he's got to stop. That's all I know. Otherwise he's going to lose everything. And he knows it. If that doesn't get through to him, I don't know what will."

"Me neither, Don."

"Well, if you need anything else, call me."

"Thank you, Don. I'll talk to you later," Trina said, hanging up the phone.

Don's revelation was too large for Trina to swallow in one bite. With the door to the office closed, her children's sweet voices a room away, she paced, contemplated, and finally got down on her knees and prayed.

"Oh, and I want to say one more thing before I go, Phil. I just want to tell my wife, Casey, that I love her. Case, I couldn't have done it without you, baby," Brent said looking directly into the camera.

As Brent walked away from the Flyers sports announcer, Casey felt glued to the small television set in her home office. Smiling, she switched off the TV, stood up, stretched her long, tight limbs and headed to the kitchen. Brent could be so thoughtful and sweet at times. Certain times, Casey reminded herself. He was so romantic, one of those men who never failed to remember birthdays, Valentine's Day, or holidays. He seemed to look for occasions to send her exotic flowers. Why couldn't she make up her mind to put all that trouble behind them? What held her back?

Because I have a right to be pissed off at his lying ass! Don't I?

Casey pulled out the hazelnut coffee beans from the refrigerator and poured them into the coffee grinder. She hoped that a full pot would be enough to keep her awake during the long night of work that lay before her. She had a challenging case involving a playwright who was fighting to keep the nudity and sex scenes in his production when it debuted on Broadway in one month.

Thinking of an evening a few years before when she had just settled a particularly stressful case, Casey actually laughed aloud. She had arrived home to find a trail of candles on the floor leading to the master bathroom. Casey had followed the lights until she reached Brent in their circular Jacuzzi filled with bubbles, an oversized red bow around his neck. His final and, Casey admitted, most succulent offering was the huge erection that beckoned to her. Standing in the tub, covered in white bubbles, he had looked absolutely gorgeous and vulnerable at the same time. It had only been a matter of seconds before Casey ripped off her clothes and joined him.

When she had jumped in the steamy water, Brent had smothered her with wet kisses. He had grabbed her face in between both of his hands and whispered in her ear that it was the perfect night for making a baby.

The thought of spending an evening like that with Brent made her heart race. They had shared a closeness that most couples only fantasized about ever having, yet it seemed like years since they had experienced a truly intimate moment. That was, of course, Brent's fault. Why had he ruined everything for them? Or was it his fault? Maybe she should think again.

Casey carefully measured water for the coffee and wondered if there was something she could have done differently to change the course their marriage had taken. Was it her fault too? After her miscarriage, Casey had to admit that she had become cold toward Brent. For months she would feel unsettled when he even touched her. And when Casey had finally agreed to having sex with Brent again, it was for the sole mission of him impregnating her. She had become obsessed with getting pregnant, and everything in her life had begun to center around her cycle.

Their lovemaking had been so mechanical back then, she wondered what part her attitude had played in driving Brent into the arms of another woman.

Not that Brent's one-night stand could ever be excused. But occasionally Casey could not help but think how different things would have been between them if she had not become so fanatic about having a child. Had she pushed him away?

Casey jumped at the sound of the doorbell ringing. The red digital numbers on the electronic coffeemaker read 11:15 P.M. Casey hoped it was not one of her neighbors coming over to congratulate her on the Flyers' win. It would not have been unusual for one of the young boys who lived in the building to show up at the door trying to get first dibs on the pair of gym shoes Brent had worn in the win over the Heat.

Casey walked slowly down the long, dimly lit hallway decorated with landscape oil paintings and two beautiful Romare Bearden works they had collected at auctions and estate sales over the years. She peered through the little peephole in the mahogany door and saw the green uniform hat of one of the building's doormen.

"Yes?" Casey said from inside her apartment.

"Mrs. Rogers, is that you?" a familiar voice answered.

"Yes," Casey said, curious as to what he was doing at her door at such a late hour.

"It's me, Joe. I'm sorry to come up here so late, but I didn't know what else to do. I have a little girl out here that I'm supposed to drop off with you and Mr. Rogers," Joe tentatively said.

"A little girl?" Casey asked in disbelief as she simultaneously swung open the door. She looked at Joe and then down at the little girl standing beside him.

Before her, dressed in miniature Levi's jean overalls with a yellow turtleneck, was a frightened child, fighting back tears. The poor thing had on sandals, exposing chubby toes, which had to be cold on such a windy night. She had two ponytails with curly sprouts framing her round face.

"Who brought her here, Joe?" Casey asked, unable to take her eyes off the little girl. She definitely had Brent's distinct eyes, but her coloring had a lighter cocoa shade. There was no doubt in Casey's mind that this child was Nikki. But what was she doing in front of her door?

"Her mother, I'm pretty sure. She was calling her Mama."

At the mention of Nikki's mother, Casey noticed the little girl's bottom lip begin to quiver and her eyes well up with fresh tears. Casey was at a loss. She wanted to find out more about the circumstances of Nikki arriving at their doorstep, but she did not want to upset her any more.

"Is this . . . woman who dropped her off still downstairs?" Casey asked, moving closer.

"No. When I told her that you were upstairs, she said that you and Mr. Rogers were expecting this little girl to visit and then she got back into a cab and left. Just like that. She was gone as quick as she came, and she handed the child over to me."

"When's my mama coming back?" Nikki cried.

Casey's heart went out to the small child standing at her door, but she had no idea what to do with Brent's little surprise package.

"Well, did she leave a bag for her or anything?" Casey asked.

"Nothing, ma'am. Like I said, that's why I came up here so late and all. So here you go," Joe said, pulling Nikki's hand toward Casey.

Joe let go of Nikki and headed back to the elevator as Nikki ran up behind him.

"Mama's downstairs. I go see my mama," Nikki said tearfully, clinging to Joe's sleeve.

Casey felt confused watching this little girl. Her head told her Brent never could have planned this visit without informing her. Her heart held back.

Casey walked toward Nikki until she was only inches from her and got down on her knees so she could be at the same eye level.

"Nikki, my name is Casey. Mommy thought you might like to visit with me and Brent . . . your father for a little while. Why don't you come inside with me." Casey stretched out her hand for Nikki to take.

"Where's Mama?" Nikki asked.

"She's coming back later." Casey realized that she needed to employ a different tactic. "Nikki, I was thinking. I have some ice cream inside and maybe you'd like to share some with me until your mama gets back."

Casey saw a twinge of interest spread across Nikki's face.

"Chocolate ice cream?"

"I think I might be able to find some chocolate in the freezer if you help me," Casey said, looking at Nikki hopefully. "You think you could help me find it?"

Casey sighed with relief as Nikki nodded her head yes. Holding the little girl's hand, the two of them went inside the apartment into the bright kitchen. As they reached the refrigerator, Casey picked up Nikki and placed her on her hip so they could look in the freezer together.

"Let's see, we have vanilla," Casey said, peering inside the freezer.

"Nooo. Chocolate," Nikki insisted.

"We have butter pecan," Casey said, looking at Nikki.

"Yucky," Nikki said, scrunching up her face.

"Ohhh, look what I found. I see some chocolate, waaay in the back."

"Yaaay!" Nikki hollered as she bounced up and down on Casey's hip.

Casey removed the Häagen Dazs chocolate ice cream and placed it on the work island in the center of the kitchen. She looked down at Nikki as she rested her small head on Casey's shoulder.

"You want it on a cone or in a bowl?" Casey said. She felt Nikki yawn against her shoulder.

"A cone," Nikki said with her small voice.

"Okay, sweetie, you sit here while I scoop it out," Casey said, placing Nikki on one of the barstools surrounding the kitchen island.

"Nooo. I want to stay with you," Nikki said, tightly grasping Casey's neck.

Just as Casey was reaching into the kitchen drawer to get the ice cream scooper, the phone rang. What next? Who could be calling at this hour? She was beginning to feel as if her apartment were Grand Central Station.

Casey snatched up the phone and abruptly said, "Yes?"

"Well, hello to you too," Brent responded on the other end of the line, ecstatic, undoubtedly about the win.

Casey had no intention of wasting any time getting to the point. "Brent, did you know that we were expecting a visitor this evening?" Casey asked, not wanting to get Nikki upset.

"A visitor?" Brent asked, sounding perplexed.

"Yes. Nikki's here."

"Nikki? There, at the apartment?" Brent said, clearly surprised.

"That's right. In fact, she's right here with me. We're about to have some ice cream." Casey tried to keep her voice level as she switched Nikki to her other hip.

"I didn't know anything about this, Casey. I promise you. How'd she get there?"

"We'll talk about it when you get home. I don't want the little ears to hear. You know what I'm saying? But I think it's safe to say she'll be here when you arrive. Now I have to go. I'll see you when you get home." Casey hung up quickly.

Casey managed to shovel a scoop of ice cream onto the sugar cone and place it in Nikki's outstretched hand. So much for her coffee and work.

Were the bombshells ever going to stop dropping? Marriage to Brent carried so much extra baggage, and Casey saw no end in sight. Now here was another victim, an innocent little girl. Casey watched Nikki eagerly lick at her ice cream, completely unaware of whose home she was in or why. As far as she knew, she'd been left with a complete stranger. It was so unfair to everyone involved.

Shivers raced down the Flyer's spine as Phil massaged his neck. Phil had learned his erogenous zones in a matter of months, and the effect was frightening. The athlete moaned involuntarily as his lover aroused him with his gentle touch.

He and Phil had begun flirting with one another nine months ago. They had started working closely together doing postgame commentary: he, the seasoned player, and Phil, the polished sportscaster. From there, the rest had inevitably followed.

"Three times in one morning is more than I can handle. You act like I wasn't working my ass off last night whippin' the Heat. It's tough work making it to the Eastern Conference finals. And then I had to get on that excuse of a private plane with those small seats, and now you wanna wear me out too," he said, turning over on his side, directly facing Phil.

"Should I get out the violin now or later?"

"And it's so damn early in the morning," he continued, enjoying every stolen moment with his lover.

"Bitch, bitch, bitch. Since when did you care about the time of day? Plus you know what they say about the early bird . . . and I think you've caught it . . . quite well, I might add. So stop fighting it," Phil said, caressing his hairy chest. "That's not such a hard thing to do, is it?"

"You play dirty; you know it's very hard," he shot back playfully.

"Then I'm on my job."

"Ahh, this is your job now? So I'm work for you, huh?"

"Yup, I've been working on you since the day I interviewed you after the Detroit Pistons game when you missed that easy layup that cost the Flyers the game," Phil teased.

"I was fouled; I should have had two free throws. Hell, Grant Hill should have been called for a flagrant on that play," he said indignantly.

"Famous last lines of all you athletes." Phil laughed, tossing a pillow over his face.

He looked at the dark, sleek body of his lover. He boasted a fair toffee complexion and hazel eyes, which contrasted with Phil's mahogany-colored skin and seductive bedroom eyes. He had slept with two other men, but Phil was different. The other two were quick, back-drawer affairs, and when they were over, he had pushed the incidents out of his mind. But with Phil, he experienced a range of feelings. He had never felt so relaxed and fully himself. It was the first time he completely let go of his physical self-control. He was so used to maintaining the control, he never trusted himself to fully be free with a man or a woman. But now he let Phil take over and he was loving it—even if it was for only stolen moments. Phil was like a jolt of energy to his mind, body, and soul. The lackluster life that had previously held him captive was gone. He was free. Well, almost. There was still his woman to consider—as if they didn't have enough problems already.

As wonderful as he felt, he could not shake his uneasiness. He was a cauldron of hot water placed on the stove to boil. Sooner or later he'd have to tell her something, and how was she going to accept the fact that he was bisexual, or probably more true, gay? He could barely say the word himself. He and his woman had a long history together, and it pained him to think about hurting her.

And what about his career? Was the world ready for an openly gay basketball player? Was the NBA ready? Sure, Dennis Rodman could dress up as a woman, but everyone knew he was still sleeping with women, including his tabloid affair with Madonna.

"Hey, you okay?" Phil was caressing him from behind. "Where did you drift off to?"

"I'll be all right. Listen, I better get going," he said, sitting up and reaching for his silk boxer shorts, which had fallen to the foot of the bed. "I have a golf date."

"You feeling bad about sneaking out? You think we went overboard? You feeling guilty? Talk to me," Phil implored.

"Yes and no," he said, standing up and pulling on his underwear.

"You want to elaborate? Are you confused or what?"

"I wish I were confused; I think that would make matters easier. The fact that I'm feeling so certain about us scares me. I even told Paul I *thought* I was gay," he said, shaking his head.

"I know how you feel; the truth of who you are is a scary thing. I went through it eleven years ago when I came out. Now my family and friends know and I feel relieved more than anything. Hell, the rest of the world could find out about me and I would care less."

He felt his whole body become rigid. "But you're not a player."

"No, but I'm in sports."

"It's different. Athletes have to keep up public images."

"You can still come out—it's 1998, after all," Phil said.

"Who said anything about coming out?"

"Hey, I'm on your side. You know that, don't you? I'm telling you what I went through, not what you should or should not do. You're the one who decided to confess to Paul that you're gay."

"But I only told Paul. That doesn't mean I'm gonna tell the world. I have a lot at stake; I have my family to think about, my friends, this racist, homophobic Hightower character who's trying to buy the Flyers—hell, my fans. I'd be risking all that and I'm not even positive that I'm gay," he said defensively.

"Now you're confused. Dennis Rodman may not be gay, but you, my dear, are as gay as I am. And on that note, I'm going to work."

"I still have my woman," he said, sounding like an adolescent.

"You're still in denial," Phil said, pulling his white T-shirt over his head.

"Phil, you tricked me into this whole affair. You turned me out."

"Boy, you were ripe for the picking. I only did what you were aching for me to do," Phil said, zipping his Lucky You jeans.

"I told you about talking to me in that tone, like I'm your subordinate or something," he said, pretending to reprimand Phil.

"You are my subordinate. That's why you're my *co*host and not the head host, the top dog, like me."

"You like being on top of the situation, huh?" he asked, thinking how sexy Phil was to him.

"I can be on the bottom sometimes too," Phil said as he approached him and kissed him full on the lips.

"You're a tease," he said, moving to the door of Phil's apartment. Reaching the foyer area, he suddenly did not want to leave. "So are you going to disappear later on tonight, as usual?"

"Why, do you have a better suggestion?" Phil asked playfully.

"Go to dinner with me."

"You mean you don't have any plans with your significant other?"

"We haven't made any plans yet; besides, it would be easy to explain to her that you and I have business to discuss. She may be busy herself. It's not like she has all the time in the world for me either."

"I don't know, let's play it by ear. After this early morning romp, I don't know if I could keep my hands off of you in a restaurant. Just call me later. Now get out of here. I've got work to do. I'm the one who has the hard part of our job. All you have to do is run up and down the court and then sit in front of the camera talking about a subject you love." Phil kissed him one last time.

He slowly closed the door as he left, willing it to remain open even as he was pulling it shut. He wanted to be with Phil all the time.

He tried to reason with his fear. Even if someone did guess their secret, it would only be speculation. He and Phil had a legitimate business relationship. Besides, one unsubstantiated rumor was not going to hurt his career, but it was becoming painfully clear that being without Phil would definitely hurt his life.

"Fore! Fore!" Brent shouted seconds after he swung his Big Bertha driver. He hoped no one was hit with his golf ball.

Brent looked over his shoulders, to see Paul and Coach trying to stifle their laughter. Jake, his partner for the day, just looked pissed.

"Thanks Brent. I guess we'll have a chance to win this match after all," Coach Mitchell said, winking at Paul as he headed toward the tee. Coach looked like he should have been on the cover of *Golf World*, with his plaid Kangol hat, cream-colored pants, and matching crew-neck sweater. No matter what Coach's surroundings were, he always managed to look like he belonged.

"It was my pleasure," Brent responded sarcastically as he stepped away from the tee box and walked toward Paul and Jake.

"Don't worry about it, partner; the gusty winds on this hole sometimes catch the balls and carry them off. And today is a lot windier than usual," Jake said, condescendingly patting Brent on the back.

"The wind carries the balls that far left?" Paul said, raising his eyebrows in disbelief.

"Both of you can kiss my ass," Brent said, handing the golf club to his caddie.

Brent could not remember the last time he hit a golf ball so badly. His mind was not on the game. When he had arrived home last night from Miami, Casey was asleep. When he'd awoken at five o'clock this morning, she had already left for work. He had wanted to explain to her that he had nothing to do with Nikki's unexpected visit. But why would she believe him? No matter what he said to her, she was bound to believe the worst. Yet despite the circumstances, Brent had to admit to himself that he was relieved that Casey had finally met his daughter.

Brent had left Nikki with their live-in housekeeper, Martha, and had taken a needed reprieve from the apartment himself before his golf outing. Strangely enough, Coach had not scheduled practice for the day even though their first game of the Eastern Conference finals against the Chicago Bulls was only two days away. He insisted they all needed time off and a round of golf to relax. Brent was glad to have the free day, but would have much preferred to spend his time at home with Nikki. Yet here he was playing this command performance at the Tuxedo Golf Club.

Coach's swing was virtually flawless, and his ball went about 290 yards, landing in the center of the fairway.

"Would you look at my partner?" Paul gibed, giving Coach a high five as he stepped away from the tee.

"Somebody has to take up the slack for you," Brent shot back.

"Lucky shot, Coach," Jake said.

Coach tossed his driver to his overweight young caddie, who was so awestruck by the famous foursome that he was in outer space. The group scattered toward their respective balls.

"You sure you okay walking on that knee, Paul? You wouldn't rather take a golf cart?" Jake asked.

"Let him be. It'll toughen him up," Coach said, waving off Jake's question with his hand. "What do you want, for him to be riding around in one of those senior-citizen golf carts with the orange handicap flags sticking out the back?"

"Actually, walking helps. My knees are just stiff and swollen from that plane ride," Paul said as they began to ascend a hill.

The Flyers had flown into a small private airport the night before. The trip back from Miami had been a loud, joyful ride as the players celebrated their win thirty thousand feet above the ground.

"Yeah, those charter plane seats are the worst," Brent said. "The Flyers need to stop using that cheap company with their beat-up airplanes and just get up off the dime and buy a luxury jet. The team sure makes enough money from the licensing deal and NBA properties."

"Or, with as much flying as we do, at least charter a plane that only has first-class seats instead of a few guys getting the good seats and most guys having to sit in coach," said Paul.

"Well, you know how old man Hirshfield can be. Private planes are not his priority. He's no Leonard Hightower when it comes to spending money," said Jake.

"Well, thank goodness money's not everything to Hirshfield," Paul said.

"You know Hal. He pinches pennies like he's about to enter the poorhouse," joked Coach.

Brent did a double take after Coach's comment. Mitchell was the second highest paid coach in the NBA, and the New York Flyers were notorious for outbidding other teams to get the players they wanted and to keep the players they had.

"Your ball's over here, Mr. Rogers!" Brent's caddie shouted from behind a clump of bushes.

"I'm gonna drop another one," Brent shouted back.

"Good move," Paul said.

"Don't forget to add your extra strokes, Brent," Coach added.

The caddie dropped the ball in the shorter brush area.

"What should I use?" Brent asked his caddie.

"You've got about two hundred and twenty yards to the front of the green, and this rough is kind of thick. I say just punch it out with your six or seven iron. If you can hit your utility wood, give that a try," the caddie said, pulling out all three clubs from Brent's bag.

Brent decided on his six iron and took a couple of practice swings before approaching the ball. As soon as he struck it, he knew he had hit a perfect shot.

"Now, I'd say that's a damn fine recovery, partner," Jake said, giving Brent the thumbs-up.

"Eat my dust!" Brent said to Paul and Coach as he handed his club back to his young caddie.

"Great shot, Mr. Rogers." The caddie grinned as he wiped off Brent's iron with a towel.

The group began moving forward in search of Paul's ball.

"So what's going on with Hirshfield and Hightower?" asked Brent. "I hear Leonard Hightower has become relentless with Hal. The word is, he's wearing him down."

Jake looked from Brent to Paul and then said, "I think they might be close to reaching a deal."

"No way, Jake. I don't believe it. Hal gave us his word that he'd wait to see if we could bring home a championship," Brent said quickly.

"I've heard Hightower's awfully determined as well. They say he's not going to back down until the Flyers are his own," Coach added.

"Well, that's why we're going to win it all and New York can thumb their noses at him. Once we get past Chicago, it should be smooth sailing. Ain't that right, Coach? Just like us whippin' Brent and Jake," Paul said, looking at Coach.

"That's the plan," Coach said, looking toward the green.

"Well, that sure is my plan. I'm going to work out as soon as we finish up here," Paul said, glancing at Brent.

"I am too," Brent said.

"You going up to the gym?" Paul asked.

"No. I'm gonna work out at home. I need to get back there pretty soon."

"You mean to tell me you fellas aren't going to join me for a round of beers back at the clubhouse after the match?" Jake said. "Coach, you're not that tough on them, are you? They just made it to the Eastern Conference finals. Surely they're entitled to a little celebration."

"Yeah, but I don't want it to be a premature celebration. There'll be plenty of time for drinking after we win the championship," Brent said, looking at Paul and then at Jake.

"Oh, what are you, a wussy now, Brent? A few beers aren't going to hurt you," Coach said.

"What's up, Coach? You trying a new coaching method or something?" Paul asked, just as Brent opened his mouth.

"Listen, fellas," Coach began. "All I'm trying to avoid is you guys getting so riled up that you psych yourselves out of winning like you've done in the past. I just want you guys to play as hard as you normally do without choking."

Mitchell removed his golf glove and started rubbing his left hand before he continued. "We finished the regular season with the best record in the NBA, and I don't want you to start doing things differently now or you'll build these guys up to be larger than they were during the regular season."

"No disrespect, Coach, but during the play-offs, the Chicago Bulls *are* larger than life. We all know it's a whole different ball game when guys are playing for the ring. It's on a whole different level, or at least it should be for the real winners," Brent said, a bit taken aback by Coach's faulty logic.

"Here's your ball, Mr. Thomas," Paul's caddie hollered from behind a large oak tree.

Paul and Coach moved toward Paul's ball to discuss the strategy for Paul's upcoming shot with the caddie. Brent was glad for the break in the conversation. He hoped that Coach wasn't slipping and losing his competitive edge as he got older. Next to Brent's marriage and children, winning a championship was the most important goal in the world to him. He wanted it badly and he planned on getting it with the New York *City* Flyers.

There was no place on earth that Dawn would rather be than sitting in between Michael's legs on their king-size bed. Erykah Badu was playing softly in the background, and the smell of apricot candles floated through the air. It was a rare lazy afternoon that she and Michael were able to spend together, but it could have been any time of the day for all Dawn knew or cared. She had lost track.

Dawn leaned her head back so Michael could gently massage her scalp and neck with his large, skillful hands. A shiver shot down Dawn's spine as he peeled off her robe, exposing her bare shoulders and back. Dawn stopped breathing as Michael moved her hair aside and began lightly stroking her neck. Then he placed his lips against her skin, and she yearned to taste him. But when Dawn tried to turn around and meet his lips, Michael would not allow it. He was torturing her.

Michael continued to caress her shoulders with kisses that felt like butterflies fluttering against her bare skin. She didn't want the moment to end. His touch, his passion: they were something she relished beyond comprehension. To call it love seemed insufficient. With him, she felt enraptured.

A moan escaped Dawn's mouth as Michael completely removed her robe and carefully turned her over on her stomach.

"You cold baby?" he asked, as goose bumps rose on Dawn's back.

"Just a little," she whispered, keeping her face pressed against the silky sheets.

"I'll warm you up," Michael said, opening his robe.

Dawn watched him reach into the drawer on the side of their bed and remove a bottle of almond massage oil. He poured out a handful of the liquid and began quickly rubbing it between his hands, generating heat in the process. Dawn stared at him, and he stared back, smiling. Her heart skipped a beat at this simple reciprocation. Michael could light up a room with his charm and movie-star good looks. He was so intense with all of his endeavors, especially the art of making love. Every time they shared themselves with one another, Dawn felt transported.

As Michael continued to warm his hands with the oil, Dawn let her eyes rove over his Adonis-like physique. Although Michael was lean, he was perfectly proportioned. He reeked of manliness, with his muscular pectorals and washboard stomach. He had very little hair on his chest, arms, or legs. And he possessed the smoothest skin Dawn had ever touched in her life.

The instant Michael placed his hot hands on Dawn's cool back, she closed her eyes in deep appreciation for his tenderness. He began to massage her back in slow, circular motions.

"I'm still cold, Michael," Dawn purred.

"Not for long," Michael said as he covered her body with his own and began sliding his chest up and down her back.

The sensations caused by the touch of his body against hers sent electric jolts down to the tips of her toes. He continued to meld with her before he began to feverishly suck at her neck. Michael had not even entered her yet and she felt close to exploding. She vacillated between wanting him to make slow, passionate love to her and needing him to screw her brains out.

Just when she thought she couldn't handle any more, he ran his tongue down her spine until he reached the base of her back. As he slowly turned her over, she opened her eyes to see Michael gazing intently while he eased his way over her naval, down her abdomen. The last she saw of his intense eyes was right before he dove his head in between her legs.

Dawn lost track of how many times Michael brought her body and soul to climax, but by the time they finished devouring each other, it was completely dark outside. The only light in their bedroom came from the candles around the bed. The Erykah Badu CD had ended hours before, leaving them in silence.

Lying on her side, Dawn looked at Michael as he quietly breathed next to her. She wished it were possible to freeze time.

"Hey, you," Michael said as Dawn leaned in and kissed his shut eyelids.

His mere touch caused a surge of raw emotions to surface. She was suddenly consumed with a yearning to have this man's children and grow old with him. Dawn inched closer to Michael and pressed her body against his.

"I love you," Dawn whispered in his ear.

"I love you," Michael said, smiling with his eyes still shut.

"I love you more," Dawn said

"No, I love you more, damn it," Michael playfully said, rubbing Dawn's thigh.

"Oh, you do? Prove it, then," Dawn said.

"I don't have the energy to prove anything else tonight. You wore me out, girl. I got to save some for the Bulls."

"I have another way you can prove it," Dawn said, running her fingers up and down his chest.

"Like what?"

Dawn took a deep breath before she answered. "Marry me when the play-offs are over. We don't have to have a big wedding. I wouldn't even mind eloping."

Dawn felt Michael's whole body stiffen.

"Dawn, I am going to marry you, but right now I'm trying to concentrate on winning an NBA championship, not plan a wedding. You know what I'm saying, baby?"

"You don't have to plan anything. I'll take care of it all," Dawn quickly countered.

"I don't even know when the season's gonna be over. It all depends on how far we go. Let's just wait and see what happens," Michael said evasively.

"I can plan it for after the last possible date the play-offs could go until."

"But then I may have appearances to do and commercials to shoot. I need to talk to Jake and see what he has planned for me," Michael said, sitting up as Dawn's hand fell off his chest.

"Well, what about your own plans?"

Dawn watched Michael stand up and sit on the edge of the sofa next to the bed and run his hands over his head in exasperation.

"Dawn, what I have planned is to concentrate on beating the Bulls tomorrow night. We've already won the first game, and with Scottie Pippen out now, we have an even better chance of winning the whole series. If we can beat them tomorrow, we'll go to Chicago two up on them, heading into their arena. We need every advantage we can get. After that, it should be smooth sailing."

Dawn looked at him, unconvinced. "Michael, what does that have to do with us getting married when the season is over?"

"Dawn, the Flyers have never won a championship before, and if we don't win it this year, we're gonna be sold and moved to Albany. Do you realize the pressure we're under? That I'm under? I don't have the mental energy to think about us getting married right now. Why can't you ever just leave well enough alone?" Michael walked to the dresser and snatched it open.

"Why do you always have to blow me off when I bring up marriage?" Dawn said, jumping out of bed.

"Damn, Dawn! You had to ruin a perfectly enjoyable day bringing up this shit again! Does every discussion of ours have to come back to marriage?" Michael said as he pulled on his Flyers sweatpants and grabbed a sweatshirt out of the same drawer.

"You know, Michael, sometimes I wish you never even proposed to me. What the hell was the point?" Dawn said, getting off the bed and leaving the bedroom.

She heard Michael running up behind her. "You know what, Dawn? I feel the same way. Thanks for fucking up the one day I had to relax. If my head is too screwed to practice tomorrow, I'll tell Coach who he has to thank for it." Michael pulled a baseball cap onto his head and walked toward the front door. Dawn was sure he'd go back to the arena to shoot some balls until he cooled off.

"Your day? Yeah, well, thanks for fucking up my life!" Dawn shouted after Michael as he stormed out of their apartment.

Dawn felt like throwing something, but the first thing that came to hand was a small statue she had bought during her senior year at the San Jose Flea Market. This did not help to assuage her anger. She was so damn tired of begging him to marry her. He made her feel like a pest.

When he had proposed to her the previous summer, marriage had been the furthest thing from her mind. Now that she was taking his proposal seriously, he was treating her as if she were a gnat that he wanted out of his hair.

She was not due back at the hospital until tomorrow, but Dawn was too upset to sit around the apartment all day. She desperately needed a distraction. She went back into their bedroom and turned on the lights. She began to walk around the room and blow out all the candles. It was hard to believe that only moments ago, they were basking in the afterglow of their lovemaking, and now she was so mad she could strangle him. Dawn sat on the edge of the bed and blew out the last candle. She did not want to move.

He had so much nerve. Dawn rested her elbow on the bedside table and contemplated their relationship and what she wanted to do about his reluctance to fully commit. As she sat in that position staring out the window at the New York City skyline, she began fiddling with the book of matches that Michael had used to light the candles.

She felt powerless. He was the one setting the limits of their relationship, and there seemed to be nothing she could do to get him to take it to the next level.

Dawn opened up the matches and lit one and then another in frustration, allowing them to burn down almost to nothing before she threw them into the metal garbage can next to the bed. She looked at the cover of the matches, which read SCORES GENTLEMAN'S CLUB.

Dawn began inspecting the matches more carefully and noticed the name 'Sandi' with a telephone number written inside the book. She could not believe that Michael had taken another woman's number, and at a strip club of all places! What the hell was wrong with him! She'd told him so many times of the anguish her father's cheating had caused, the havoc it had wreaked on her mother's life—and hers. She could be patient with his career, but she wouldn't allow unfaithfulness.

Before today, between her schedule at the hospital and his with basketball, they hadn't shared any real quality time alone. They needed more of that. He was probably feeling lonely with her working so much. That was why he had taken another girl's number. It had to be. Michael was her man. And no matter how much they argued, she knew that he genuinely loved her. They just needed some time away from New Jersey, from their apartment. They needed a change of scenery—something to snazz up their relationship, to put the fire back into it.

Dawn knew with her long hours at the hospital, she often neglected her appearance when they were at home together. Maybe she would take a trip to Victoria's Secret. Michael had so many young, beautiful women throwing themselves at him, she should have known that it was only a matter of time before he took one of their numbers. Hopefully that was all he had done. Dawn needed to give more attention to her looks and their relationship. She thought about the days off from work she had coming up and how the two of them could use them. Suddenly she knew what she had to do to get their relationship back on track. She wasn't losing her man.

"We all indeed have a choice!" Reverend Lewis said as his deep, rich voice reverberated throughout the church, capturing the attention of even the most skeptical members of the congregation. He had that effect on people.

Reverend Lewis was not about mere rhetoric.

"You can either ask the Lord to help you steer clear of sin and temptation or let the devil guide you to its doorstep. Ask the Lord, ask Him, 'cause He's there, He's here, He's in all of you. Are you open to Him? Settle up! Settle up with God today." Reverend Lewis's voice rang out among the pews.

"As long as there's a good, there's going to be an evil, and we have to make a conscious decision in our lives right now as to which side we want to be walking come Judgment Day. And don't nobody in this world know when that day gonna be. That's right. Though the light of God illuminates from within us—we are all walkin' in the shadow of death. Settle up with the Lord today! I am tellin' you, He's waitin'."

The reverend slammed one hand down on the podium as he stood there preaching.

Paul turned to look at Lorraine as he heard her say, "Amen" in response to the sermon. He placed one arm around his diminutive wife's shoulders as she glanced up at him smiling.

He had been thrilled when Lorraine told him last night that she didn't have to work in the morning. It had been weeks since they had gone to Sunday morning service together. Instead, Paul had been relying lately on his own daily Word readings and the infrequent Bible studies he held during the Flyers' road trips for answers to his own inner turmoil. It bothered him that more of his teammates didn't join in on his sessions. Some of them outright ignored him whenever they thought he was in his preaching mode. In actuality, he was just trying to help spread the Word.

Thinking about meaningful coincidences, Paul was astounded how much Reverend Lewis's words touched directly upon his own life. He's trying to tell me something, Paul thought as he envisioned God using the reverend as a medium. Paul just wasn't quite sure how to make sense of all that was going on in his life right now.

"Even with all the sinister things you may see happening around you," Paul heard the reverend continue, "it's up to you to stay clear of the negativity. Don't let yourself be drawn into the fire, not even for a second. I know it can look bright and pretty with hot, dancing flames that seem to beckon you, but as God is my witness, you'll walk away scarred."

Giving Lorraine's shoulder a light squeeze, Paul turned to look at her. She was staring at the reverend as if she were in a trance. Paul briefly wondered what Reverend Lewis's sermon meant to her.

As he reflected on the reverend's words, it became clear to Paul that there were definitely some negative external forces at play in his life. Not that Paul expected the answers to everything, but he could not deny that there seemed to be a number of unexplained occurrences lately—at home and at work. It dawned on Paul that if he didn't bow his head and ask the Lord for assistance in walking a clear path, he would be caught in the eye of the New York Flyers hurricane. That was the last thing he needed right now, especially when he knew something had been troubling Lorraine recently.

Paul heard the reverend draw to a close. "Let's not forget to pray for our elderly and infirm brothers and sisters who couldn't be with us here today. Open up your heart to the Lord and those around you." Paul felt Lorraine press his hand as the offering basket was pushed in front of them. He dropped a hundred-dollar bill into the container and reminded himself to write a hefty check for the church as soon as he got home.

"And for Brother Paul Thomas . . ."

Paul lifted his head at the mention of his name.

"We pray for you and your teammates as you go after that championship title. Go, Flyers!"

Paul lifted one hand in thanks as various "amens" resounded throughout the church.

Giving a parting thought to Reverend Lewis's sermon, Paul could not shake the feeling that time was running out. He didn't know if it was anxiety over having to play the Chicago Bulls on their own turf or the look he saw in Lorraine's eyes throughout the service.

It should be a sin for a woman to be that fine, thought Michael, grinning. As Sandi Cole sashayed across the hotel's splendid lobby, Michael saw people stop to stare and gawk at the supermodel famous for her exotic looks and Copper Tan commercials.

Chicago's Bellevue Hotel was well known on Michigan Avenue for its rich and famous celebrity clientele. The various sports teams that traveled to Chicago often resided at the Bellevue the night before meeting their opponents. For years the New York Flyers had made the hotel's luxurious accommodations their home away from home.

Doormen dressed in royal blue attire and adorned with gold tassels and high black top hats opened the massive polished gold lobby doors twenty-four hours a day for actors, athletes, politicians, and models. It was a private and impressive place, perfect for what the Flyers' star rookie, Michael Brown, had in mind.

From where Michael sat perched on a shiny chrome and leather barstool, he signaled the bartender for another Amstel Light. He turned around as he heard a subtle clicking sound. He saw Sandi standing on the other side of the etched window, tapping her carefully manicured fire-engine red nails on the glass, trying to get his attention.

Smiling broadly, Michael motioned for Sandi to walk around and join him in the lobby bar. This was the perfect opportunity for him to show off Sandi's fine ass to two of his teammates who were sitting at a nearby cocktail table with their own "on-the-road booty." But Michael's piece blew theirs away. She was a perfect physical specimen. Michael quickly glanced at his reflection in the mirrored wall behind the bar. Giving himself one of his infamous *I'm so cool* looks, he turned around just in time to see Sandi stop and strike a perfect model's pose in front of him.

"Sandi! Look at you, you look good enough to eat," Michael began, laughing as he took Sandi in his arms and hugged her. "Of course, I don't know how big my appetite will be. I gotta be ready for the Bulls tomorrow."

"Oh? Really?" Sandi asked as she pushed against the star ballplayer so she could look up at him. "Well, I'm hungry enough for the both of us. I'll do all the eating myself." She smiled coyly and twisted a long lock of her auburn hair around her finger.

Michael liked Sandi's quick literal interpretation of his words. She wasn't the type to dig too deep searching for something that wasn't there. Unlike someone else I know, he thought as he remembered his last argument with Dawn. He and Sandi could just free-flow together.

"So," Michael asked. "How was your trip?"

"Fine, I guess," Sandi answered. "I hate airplanes, though."

"Yeah, I know. They can get pretty scary when there's turbulence. Was your flight rough?"

"Rough? Oh, no. I don't like planes because all that stale, dry, recycled air is bad for my skin," Sandi said, stopping for a moment to peer at her own reflection in the mirror.

The two of them stood there like that for a long moment looking at their reflections.

Damn, Michael thought, we sure look good together.

"We look good together, huh?" Sandi asked, shaking her mane of curls into place. "We'd make some pretty babies." She smiled up at him and licked her full, glossy lips.

"Umm," Michael stuttered, "I don't think I'm ready for kids yet."

"Yeah, well, who knows what the future has in store," Sandi nonchalantly tossed back at him.

"What are you drinking tonight?" Michael was anxious to get a few drinks into his date so that he could take her up to his room and relax.

Sandi had met Michael on the road on more than a few occasions after their initial meeting at a popular New York strip club one night after a game. Sandi was open-minded and was not the type of woman who got jealous about him going to gentlemen's clubs. Hell, she enjoyed a good lap dance herself. Michael knew from experience that Sandi was an expert lover, especially when she was slightly intoxicated. She might even do a little dance for him tonight.

It had been easy to convince himself that he had a good thing going with the beautiful model. As he'd rationalized on more than one occasion, most of the guys cheated, and he wasn't even married—and wouldn't be if he could help it. The two other Flyers in the lobby bar were very married. But he'd learned quickly, the "side girl" and the "main woman" were separate. The two had nothing to do with each other.

With Sandi there were no strings attached, no questions asked, nothing, in fact, but a round-trip first-class airline ticket and some of the best sex he had ever had. What could be better? he asked himself as he brushed away her nagging comment about them making pretty babies.

They sat together at the bar drinking and talking for a couple of hours. By the time Michael helped Sandi gather her overnight bag and belongings from the bell captain's desk, both of them were drunk and ready to retire to Michael's suite and king-sized bed.

He had Sandi's black Chanel duffel bag slung over one shoulder and one arm around her waist when he stepped forward to push the button for the elevator. Just as Michael held the door open for Sandi and stepped into the elevator himself, he turned around to press the button for his floor. The button lit up and Michael dropped her bag as he turned around and gently pushed Sandi up against the elevator's mirrored rear wall. As he bent to kiss his date fully on her delicious open mouth, something in the mirror caught Michael's attention. The doors had not closed completely as Michael looked up in horror at the reflection.

The young star immediately recognized his fiancée striding across the lobby, clutching her own overnight bags. She stared directly at Michael and Sandi, looking shell-shocked.

As the elevator doors closed, Michael stood there feeling deflated and oblivious to Sandi's persistent tugging fingers. For once in his life, he didn't know what to do.

Michael sat by himself in the front of the bus on the way to the Chicago Bull's new arena for shoot-around practice. He wanted to be alone. He could hear his teammates' loud talk and was already, after only one year in the league, familiar with the various topics of conversation swirling around him.

Some of his colleagues would be engaging in ticket switching for tonight's matchup against the Bulls. This, Michael learned early on, was a simple matter of swapping tickets with your teammates so that no one's wife, fiancée, girlfriend, mistress, or some miscellaneous groupie came in contact with someone the player did not anticipate having at the game. Michael remembered feeling as if he was a true Flyer the first time one of his teammates had approached him to switch tickets. He had proudly handed over his seats in exchange for his comrade's tickets.

Some of the guys, Michael knew, would be discussing their latest road-trip conquest, most often referred to as "roadkill."

After last night, Michael felt like putting all of his own sextracurricular activities on hold. Somehow it wasn't as fun when he got busted. He figured Dawn must have had a few days off from work and had planned on surprising him in Chicago. After Michael had gotten over the initial shock of seeing Dawn in the hotel lobby, he had rushed Sandi up into his room and left her there, telling her he'd be right back. By the time he'd gotten back down to the lobby, Dawn was nowhere to be found. He searched the hotel, and if she'd checked in, she hadn't registered under her name. Michael had been calling their apartment all morning trying to reach her.

When he'd returned to his room hours later last night, he'd found Sandi prepared to go and stay with a girlfriend of hers who lived nearby. He'd been grateful and relieved that she'd realized she was no longer a welcome visitor, first-class plane ticket or not.

"Yo, Mike! Whassup, man? You awfully quiet today. That fine-ass honey you was with last night wore you out, huh?" Michael's teammate Kyle started cracking up at his own comments.

"Whatever it is, brother, you better shake it off. We need you to kick some ass tonight," Brent said from his seat in the rear of the bus.

Michael didn't even turn around.

"Michael? You all right, man?" Collin asked, tapping him on the shoulder from the seat directly behind him.

Michael sighed deeply and turned around to face Collin. "Naw, man." He shook his head and looked out the window. "I fucked up. I fucked up real bad this time."

"You wanna talk about it?" Collin asked gently.

Michael was quiet for a long moment before answering. "My girl showed up," he said softly.

"What? What happened?" Collin asked, leaning in toward the seat in front of him.

"My girl showed up. I got caught," Michael repeated loudly.

"Damn, Mike!" Kyle interrupted. "How'd you let that shit happen? You know the rules; no women on the road. Well, at least not the ones you're serious about."

"Man, I couldn't help it. She surprised me. What the fuck was I supposed to do?" Michael knew his teammates gossiped more than the wives, and wished he'd kept his mouth shut.

"Man, fuck that! You do your own thing! She ain't going nowhere. Where else is she going to be able to live large, shop all the time, and drive dope-ass cars?" one of his other teammates demanded of him, obviously thinking the problem had become a community affair. "And I speak from experience. Look at how many times my wife walked out on me and came running back with her tail between her legs. And they want to call us dogs!" He howled with laughter.

"For real, Michael," a voice chimed in from the card-playing section of the bus. "He's right. Your girl probably just wanted a little bit of drama so you'd feel sorry for her and get her a fat gift. Don't even worry about it, man."

"That's right, dude. Add a little cash to her stash; that's the only reason they stay with us anyway, all the money we make," someone else chimed in.

It was hard, but Michael tried to ignore his teammates. Everyone seemed to have some type of advice for him, but he knew Dawn well enough to know that if he followed in their footsteps, he would lose her forever. Plus they were wrong. Dawn was not like the women they were talking about; she genuinely loved him. This just needed to blow over, but as Michael thought about it, he figured maybe a gift would speed up the forgiveness process.

Michael looked up as he felt Collin slide into the seat next to him. "Okay, so what's your take on my situation?" Michael asked the veteran.

Michael was actually glad that Collin had sat down next to him. He had a lot of respect for Collin and admired his maturity and composure. Collin tended to keep to himself, especially lately, and Michael was slowly beginning to understand why, free-agency blues or not. Collin DuMott was on an entirely different level from the rest of his teammates, with the possible exceptions of Paul and Brent.

"Funny, I was going to ask you the exact same thing," Collin answered. Before Michael could respond, Collin continued. "Before you let your teammates tell you how to handle your affairs, you might want to ask yourself how you think *Michael* should manage *Michael's* business. These guys don't know your fiancée. Hell, they barely know you. Some of us have been playing together for years, but we all get so caught up in our careers and winning and making more money, it's rare that we ever take the time out to really get to know one another."

Michael slowly nodded his head.

"You let them convince you your lady is no different from any other woman and you'll be just like the rest of them: spineless, selfish, egocentric jerks," Collin continued.

Michael agreed with everything Collin was saying. Still, he was not sure how he was supposed to apply it to his situation with Dawn.

"So many guys are just so happy to be part of the league that they'll do whatever it takes to fit in. That includes adopting the league's stereotypes of women. That's one of the reasons why so many of our relationships are fucked-up. Just because the majority of men in the league cheat doesn't make it right. It just means that a lot of men are out there dogging their women. Nothing more, nothing less," Collin said disgustedly.

Collin paused for a moment. It occurred to Michael that Collin sounded as if he may have been rehearsing these lines to himself. Michael wondered just who it was Collin was trying to convince, himself or Michael.

"I'm not saying that I'm any different from any other guy in the league," Collin said. "There've been times when I jumped on someone else's bandwagon myself. But there's something to be said for knowing the difference between right and wrong and knowing what's appropriate or inappropriate for your own relationship. Otherwise, you end up walking in other people's footsteps. You've heard what's good for the goose is not always good for the gander?"

Michael was beginning to understand what Collin was saying.

"You'll wind up trying to convince people you love that you can do no wrong, saying to yourself, since everyone else is doing it, it must be right. In the long run, you'll either end up in a relationship where your woman won't respect you and she'll be afraid to have any expectations of you. Or you'll be in and out of meaningless relationships, hurting yourself and others over and over again," Collin said.

This was all so heavy for Michael. It was like a huge dose of reality that he wasn't ready to swallow. "What's wrong with meaningless relationships?" he sardonically asked.

"Hey, if you think that would make you happy, then go for—"

"No, seriously, I hear what you're sayin', man," Michael interrupted, feeling as if his head were spinning. "But I don't really know how to deal with this stuff. I mean I know I love Dawn and I want to marry her . . . one day. But what if some of the things I'm hearing are true? Maybe I am too young to even be thinking about getting married. Maybe I do need to just sit back and enjoy the lifestyle with all its perks, and see what else is out there."

Michael shook his head back and forth. "I don't know, Collin. I mean shit, just about every guy on this team cheats. We all see it, everybody's doing it. It's accepted, it's cool, and if you're one of the few who's not down with that, then they call you a fag or say you're pussy-whipped at home or somethin'. Even you, Collin, they think you're different 'cause you're so devoted to Remy—not that anyone could blame you. But it's like when you're in Rome, you do as the Romans do, and if you don't, you just get dogged out."

"Look, I know it's hard," Collin told him. "The pressure to do what's right according to you or what's right according to your boys; it's a tough position. You're young too. You're probably not even sure exactly what it is you want out of life, much less one relationship. Take your time, man. You're going to end up doing what you want to do anyway. Just make sure the decision's yours."

"Thanks, man," Michael said as he lightly tapped Collin's fist with his own. "For everything."

Michael had said more than he should have, but he was getting tired of people telling him what he should do. Even if he was able to find a solution, it would not matter. In his mind, he was in a no-win situation. He wanted Dawn to still be his woman, but she would have to be patient and willing to give him time before he was ready for marriage, or faithfulness for that matter. Michael only wondered if Dawn would remain with him under those terms.

The crowd in the Mecca was on its feet as the referee called a foul against Michael Jordan, who had just slapped Steve Tucker's wrist in an attempt to steal the ball while Steve tried to make a shot. Now Jordan was visibly furious as Steve approached the foul line to shoot his two free throws.

Steve could hear Jordan yelling, "That was bullshit, Tom, you know that call was bullshit! I ain't touch him!"

The referee just ignored the star.

Steve's adrenaline was pumping like crazy as he prepared to take the two shots. If he made the baskets, the Flyers would go to the NBA championship series. There were only four seconds left in the game, and the Flyers were one point ahead of the Bulls.

Steve bounced the ball up and down as the home crowd quieted so he could concentrate.

"Ain't it about time for you guys to choke again?" Jordan taunted Steve just as he released his first shot.

As soon as the ball left his hands, he knew that the shot was good, and so did the fans as they erupted into wild cheers. Steve lifted up his hands to receive high fives from Brent and Collin while the referee waited to toss the ball back to Steve.

"Naw, man, we just trying to get one of what you have already," Steve pointedly said, looking at Jordan with a mixture of respect and fierce competitiveness.

As Steve bounced the ball again, he looked out into the stands to see Stephanie's reassuring smile. He was so grateful that she was a part of his life now and that the chapter with Kelly was finally behind him for good. As much as Steve longed to advance to the championship, even more, he wanted to make Stephanie proud of him. Saying a silent prayer, Steve released his second shot. The ball seemed to move in slow motion. As the leather sphere reached the rim, it rattled around and around for what seemed like an eternity before finally toppling inside the basket.

Everyone in the Mecca was on their feet as the Flyers quickly returned to defense. Since both teams were out of time-outs, the Bulls were immediately back on offense as Ron Harper threw a long pass downcourt to Michael Jordan. The Flyers defense swarmed Jordan as if he were honey and they were bees. Realizing that there was no way he could get a shot off, Jordan attempted to throw the ball to a very wide-open Steve Kerr. Paul obviously read Jordan's mind as he jumped in the line of the pass and practically stole the ball from Kerr's hands. Paul dashed down the court, making an easy layup just as the buzzer signaled the game was over and the Flyers had officially become the Eastern Conference champions.

Steve felt euphoric as he jumped up and down and ran up the court toward Paul where all of the other guys had begun to converge around him in celebration. Steve looked around to hug Coach, but Mitchell was nowhere in sight.

The media did not waste any time getting on the court as they began filming. Steve knew the New York media well enough to know what their angle would be on this defeat: the team that eliminated the Bulls.

Amidst more high fives than he could count, congratulatory slaps on the back, and cameras shoved in his face, Steve headed off the court toward the locker room on a high he had never before experienced. He could not stop smiling thinking about going to the NBA finals and the fact that he had played a big part in getting the team this far. Just as Steve made it through the mouth of the tunnel, he began envisioning tomorrow's headlines, heralding him as THE FLYER WHO SAVED THE DAY or TUCKER DETHRONES THE BULLS.

Steve was having a difficult time reaching the locker-room door with all of the reporters swarming his path. They seemed to be as worked up as the players.

"Excuse me, Steve Tucker?" Someone grasped Steve's arm.

Steve turned around to discover a police officer holding on to his arm. The cop was about a foot shorter than Steve.

"I'll be all right Officer, the crowd's a little excited about the win, that's all. They'll clear out in a few minutes," Steve said as he tried to continue on his way.

When the officer failed to release his grip, Steve looked back and said more brusquely, "I said I'm fine."

"Mr. Tucker, I'm afraid that my partner and I are going to have to detain you," the short officer said, motioning for someone else to join him.

"Detain me? For what?" Steve asked.

"We have a warrant for your arrest."

"For my arrest? Is this some kind of joke?" Steve said, looking around for the culprit who was responsible for this untimely prank.

"I'm afraid not."

Steve began to laugh.

"Mr. Tucker, you're going to have to come with us," the second officer said as he approached his partner.

This had to be a joke, and a bad one at that.

"Okay, fellas, whoever sent you, tell them it's bad timing, but they can catch me on another night. I've got a shower to take and interviews to give after that." Steve turned to leave again, when the other officer grabbed his elbow.

"You can shower later. Now you're going to Central Booking," the short officer said.

"Joke's over; now, let go of my arm," Steve said as he noticed a crowd of reporters begin to converge around them.

"Mr. Tucker, are you all right?" one of the Mecca's uniformed security guards asked as he moved into the center of the crowd to where Steve was standing with the two New York City police officers.

"Actually, I'm not. I'm being harassed by Barney Fife and his sidekick."

"Mr. Tucker, I'm Officer Hernandez and this is Officer Smith." The shorter officer pulled out his badge, and his partner followed suit. "Here's a copy of the warrant for your arrest. Now, you can come quietly without making a scene, or you can give these bloodthirsty reporters something else to write about in tomorrow's papers."

Steve glanced around the room as bulbs began to flash and reporters started moving their mikes in on him and the police officers. Steve felt as if he were in the twilight zone.

"What are the grounds for my arrest?" Steve asked, realizing that they were serious.

"Assault and battery," Officer Smith said.

"Now, let's try and make this as painless as possible. I need you to place your hands behind your back," Officer Hernandez said with a smirk on his face.

"You mean you're going to handcuff me, right here in front of all these reporters? I haven't even done anything! This is crazy!" Steve said incredulously.

"It's routine procedure. We can't make special allowances, even for a Flyer. Even you guys have to come down to earth sometimes," Officer Hernandez said.

The cops were loving every moment of bringing down a star—that was clear. Steve could not believe this was happening to him. There had to be some sort of mistake. Quickly, desperately, he searched the room for Coach or Jake, anyone to help.

"Well, can't I at least change out of my uniform?" Steve asked as the photographers went into feeding-frenzy mode, getting shots of him in handcuffs.

Steve thanked God when he saw Brent approaching as the officers began to lead him away from the swarm of reporters.

"Hey! Hey! What's going on here?" Brent said, running up. "Steve, what's going on, man?"

"Brent, call Jake for me . . . Get that damn mike out of my face," Steve said as a reporter shoved a microphone up to his mouth. "Tell him to meet me down at the . . . Can you guys at least tell me what precinct you're taking me to?" Steve asked the officers.

"Central Booking, like I told you," Officer Smith answered curtly, as he continued to pull Steve toward the arena exit.

"Officers, why are you arresting Mr. Tucker?" a female reporter asked with pen in hand, anxious to scoop the other beat writers.

"Brent, tell Jake to meet me at Central Booking ASAP," Steve pleaded.

"What's going on, man?" Brent asked, ignoring the reporters as he followed the officers leading Steve away.

"Brent, with God as my witness, I have no idea what this is about."

"All right, man. I'll take care of this right away, and if I can't reach Jake, I'll think of something else, but we'll get you out of there, man. Don't worry. If I have to come down there myself, I will," Brent shouted after Steve as he left the Mecca surrounded by officers and followed by a flock of journalists.

"Thanks, man," Steve hollered over his shoulder as the door slammed behind him.

Steve had not shut his eyes the whole night. He'd been kept awake by nightmare visions of Kelly and the last night he was at the house in Englewood. She'd retaliated for the eviction.

He had never spent a night in a jail cell before, and he could not believe that he had just done so, thanks to that lying bitch Kelly. Steve berated himself as he paced back and forth waiting for the clerk to return his personal effects. He should have learned his lesson the first time she lied—once a liar, always a liar.

Kelly had filed a report that he had beaten her up a few hours before the game. Somehow she'd even found a witness to corroborate her lie. An officer arrived to remove him from the holding cell.

"Hey, star baller, you've been sprung—temporarily." At that

moment Steve was sure he'd never donate money to the PAL Association again.

As Steve was handed his uniform and NBA tube socks from the clerk, he felt as if he could kick Kelly's ass.

"My gym shoes are missing," Steve said to the giggling clerk sitting behind the counter.

"I didn't have any gym shoes listed in your inventory, Mr. Tucker," the clerk said, trying to suppress a smile.

"Oh, so I guess I just came in here barefoot when they arrested me off the basketball court. This is fucking ridiculous. Fuck it!" Steve said as he walked away from the counter and sat down to wait for Jake.

First I get arrested after the greatest night of my career, then I spend the night in jail, some imbecile steals my gym shoes, and now I have to leave here in socks.

Steve stood up again, too angry to remain seated. What the hell had taken Jake so long to get him out of jail anyway? He sure was around when it was time for him to collect his agent fees or when there was a celebrity-studded event, but he couldn't even send one of his flunkies to post bail for Steve; he'd just left him there till this morning.

Damn! Stephanie had probably worried herself all night, and Steve was sure no one had had the thoughtfulness to call her. She'd probably read about him in the morning's papers. Steve knew his name was smeared all over the *Post* and the *Daily News*. He shuddered just thinking about the headlines.

"Steve! You all right, man?" Brent said, appearing in the waiting area, accompanied by Paul.

Steve turned to see his teammates and felt so relieved at the sight of their faces that he had to hold back tears.

"What are you all doing, slumming? Is Jake with y'all?" Steve asked.

In unison they shook their heads, obviously reluctant to answer him.

"We brought your clothes from your locker. Why don't you go and get changed, and we'll talk in the car," Paul said, handing Steve his bag.

*　　*　　*

"It's a madhouse out there," Steve said, looking out the window at all the reporters swarming the car. "I'd hate to see what the papers look like."

Steve began to rub his temples as he leaned back on the soft leather seats of Brent's Bentley.

"Yeah, the papers are real ugly," Paul said from the backseat.

"That bad?" Steve asked, unsure how much he wanted to know.

"Steve, she jacked you up . . . a real hack job," Brent said, shaking his head.

"Damn! That girl is crazy. Now I want to seriously hurt her." Steve was fuming.

"I wouldn't repeat that to anybody else if I were you, Steve," Brent advised.

Steve looked out the window as they sped through the city toward his apartment.

"Thanks for busting me out, guys. What happened to Jake anyway? I know he's around."

"I called and left several messages for him all night until I finally reached him at home about three in the morning. He was asleep and told me he would call me when he woke up. Can you believe that shit?" Brent said.

"And he knew I had been arrested?" Steve asked in disbelief.

"Yup."

"What the hell is wrong with him?" Steve asked. He felt betrayed, big time. And pissed off.

"That's precisely what Paul and I are trying to figure out. He even tried to give me some lame excuse, claiming that there was nothing he could do until the morning anyway. That's when I called in a few favors of my own and decided to handle this myself," Brent said as he turned onto the West Side Highway.

"Now I want to hurt him too," Steve said, punching his fist into the palm of his hand.

"I can't say that I blame you, man," Paul said.

"Our win's gonna be tarnished because of this crap," Steve said, wishing that he had never met Kelly. "I hurt you guys."

"You can't worry about that right now. You have to think about clearing your name and doing some damage control. The press is eating you alive right now," Paul said.

"Whatever the papers say, you all know that I didn't touch that girl. Y'all do know that, don't you?" Steve asked, looking back at Paul and then at Brent.

Brent cleared his throat before he answered. "First, let me say that I know you didn't hurt Kelly in any way except by maybe not giving her all the money she wanted. And second, I hope you don't take this personally, but I knew she was bad news from the first time I ever met her. She was up to no good from the get-go. Just remember there's a way out of this, and we're gonna figure it out."

"I hope so," Steve said, staring out the front window.

"We've got to, man. We need you with us to kick the Lakers' ass in the finals. We're not trying to be playing up in Albany next year," Paul said, reaching over the seat and grasping Steve's shoulders.

Steve wished he could be as optimistic as Brent and Paul, but he knew how vindictive Kelly could be when she was scorned. There was no telling how far she would carry this charade. Her new focus in life must be to ruin him. And when Kelly focused, she could shoot you down like a high-powered rifle—hot, quick, painful, total destruction. Man, where had his head been?

"The media found out? How?" Brent demanded incredulously. Casey's mouth dropped open as she turned to look at Hal. Oh my God, she thought, glancing at Paul and Lorraine, who were also talking with Hal. This was the last thing the Flyers needed right now.

"Hal, do you know who leaked it?" Paul asked.

"No," Hal said, obviously upset. "Although I do have a few names in mind.

For the first time, Casey noticed how much older Hal looked than when she first met him over eight years ago. The season had certainly taken its toll on the Flyers' owner, and Casey felt sorry for him. She knew the Hirshfield history with the New York Flyers, and her heart went out to him as she imagined the burden he must be faced with having to consider selling his family's legacy.

"Do you think it was Hightower, trying to put pressure on you now that we've made it to the final round?" Brent asked.

218

"Could be, could be not," Hal thoughtfully responded, thrusting his weathered hands in his pockets. "It could have been any number of people, although I don't see what incentive Hightower would have to let something like this out."

"Yeah, if it was Hightower's people, they'd just be setting themselves up for a bidding war. That wouldn't be too smart," Paul added.

"You're right, Paul. I doubt that Hightower wants to sabotage his own offer. He's already thirty percent higher than the market value of the team. Even though he may have all the money in the world, he's still a businessman; it could become obscenely expensive if a bidding war resulted. I'm just sorry any of this has to even be going on," Hal said tiredly.

"I have to confess, Hal, it could have been just about anyone. After that meeting you held, I had to tell the rest of the guys." Brent looked around at Paul, Casey, and Lorraine with a guilty expression on his face. "It didn't seem right for them not to know what was really at stake," he finished, holding his hands helplessly out in front of himself.

"You're right, Brent," Hal said, nodding in agreement. "I probably should have held a team meeting anyway. It was only fair that everyone should've known what was going on."

"I agree, man," Paul said, looking at Brent. "You did the right thing."

"Well," Lorraine added. "If all the guys know, then that means all of the wives and girlfriends know too. Maybe even players and wives from other teams. With all those people knowing about Hightower's offer, we may never find out who leaked it to the media."

"It really doesn't matter at this point," Hal said. "Right now I'm more concerned about damage control. CNN–Sports Illustrated and ESPN have already aired it, and I heard the local stations are going to be airing their version of the full story on tonight's news. But what's most troubling to me is the phone calls from our season ticket holders. Some are already demanding refunds for next year. Not to mention our sponsors are in an uproar. A couple have even threatened to terminate relationships with the team. They don't even want to think about the 'Albany Flyers.' " Hal finished.

"What are you going to do, Hal?" Casey asked, noticing how dejected he looked.

"I'm not sure right now," Hal said. "Tonight's dinner was supposed to be a celebration. The team's come so far. Now, with this leak and in light of Steve's arrest, the press is going to have a field day. I'm not sure if I shouldn't just go ahead and accept Hightower's offer while it's still in the best interest of the team."

"Hal," Brent interrupted, clearly upset, "his offer was never in our best interest. You can't give up on us now. I told you up front that we could win the championship, and we're almost there! Steve's part of the team, and we still have a chance to kick the Lakers' asses." Brent was determined to convince Hal to let the Flyers lay the path for the team's destiny.

"Brent's right, Hal," Paul said. "We didn't come this far to watch you hand the Flyers over on a silver platter. We have a real chance at bringing home the championship, and once that happens, you can tell Hightower to kiss off."

"We'll see. A lot will probably be determined by the outcome of the game tomorrow night. I'm not sure how our big sponsors will react if the team loses now that they know about the potential sale. If they pull out on us now, there's no question I'll have to accept Hightower's offer," Hal explained.

"But come on, let's go inside," Hal said, placing his hands lightly on Casey's and Lorraine's shoulders. "Dinner is probably being served, and I know Coach has a speech to make tonight. I don't want you guys to worry too much about all of this; you have enough to handle out on the court."

Hal and the two women led the way into the private banquet room at the St. Regis Hotel where Hal and Coach had arranged for a team dinner to celebrate winning the Eastern Conference title. The dining room was beautiful, filled with Louis XV tables and chairs. Casey saw Remy and Collin sitting at a table alone, waving for them to join them. Hal walked off to his table, and Casey led her group across the room.

"Hey, man, what's up?" Brent said to Collin as he held Casey's chair out for her. He leaned down to kiss Remy on her cheek and sat down.

Paul and Lorraine exchanged greetings with Collin and Remy. Casey noticed Collin seemed a little more subdued than usual, and assumed that the leak to the media had done little to improve his free-agency status. If anything, it would prolong any talks of renegotiation with the Flyers. In light of the team's concerns, Casey realized, Collin DuMott would not be a priority.

"Casey, I told you that dress would be perfect for tonight," Remy said to her friend as she leaned over to kiss Casey's cheek.

The two women had gone on a last-minute shopping spree at Macy's earlier in the day. Remy had flown into town from her mini tour early that morning so she could accompany Collin this evening. They'd both agreed to ignore Alexis's conservative dress code and splurged on chic, sexy designer outfits for the team dinner.

Casey had wanted something that was form-fitting so she could show off her new figure. She had started weight training at the local Equinox Fitness Club three months ago and was noticing firmness and muscles she'd never had before.

The dress she wore was a sleeveless dark red Nicole Doss original that fit her well. The dress dipped dangerously low both in the front and the back, and her figure was accentuated by a long slit that stretched from the top of one thigh down to the top strap of her sexy high-heeled Giorgio sandal. Casey completed her sleek look by wearing her hair slicked back into an intricate twist she had seen modeled on the runway at a recent New York spring collection fashion show. A sparkling diamond stud decorated each ear, and her only other piece of jewelry besides her simple platinum wedding band was a diamond-encrusted Ebel watch.

"Thanks, girl, but you don't look too shabby yourself," Casey said, winking at Remy.

Remy looked stunning in a Chanel gown by Karl Lagerfeld. The cream-colored tight bodice created a beautiful contrast with Remy's light brown-sugar coloring. Her dark brown eyes were offset with an intricate collar of Swarovski pastel-tinted crystals. The silk material of the dress had an iridescent shimmer that made Remy appear to have lights shining from within the folds of her gown. Her dress, like Casey's, fit her perfectly and displayed her naturally model-like figure in a sexy but classy manner.

"Man," said Collin as he looked at his two teammates. "I can't believe the season's just about over."

"Yeah, well, we ain't finished yet, not till we get our rings," Brent declared, holding up his unadorned right hand.

"You got that right," Paul chimed in. "I'm not walking away empty-handed."

"You'll still have me, baby," Lorraine said as she smiled up at her husband. Paul laughed and put his arm around her chair, pulling her closer to him.

"Has Coach been brainwashing you with his 'win, at all cost' speeches?" Casey asked, looking around the table at the guys.

"I know, he never seems to stop with all that psychological mind-game stuff," Lorraine said. "Remember the videotapes he sent you guys last summer showcasing your worst moments of the season?" She shook her head and took Paul's hand in hers. "He's crazy."

"Probably not crazy, but definitely a control freak," Remy added.

"Actually, Coach has been kind of low key lately, definitely not his usual self," Brent said.

"Really . . . you'd think he'd be feeding us that psycho basketball babble, but you're right, Brent. He hasn't really stepped up the way he usually does," said Collin.

"Well, you never know with Coach," added Paul, matter-of-factly. "I'm sure as far as he's concerned, there's some method to his madness."

"Maybe," Casey said, "he's just trying out a new coaching technique, experimenting with the 'leave well enough alone' theory."

"Yeah, well, maybe we all should try that theory out every now and then," Brent added, staring at his wife.

Casey shifted her eyes and looked across the room. She knew her husband's comment was directed at her and the way she had been handling their relationship lately. If only it were that simple, she thought.

Casey could not seem to stop picking apart her life with Brent. She constantly scrutinized and questioned every facet of their relationship.

Ever since her encounter with Gregory Patrick at Panthers Night-club, Casey had been torturing herself by questioning her own motives and reasons for staying with her husband. She felt that something had to be wrong with her in light of her inexcusable behavior that night, and often wondered if she purposely brought herself down to that level in an effort to convince herself that she was no better than her husband.

Maybe, Casey thought, if she convinced herself that everyone cheated in some way every now and then, including herself, then it was okay. Still, Casey knew she was not fooling anyone but herself. Cheating was wrong, and what she'd gotten herself into that night at Panthers was wrong. She loved her husband more than anything else in the world and wanted nothing more than to be able to trust him again. She just didn't know how to make that happen.

Casey's thoughts were interrupted as she felt Remy tapping her on the arm, trying to get her attention.

"Here comes your girl," Remy whispered loudly in her ear.

"Where'd you learn how to whisper?" Casey asked her friend, drawing back from her. "In a helicopter?"

As Remy started to snicker, Casey turned around in her chair to see to whom Remy was referring.

"Oh my goodness," Casey heard Lorraine mumble as she quickly shifted in her seat, giving Paul her full attention.

"Hello, everyone!" Robin Stillman gushed as she raced around the table double-kissing their cheeks, as she had no doubt carefully watched Alexis do on countless occasions.

"Hi, Robin," they all chimed in unison.

"How are you doing?" asked Casey, ignoring Remy as she saw her friend roll her eyes.

Casey knew how Remy felt about the Flyers' gossip queen and didn't want to subject her friend to Robin's tasteless banter. Remy had been hesitant about accepting Collin's invitation to the dinner tonight, with the distance that had crept between them recently. Plus she was in the midst of her mini tour. Casey was the one who had urged Remy to use her two days off to fly into town and stand by Collin's side for the evening.

It had not been an easy task convincing Remy that Collin was probably more stressed out over Flyers management not approaching him to re-sign with the team than he was letting on to Remy. His entire career as a professional athlete was on the line.

"I don't know, Casey," Remy confided to her friend. "It just seems like

we're drifting further and further apart. No matter how hard I try to get him to talk about things, he keeps resisting."

"I know it doesn't make it right Remy, but have you ever considered how difficult it must be for any man, not just Collin DuMott, to have to share with a superstar like yourself concerns about not having a job?" Casey asked.

"Come on, Casey. You know me better than that. I've never made anyone, especially him, feel like they have to measure up against me." Casey knew Remy was hurt and angry and she didn't like to see her friend in pain.

"Girl, you know that's not what I'm saying," Casey counseled her friend. *"We both know all's not fair in love and war and you just have to remember that most men have their pride and egos and we women often have to tread very carefully when these get in the way of our emotions."*

Their conversation was two days ago and it still didn't change how Remy felt. She was hurt and angered by Collin's actions and felt like she deserved an explanation after three years together. Casey agreed with her friend to a degree, but she also believed, as she had reminded Remy, that Collin would probably start to deal with his issues once the Flyers' season was over. She knew that patience was not one of Remy's virtues, but even Casey recognized that her dearest friend was going to have to give Collin both time and space if she wanted things to work out between them.

Casey felt Robin hug her shoulder. "I'm simply marvelous, Casey, thanks. You ladies look gorgeous, but I see you and Remy seem to have deviated from Alexis's dress code, hmm?"

Out of the corner of one eye, Casey saw Lorraine peek over at them and attempt to hide a smile. She had dressed in a simple black sheath with a beautiful strand of gray pearls.

"Lorraine, I see you seem to have remembered our rules. Good girl!" Robin said, gleefully clasping both hands together.

"Hey, whatever it takes for the Flyers to win the championship," Lorraine said with a shrug of her slim brown shoulders.

"Wow," Collin said with a soft whistle. "Mrs. Coach really got to you ladies, huh?"

"Man, Remy didn't tell you?" interjected Brent. "Alexis went off on all the women, telling them how to dress, walk, talk—"

"Brent!" Casey said, giving her husband a swift kick under the table. "That's not exactly what was said; she wasn't that bad. So, Robin," she quickly continued, noticing Paul trying to stifle his wife's laughter. "Do you have any idea what Coach is going to talk about tonight? No one here at this table seems to have a clue."

Casey forced herself to keep a straight face as Robin subconsciously shifted into her gossiper's stance. Leaning down in between Casey and Remy, Robin hunched her shoulders forward, causing a clump of her stiff hair to fall over and create a right angle with her forehead.

"Well, from what I've heard, he's going to give some type of pep talk to help keep the guys unified. Especially after the night before last, Steve getting arrested and all . . . Speaking of which, I can't believe he didn't even show up tonight!" Robin paused to catch her breath. "By the way," she continued, obviously reluctant to lose an audience, "have you guys heard the latest?"

Casey saw Remy watch with disgust as Robin smacked her lips in eager anticipation of spilling out her latest piece of juicy gossip. It was amazing to Casey that a grown woman could be so fascinated by everyone else's personal business. But then she reminded herself that there were actually people who made a profession out of it.

"The latest what, Robin?" Alexis asked, barging in. "Shouldn't you be sitting with your husband over at the coaching staff's table?" she inquired in a sugar-coated voice with one perfectly tweezed eyebrow arched.

"Ta-ta, everyone," Robin said as she lamely wriggled her fingers at no one in particular and walked off sheepishly.

"Well, now, how are our boys doing tonight?" Alexis asked, giving everyone at the table one of her famous once-overs. To Casey's dismay, she watched as each of the guys stood up in turn to kiss and greet the coach's wife.

Even as she cringed inside, Casey could not help but marvel at how Alexis always managed to present such a dignified and cool front even when she was being a bitch.

"Remy, it's always good to see you. Glad that you could come into town from your tour, and of course, you're looking splendid as ever." Alexis leaned down and kissed Remy on her cheeks.

"Hello, Alexis. Touché," Remy said lightly.

"Lorraine, dear, it's always such a pleasure." Alexis refrained from the double whammy on the cheeks and instead patted Lorraine's hand. "How's the clinic treating you?"

"Actually, I work at a hospital . . . as a nurse, and I'm doing just fine, Alexis. Thanks for asking," Lorraine responded, looking sullen.

"Oh, goodness, for some reason I thought you were doing volunteer work. Well, whatever it is, I'm sure you're excellent at it," Alexis said dismissively before continuing. "Casey, darling, it's obvious life is treating you well. You look stunning, as always!" Alexis kissed Casey on both cheeks and stood looming over the table.

"Hello, Alexis, it's good to see you too. The Flyers ought to have more occasions like tonight when we can all get together. This is so much fun." Casey felt a spiked heel digging into her foot under the table and pictured the high-heeled, strappy pump Remy had on puncturing her skin.

"Casey, sweetie, may I speak with you for a moment . . . alone? There's something I need to ask you." Alexis stood aside, giving Casey space to scoot back her chair.

Casey could feel everyone's eyes on them as she and Alexis retreated to a corner of the room. Casey just knew that Alexis was going to say something about her dress and probably question her as to Dawn's and Trina's whereabouts.

Stay cool Casey, stay cool, she reminded herself.

"Do you have any idea what's going on with Michael and Dawn?" Alexis inquired, peering into Casey's eyes.

Just as I thought, Casey said to herself. She knew Alexis had to have heard what happened in Chicago with Michael and Dawn. Everyone knew. There were no secrets with the Flyers.

"Well, Alexis, after she surprised him in Chicago . . . You have heard, haven't you?"

Alexis nodded her head.

"Well, why do you want to know what's going on with them?"

Casey asked, feeling a little guilty about not calling Dawn. She had wanted to telephone her when she heard about the scandal to let her friend know that she was there if she needed someone to talk to, but she didn't want to impose herself on Dawn either. She figured it would be better to give Dawn her space and be there if called upon.

"Oh, it's nothing much; well, nothing that can't be handled with a little talking to," Alexis continued. "I just wondered if Dawn was going to keep bothering Michael now. I mean she obviously doesn't realize what a valuable commodity he is to the Flyers—he's the future of this team and he certainly doesn't need any distractions right now.

"I better go, dear; I see Coach is getting ready to take the stage."

Casey was speechless as she watched Alexis glide off across the room. The audacity of that woman! She wondered, not for the first time, just what kind of a monster Alexis really was. Casey never would have put anything past Alexis, but this was outrageous. *What happens between Michael and Dawn ought to be their business, you bitch*, Casey thought as she walked slowly back to her table. Win or lose, she couldn't wait for the Flyers to finish their season.

Casey watched as Alexis stared up at her husband in utter reverence with tears glistening in her eyes. She nodded her head as he spoke as if affirming his every word.

"To every athlete here, you know your role. When you walk out on that court, you're expected to give two hundred percent of sheer athletic ability to ensure that every game in this final round is played to win. It is on your twelve sets of shoulders that the heaviest burden has been placed. It is your job to carry the entire team across the finish line."

Casey noticed people smiling and nodding their heads in agreement at Coach's words.

"It is your job," Coach repeated, "to carry the entire team across the finish line. Our trainers, coaching staff, and team managers, you all have your own duties to carry out. Whether it's healing an injury, educating players on the various game plays, or making sure each player has a pair of game shoes for every game, if any one person chooses to carry out their task in a deficient manner, the entire team is affected and our goal becomes threatened.

"Here's to our team, the New York Flyers, and winning the NBA championship!" Coach finished.

Casey looked around the table. Everyone looked stunned and confused by what they had just heard.

"What kind of bullshit speech was that?" Brent said, looking at Paul and Collin.

"I don't know," Paul replied, "but Hal doesn't seem too thrilled by it either." He flipped his head toward a corner of the room where Hal stood conversing with Coach.

It was obvious to Casey that Hal was disgruntled and he was clearly expressing his displeasure to Coach. Coach, on the other hand, looked passive and unimpressed with whatever it was the team's owner was saying to him.

"This is weird, man; something's not right here," Brent said, shaking his head.

Casey had to agree with her husband. It wasn't like Coach to give a speech that lacked fire and intensity the way his speech did tonight. Both Coach and Alexis were acting strange, Casey realized, and she wondered what was really going on.

"Oh, Casey, I don't know how I'm gonna tell Rick. I've started to say something a thousand times, but I can never get it out," Trina said, twisting a napkin in her hands.

"Why would he be that upset about it? You can't hide your pregnancy too much longer," Casey said, looking down at Trina's midsection.

Casey had debated whether to even attend the game tonight, but she had not wanted to raise any eyebrows by being conspicuously absent. It was the first game of the championship, after all, and there was a part of her that felt obligated to support Brent even though she had to go to work in the morning. Although Alexis had not been as vocal as usual at the team dinner the night before, it was plain to Casey what her expectations were. Alexis had made them very clear to her before the play-offs began. She had also promised Alexis that she would be at every championship home game to keep the other wives in line, a role she had increasingly come to regret.

With the napkin torn to ribbons, Trina was now wringing her hands and looking around the Family Lounge anxiously. "Rick has told me time and time again that we can't afford to have any more children," Trina said, lowering her voice as more people filed into the lounge. "You know Rick. He has a temper on him." She shook her head.

"I've seen his temper on the court, but would he actually be upset about having another child? That's hard for me to believe," Casey said, not being able to imagine someone not being excited about a pregnancy. She pushed away her own feelings of longing. "Trina, I'm not trying to tell you how to deal with your husband, but that's absurd. First of all, I think he played a big part in you getting pregnant, and second, Rick makes more than enough money to support ten kids. Goodness, what is wrong with these men?" Casey added, more to herself than to Trina.

"Actually, Casey," Trina started, and then stopped as Michael Brown's mother, father, and brother drew close to the nearby picture window so they could see Toni Braxton sing the national anthem on the court below.

Trina scooted in closer to Casey before continuing. "There's something else I haven't told you. Rick's been spending his money as fast as he makes it . . . on gambling. I couldn't even borrow the money from my bank to start my dessert catering business," Trina said in embarrassment.

"He messed your credit up that badly with his gambling?" Casey asked, her heart going out to Trina.

Trina nodded her head.

"What did he have to say about it?"

"Nothing," Trina said, averting her eyes.

"Nothing?"

"I haven't said anything to him yet. I'm too afraid. He doesn't know that I found out about his gambling problem. His agent told me. Rick would be furious for my meddling in his business if I mentioned it to him."

"His business? Has he forgotten that—" Casey began, and abruptly stopped herself as the Gossip Queen, Robin Stillman, assistant to First Lady Alexis, plopped herself down at their table. It was pathetic, Casey thought, how Robin mirrored Alexis Mitchell's image, except Robin was the black version of Mrs. Coach. She tried so hard to be like Alexis, from the way she dressed to her mannerisms to her flawless costume jewelry, which was copied from her idol's original pieces.

"I hope I'm not disturbing you girls." Robin was not an unattractive woman, though her gossipy character often caused people to describe her as such. She was midfortyish and always looked like she had just spent the day at a Georgette Klinger day spa. Her hair and makeup always looked professionally done, and her smooth brown complexion stayed clear.

Trina looked at Casey and rolled her eyes, ignoring Robin.

"No, Robin, I'm about to go downstairs in a minute anyway," Casey said, clearing the table of her napkin, Coke can, and utensils.

"Aren't you going to wait for Remy to get here? You usually do."

"She only came into town for the team dinner party, then she flew right back out. She's on a mini tour right now." Casey was careful to keep any inflection out of her tone.

"Really? You mean to tell me she's going to miss the entire championship series?" Robin raised her eyebrows in what could only be described as a smirk—Robin's eyebrows were sneering!

Casey knew Robin was well aware that Remy had returned to her tour. But her goal in life was to know everyone's business and report back, trying in the process to poison Alexis's opinion of them.

"She's just hitting a few major cities, so she may get to see the last couple of games."

"Ohh, I see. What about Lorraine and Dawn? What's their—Oh, pardon me, we all know why Dawn isn't here," Robin snickered. "I warned her not to pop up on the road. Poor girl, she'll learn. But what about Lorraine? What's her excuse? Alexis is not going to be pleased."

Casey tried not to snap at Robin as she ignored her comment about Dawn.

"Their excuse? They both work. You know, they have jobs. And most of the time, their hours are unpredictable."

If Casey had been Kelly, say, or maybe Trina when she got angry at the referees for making calls against Rick, she would, without a second's thought, have wrestled Miss Nosy Body to the ground—and maybe squashed a grapefruit half in her face to match Robin's sour attitude.

Robin had the hide of an elephant and she was like the Energizer Bunny: she kept going and going until she got what she wanted.

"Well, we all know why Kelly's not here too, don't we?" Robin began with a wicked laugh. "The whole city knows!"

"Do we?" Trina dryly said to Robin.

"Come on now, Robin, why would she show up after pressing charges against Steve?" Casey said, looking at Robin as if she had lost her mind. "If she showed up, the whole team would lock her out. There isn't a member of the team who believes her story, whether there's any truth to it or not."

"Truth! Ha! There's no truth to her story. She's been pulling the wool over all of our eyes," Robin said, nodding her head as if agreeing with herself.

"Well, none of us know what really happened," Casey said. Even though she believed Steve was innocent, she felt a twinge of loyalty to Kelly.

"Kelly has been completely discredited as far as I'm concerned. I can't believe that she lied to all of us about Diamond being Steve's daughter. Now, that's wrong," Trina said.

"How much do you think she and Daryl got for that story to the *Daily News*?" Robin asked.

"Really, Robin! You don't know that Kelly had anything to do with Daryl's exposé to the papers. He could have just been trying to make a quick buck on his own. Not that it makes it right."

"Talk about making a quick buck, Casey, isn't that what Kelly has been doing since Diamond was born? Making money at her child's expense? Claiming her daughter was somebody else's child?" Robin said matter-of-factly, pulling out her case and fixing her lipstick.

"My God, Robin," Casey said, feeling her stomach turn.

"Well, truly, Casey. How do you think poor Steve feels in all of this? Having that copy of the paternity report plastered on the front of the *Daily News*, proving without a doubt that the daughter everyone *else* thought was Steve Tucker's child was actually fathered by this Daryl character. And that horror show of a person Daryl saying that

Steve thought he could steal his daughter from him just because he was a big-time sports star. I mean, it's absolutely scandalous! And I don't care what anyone thinks, I bet Kelly and Daryl are in cahoots in this whole fiasco. This was probably her last-ditch effort to milk the situation since Steve dumped her."

Casey had felt hurt and betrayed since the truth had come out. She was in shock. She did not understand why Kelly would tell such a huge lie to everyone. Was that why Steve had broken off their engagement?

Casey couldn't completely turn her back on Kelly, though, not yet. "All that doesn't mean she was lying about him battering her, and you know what? I really don't feel comfortable talking about this. Kelly's not here to defend herself. Let's just drop it."

"You know what they say," Robin said, ignoring her, "once a liar, always a liar. Why would Kelly be telling the truth now?" Robin placed her lipstick back in her purse.

Trina stood up and looked directly at Robin. "You know what they say, Robin: once a gossip, always a gossip."

It looked like Trina had pierced the elephant's hide. Casey only wished Trina could stand up to Rick in the same manner she did to Robin.

Casey followed suit and quickly rose from the table as Robin was still recovering from Trina's verbal blow.

"You heading down, Trina?" Casey asked.

"I guess so. The air is bothering me in here." Trina said, crinkling her nose.

Casey was surprised and felt pride for Trina as they worked their way toward the Family Lounge exit.

"Now, Trina, if we could only get you to handle Rick like that," Casey said.

"Who are you telling?" Trina laughed.

"You'll do it when you're ready." Casey felt bad for the new friend she'd made this season. Here she was, a pregnant housewife trying to take care of her family and start her own business with no support from her husband. Not only a nonsupportive husband, but one who had a huge gambling problem as well. Yet Trina was still trying to move forward with her life. Casey admired her courage. Maybe it was time for her to take a trip to the Land of Oz and get a little of her own from the Wizard.

Casey sat in her seat and wished she could feel some of the excitement that permeated the Mecca. There was a buzz in the air as the Flyer City Dancers, dressed in miniature Statue of Liberty outfits, passed out purple and black towels to the excited crowd. Hoping to psych herself up, she glanced around at the other courtside seat occupants. There were so many celebrities in attendance, it could have easily been a night at the Oscars or the MTV Awards. Shaquille O'Neal and the Los Angeles Lakers facing off against Brent Rogers and the New York Flyers in the NBA finals was enough to get Michael Jackson, Bill Cosby, Tom Cruise, Demi Moore, Whoopi Goldberg, and Vanessa Williams to show up at the Mecca. And more superstars were there, Casey was sure.

Once again Leonard Hightower was sitting boldly in Star Row, flanked by his muscular, redheaded henchman on one side and his stunning child bride on the other side. Casey wondered how long it would take for this young beauty to become a member of the Second Wives Club. Hightower had shown up at every game since the playoffs began. He always arrived in a flurry, making a big scene with Secret Service–like escorts and media blitzes attempting to converge around him whenever there was a time-out on the floor. Casey noted, though, he never spoke directly to the press at the games. Rather he calmly sat back rubbing his young wife's leg and licking his chops.

Casey's mood didn't lift, though, especially after she'd seen Hightower and his cronies. He was unrelenting. Many of the celebrities waved and smiled at her, but she was lost in her thoughts about Brent, their marriage, and what it would mean if the team was sold and relocated. She had no intention of leaving her job in New York City. What would that mean for Brent's roving eye or even hers, she thought, recalling the debacle with Gregory Patrick. But Brent had taken it further than her—a lot further. Not only had Brent been unfaithful to her, but he had lied to her one too many times. It seemed as if a true reconciliation was next to impossible, at least on her part. How could she ever trust him again?

Nikki's mother had still not returned and had since asked Brent if they could keep her for a while. Casey had no idea what "a while" actually meant. At first Casey thought she would hate the intrusion. She had four cases going, along with her controversial photographer's censorship hearing, which was looming before her. Taking care of Nikki for only a short while meant it would be pointless to look for good day care. They settled for their live-in housekeeper, Martha, and the teenage baby-sitter who looked after Brent, Jr., when he was in town. Martha usually looked after Nikki while Casey was working, but she knew Martha wasn't stimulating Nikki's intellect. Casey had actually taken a few sick days and watched Nikki herself at home. But as it turned out, Casey didn't mind Nikki living with them. She was actually a sweet, well-behaved little girl, but Casey was still convinced that Brent had planned the entire visit. She didn't believe Nikki's mother's claims of being ill as the catalyst for this extended stay. Casey was tired of second-guessing everything Brent said or did.

"Casey," said a man's voice from beside her.

"Yes?"

"I think your husband is trying to get your attention."

Casey turned toward where the man was pointing and saw Brent across the court. "Thanks," she said as Brent waved to her. Then he blew her a kiss.

Casey suppressed a smile as she blew a kiss back to her husband. Why did he have to be so romantic when she was angry at him? He continued to stare at her for what seemed like minutes, and finally he began to make silly faces until she broke into a smile.

Casey turned away from him as the announcer, Bud Zanny, began to unenthusiastically introduce the Los Angeles Lakers. She spotted Alexis standing behind the Flyers' bench, looking impeccable as usual. She was wearing a dramatic flowing camel-colored Valentino coat dress. The fabric stopped inches below the top of a pair of long black suede boots. She realized that she had not noticed Alexis in the Family Lounge before the game started, which was unusual. Normally Alexis would be right in there taking stock of all the wives like dogs before a show. Her absence tonight was even more peculiar as this was the first game of the finals.

Alexis stared at her husband, completely enraptured, as he assembled his players to get them ready for their official introduction. Alexis's awe of her husband was larger than life. A painting of them would have had to portray her as only a shadow standing behind the man. Alexis had remained by his side for all these years despite his relentless philandering and who knew what else.

Alexis embodied one of Casey's worst fears: she was scared that she might become like a shadow standing behind her husband. Oh, that's absurd, she told herself for the millionth time. Casey would never lose herself in Brent or his career, nor would she want to overlook his infidelities. Still, a little voice inside her continued to nag: she did stay after Brent's one-night stand. Was she becoming desensitized? The thought was chilling.

The lights dimmed for the laser show that preceded the introduction of the Flyers.

As Casey watched the ceremonies, she noticed that although Steve was suited up, he was not among the starting players introduced now. Coach must be punishing Steve for Kelly's assault-and-battery charge—true or not. At any other time during the season, it would not be surprising for Coach to use such tactics to put a player in his place, but now? It was risky to say the least.

In Steve's absence, Rick Belleville, the second-string center, was going to jump for the ball against Shaquille O'Neal. Rick was clearly too short and too old to be a fair match against the Shaq. Why hadn't Coach substituted Kyle? He sometimes played backup center. The Flyers may as well have just handed the ball to the Lakers.

The game progressed at a faster pace than usual, with the Flyers and the Lakers basically trading baskets. Shaquille was responsible for the majority of the Lakers' points. One of the strengths of the Flyers was their deep bench, which was stocked with experienced veterans; the Lakers had a younger team, but they had less play-off experience, a mandatory ingredient to winning an NBA championship.

Throughout most of the game, there was never more than a five-point difference in the score. With Steve Tucker on the bench, Shaquille was having his way with Rick Belleville, dunking over him almost every time he went to the basket. He was also outrebounding him, fifteen to three. Casey kind of felt sorry for Rick. It was embarrassing for him, especially since the crowd had begun to chant Steve Tucker's name, in hopes of him replacing Rick in the game.

What was the coach thinking? He even could have tried a technique the Flyers had used in the past when both their centers, Steve and Rick, had been injured or having off nights: he could have rotated Brent or Collin into the center position; both were better rebounders than Rick. If Coach wanted the team to win the title, now was not the time to be teaching costly lessons.

Fortunately, Brent, Paul, and Michael were taking up the slack, keeping the Flyers in the game. Collin, who was regularly a force, seemed strangely lethargic, even distracted, tonight. Casey kept catching him glancing across the court into the stands. Collin needed to be concentrating on the game he was playing.

Oh, Brent wanted the championship! He had grown up a fan of the New York Flyers, and since joining the team, it had become his goal to bring a championship to the team he had loved as a child. It was what he had been waiting for his entire life. Despite all of her unresolved issues about their marriage, Casey prayed that Brent could get his wish.

The game of basketball was not merely about the money for Brent. He was a competitor and he hated to lose more than anything. Brent even played his heart out during the preseason, which was rare for most players. Brent couldn't stand to lose in a game of Scrabble!

When Paul Thomas got possession of the ball with twenty seconds left to play in the game, Casey leapt to her feet with the rest of the screaming crowd at the Mecca.

Paul ran down past the half-court line and guarded the ball as if his life depended on it. The Flyers were four points in the lead, and Casey suspected he'd hold on to the ball unless he was fouled. In the split second Eddie Jones attempted to steal it with thirteen seconds left, Paul passed the ball to Brent, who quickly passed it to Collin, who kicked it back out to Paul. The Lakers failed in their attempt to foul one of the Flyers in order to stop the clock. The buzzer signaled the end of the game, and the masses in the Mecca were in a frenzy as confetti was thrown around the stands by the Statue of Liberty–clad dancers.

* * *

Alexis slowly approached Casey as she stood outside the locker room waiting for Brent. They had decided before the game to pick up some carry-out Chinese food and take it home to have a family dinner with Nikki.

Casey braced herself for Alexis's interrogation about the other wives. Where was Dawn? And why hadn't Lorraine made it? No doubt Robin Stillman had debriefed Alexis about all the gossip in the lounge.

"Hello, Casey. You look divine," Alexis said as she gave her customary phony European kisses.

"Thank you, Alexis. You look great yourself."

Truthfully, Alexis looked more distracted than fantastic. Normally she would have been elated about a win, especially in the finals. Casey noticed that Alexis kept looking at the locker-room entrance and then at her watch. She then started fidgeting with her hair and adjusting her sparkling diamond charm bracelet.

What was up with Alexis? Casey was ready for her tonight and was almost disappointed. She had a few lines rehearsed to explain why Dawn, Lorraine, and Remy were not at the game. Casey had planned on explaining to Alexis that they all had to work. She wanted to rub it in that those wives and fiancées had jobs of their own, that their schedules did not center around their husbands'. That would get under Alexis's skin.

"It was good seeing you, Casey; take care," Alexis said, not even looking at Casey as she hurried off toward Coach, who was quickly leaving the locker room.

Weird, Casey thought. What had gotten into Alexis? Maybe she was sick. God, Casey felt terrible thinking those mean thoughts while Alexis was under the weather. Oh hell, she and Coach were probably running off to do "The Late Show with David Letterman," albeit a little prematurely. The Mitchells could at least have waited to ensure that the Flyers actually won the championship first, considering the team's history in the finals, Casey thought.

"Dawn, dear, how are you?" Alexis gushed as she floated through the revolving door at the Four Seasons.

Dawn smiled through her exhaustion and pain, dutifully going through the kiss routine.

"I'm okay, Alexis, just a little beat. And you?" Dawn said, noticing Alexis's driver return to the long black limousine and pull away.

"To the Grill Room," Alexis said, taking Dawn's elbow. "Follow me, dear."

The maître d' approached them and said, "It's a pleasure to see you, Madame Mitchell. May I take your wrap downstairs to the cloakroom for you?"

"No, thank you, I'd prefer to keep it," Alexis said, casting her wool crepe cloak dramatically over her arm.

"I have your favorite table reserved, madame. If you'd kindly follow me," the maître d' said with a click of his heels as he escorted them to the best table.

Dawn noticed that virtually everyone in the restaurant looked up from their meals as they passed by to get a glimpse of Mrs. Mike Mitchell. Dawn felt like Alexis's underdressed step-daughter in her wrinkled linen pantsuit and no jewelry other than her small diamond studs. Feeling like a zombie when they reached their table, Dawn gladly took the offered seat. She stifled a yawn as a crisp white linen napkin was spread across her lap. She had just finished a thirty-six hour shift at the hospital; anything was better than being in the apartment with Michael. Even though they still lived together, she had not spoken to him since busting him with that other woman in Chicago. She didn't know what to say. Hadn't she seen enough? And as much as he had tried to explain and apologize, what could he really say other than "I fucked up"?

Dawn had seriously contemplated breaking the lunch date with Alexis, but it would have been her third time canceling. And there was a small part of Dawn that secretly fantasized Alexis was going to pass on a message from Coach that Michael had been miserable since she caught him red-handed and that he was ready to get married now to prove his undying love for her.

Picking up the menu in front of her, Dawn did not even feel like reading it. She would have much preferred having a quick McDonald's cheeseburger.

"Dawn, you've got to try the spinach strudel. It's heaven to start with, and then I'd suggest the grilled swordfish with the glazed *pomme de terres.*"

"Sounds good to me," Dawn said, closing her menu, glad to have one less decision to make.

As the waiter poured them each a glass of Chardonnay, Dawn watched Alexis inspect and rotate the liquid around her glass before she lifted it to the center of the table in a toasting gesture.

"Cheers. This is to change and transition," Alexis said, lightly tipping her glass against Dawn's.

Taking a sip of her wine, Dawn waited silently, a trick she'd learned during her psychiatry rotation to make the other person speak.

"You look tired, Dawn."

"I feel tired, Alexis . . . You know, long hours at the hospital."

"So I hear," Alexis said, holding her wineglass with both hands as she swiveled it back and forth.

"Yep, the life of a first-year resident, it's not easy."

"I understand that's why you haven't been to a lot of the games this year," Alexis said.

Here we go, Dawn thought. She sipped her wine, her senses not even alive enough to taste it, before responding.

"Alexis," Dawn began, carefully weighing her words, "you hit the nail on the head. The life of a doctor is not conducive to moonlighting as a cheerleader."

The derogatory image of herself as bimbo cheerleader must have gotten to Alexis, and Dawn felt a small sense of satisfaction as she saw Alexis visibly flinch.

"How long is your residency?"

"Three more years."

"At the same hospital, in New York City, all that time?"

"That's right," Dawn said, snatching up a piece of sourdough bread as the waiter came and took their identical orders.

"So your schedule is going to continue like this for the next three years?" Alexis said with raised eyebrows.

"Basically, yes," Dawn said, looking directly into Alexis's eyes.

"And how are you and Michael doing?"

"Well, we're both under a lot of pressure. Our schedules are hard on the relationship." As soon as the words were out of her mouth, Dawn regretted being so frank with Alexis.

"Michael's a big part of the future of the Flyers. He could be the Flyers' franchise player one day. Do you realize the direction his career is taking? Stellar play on the court, a variety of new endorsement deals."

"New endorsements?" Dawn knew nothing about any new endorsements, but then again, she hadn't known about Miss Chicago either until busting him.

"Hilfiger, Continental Airlines, plus Disney wants to make a line of dolls. He must really not share anything with you," Alexis said, putting down her wineglass.

"He shares enough with me. As I said, we're both very busy," Dawn said defensively. Inside, though, she was reeling.

"But you don't take his career as seriously as you take your own work?" Alexis pressed.

"Alexis, with all due respect, what's your point? I have my work; Michael has his. They're both important. End of story."

"Not really, dear. You do realize that the two may not be mutually compatible, don't you?"

"How so? From where I sit, our two separate careers have nothing to do with each other."

"Perhaps it's time for you to consider his career; that is, if you still have plans to marry him."

Dawn wanted to reach across and slap Alexis's pinched face.

"Alexis, I haven't thought that far ahead, and the last time I checked, the Flyers were still in New York City. That's all I can base my decision on."

Dawn noticed a look of contempt spread across Alexis's perfectly made-up face.

"Oh, come on, Dawn. Surely you can't be that shortsighted. You need to think about these things. My God! You're engaged to a basketball star. They move around, teams move around, things change all the time, and you need to be ready to move when it's time to move . . . and if you can't do that . . . then . . . then sometimes you simply get left behind, especially when you don't follow the rules of this profession. If you want to marry him, you need to put him and his career first."

Dawn could not believe the words she'd just heard come out of Alexis's mouth.

"How dare you tell me how to run my life. And when is it up to you whether or not I marry Michael?" Dawn said, throwing her napkin on the table.

"Now, now, Dawn. Calm down. The reality of professional basketball is such that the team does dictate the personal lives of its players. And that's a fact you'd better get used to. Life is full of choices, Dawn, choices that you have to make. You choose to be the wife of a Flyer, then you choose to go along with the program, period. And as you were warned early on, that does not include surprise visits on the road, my dear."

So Alexis did know; of course, she would. Why wouldn't she know? Everybody probably knew about Michael's indiscretion. This team was like John Grisham's *The Firm!*

"Go along with the program? Are you kidding me? I have my own program, period!"

Alexis began rearranging the silverware in front of her. "I have a suggestion for you then, sweetie." She paused. "I would pay more attention to your fiancé when he's at home. Don't worry about what he does on the road. That's simply none of your business. You've discovered the hard way what accompanies the endorsements, haven't you? A lot of female attention. Namely the supermodel, what was her name? Oh yes, Sandi Cole, I believe that was it."

Suddenly Dawn was on her feet. Before she fully realized what she was doing, she'd thrown the remainder of her wine in Alexis's face.

"How dare you . . . you!" Alexis seethed as she began to wipe her face with her napkin.

"How dare *you* tell me how to run my life! Priorities mixed up . . . inattentive wife!" Dawn spat out, as her whole body shook. "I've watched you stick your nose in everyone's business all year long and I am sick and tired of it! You may bully everyone else with your highbrow bullshit and veiled threats, but I could care less about this team and even less about you! What I care about is Michael." She reached for her purse on the floor, not caring that the entire room was staring at their table. "And one more thing . . . you'd better not ever come near me again!" Dawn said, and stormed out of the Grill Room.

It was all brought back to her, as if she needed another reminder: Michael in the arms of another woman.

Lorraine involuntarily sat up in bed as she felt the sweat dripping down her neck and back. Her heart was beating so rapidly she feared she might have a heart attack. She struggled out of bed and ripped off her drenched T-shirt and shorts.

She wondered if her own again. In the last from little Crissy's asking for money, Lorraine's involve- eight years ago. The seemed scattered and were coalescing, and it was life would ever be her week the phone calls mother had increased, threatening to reveal ment in Crissy's death images that had ethereal all these years not a pretty picture.

Her head throbbed as she dragged herself into the bathroom and turned the water on full blast. If only she could wash the filth of her dreams away. She had worked the graveyard shift the night before and had been trying to get some sleep so she and Paul could spend a quiet, relaxing evening together. Now, with one of her migraines surfacing and her mind racing with images that were either real or dreams, she did not know if she could muster a facade for anyone, especially her husband. Maybe it was better for her to be alone.

The steaming hot blasts of water offered Lorraine a small sense of relief. The image had been so real: In it she'd been a nurse making every effort possible to stop the child from dying. Crissy had kept calling Lorraine's name to help her, to get her mother, to do something, anything. Yet everything Lorraine had tried failed.

Had Lorraine done everything in her power to help Crissy? Yes—everything except put her murderers away. Instead, Lorraine had chosen to save her own skin. She had opted for the path of a coward. The fact that she'd been only sixteen years old at the time was no excuse for her selfish behavior.

Picking up the bottle of sea-salt scrub, Lorraine rubbed it all over her body until she stung and then she continued to scrub until her skin felt raw. She wanted to scream out in anguish at the pain torturing her mind, body, and soul.

Sitting down on the marble shower bench, Lorraine curled over as her body was racked with agony. She rocked herself back and forth as the water beat on her head in steady streams.

Come on, Lorraine, you've got to get yourself up. You've got to get a handle. Get up, girl. Lorraine tried to regain a semblance of composure before Paul returned home. She could not let him see her in this condition. He was under enough pressure with his team.

Finally she opened the shower door and grabbed her terry cloth robe. Slipping her arms into the folds of the material, Lorraine felt the moisture soak into the soft fabric. Just as she reached for a towel, the phone rang. She froze standing next to the ringing phone on the wall of her bathroom. But maybe it was Paul on his way home from practice, wanting to know if he should pick up something for dinner—or maybe he just needed her that minute.

Lorraine tentatively picked up the phone and held it to her ear for a few seconds before speaking. "Hello," she said softly.

"Off from work, huh?" a woman's voice said on the other end of the line.

Crissy's mother. "Please stop calling here—"

"A nurse! Pretty impressive. You save any lives lately?" the woman said. "And married to that nice rich athlete—"

"Please, just tell me what you want," Lorraine said as her heartbeat began to quicken.

"I want my baby back, but you couldn't save her! What, you think you some damn do-gooder now? Not good enough!" The woman's voice shook with anger.

"What do you want from me? Why can't you just leave me alone?" Lorraine cried.

"Leave you alone? I'll never leave you alone! After all these years, I was sure that you were already in hell for what you did. But I see your little fairy-tale life has continued. Here I get to see your husband's smiling face in the paper on my doorstep every morning complaining about his team trying to win a championship. And you let those animals get away with murdering my baby! And nobody complained about nothin' then. Just another dead baby."

Lorraine thought back to the night early in the season when she couldn't bring herself to leave another little dead black child. "No! There wasn't anything I could do—please, you've got to believe me," Lorraine said in anguish.

"Shut up, you liar! You lied to the police when they questioned you, and those bastards got off scot-free, and now you think your little life should go on like you're some damn Cinderella. Not anymore, Lorraine Thomas! I think it's high time that the world knew that Paul Thomas of the New York Flyers is married to a lying, selfish . . . murdering . . . You were what they call, an accomplice—"

"Lorraine! Lorraine!" Paul said, suddenly walking up behind her in the bathroom.

Lorraine was so startled that she dropped the phone on the bathroom floor. "Paul," she barely uttered.

"What's going on? Who's that on the phone?" Paul said, looking down at the dangling telephone. He made to pick it up, but she stopped him, quickly replacing the phone in its cradle.

"What?" Lorraine said, not meeting Paul's gaze.

"The phone. Who was that on the phone, Lorraine?" Paul said, inching toward her.

"The phone? Oh . . . it was just a prank call."

"A prank call? You look like you've just seen a ghost. I heard you yelling. Tell me what's going on."

"Nothing," Lorraine lied.

"Lorraine, what's wrong with you? Whatever it is, you can tell me. I'm your husband, baby. It's me, Paul, remember?"

Lorraine tried to push away the woman's voice. She felt close to collapsing, but she was afraid to turn to Paul. What if he didn't understand? Her past could ruin his image, maybe even his career in New York. What would happen then?

"Baby?"

Lorraine turned toward the sink, concentrating on brushing her teeth.

Leave, Paul, please.

Her thoughts flashed back to last Sunday when she sat in church with Paul. Reverend Lewis's words were coming back to haunt her; she had no other choice. Lorraine knew she was going to have to open her heart to the Lord for guidance through the forest of pain and misery in which she had become lost.

"Baby?"

Trina was worried about Rick. He'd checked into the Regency Hotel on Park Avenue after the first championship game. He'd told Trina that he needed some space so he could concentrate on his game. Even though the Flyers were the victors in the first game against the Lakers, Trina knew Rick's ego had been deeply bruised. Shaquille O'Neal had run circles around him, making him look like an old man trying to play a young boy's game. Rick was a four-teen-year basketball veteran, and the Flyers had only signed him to a one-year contract. He was at the stage in his career when every game was a test to prove that he was still worthy to be in the NBA.

With Rick so close but not at home, the house felt strange to Trina. They'd been through difficult times before, but even Trina's faith in their marriage felt a bit shaken. It was all so complex. She knew she could no longer wait to tell him about her pregnancy. She was five months along, scheduled to find out the sex of their baby next week, and she needed to share that with Rick—whether or not he wanted another child.

Trina had been unable to reach him at the Regency Hotel because he'd had his incoming calls blocked. She had left a couple of messages for him, and when he had finally telephoned back, she'd missed his call, having gone to pick up Monica from school. The only message he'd left was for Trina to pack him a suitcase for his upcoming road trip to Los Angeles.

Trina placed her special homemade sweet-potato pie in the oven and then headed toward the family room. It looked like a tornado had struck. She could scarcely see the lavender carpeting beneath the kids' toys. Marcus was absorbed with his latest electronic gadget, building his own Giga pet, and Monica was busy combing her Moesha doll's hair. Aunt Thelma, who was visiting from Tennessee, was content to sit in Rick's La-Z-Boy as she fiddled with her Discman and classic jazz CDs. Trina looked at her aunt and smiled. Aunt Thelma's salt-and-pepper Afro, which she'd worn since the sixties, was flattened by the headphones and she was rocking back and forth, undoubtedly listening to a scatting Ella Fitzgerald.

The older woman eased out of the recliner and danced into the kitchen. She was shuffling her feet back and forth, doing the jig.

"Stop looking out that window, child," Aunt Thelma said in her no-nonsense manner.

"Ain't nobody looking out the window," Trina said.

"Every two minutes you're looking out there."

"How would you know, old woman? You had your eyes closed."

"I know what I saw," Aunt Thelma said as she began removing silverware from the dishwasher in between dance moves. "Stop worrying about that boy. You got better things to do with your time—like thinking about Marcus, Monica, and the little one on the way. I don't care if he is your husband; he ain't worth a dime."

"Auntie, don't be talking about Rick like that in our house."

"Tree, I love you like the child I never had." Aunt Thelma called Trina by her childhood pet name. "And I don't mean no disrespect to you, but I'm gonna be frank with you like nobody else has. That boy ain't good for nothing except paying the bills, and you can get those taken care of better without him holding the purse strings over your head," Aunt Thelma spat out, with her southern accent more pronounced than usual.

"Well, I love him, even with all his faults," Trina countered, even though her aunt was probably speaking the truth.

"How can you be married to a man you're not even comfortable enough with to tell that you're pregnant? What's that all about?"

"I'm gonna tell him . . . when the time is right."

"When, Trina? When you're in labor? You never stand up to him."

"It's gonna get straightened out," Trina said resolutely.

"Listen to me, Tree. At least think about your kids. What do you think Monica is ever gonna expect of a man, seeing how her daddy treats her mama? And what about Marcus? How you think he gonna treat women when he gets older? Do you even care about that?"

Trina did not know how to respond. So she looked out her window.

"Daddy's here! Daddy's here, Mommy!" Monica screamed, running into the foyer.

"Let me take care of my affairs, Auntie," Trina said, yanking off her apron and smoothing her hair with her hands. "Now, how do I look?"

"Girl, scrape your pride off the ground," said Thelma, grasping Trina around the wrist. "Look at me, girl. Don't beg that man for nothing, except maybe to let you be."

"Ain't nobody begging. Now, you let me be, old woman," Trina said, breaking free and rushing past her aunt into the entrance hall.

Marcus and Monica beat Trina into the foyer to greet Rick. He brought Marcus a bag full of the latest video games, and Monica some baby dolls. Monica was clinging to Rick, showering him with kisses. Trina liked watching Rick with their children. It was clear they adored their father. She stood back and pulled at her oversized sweater, suddenly becoming self-conscious of her ever-enlarging stomach.

Monica continued to hug and kiss her father as Marcus chattered away about his last soccer game, giving Rick a play-by-play report.

"All right, you two, Daddy's got to get a few things upstairs," Rick told them, putting Monica back down.

Rick turned toward Trina and looked at her quickly before he spoke. "You gather some clothes together for me to take to L.A. yet?"

"You didn't say when you were coming by, but I'm almost finished packing for you," Trina explained, noticing his freshly cut hair, which told her he had not deviated from his road-trip routine.

"That's all right, I'll finish it myself," Rick said, walking past Trina up the staircase to their bedroom.

Trina scurried behind him, staring at the perfect buzz line at the back of his head. She did not want to lose the opportunity to talk to him. Following Rick into the bedroom, she closed the door behind her, in case Aunt Thelma decided to eavesdrop.

Trina watched Rick lay out his wardrobe bag, walking back and forth between the closet and the bed, throwing clothes into his luggage. Naturally he did not forget to pack the brand-new Calvin Klein underwear for his road trip, unlike when he was at home with his drawers full of holes. She remained transfixed in her spot by the door, not having the slightest idea how to proceed. Rick seemed so preoccupied as he packed, she felt as if she would be intruding.

"So when are you scheduled to leave?" Trina asked, shifting from side to side.

"The day after tomorrow," Rick said, not missing a beat in his packing.

"You plan on staying in the hotel even when you get back from L.A.?"

"I don't know, Trina. That depends on if we're still playing then. The series could be over if we beat the Lakers tomorrow night and then beat them twice in L.A. So I really couldn't tell you. Now, let's see, do I want to take my gray suit?" Rick said to himself, holding up the suit to his chest and looking in the mirror.

"You feeling any better?"

"I'm fine; nothing was wrong with me. I just need full concentration on my game. It helps to be alone."

"Oh," Trina began as she walked toward the bed.

"And that should about do it," Rick said, throwing a pair of black Bally loafers in his bag.

Trina sat down on the edge of the bed and watched Rick zip up the garment bag and fold it over.

"Rick, before you go . . . I need to talk to you about something."

Trina had gotten herself into a bind waiting so long to tell him. With the rest of the championship series ahead . . . well, this sure wasn't the time. Maybe . . . Thelma's advice about what message she was sending her children reverberated.

"You can stop right now if it's that baking business. I told you no." Rick was shaking his head.

"No, Rick, it's not about that; it's something else . . ."

"Come on, spit it out. I don't have all day. I need to get an extra workout in before my dinner," Rick said, walking toward the door.

"Rick, could you please just sit down a minute?"

"Trina, I don't need to—"

"Rick, please, please, would you just have a seat?" Trina said.

Rick reluctantly dropped his bag and took a seat on the chaise lounge across from the bed.

"What's going on, Trina?"

"Rick, I know how you feel about this, but there's nothing we can do about it now 'cause it's done . . . I'm gonna . . . We're gonna have another baby," Trina said, dropping her eyes to her lap.

"I hope I heard you incorrectly."

"You heard me right. I'm almost five months along."

"Five months pregnant! How did this happen? Don't you use your diaphragm anymore?"

"I don't remember when it happened, but it was probably one morning when I was too groggy to be thinking about something like that."

"Well, damn. Ain't that a fine thing to forget about. I don't even remember doing anything with you," Rick said, shaking his head.

"Well, I'm pregnant and we got to deal with it."

"You sure have perfect timing telling me this," Rick said, standing up as he began to pace.

"I guess as far as you're concerned, there'd never be a good time to tell you." Trina felt the anger rising in her throat.

"I got a lot going on right now, Trina. You know I'm not gonna be making money like this forever. This is the last year. Hell, this is the last few weeks I'll be making money like this. We can't afford to be spitting out babies. Not to mention all the debt we have now," Rick said as he began to pace even faster.

Thanks to you, she wanted to scream—but she loved him. He was her man.

Trina noticed Rick breaking into a sweat.

"Well, we'll manage somehow, Rick. We don't have a choice."

"Trina, you had a choice. You act like money grows on trees."

Trina could not believe the gall of Rick. She was not the only one he was depriving now. It was their unborn child. Her maternal instinct was ignited and she felt a rumbling ferociousness rising up in her.

"Rick Belleville! You're the one who acts like money grows on trees! I'm not the one who has over a million dollars in gambling debts," Trina said, no longer wanting to stop herself from mentioning the forbidden subject.

Rick stopped in his tracks with widened eyes and stared at Trina, stupefied. He started to speak two or three times but couldn't get a complete sentence out.

"Trina . . . I . . . I don't know where you heard that from, but I don't owe no million dollars to nobody. I told you about meddling in my business," Rick sputtered.

"Rick, cut the crap. I know you've been spending our money as fast as you get it and—"

"Our money? I'm the one out there workin' my ass off on the basketball court every night."

"I'm so tired of hearing that bull. Yes! Yes, our money! My money too, damn it! And our kids' money! And this one here in my stomach, it belongs to him or her too, and I'm not going to sit back and let you lose it all at the tables or anyplace else for that matter." Trina was now on her feet, staring Rick down.

"Girl, I don't know what you been sniffing, but you talking out the wrong side of your mouth. You better stop listening to your crazy aunt Thelma. You gettin' a little too big for your britches."

"Shut up, Rick! This is the most sense I've made in fourteen years. I'm telling you now, you need to get some help about your gambling problem, and I don't mean by going to the casino to win back our money. You need to get some professional help," Trina finished, suddenly feeling empowered for the first time in years.

"You been talking to Coach, haven't you? Y'all can kiss—"

"Rick, I'm not playing with you," Trina interrupted him. "We have a family to think about. I don't know when it happened, but somewhere along the line, you forgot what we're supposed to mean to each other. Now, I'm telling you this because I love you. You better get some help for your sake and for our family's."

"Or what?" Rick challenged.

Trina forced herself to close her eyes and count backward from ten before she responded to Rick. She knew that she'd better be certain about what came out of her mouth next, because the future of her family depended upon it. Trina grasped the four-poster bed to brace herself.

"Rick, I know that this is going to hurt me a whole lot more than it's going to hurt you, but you're not welcome back in this house until you take care of your problem. You're not going to run this family into the ground with your destructive behavior."

"I'm not welcome in this house! Who you talking to?" Rick said, looking at Trina as if she had lost her mind.

"I'm talking to you, Rick Belleville, and I mean that. So maybe you ought to pack a few extra things before you go," Trina said, pushing past him as she walked toward the door.

Rick spun around as Trina reached it. "Hey! Where do you think you're going?"

"I'm going to take care of my family and my business," Trina yelled over her shoulder as she left their bedroom and slammed the door in Rick's face.

By the time Trina reached the bottom of the stairs, her legs felt like rubber. She did not know where she'd found the strength to tell Rick off, but she'd known she had to do it. Now, she only hoped she had not lost him forever.

Michael Brown flexed his arms and tightened his stomach muscles as he stood in front of the full-length mirror of the Flyers' locker room. He had just finished working out, and his pectorals were pumped from the six sets of chest presses. Michael was trying to decide which angles were his best. His contract with Tommy Hilfiger was to lead an adver-tising campaign for a new line of under-wear, and Michael was scheduled to begin shooting as soon as the championship series was over.

As Michael gazed at his reflection in the mirror, he imagined his face and body plastered all over buses, billboards, and magazines. It was a heady feeling for the young rookie. And considering how well he had been playing throughout the entire play-offs, he was a shoo-in to be Rookie of the Year. If they could only win the championship, all of his goals would be met, his business for the year finished. Well, almost.

There was the issue of his fiancée. He and Dawn still had not spoken to each other since she'd popped in on him in Chicago and seen him with Sandi. Well, Dawn had not spoken to him. He had apologized, pleaded, and even bought her a tennis bracelet, but she wouldn't even acknowledge his presence—and they were living together. Finally he had stopped trying. Dawn was probably waiting for him to say, "Okay, we can get married now," but that wasn't going to happen any time soon. He needed all of his energies focused on the play-offs—not trying to win back her affections. That could wait. She was probably just trying to pay him back now by sleeping in the guest bedroom. Thinking about it, though, Michael couldn't deny that he missed being next to her warm body at night. If she'd just give him some time, until after the championship, then he'd think about marriage—maybe. He had other priorities right now, and marriage was not one of them. Hell, commitment wasn't either. Michael wished Dawn could learn to accept that. It would certainly make things much easier on him. Well, I'm not about to try and fix my relationship during the rest of the series, Michael thought.

Stepping closer to the mirror, he smiled broadly, exposing all of his perfect white teeth. No, he thought, they probably won't have me smiling for these pictures. They'll want me to look sexy, I bet. Michael took a step back and tried his best Tyson imitation pose, trying to look very serious and then breaking back into a huge grin.

"Rehearsing for something?" Coach said, stepping up behind Michael.

Michael's whole face felt flushed as he saw Coach and Jake.

"You starring in a movie I don't know about, Michael?" Jake laughed.

"Ahh, no, just . . . thought I had something stuck in my teeth," Michael said in a fluster.

"Putting in a little overtime, huh, champ?" Coach asked, taking a seat on one of the locker-room benches.

Michael liked whenever Coach referred to him as "champ." In fact, every time Coach paid extra attention to Michael, he felt special. The guys on the team joked that Michael was Coach's son. Michael scoffed at their remarks, but was secretly flattered that he was one of Coach's favorites.

"You know me, Coach; just trying to be in shape to win the championship." Michael grinned.

"Well, don't wear yourself out, Michael. You need to save some energy for the court and the years you have ahead," Coach said.

"That's right, Michael, you don't want to burn yourself out," Jake said, leaning against one of the lockers.

"Oh, I'm not. I feel great. I'm ready to school that little boy Kobe Bryant tomorrow night," Michael said confidently.

"Look who's talking, rookie. Getting a little cocky, huh?" Jake's chuckle had an edge.

"Naw. I'm not cocky. I just have a job to do, you know; I have to get my head together."

"Oh, I like cocky," Coach said pensively. "I like cocky a lot, especially in my future star."

Michael felt his chest swell with pride. The legendary Mike Mitchell saw him as the future star of the team. Coach did not make comments like that very often to his players. The last guy he probably said that to had to have been Brent Rogers.

"Thanks, Coach. I'm glad you have that much confidence in me," said Michael quietly, a little humbly, but damn, he wanted to shout!

"So you say you have to get your head together. Everything all right on the home front after the Chicago incident?" Coach asked.

"How did you . . ."

"I make it my business to know these things," Coach said.

Man! Coach must have been reading his mind when he came into the locker room. That's another thing Michael respected about Mitchell. His team was like family. He cared about his players' personal lives and he knew how private matters could affect performance on the court. Michael knew that a lot of the guys thought he was a control fanatic, but Mike Mitchell was really just a winner. He had a strenuous work ethic and he cared about his players on and off the court. It seemed to Michael that most of the other guys did not recognize the side of Coach that Michael saw.

"Pressure at home from the little fiancée after she caught you?" Jake said, stepping forward.

"Well," Michael began, not sure how much he should discuss with them, "you know how it can be sometimes when . . ."

"When they're just dying to walk down that endless aisle of hell," Jake said, finishing Michael's sentence.

"Exactly. And Dawn, she's . . . she's not your typical lady . . . Sometimes she's just so . . . so . . ."

"Headstrong?" Coach suggested.

"Headstrong! Now, that's a good description, especially since she came to Chicago. Now she's being so bullheaded, she won't even speak to me," Michael said, pointing at Coach in affirmation. He watched as Coach shook his head.

"That's a shame. Now do you see one of the reasons why I have my strict rules about your women not being allowed on the road?"

"Do I ever."

"It helps to keep domestic matters separate from . . . from extracurricular activities on the road," Jake concurred. "Things run smoother that way. Trust me and Coach on that one."

"But Dawn surprised me," Michael protested.

"That's your responsibility, Michael. You have to learn to keep your woman in check, or have the type of woman you can keep in line," Jake said.

"But I feel sorry for you, champ, I really do," Coach said. "You're under a whole lot of pressure right now. I know having a woman like that has got to be difficult at times, especially with the other . . . differences between the two of you."

"You're telling me. Hell, I live with her," Michael said, looking at Coach.

"Michael, come on. You know what Coach is saying. Different cultures, different races," Jake interjected.

"Our problems don't have anything to do with that," Michael said.

"Maybe not now, Michael . . . but in the future, you just never know what may come up. May cause some problems down the line," warned Jake.

"I doubt it, Jake. Aren't those attitudes kind of old?"

"Depends on who you ask."

"Hell, half the players in the NBA are married to women outside of their race," Michael began, looking from Jake to Coach and back again. "I don't see how that would ever make a difference."

"Not so fast, Michael. I warned you about live-in arrangements, remember? But you didn't want to listen to good ole Jake back then. Now you got trouble between you two. I'd never steer you wrong, kiddo, and I'm telling you those other differences will make a difference down the line."

Michael pulled his hand towel around his neck. "You may have been right about the living-together thing, but there's nothing I can do about it now. We live together and it's not really that bad . . . just when we argue . . . or don't speak at all," Michael said, realizing that was worse.

"So this is a permanent situation?" Coach asked, raising his eyebrows.

"What? Us living together?"

"Yes, you plan on living together forever?" Coach pressed.

"I don't know. I guess one day maybe I'd like for us to get married," Michael said, shrugging his shoulders.

"Marriage is a huge step. One of the biggest you'll ever make in your life. There's a lot more involved to getting married than you realize. You have to think about your estate planning, your prenuptial agreement; the list goes on and on," Jake said.

"Prenuptial agreement! If I do marry, I wouldn't dare ask Dawn or any other woman to sign any contract," Michael said vehemently.

"Don't be naive, Michael. What you're telling me is that you're willing to share everything you own fifty-fifty just because some woman is telling you she loves you? I thought you were a lot smarter than most of the other guys. Come on, you even went to Stanford, for goodness' sake!" Jake said, lifting his tortoiseshell glasses from the end of his nose.

"Jake, I'd watch what I say if I were you. You're treading on some thin ice here," Michael warned. "Did you have your wife sign any agreement?"

"Listen, Michael," Jake said, ignoring his client's question. I just don't want you to make a big mistake. Things can get real ugly when people's emotions are on the line, and all I'm saying is that you've got to protect yourself up front."

"Jake, he said he's not getting married right now; lay off. All this talk is a bit premature, wouldn't you agree?" Coach said rhetorically. "Michael, you're young. What are you, twenty-one, twenty-two? All we're saying is, don't rush into anything. The only thing you should really be thinking about now is your future as a basketball player." Coach's look was intense.

"You have to look at all possible scenarios, Michael," Jake said. "There is the possibility that the team will be sold and relocated, even if the Flyers do win the championship."

"But I heard that—"

"Everyone in this organization has heard that the team might not be sold if we win the championship, but Hal hasn't put anything in writing," Coach said. "Hell, he could go back on his word for all we know, with everything Hightower is offering. You've got to be ready for any possibility, and you have to make smart decisions about where Dawn fits in; that's what Jake's saying." Mitchell's blunt words intimidated Michael. He had the urge to put his back against the wall so he wouldn't get jumped, mentally, from behind.

"It's such a lucrative deal that Hightower is offering, Hal may just want to wash his hands of the team and take the money and run . . . At least, from what I hear, that could be the case," Jake said, quickly glancing at Coach.

Michael cast his eyes downward thinking about all the personal implications of the team being sold and moved.

"The almighty dollar, son. The almighty dollar. It makes people do crazy things," said Coach, patting Michael on the back.

"That, it does," Jake said almost in unison, approaching Michael and giving his shoulder a quick squeeze before heading out of the locker room.

"Heads up, Michael," Coach began. "No matter what happens, you're still the future of this team if you play your cards right. See you tomorrow, champ."

Michael stood there, alone. Why did he feel as if he'd just been double-teamed?

"I'm telling you, it's not ripe," Phil said, looking at the tomato in his hand.

"How would you know? You haven't even felt it," he said, glancing at Phil sideways.

"Some things you can just tell by looking at them . . . whether they're good or not," Phil said, winking at him.

"Is that from per- sonal experience?"

"I'll never tell."

"Is that so?" he said, putting the tomato back in the pile.

He and Phil were grocery shopping for their dinner. The time he spent with Phil had a way of eclipsing everything else going on in his life. With the exception of the occasional stares of people who recognized him as well as Phil in Dean & DeLuca, the chichi Greenwich Village shop, he was totally relaxed. Here it was, the night before the second game of the championship, and he felt peaceful, as if he were on summer vacation instead of in the NBA finals.

"Excuse me, sir, would you mind autographing my hat?" a freckle-faced man wearing a New York Flyers hat asked him. As he removed the cap, he revealed a full head of red hair.

Well, he was almost relaxed. He and Phil would probably have to run away to a remote island to have complete privacy. Still, the man's gesture touched him. He hadn't forgotten that it was the fans who supported the Flyers—well, sometimes, at least.

"Sure," he began, smiling at Phil, who was still inspecting the tomatoes. "Do you have a pen I can use?"

"Oh, yeah, just let me find it." The man began searching in the pockets of his plaid pants and then opened up his large tote bag and pulled out a felt-tip pen. "Here you go."

He grasped the pen and signed his name and playing number on the hat.

"Thank you so much; I'm going to give this hat to my son," the man said excitedly as he walked away, leaving him feeling as if he'd done his good deed for the day.

"How come he didn't want my autograph?" Phil laughed.

"He probably doesn't watch your show," he said.

"Yeah, my popularity has declined since I got this new co-anchor."

"Is that right?"

"Yeah, the network forced him on me. Somebody high up must have thought he was cute, but, man, have the ratings plummeted since he's come aboard." Phil shook his head back and forth.

For the past two weeks, the two of them had been enjoying quiet evenings at Phil's apartment, depending on his woman's schedule. Of late, each conversation he had with her became more strained than the last. After the obligatory niceties, their talks were plagued by awkward pauses. They both knew something was amiss, but neither wanted to acknowledge anything.

"Now, here's a ripe one," Phil said, holding up a shiny red tomato and then tossing it to him. "See the difference."

As he caught the tomato, he punctured it with his fingers and tomato juice and seeds began oozing down his hand. "No, actually, I can feel the difference, shithead."

"I'm not paying for that one." Phil laughed as he quickly walked away, pretending they weren't together.

Each moment he spent with Phil felt more right than the last. They were completely at ease with one another, whether they were at Phil's apartment hanging out, at work on their postgame broadcast, or simply grocery shopping together. The chemistry that flowed between them worked like magic. More than anything, what tugged at his heart the most was the joy he felt just being in Phil's company; it was also what scared him. This relationship was not some sexual fling that he could shake like a cold. The feelings he had for Phil were the real deal.

He knew that time was running out. He could not continue to deceive his woman. He cared about her enough to tell her the truth. Hell, he cared enough about being truthful with anyone. The lying had gone on long enough.

"Hey, need a towel?" Phil said, returning with some napkins for him. "Sorry about the mess."

"Sure you are," he said, wiping the tomato from his hand.

As he watched Phil walk toward the peppers and begin to sift through them, he began picking through the tomatoes, looking for the softest he could find. Ah—victory! Finding a particularly mushy tomato, he put it behind his back and headed for Phil. He looked to his left and then to his right; no one was watching. He bit his lip to keep from laughing as he inched up behind Phil and stood there for a couple of seconds, planning his attack. Not giving Phil an opportunity to defend himself, he lifted up his lover's sweater and smeared the tomato all over his stomach.

"You . . ." Phil began, but stopped in midsentence as light suddenly flashed in their faces.

Before either of them had a chance to react, the redheaded man with the plaid pants and New York Flyers baseball cap shocked them both again with the flashing bulb of a camera.

"What the hell?" he said, clearly startled.

By the time he regained his composure, the man was moving fast out the front door of Dean & DeLuca.

He and Phil looked at each other, startled; it wasn't difficult to figure out how this scenario would play itself out.

"What the hell!" Phil said as he held his sweater away from his stomach.

"Shit!" he said, blinking his eyes, trying to regain full vision after the bulb had flashed in his face.

"You and your fans. I don't think I'm going to be seeing you anymore after tonight. You're too much trouble." Phil giggled, an obvious attempt to lighten the mood. "Let me have one of those napkins I gave you."

He handed Phil the rest of the napkins, and Phil began to clean his tight stomach.

"Let's get out of here," he said, suddenly nervous.

"What about the groceries?"

"I think I might need to get home," he said as they headed for the door.

The two men walked down the street side by side, suddenly careful not to brush bodies too closely.

The sauna's intense dry heat had become a necessity for Paul over the last couple of years as the tendinitis in his knees worsened. He leaned his head back against the hot cedar wall and looked over Brent's shoulder as he finished the article in the *Post*. Brent closed the paper and looked at the cover photograph for the third time, a mixture of disbelief and disgust flashing across his face.

"What is this shit all about?" Brent said as he continued to study the picture on the cover of the *New York Post*.

Paul had seen the paper that morning at the bagel shop. Not that he had to actually see it for himself. The whole city was talking about the article. Collin DuMott and Phil Johnson, the Flyers' pride power forward and the Mecca's guru of sports commentating, Collin's body pressed against Phil's from behind, his hand up the front of Phil's sweater. Unfortunately, they looked like a picture of bliss.

" 'Lovers at Play?' " Brent said reading aloud the paper's headline.

Paul looked at Brent through the sauna's haze.

"Can you believe this? I just can't believe it!" Brent said, shaking his head. "No way. I don't believe Collin's gay. Do you believe this crap?"

Paul did not respond for a few seconds as Brent opened the paper again and started reading the article.

"I mean, this is crazy. It says that Collin and Phil have been seen nuzzling each other on line at Dean and DeLuca, and holding hands and caressing at a neighboring coffee shop, gazing into each other's eyes. What's that all about?" Brent asked incredulously.

"You can't believe everything you read," Paul said, trying to defuse the article even though he wondered if he should just tell Brent the truth about Collin anyway.

"Yeah, but, Paul, it's so out there. Look at this—it refers to them as lovers, that they've also been spotted taking cozy walks together in Central Park. It's so hard for me to believe this. I mean, Remy's one of the finest women I've ever seen. Why would Collin want some man flexing beside him?" Brent said, setting the paper down next to him.

"Come on, Brent; if Collin is really gay, then I guess a woman's tits and ass wouldn't matter."

"But you don't think he's gay, do you?"

Paul would not betray Collin's trust, but it was difficult to look Brent in the eyes and outright lie to him. "I . . . I don't know. What if he is? Should it make a difference?" Paul asked, flipping it back to Brent.

"No. I mean yeah," Brent began, clearly flustered. "You mean to tell me it wouldn't make a difference to you? I mean, you of all people don't think it's sacrilegious? I don't know. It's just something I would have liked to know about one of my own teammates, that's all."

"Just because he's your teammate doesn't mean that he would tell you he's gay, especially if he thought you or anyone else might have a negative reaction. It's not like the two of you were ever that close," Paul said, feeling defensive for Collin.

"Yeah, I know, but Casey and Remy are pretty tight. We've been out together lots of times—never noticed anything strange. I guess it just seems like something I should have known. It's so damn shocking," Brent said, wiping the sweat from his forehead.

"How could you really know unless he told you himself? It's not like he'd be wearing a gay badge." Even as Paul said this, he remembered how flabbergasted he had been when Collin confided in him.

The two of them sat in silent contemplation as the heat penetrated Paul's worn-down body. The smallest guy on the team felt as if the weight of the world were coming down on him: between worrying about Lorraine and the team, he didn't know if he could take another complication.

As a gust of cold air swept into the sauna, Paul shook himself from his private worries. Paul and Brent both sat forward as Coach stormed in with a copy of the *Post* article under one arm. Taking a seat on the upper bench, Coach grimly shook his head as he looked back and forth between the two of them.

In all the years Paul had known Coach, he had never seen him look so angry. He seemed to have lost all of his composure. His hair was in complete disarray; he had a five-o'clock shadow on his face and it was only eight-thirty in the morning. He hadn't even bothered to cover his nakedness with a towel. Not like the oh-so-refined Mr. Mitchell at all.

"Would somebody please . . . please tell me what the hell is going on around here?" Coach said, taking the newspaper and slamming himself down on the sauna seat. Comically, the hot bench burned his privates, and Paul saw Brent look away quickly to cover his smile.

"First Rick is hunted down by half the pit bosses in Atlantic City for gambling debts up the wazoo; then Steve gets plastered all over the papers with assault charges; and now the *Post* is claiming Collin is a queer!" Coach threw the paper against the wall.

Belleville's gambling problem was a very well kept secret within the team, and Paul was surprised Coach mentioned it now. What was the point of busting the guy's privacy and further demoralizing him? Somebody needed to give Mitchell some sensitivity training. That was for sure. And maybe when the championship was theirs, he'd go to Hal and say so.

"Not the best timing for all this to be going down," Brent said.

"That's a fucking understatement! We may have made it to the finals, but this team is the shame of the NBA!" Coach fumed.

"Is there some sort of damage control that the publicity department can put into action?" Paul asked hopefully.

"Or maybe the legal department could demand some sort of retraction statement from the *Post*," Brent suggested.

"Damage control? Retraction statements? Hell, we'd have to get injunctions against damn near every radio station and Associated Press paper in the country. This story has spread like wildfire." Coach began shaking his head. "Not good, not good at all, guys!"

The three of them sat pensively in the blistering heat.

"Well, for starters, we can't let this distract us from the game tonight. We've got to get another win before we head out to the Forum," Paul said.

"That's easier said than done," Coach countered.

"Look, Coach. We've come this far and we're not going to let some snow job in the *Post* stop us from getting what we've been working for all season long. It's as simple as that," Brent said.

Paul nodded his head. "I agree with Brent. We've got to take this by the horns and keep moving forward. I think the rest of the team should be briefed on how to comment to the media, and other than that, we need to practice our asses off today and concentrate on winning tonight. What else can we do?" Paul said, but Coach was shaking his head.

"Negative. Feeding into this with the rest of the team would only make matters worse. We just gotta play like we've never played before, period. You guys really don't understand the full implications of this, do you?" Coach began as he ran his fingers through his curly grayish blond hair. "I've got Commissioner McDeavitt breathing down my neck, and every owner in the NBA pressuring me to . . ." Coach began.

"To what?" Paul asked.

"To act on this," Coach solemnly said.

"To act on it how?" Brent asked.

"Listen. The NBA has an image to protect. The league already has a bad rap for the fighting, the trash talking, the drug-possession charges of certain players, domestic-abuse issues . . . The list goes on. Commissioner McDeavitt wants the league's image squeaky clean. That's why

Hightower would be a perfect owner in his eyes—no wife beaters, substance abusers, gamblers, faggots, whatever, are allowed on his teams."

"Yeah, only racists and supremacists. Now, there's a step up for the sport's image!" Brent stood, his face revealing the same spectrum of anxiety, fear, pressure, fury, and hopelessness that Paul felt—play your heart out and ruin your body, and in the end somebody's opinion or value judgment, right or wrong, could screw you.

"Forget the speeches, Mr. Big Man—right now what we've got is a reputation as a league filled with thugs and degenerates. If you want to know what I think, I think the value of this league is going to go straight down—and that, my children, means money."

"Coach," Paul said, "I think we'd all agree that we care about the game as much as the commissioner, probably more. Those incidents you mentioned involve only a handful of players, and they're the exception rather than the norm. You know how the media blows these incidents way out of proportion. There's nothing we can do about that."

"Unfortunately for us, the majority of that handful happens to be on this team," Coach said in disgust.

"Coach Mitchell." Paul felt using his proper name might make Coach feel respected. "Everything you say may be true, but we need to think about solutions. We already know what the problems are." Paul massaged his swollen knees.

"That's why I wanted to tell you guys this first so you won't be surprised tonight. But . . . I've been forced to make some tough judgment calls." Coach avoided eye contact with Paul and Brent. "If we want this game to be run fairly and not by the referees, I'm going to be forced to have a few of the guys who are normally in the rotation sit out for a while."

"Bench a few of the guys?" Paul said, standing up in the middle of the sauna as his sweat dripped to the floor.

"Like you did with Steve the other night? No way, Coach; that almost cost us the first game," Brent said, shaking his head.

"I don't have a choice," Coach said.

"What do you mean you don't have a choice? You're the coach of this team. You play who you want to play," Brent said.

"Not anymore. Not with everything that's happened. At the moment, public opinion rules this team. Do you realize how many millions of people around the world watch the NBA finals? And do you know how bad it looks for the NBA's image to have a woman beater—"

"Alleged woman beater," Paul quickly corrected, interrupting Coach.

"Whatever," Coach continued, "and a gay jock playing on a championship contending team. It sends the message to the world that the NBA condones this type of behavior in its boys. Commissioner McDeavitt won't stand for it, believe me."

"What are you saying? That Collin shouldn't play because he's gay? Hell, look at Dennis Rodman. He boasted in his book that he was dating a transvestite, and that didn't stop Phil Jackson from playing him in numerous championship games." Brent was standing now.

"Rodman's situation is different. No one takes him seriously. He's just seen as an entertainer, with all his different hair colors and shenanigans. The guys in the main office brush him off as a joke. Collin and Phil have been depicted as stars in some Hollywood love story. And if Collin is actually gay, that would be a threat to the whole status quo," Coach said.

"Well, maybe it's time that the 'status quo' is threatened," Paul said, surprised at himself as he spoke the words.

"Paul, I don't think you want to risk that right now." Coach gave Paul a decidedly mean stare.

"Well, our chances of winning a championship are drastically reduced without Collin and Steve playing anyway," Paul said, not believing that Coach was trying to bench two of their starters in the finals.

"The two of you obviously don't understand. Let me put it like this: I've been all but ordered not to play them by the powers that be. I guarantee you both, the repercussions of me going against that could be more detrimental than if I let them play."

"How?" Brent said, looking at Paul skeptically.

"Sponsors will pull their advertisements and . . . and you know just like I do that the referees have probably been pressured to not make any calls in our favor . . . and the game would just be taken out of our hands," Coach quickly finished.

"You know what it seems like to me, Coach?" Brent said as Coach opened the sauna-room door. "It seems to me that it's already been taken out of our hands."

"Yeah, I'm sorry to say, fellas, that seems to be the case. See you at practice. Keep your heads up," Coach said, sucking in his lips and walking past Paul.

Once they were alone, Paul said, "Brent?"

"Yeah, man."

"Why do you think Coach fed us that crock?"

"I have no idea, but that had to be the most bullshit I've ever heard him shovel. Something strange is going on."

Dawn sat on the living room sofa watching Michael quietly as he dashed back and forth between the kitchen and the laundry room. He had placed a sausage muffin in the microwave and was trying to find a pair of matching sweat socks in the dryer at the same time.

She'd done a great deal of soul-searching during the last couple of weeks of silence between them. The decision she'd reached had not been easy, but it had been necessary just the same.

She had gathered some essential personal items and was ready to move into the medical-resident housing complex at Columbia University until she found an affordable apartment in the city. She had exhausted all of her emotional energy dealing with Michael. First, he'd begged, whined, and cajoled, trying to convince her that nothing had been going on between him and that model even though she'd flat out busted them together. He had not admitted to anything about their relationship, certainly not to having become blinded by all his endorsements, money, and promised glory. Since arriving in New York, other than being a wonderful lover, Michael had been missing in action where their relationship was concerned. Dawn had not been able to get through to him before he'd cheated on her, and afterward, she hadn't even tried. It hurt too much and she was tired of hurting.

As the microwave timer buzzed, Michael flung the door open and grabbed the hot muffin. Dawn watched him blow on his steaming hot breakfast and then toss it onto the granite kitchen countertop. This was the longest time she had been in his presence since the Chicago incident.

Michael had to notice her sitting in the living room watching him, but he would never let on. He was even more stubborn than she was now. Dawn knew that he would not speak to her until she broke the silence. She was certain that he assumed his initial begging and diamond-tennis-bracelet guilt bribe should have been sufficient for her to stop sulking. She knew he really thought she should just get over it. Normally she would have been the peacemaker in their relationship, but that role had begun to feel stale. She was not interested in keeping score. She simply wanted to tell him she was leaving. Watching him greedily gobble down his food, Dawn knew that Michael could have easily continued with this game of silence for months. She had outgrown these childish tactics.

She let him finish eating his breakfast and figured that now was the best time to break the news to him. Just as Michael rinsed off his hands at the kitchen sink, Dawn rose from the couch and walked toward him.

Standing with the kitchen counter between them, Michael gave her one of those killer smiles that usually made her heart melt.

"So you finally ready to kiss and make up now?" Michael said, continuing to grin.

Dawn smiled weakly, unable to speak.

"I know these past few weeks have been hard. Let's just forget about it and move on," Michael said, still grinning from ear to ear.

Dawn managed to shake her head as she felt the tears sting her eyes.

"What's wrong, baby?" Michael said, moving around the kitchen counter toward her.

Dawn instinctively backed away from him before he could reach her. "Michael, don't . . ." Dawn began, fighting back the tears. "Please, don't make this any harder than it already is."

Michael stopped a few feet short of Dawn and stared at her. "You're scaring me, Dawn. You're looking at me like you don't even know me," Michael said, taking another step forward.

Dawn lifted her balled-up left fist and held it in midair for a few seconds before speaking. "Michael . . . I love you. I admire you, I don't think I'll ever get over you, but I'm going to have to give this back to you," Dawn said as she opened her fist and placed the five-carat diamond engagement ring on the kitchen counter.

Michael only stared in disbelief. "I . . . I don't understand, Dawn."

"I know you don't, Michael," Dawn said, unable to stop a lone tear from rolling down her flushed cheek.

"But, Dawn . . . I told you that girl in Chicago didn't mean nothing to me. I told you she was just going to be in a photo shoot with me. That's all it was. Why you gotta go and give me the ring back? It wasn't that deep," Michael said, sounding flustered.

"Exactly, Michael. It was not that deep, for you. That's the problem. You don't get it. You just aren't listening," Dawn said, walking back toward the couch to pick up her small duffel.

Michael ran up behind her and snatched the bag out of her hand. "What do you think you're doing?" Michael said, still holding her luggage.

"Michael, you should thank me. I'm letting you off easy. Now you don't have to hear my nagging anymore." Dawn reached for her bag.

Michael pulled the bag so it was out of her reach. "Come on, Dawn. You don't want to leave. Everything's gonna be all right. We can have a nice dinner tonight after the game and then we can come home and snuggle . . . Well, not tonight 'cause I'm leavin', but . . . but maybe when I get back from Los Angeles. Come on, baby. I know this isn't what you want," Michael pleaded.

"You're right. It's not what I want . . ." Dawn began.

"And neither do I. We can work this out."

"And after you get back from California, then what? What do we do then?" Dawn asked, already knowing what his answer would be.

"Then it's me and you. We'll concentrate on our relationship. I promise."

"Until your next flavor of the month or your next call from Jake or your next photo shoot or until you have some other basketball-related commitment that causes you to run off and leave me again. Until you can put off marriage once again. I don't want your broken promises anymore. I'm sick of trying to convince you that I'm worthy enough to marry. I'm sick of the people in your life making decisions for you and for me. All this extra stuff that comes along with you wanting to be the biggest sports star in the world, which Nike ad you get next, which billboard you're going to grace next—all that stuff is frivolous and has no place in a relationship. At least not with me. I just wanted you. I'm tired of always coming second in your life, Michael," Dawn said, resolutely shaking her head.

"Dawn, what about your work? As much time as you spend at that hospital, it's not like you put me first either," Michael countered.

"Stop trying to bullshit me again, Michael. You're just rationalizing your behavior. You know that's different. When I'm at the hospital, that's work, and I leave it there where it belongs. When I'm at home with you, I'm all yours. And you know what else? I'm ready, willing, and able to be all yours for the rest of my life. You can't say the same thing. You're not ready for a committed relationship, Michael, but I am and I want it from you. Can you say you want the same thing from me?" Dawn said as she stared at the only man she'd ever truly loved.

Michael dejectedly sat down on the sofa and dropped Dawn's bag to the floor.

"I didn't think so," Dawn said, leaning down to retrieve her bag as Michael grasped her arm.

Dawn remained in the same position for a few moments as her eyes and Michael's locked in unspoken understanding. Pulling herself back up, Dawn smiled at Michael through her pain.

"Dawn, wait . . . don't," Michael said.

Dawn leaned down once more and gave him a deep kiss full on the mouth before she pulled away for the last time. "Michael. It's okay. It really is. You'll be fine. Our relationship has run its course. That happens. I guess it's a part of growing up." Her own words ripped at her heart.

She stared at Michael long and hard once more before she left the apartment that used to be theirs. He looked to her like a distraught little boy who had just lost his first pet, and as she walked out the front door, she knew he would be fine. As the tears relentlessly streamed down her face, she only hoped she would recover.

Remy's hand shook uncontrollably as she inserted the key in the door. Collin had given it to her the year before, telling her that she was always welcome in his home. Popping in on Collin without calling first had never been her style, but on this particular occasion she did not care about such formalities.

Liza, her agent, had telephoned her earlier this morning in Toronto and told her about the *New York Post* article.

Collin had not left Remy any other choice except to find out the truth for herself.

As Remy eased the door open, she heard talking that sounded like it was coming from the library. Stepping inside Collin's foyer, she softly shut the thick oak door behind her. As much as Remy believed she had a right to know what was really going on, she still felt as if she was sneaking up on Collin.

After Liza had read the article to Remy and described the photo, Remy knew she had to confront Collin in person. She had fled her hotel room determined to catch the first flight to New York. An array of emotions had raced through her mind as she sat on the airplane. For months now, she had to admit that her conversations with Collin had been strained. Even though an unspoken distance had crept between them, Remy had assumed the main reason for his aloofness was the Flyers' play-off pressures, not that he was having a relationship with someone else—well, she had to admit the thought had crossed her mind. But never did she suspect that it was with another man. It was just too devastating to believe.

As she walked through the dimly lit foyer toward the library, the unmistakable smell of blueberry bagels drifted through the air. She and Collin use to eat them whenever she spent the night. Now she became increasingly nervous as she physically neared the man she had been so emotionally tied to over the last three years. She had no idea what she was going to say.

When she entered the cherry-wood library, Collin was sitting on his hunter green leather sofa with the phone in one hand and the other one reassuringly on Phil's shoulder as if he were consoling him. Phil was sitting at Collin's feet on the floor in front of the coffee table, reading a magazine. The picture worth a thousand words was right there before her—domestic bliss. Pain sliced through her. Remy felt sick to her stomach. She felt humiliated and betrayed. The two men worked together. Phil had always been so friendly toward her. She had thought he and Collin were like brothers. It was embarrassing watching the two men in such an intimate scene. The lone, strong woman who had for the first time in a relationship lowered her shield of armor felt a thousand things. Remy used to be the one sitting between Collin's legs on the floor; now she was an intruder. Too stunned to say anything, she remained transfixed.

She searched for words that refused to come. This could not be happening.

Remy closed her eyes for a moment in hopes of regaining her composure. When she opened them, Phil was sitting up ramrod-straight staring at her. Collin abruptly hung up the phone. No one said anything as time was suspended and the room took on a surreal quality.

Both men rose at the same time—fumbling, looking ashamed and guilty. They were both parties to the deceit. Collin took a few steps toward Remy, while Phil began straightening the papers on the coffee table.

Remy's eyes bored into Collin's, questioningly. Why? Why hadn't he told her? Numbness crept inside her, replacing the hysteria and nervousness she had felt in the taxi ride on her way from Kennedy Airport. As her defense mechanisms were kicking in, Collin continued to walk toward her with sorrow in his eyes.

"I . . . I think I better go," Phil said, grabbing a sweater that had been flung over a wing chair in the corner of the library.

Phil did not look at Remy or Collin as he brushed past them leaving the room. The effect of his presence lingered on.

Remy felt as if her knees were going to buckle. She leaned against the wall closest to the door, farthest from Collin. Betrayal had previously been foreign to her; now the feeling penetrated her heart.

"Remy . . ." Collin began, with his hands up in the air as if offering something. "Remy. I'm so sorry about this. I never meant for this to happen, but—"

Remy held up her hand to silence him. "How long have you been lying to me?"

"Remy, it was not like that . . . I . . ."

"How long, Collin? How long has this *affair*," Remy said, spitting out the word "affair" with contempt, "been going on between the two of you?"

"Remy, it's not an affair," Collin said flatly.

"Well, whatever you want to call it!" Remy's rage broke through the numb, hollow, empty space and propelled her. "Have you been doing it right under my nose all this time? That would certainly be convenient with all the late night business meetings the two of you had."

"Remy, please," Collin began.

"Or did you just wait until I was out of town so you could sneak around behind my back?" Remy said, strong enough inside now to move away from the wall.

"Please, Remy, it's much more complicated than that. I don't expect you to understand right away, but please give me a chance to explain. You have every right to be angry."

"How did it work, Collin? Huh?" Remy said, beginning to piece things together. "No wonder you always looked so damn giddy on your postgame shows. You got to be with your lover, didn't you? Let's see, what did the article say? That the two of you have been seen gazing into each other's eyes all around town. Is that it? Did you take your boyfriend to our spots, too, or did you pick some new hang-outs?" Remy said, feeling the rage strengthening her.

Collin fell back down onto the sofa and began rubbing his temples. "All right, Remy."

"All right, Remy, what? Is this the point where I finally get the truth or do I have to read about it in part two of the *Post* exclusive, 'Lovers at Play—Again'?" Remy said, mocking the headline as she walked into the library and snatched up a copy of the *New York Post* lying on the coffee table.

Remy studied the photograph of Collin and Phil on the cover and began shaking her head back and forth. "Did you think about how I would have to pick my humiliated ass off the floor? About my image, my career? Oh, and let's not forget about my feelings."

Gently he took the paper from her. "The freak show's over. I have no excuse, I'm sorry—I couldn't stop it. Please, Remy, I couldn't help what I felt."

"Couldn't you have postponed the public displays of affection until you at least broke it off with your girlfriend?" Remy said, clutching her hands together so hard her knuckles turned white.

"Remy—"

"So now what?" Remy said, looking at Collin with her head cocked to the side.

Collin did not respond.

"Well? How do I go on, Collin? How do I hold my head up—and maybe go on to trust another man?"

"Stop, Remy."

" 'Stop, Remy?' When was Remy going to find out the truth? I ought to be thankful to the *Post*. I might not have ever known the true Collin."

"Remy . . ." Collin struggled as he covered his face with both hands and began to cry.

Remy looked at this mammoth jock of a man so visibly tormented. "Collin, how long have you known that you're gay?"

"Remy, I'm so sorry. I'm so sorry that I lied to you," Collin said in anguish, still covering his face.

"How long have you known, Collin?" Remy pressed.

Remy watched as Collin began to rock back and forth on the couch.

"Collin? Was it before we even started dating?"

Collin slowly removed his hands from his face, revealing red eyes and damp cheeks. "Probably. It probably was."

"That's all I needed to hear. Good-bye, Collin," Remy said, turning on her heel.

Remy hurried out of his apartment and into the hallway. Banging on the elevator call button, she tried to control the emotions and tears that were welling up within her. She felt as if her best friend, her lover, and a part of herself had just died.

"Who wants to get their ass kicked? It's all about the Benjamins' baby!" Steve said, throwing a crisp hundred-dollar bill on the airplane seat next to Brent.

"Didn't we get our asses kicked enough for one night?" Brent said, completely disinterested in the card game and wanting to stay engrossed in the latest book he was reading, *Invisible Life*, by E. Lynn Harris. The Flyers had lost game two to the Lakers, 78–109. No one was shooting well, least of all Brent. Good as his word, Coach had benched both Collin and Steve.

"Might as well take our minds off of it. There's nothing we can do about our fucked-up coach this late in the series," Steve said as he began to shuffle a deck of cards. "How 'bout you, Paul? You feel like a game of blackjack?"

"I don't feel like doing shit except strangling Coach," Paul said in disgust as he stared out the window.

Steve walked to Rick's seat. "Rick, my man! Now, I know you're good for a game. I think tonight might be your lucky night. I'll even start with two hundred for you," Steve said, leaning back and winking at Brent.

Brent shook his head as Steve attempted to entice Rick. Everyone knew Rick never turned down an offer to win some money. The whole team knew about Rick's gambling problems and his mounting debts.

"What? You hear that, fellas? Rick doesn't want to win any money tonight!" Steve said, looking back over his shoulder toward Brent and Paul. "Are you feeling all right, Rick?" Steve teased as he placed his hand up against Rick's forehead.

"Get your hand off me, man!" Rick began, smacking Steve's hand away. "I'm trying to get some sleep. Just 'cause you didn't play tonight don't mean nobody else ain't tired. Shit, you try guarding Shaquille's big ass for forty minutes in one night."

"All right, man. That's cool. You don't got to get so sensitive." Steve got up and started walking back toward Brent. "That's never stopped you before, but that's cool." Steve sat on the edge of Brent's seat and grinned sheepishly.

"Serves you right, trying to take advantage of him," Brent said.

"What are you so damn chipper about, Steve?" Paul asked. "Coach railroaded your ass and Collin's ass and cost us a game."

"I'm not happy. I'm mad as hell, too, but shit, what can I do about him benching me? He won't even talk to me, and I've tried, believe me. You know what a control freak he is. I guess he thinks he's teaching me a lesson or something."

"Yeah, well, it's gonna be a lesson that he regrets when we lose the championship, 'cause Rick can't keep up with Shaquille for five more games—if we make it that far," Brent said.

"Coach is gonna have to put you back in the rotation, Steve. That's all there is to it," Paul said seriously.

"Yeah, well, you try telling him that," Steve said, putting the deck of cards on Brent's tray.

"We already did, this morning, in fact," Brent said, glancing at Paul sitting across the row from him. Brent hesitated telling Steve about the conversation in the sauna, but then figured the players were all in this together.

Steve looked back and forth between Paul and Brent. "This morning? Y'all knew he wasn't going to play me this morning?"

Brent and Paul both nodded their heads.

"Because of Kelly's goddamn charges?" Steve demanded.

"He said it was an embarrassment to the NBA to have you playing in the finals amidst all the controversy in the press surrounding her allegations," Brent answered.

"What bullshit! Well, Coach may not be able to play that angle for long. I was finally able to reach Kelly yesterday, and she's agreed to meet me when I get back from L.A. I think I may be able to talk her into dropping the charges," Steve said.

"Why didn't you say something?" Paul asked.

"I just did."

"Well, according to Coach's logic, he can't keep benching you if Kelly drops the charges," Brent said as an idea began to emerge. "Is she going to make a public retraction statement?"

"I don't know, I didn't ask her all that."

"You know what, Brent?" Paul interrupted. "Even if she doesn't make a public retraction, we could get some leaks in the paper to print that reliable sources report that the trumped-up assault charges against Steve Tucker are being dropped," Paul said, looking at Brent.

"This way, Coach's NBA 'negative image reason' for benching Steve can justifiably be shot down," Brent said, finishing Paul's thought.

"Couldn't we ask Jake to use some of his connections?" asked Paul.

"Hell, that bastard didn't even help me get out of jail. Fuck him," Steve said.

"Jake represents Coach too; and it seems the troll always sides with Coach when push comes to shove," Brent said.

"It's bullshit that Coach benched his All-Star forward during the NBA championship because he's allegedly gay," Paul said. "That, coupled with you being benched, Steve, is almost enough to guarantee us losing."

"Well, Collin didn't help matters by skipping practice this morning," Steve said.

"My God, Steve, the most embarrassing photo of his life was plastered all over the city; give him a break! Would you have come to work if a picture of you was like that all over town?" Paul said curtly.

"Listen, you two. Never mind that stuff right now," Brent interrupted. "Collin missing practice this morning had nothing to do with him being benched tonight. Coach told us this morning, before practice, that he planned on taking Collin out of the rotation before Collin had even skipped practice."

"I've been thinking about how Coach was talking about how sponsors were going to pull out if Collin played in the game and how the so-called 'powers that be' were making all of these decisions," Paul said. "The *Post* article just came out this morning. How could he have talked to all those sponsors, Commissioner McDeavitt, and the powers that be by, say . . . seven-thirty in the morning, Eastern time. I don't think that's possible. And even if he had talked to them, how would they have reached such monumental decisions so quickly—like pulling million-dollar advertising spots for the game tonight? It's bullshit. Coach has been acting funny ever since we made it to the Eastern Conference finals. I've got a mind to call those sponsors myself."

"Whoa. What are y'all talking about? I'm lost," Steve said, looking bewildered.

"It's like . . . like Coach was deliberately trying to make us lose, and blow air up our asses trying to cover his own," Brent said.

"But I don't understand why Coach would do that. He's always been about winning at all costs. Coach's whole MO is winning," Steve said.

"Winning at all costs. Winning at all costs," Brent repeated. "But not tonight. Tonight he was not about winning at all costs. Ever since I've known Coach, that's how he operated—doing anything and everything for the big win, even the small ones. Hell, the dirtier and harder a guy played on the court, the more time Coach would give him. He even gave tips on how to foul the shit out of an opponent without getting caught by the refs. The coach I know would have never let an accusation of domestic abuse keep one of his best players out of a game. Hell, he'd normally be the first one in front of the camera denying all of the allegations on behalf of his player. And he'd keep the team running normally until further investigation into the matter. He wouldn't risk losing. Shit! He's covered up past incidents similar to this. Steve, you're not the first Flyer ever accused of domestic violence." Brent was trembling when he finished.

"And he tried to give us this bogus argument that the NBA has an image to protect and that Commissioner McDeavitt is breathing down his neck," Paul chimed in.

"Paul, since when has Coach been intimidated by the commissioner?" Brent asked.

"Never, as far as I can remember. The two of them have gone head to head for years. Coach loves a good fight, and if it's with Commissioner McDeavitt, all the better," Paul responded.

"Exactly," Brent said.

"He's bullshitting us, but why?" Paul said. "Why doesn't Coach want us to win?"

"Maybe Coach *is* playing to win," Brent slowly said. "Maybe there's just another game going on that we don't know about."

Trina sat alone amidst three other couples in the waiting room of her obstetrician's office. She had grown accustomed to these solo visits to the doctor.

Trina removed her grocery list from her black leather Coach sack purse. She had several items to pick up for the desserts; already she had more orders than she could possibly fill. She'd sent around samples and an advertisement to all the owner-run bak- eries and local caterers in Stamford and Greenwich, Connecti- cut. This was prime wed- ding and graduation season, so the caterers welcomed the extra supply of desserts. It probably didn't hurt that she was Rick Belleville's wife. Trina just prayed she'd be successful.

Trina had managed to secure a short-term business loan, using the house as collateral. Rick's agent had helped her set up a repayment plan for Rick's debt. He'd also told her that Rick had been attending Gambler's Anonymous, though how often, Trina wondered. He was in the middle of the NBA championship round. Besides, she knew if Rick was to change, it wouldn't happen overnight.

"Mrs. Belleville. Mrs. Belleville," one of the nurses called from behind a glass wall.

"Yes. That's me," she answered, not wanting to draw attention to herself.

"Dr. McCray is ready for you now."

Trina never understood why doctors called for patients when they were not ready to see them. She had gotten undressed from the waist down and was sitting on the edge of the hard examination table dangling her legs. The cloth gown she'd been given only covered the front of her body. Trina was embarrassed when she glanced down at her ashy feet and chipped burgundy toenail polish. She was getting antsy and cold sitting in the sterile room half dressed.

The previous excitement Trina had experienced when she'd been pregnant with Monica and Marcus was absent. She was moments away from finding out the sex of her baby and she felt little emotion. Trina had been moving in lackluster circles ever since Rick had gone. If it were not for the kids' needs and Aunt Thelma's easy companionship, she may have never gotten out of bed. She missed the certainty of knowing that Rick would be there for her and their children. And she missed Rick.

Dr. Ruthie McCray finally sauntered into the room, smiling from ear to ear, with her tortoiseshell glasses only slightly obscuring her bright green eyes. As the statuesque doctor looked around the small room, Trina realized she was searching for Rick. Trina had an ache in her heart wishing that Rick could have been there to share in this moment. She stared at Dr. McCray's simple gold wedding band as she quickly read over Trina's chart and wondered if her marriage was one of wedded bliss or if she ever experienced problems with her own husband.

Trina lay back at Dr. McCray's direction and jumped when the cold gel was spread over her ever-expanding stomach.

"So Mr. Belleville won't be joining us today, huh? Trying to beat the Lakers on their turf? Well, I sure hope they can bring a championship home to New York," Dr. McCray said as she moved the Doppler mechanism in circular motions over Trina's stomach.

Trina only nodded her head.

Even at the doctor's office, partially nude, Trina was unable to escape who she was married to. In the past, questions surrounding Rick's career had flattered her. She had always thrived on his accomplishments. But recently the luster of his career had begun to fade. She had her own personal goals to accomplish; no longer was she content to bask in the glow of his light.

Suddenly there was nothing glamorous about being married to Rick Belleville, the NBA star. Reality had replaced glamour. Trina was alone, tending to a pregnancy that only one parent wanted.

"It looks like you have a little boy! See there?" Dr. McCray said, pointing to the screen displaying the fetal image. "Looks like another basketball player in the making."

"I hope not," Trina said under her breath, staring at the speckled ceiling.

"He's a busy little thing. You see him, Mrs. Belleville?"

Trina slowly turned her head toward the monitor and watched her baby's black-and-white floating image on the screen. It was hard to believe that he was swimming around inside of her. She was the holding tank for this new life, and she had no idea what their future held. She could not say with any degree of certainty that this unborn child would ever spend any birthdays or holidays with his father.

For the first time, she did not have the security of knowing she could depend on her husband when the baby came. It was a sobering feeling. At least with Monica and Marcus, she'd been able to count on his presence with some regularity. And thinking about it, really that was all he did—show his face every now and then. Trina thought about Rick's involvement with his children, and the only thing that came to mind was him picking up Monica on his shoulders occasionally or taking Marcus to practice with him every now and then.

As Trina began to ponder her husband's role as a father, she realized that Rick rarely helped the children with their homework. He never even sat on the floor and played with them. What would her unborn baby be missing other than unfulfilled expectations? No matter how much she missed him, if Rick ever wanted to come back home, he was going to have to work on a whole lot more than remedying his gambling problem. He had to learn to put family first. Trina had known long ago that she came second place. But the children deserved to be number one in their father's life.

Casey leaned back in her chair, clasping both of her hands behind her head, and stole a glance at Nikki. The little girl abruptly sat back in her miniature chair with her chubby hands locked behind her head, mimicking Casey. Quickly sitting forward, Casey placed her elbows on her desk and put her open palms under her chin. Nikki imitated her once again, resting her tiny elbows on the play table Brent had bought for her. The table had been in the kitchen, but since Nikki liked to color in Casey's home office while she worked, they had moved it there. All morning long, whenever Casey made the slightest shift of her body, Nikki would try and do the exact same thing. Even when Casey was on the phone, Nikki pretended that she was talking as well, repeating blurbs from Casey's conversation.

Nikki's mother, Shauna, had yet to return. Casey knew by now that Shauna was not suffering from any illness as she had claimed when she first dropped Nikki off on their doorstep. She simply had another agenda—one that did not include raising a child. Casey had walked in on a conversation between Brent and Nikki's mother. She had called Brent two weeks ago, claiming she had personal problems and couldn't handle Nikki in *her* life right now but that she planned on depositing Nikki with some nameless cousin in Grand Rapids, Michigan. Understandably, Brent had been outraged at the prospect of Nikki living with a strange cousin of Shauna's. He was furious at Shauna for even suggesting it. Truthfully, Brent would have been outraged at the thought of Nikki being anyplace except with him and Casey. Of course, this had been exactly what Nikki's mother was counting on— Brent's fierce love for his daughter. He had played right into her hands when he told Shauna Nikki wasn't going anywhere. Showing her colors, Shauna had reacted by putting a price tag on her own daughter's head. Casey had tried to explain to him that legally he had just as much right to be with Nikki. But Brent had been so shaken up, it didn't matter to him that what Shauna was attempting amounted to extortion. He simply wrote her a check in hopes of getting her out of their lives. Brent just didn't understand that they couldn't buy her off forever. Casey was well aware that the custodial issue regarding Nikki could ultimately only be resolved in court or arbitration. Brent didn't want to hear it, though. His only concern was for his daughter to be with them right now.

The truth was, Casey felt sorry for the innocent little girl. It was obvious that Shauna was using both Brent and Nikki. Casey didn't want to see Nikki hurt any more than she already had been.

Casey was supposed to be at work right now, but Martha was visiting her daughter who had just given birth. And the alternate babysitter had called in sick at the last minute. The timing could not have been worse. Casey was working against a deadline for one of her clients, the Harlem Renaissance Theatre Company, and she needed to file a temporary injunctive order within the next twenty-four hours against one of the major Broadway production companies. The company was trying to cancel HRTC's remaining performances of *Body and Soul* because of pressure from right-wing religious groups claiming that the subject matter of the play was lewd, lascivious, and obscene. The religious group's assertions that the production was patently offensive scared the production company into trying to censor its own partner, HRTC, in the joint venture.

Casey probably would have been more upset about the cancellation if Nikki had not gotten so excited when she found out that Casey was not going to leave. It was fortunate for Casey that she did not have any actual meetings today or she would have been forced to take Nikki to the office with her and leave her with her secretary. Now Casey only needed a messenger to come to her apartment and pick up the temporary injunctive order that she'd been able to pull up from her home computer, which was connected to her office system. Brent was not due back in town until tomorrow morning, and Casey had been taking care of Nikki in the evenings when she returned from work.

For the past week the two had been following a comfortable routine. They had dinner together each evening, then Casey would bathe her and they would play with some of Nikki's new toys until it was time for Casey to read her a bedtime story.

A couple of times Casey actually found herself rushing home, wanting to see the little girl run to the front door to greet her. Once she'd arrived home late and found Nikki in the foyer, half asleep on the floor, with the pictures she had colored for Casey clutched in her small hands. The baby-sitter had said she hadn't been able to get her to move from the spot. That nearly broke Casey's heart.

"What are you doing, little girl?" Casey said, squeezing Nikki's button nose. "Are you acting like me?"

"Yes." Nikki nodded. "I Casey. I go to work."

"Is that what you're doing? You're working like me?" Casey asked, smiling.

Nikki nodded again. "I busy. I very busy. See?" Nikki said as she tucked her head over the paper in front of her and began to scribble.

Casey quizzically looked at Nikki and wondered what she knew about Casey being busy. She was only three years old.

"Who told you I was busy?" Casey asked as Nikki continued to draw on the papers.

"See, Casey, see?" Nikki said, holding up her work for Casey's inspection.

"Oh, that's pretty, Nikki," Casey said, looking at Nikki's picture.

"It's for you, Casey. It's Nikki's work."

"Nikki. Who told you I was busy?" Casey gently asked the little girl, curious as to why she made that comment.

"Daddy say Casey busy. Daddy say Casey very busy," Nikki said, trying to sound like a reprimanding adult.

"Daddy said that?"

"Daddy say Casey busy. Be good little girl and leave Casey lone. I be quiet. I work too, Casey." Nikki started drawing another picture.

She and Brent had not exercised any birth control methods since her second miscarriage, but their efforts at getting pregnant had failed. Finally Casey's doctor had told her that because of an earlier ectopic pregnancy, her chances of ever carrying a pregnancy to term were slim. She had cried herself to sleep on many occasions thinking about the doctor's bleak prognosis, but with Brent's constant support, she was beginning to accept her situation. They had all sorts of high-tech methods to choose from, the doctor had told them. But to Casey, it wasn't an option—it didn't seem like the way babies were supposed to happen.

Now her life had taken another unexpected turn. Much to her surprise, she had begun to feel a sense of gratification and renewed purpose since Nikki came into her life. And Brent loved Nikki's being there, a part of them. He relished his role as father and was eating it up with delight. She was seeing on a constant basis a side of Brent she had glimpsed only rarely when Brent Jr. was in town. The daddy side of Brent. The nurturer, mentor—a man she liked.

"Casey, this for you too," Nikki said, handing her another work of art.

"Thank you, sweetheart. This is so pretty."

"You want me make you another, Casey?" Nikki hopefully asked.

"I'd love that."

"You would?" Nikki said as her eyes widened.

"I sure would," Casey said, beginning to feel morose.

Casey watched as Nikki worked, an intent look on her face, the crayon held tightly between her tiny fingers. She was a special little girl. There was no doubt about that.

As she stared at the child who adored her, Casey wondered if she could overcome the circumstances of Nikki's conception enough to love her with an unencumbered heart. Casey wished she had the overflowing capacity to completely love this child as her own, but she just didn't know if she was capable. When would God grant her a forgiving heart?

Steve was ringing Kelly's doorbell. She'd moved to a modest suburban town in New Jersey, outside of Philadelphia. The town-house rental she had found so fast was beautiful: a long, airy contemporary three-story unit with a connecting two-car garage. As usual, he marveled how quickly she'd pulled it all together, found a place to live and all. Kelly has landed on her feet, again, Steve thought.

He was about to press the bell again and then Kelly was standing before him. She was wearing a sleek black knit outfit, which hugged the contours of her beautiful body. She wore a row of thin gold bangles on her right arm, and Steve noticed a beautiful new diamond solitaire ring flashing on Kelly's left hand. Another unknowing victim, he mused.

"Hi, Steve, why don't you come in." Kelly stood aside and motioned Steve inside.

"Is Diamond here?"

"No, a friend of mine is watching her. I thought it might be too confusing for her to see you."

Steve was ready to jump, but resisted. There was something about Kelly's calm demeanor that made him think she was actually being straight with him. He looked around the comfortably furnished house. She had decorated in typical Kelly style. A leopard-print couch sat in the middle of the living room, flanked by two large black leather chairs. He walked into the room and noticed a trophy sitting on the fireplace mantel. Curious, he moved closer and read the engraving: 1997 *NCAA BIG EAST PLAYER OF THE YEAR.*

"Is he a friend of yours or did this just come with the house?" Steve asked, turning toward Kelly.

"Actually, both," Kelly said with a smirk on her face.

Some things never change, Steve thought.

"So what did you do with all the furniture from the other house?"

"Left it—I assumed you'd want to deal with it. Keep it—sell it, whatever. Anyway, I wanted a clean break. Why, don't you like it?"

"No, no," Steve said apologetically. "It's just that I was surprised . . ."

"At?" Kelly was smiling now.

"I don't know. I guess all you've done. So . . ."

"So I'm assuming you're here about the assault charges." Kelly paused and looked down. "Well, let's put it this way; I think I've changed my mind."

Was she going to be this easy? Steve thought. No way, not Kelly. She must have something up her sleeve. "Like I said to you on the phone, I thought we could work this out between us."

"I know, I know. Truthfully, Steve, I don't want to go over that whole mess again. What I've got to say won't take long."

"What you've got to say?" Steve was on red alert.

"Yeah, what I've got to say," Kelly said flatly.

"Why the hell you'd do it, Kelly? How about startin' there?"

"Listen, Steve, I told you, I'm not interested in going backward . . . Sometimes in life you have to . . . to do things, to make choices . . . even if they don't seem totally right at the time, but maybe under the circumstances, the choices seem a little right . . ."

"There was nothing right about any of the choices you made with me," Steve said, not believing that she was trying to justify her lies once again.

"They didn't only concern me, all right?" Kelly began, raising her voice. "I was thinking about Diamond's future . . . and you were so cold to us. You just turned your back on us, like we weren't your family—"

"*I* turned my back on you all?" Steve asked, incredulously. It was just like Kelly to switch the situation around and make herself a victim. The nerve of her. Steve forced himself to be calm. He came here to get Kelly to drop the charges, not get her angry.

"And I didn't know what else to do and . . . and they made . . . I . . . couldn't refuse . . ." Kelly sputtered.

"Whoa! What do you mean you couldn't refuse?" Steve said, wondering if she was trying to shift the blame to someone else.

"I did what I had to do, and what's done is done. Now . . . now I . . ."

"What you had to do? Kelly, what are you talking about?" Steve wondered what Kelly had gotten herself into this time. He just wished she would keep him out of it.

"Steve, that's over, that's water under the bridge."

"For you maybe. My whole career could be on the line. My reputation is already ruined. Why'd you do it, Kelly? Why?"

"I said it's over, Steve."

"What's over, Kelly? What?"

"Look, I want to get on with my life," Kelly resolutely said.

"You and me both."

"I'm willing to make a deal with you," she quickly said, casting her eyes down.

"What kind of deal?" Steve asked warily, seeing Kelly's wheels spin. She knew she had him by the balls.

"I paid for this house with the last of my savings."

"Savings?" Steve said. "Don't you mean the funds you emptied out of our joint account, Kelly?"

"Whatever, Steve. Look, I needed the money. What was I supposed to do? You abandoned us."

"Slow your roll, Kelly. How about getting a job, or going back to school? Do something productive with your life."

"That's easy for you to say. I have a child to raise, and right now I'm working hard at being a single parent. After all the fuss Daryl made in the papers, he flew the coop. I guess he thought you'd give him money. Anyway, I need some help for Diamond's school. I'll drop the charges if—well, not if—I'll drop the charges and—"

"And I will help support Diamond?" Steve paused and then said, "Of course. But, Kelly, you've got to know that I never changed the account I had set up for Diamond. I promised I would always take care of her, and I meant it."

As Steve watched the tears roll down Kelly's face, he knew there was more behind them than gratitude. He was seeing something else in her face that her words had almost revealed minutes before. But what?

"Steve, can I ask you one thing?"

He nodded his head.

"What's happened to us? I was so . . . so . . ."

"Kelly," Steve said. "Let's not even go there. Please don't start playing that role with me. We both know why things didn't work out between us, and it's not even necessary to retrace our steps on that subject."

Steve continued to study Kelly's face, thinking about what she'd said to him, or maybe more to herself, today.

"Let me ask you something, Kelly. What couldn't you refuse?"

"What are you talking about?"

"A few minutes ago you said you couldn't refuse something. What were you talking about?"

"Steve . . . don't . . ."

"You said you did what you had to do. Was it what you had to do, or was it something else?"

"What's the use going over this? I'm gonna drop the charges now anyway."

"Going over what? Tell me what there is to go over."

"Steve, there's no point. I can't . . . They'd . . . I just can't . . ."

"Kelly, did someone put you up to this? I think I have a right to know."

"Steve, just leave well enough alone. I told you it's over now."

Steve couldn't imagine why anyone would want him behind bars or to ruin his reputation, but he did know that whatever Kelly did, money was usually the motivating force behind it. And if he had any chance of getting her to talk, he'd have to speak her language.

"Kelly, you said you wanted my financial assistance. Well, right now I need your help."

"Steve . . ." Kelly began, as she turned away from him, probably so he couldn't see her smile.

"Kelly, cut it. What'll it cost me to find out?"

"Steve! It's not only about that anymore . . . I would tell you . . . I know I should tell you . . . but you say you'd give me some extra financial assistance?" Kelly looked like her mouth was watering as she turned back around.

"When you drop the charges and publicly retract your allegations."

"But then they wouldn't—"

"And," Steve cut her off, "when you tell me who's behind this."

"But, Steve . . ."

"Damn it, Kelly!" Steve's patience was just about used up, but he still had to get through to her. "That's the least you could do after turning my life upside down, not that you would care. You don't ever care about anyone except yourself."

For a flicker of a second, Steve could have sworn that he saw a look that could only be described as remorse pass over Kelly's face.

"Kelly, please. I'll hold up my end. I've been more than fair with you. Please, Kelly."

"I don't know if you really want to know."

"Who, Kelly?"

"All of them, they're all in it together."

Steve stared at Kelly, totally baffled as she slowly approached him and leaned her head forward next to his. In hushed tones, Kelly spilled out the whole story, and Steve could scarcely believe what he was hearing.

"What the . . . !" Lorraine screamed, and dropped the iron to the floor, spilling water in the process.

Paul looked at Lorraine in confusion. "Baby, it's just me," he said, troubled by the look of terror in her eyes as she turned around to face him.

"Damn, Paul! Don't that. You scared the raine said as she hell out of me," Lorraine said as she kneeled on the ground and wiped up the spilled water.

"I'm sorry. I didn't mean to frighten you," Paul said as he leaned down to help her.

He had just returned from Los Angeles, and the Flyers were in an uphill battle struggling to win the championship. The Lakers were ahead three games to two in the best-of-seven championship series. They were going to have to win the next two games at the Mecca. But Paul's faith was shaken. Coach still had not put Steve in the lineup, no matter how many times they explained to him that Kelly planned on dropping the charges. Surprisingly, Paul and Brent had even gotten some of the sports-beat writers to plant stories stating that the bogus charges against Steve Tucker were soon to be dropped. Hell, Steve was practically a hero out there—yet he was benched. And Collin also remained out of the rotation. Paul felt as if he had aged twenty years over the past week. He watched in silence as his wife continued to iron her nursing scrubs. After the Flyers' disastrous road trip, all he wanted was for her to turn and pull him into her warm embrace. She shrugged him away.

"You shouldn't walk up on people like that."

"I wasn't walking up on people, I was trying to give my wife, who I haven't seen for a week, a hug," Paul said. "But I guess that's too much to ask for these days."

"Look, just drop it, Paul. How was your road trip?" Lorraine asked, brushing off her uniform.

"You know what, Lorraine?" Paul began, feeling as if his last ounce of patience was just about to break. "Don't even worry about it. I'm going to take a nap."

Lorraine stared back. "A nap? I was trying to ask you about your trip, but you go on and take your nap."

"Fine," Paul said.

"Fine."

This is ridiculous, Paul thought. He turned back and retraced his steps into the laundry room where Lorraine was standing massaging her temples.

"Lorraine, what's going on between us? Why all the attitude with me?" Paul said.

"Paul, I don't have an attitude. You just scared me when you walked up on me like that."

"Come on, Lorraine. I know you better than that. What's wrong with you? Is it me?"

"No, Paul, it's not you."

"Is it work? Are you just stressed out from work? Is that it?"

Lorraine did not respond as she continued to rub her head.

"I know you've been working a lot of hours lately and it can't be easy. Maybe you can use some of your vacation time right now and give yourself a break for the week. Two more games and my season will be over. I won't have to go out of town anytime soon. What do you think?" Paul said, stepping in closer to Lorraine.

Lorraine seemed to grow anxious as he neared her. "Paul, I don't need a vacation," she said, backing away from him.

"Well, you need something, because you're jumping out of your skin right now."

"I need my work. I'd go crazy if I didn't go to the hospital," Lorraine said as she nervously fiddled with her hair.

"I think you need a break." Paul continued to move forward to touch his wife.

"Paul, I'm fine. You're making a big deal out of nothing. Now, would you just back off?"

It was plain she was far from fine. Her entire body language was screaming that something was wrong.

"No. I won't just back off. Something's wrong with you. You have dark circles under your eyes . . . you've lost weight . . . you're jumping at your own shadow . . . and you won't even let me near you. Something's not right. Baby, please tell me what's wrong," Paul gently asked.

Lorraine shook her head, but she still did not meet Paul's eyes. He felt at a loss. Why couldn't he get through to her?

The phone rang and Paul saw a look of horror register across Lorraine's face.

"One second," Paul worriedly said to his wife as he turned to answer the phone.

"Don't answer it!" Lorraine said with such urgency that it startled Paul.

"Why don't you want me to answer the phone?"

"Just don't pick it up. Please," Lorraine said, moving toward Paul and grasping his arms. "Just stay right here with me."

Paul stared at his wife with mounting confusion and apprehension. "Or is there someone you don't want me to talk to?"

"No one, Paul. It's no one." As much as she had avoided him before, she clutched him to her now, squeezing his arms more tightly with each ring of the phone.

"I'm answering it since you won't tell me anything. Maybe I'll ask whoever's calling what's going on," Paul said, pulling away from Lorraine, suddenly angry. Just as he reached the receiver, she ran up behind him.

"No, Paul. Don't answer it." Lorraine tried to pull the phone from his hand.

Paul ignored her and knocked her arm away as he lifted the phone to his ear. "Hello!"

"Paul? You all right?" Brent said on the other end of the line.

Paul felt the tension release from his body at the sound of his team-mate's voice.

"I'm fine, man; what's up?" Paul said, turning his back on Lorraine. It looked like she was trying to figure out who was on the phone.

"Look, we need to talk sometime before the game. You wouldn't believe what Steve just told me. I'm trippin' out here. I think I might know what's up with Coach now."

"All right," Paul began. He desperately wanted to know what was going on with his team, but right now his mind was on his wife. "Let's do that, but I can't right now."

"Hey . . . wait," Brent said into Paul's ear.

"I'll hit you back."

"Okay, man. Later," Brent said, sounding disappointed as he hung up.

Paul abruptly turned toward Lorraine and looked at her pointedly. "Lorraine, are you having an affair?"

A look of shock appeared on her face. "Absolutely not! Paul, it's not that. It's nothing like that. Baby, I promise, I would never cheat on you."

"Then what is it? Can't anybody tell the truth around here?"

Lorraine did not respond.

"My God. What is going on?" Paul began, more to himself than to Lorraine. "I can't get the truth from my agent. I don't know what the hell is going on with Coach and the whole damn team! Can't I at least count on some honesty from my wife? Like for starters, who did you think was on the phone?" Paul said as his voice began to involuntarily rise to the point of hollering. "Who did you think was calling here? And while we're at it, who was on the phone that day in the bathroom when you looked like you had seen a ghost? Lorraine, I'm telling you,

I can't take this anymore! I want the truth!" Paul said, banging his fist against the wall.

Lorraine's whole body began to shake as the tears rolled like a waterfall.

"Is it that bad, Lorraine?"

"Paul . . . it wasn't my . . ." Lorraine began in between sobs. "It wasn't my fault. I tried to help."

"What wasn't your fault?" Paul said, fearing the anguished expression on his wife's face.

"I didn't kill her. I know her mother blames me . . . but they said they would kill my mother and me if I said . . . if I said anything to the police," Lorraine cried.

Paul could not believe the words coming out of Lorraine's mouth. She was acting delusional. He walked over to the corner his wife was cowering in and cupped her face with both of his hands.

"Shhhh," he comforted her. "It'll be all right."

Soon she met Paul's eyes, and to him it looked like she was fighting off invisible demons.

"But I saw them kill her. I saw them do it."

"Lorraine, look at me. Did you witness something at the hospital, with the doctors?" he asked as she closed her eyes.

"No. The Disciples, they did it."

"You're not making sense." Paul knew he was witnessing some kind of trauma.

"They were a gang in Harlem when I was in high school."

"And what did they do?"

"They killed a little girl. Her name was Crissy. I found out later, her name was Crissy Jackson and she was her mother's only child," Lorraine said quietly.

"And you were there?"

"Yeah, I was there and I saw everything. Paul, I was in the car with the gang when they . . . shot her, and I jumped out and tried to save her, but it was too late. I was too late. I couldn't do anything else. I was only in high school. I didn't know how to save her." Lorraine covered her face.

Paul tried to hide his shock; he didn't want to upset her further.

Was this true? Did this really happen? Had she been keeping a secret this devastating from him for all these years? But why? He wondered what was making her relive the whole experience now.

"So what happened to the Disciples?"

"Nothing, thanks to me. I was too scared to tell the police anything. Oh, they questioned me and they questioned me, but all I ever said was, 'I didn't see a thing.' The Disciples put the word out on the street that if I talked, my mother was dead and then I was next. I covered my ass and that's all I did. So I never said a thing. But I knew exactly who did it. I knew their names, their addresses, their telephone numbers, what schools they went to. I had to see them every day, but I never said a thing." She repeated the refrain—a cry from her heart. Lorraine stared straight through Paul.

He was shocked at what he was hearing, but at the same time he realized that the pieces were starting to come together.

"You've been going through this by yourself all this time. Why didn't you ever tell me? You know you could have talked to me about it. I'm so sorry this happened to you. So this is the reason you've been having nightmares, isn't it?"

"Yes."

"Now, tell me, when did this happen?"

"The spring of my senior year in high school. I hadn't turned seventeen yet. Then I left to go to Howard and it just like fell out of mind. Every so often a little piece would tease at me. So I prayed on it the best I could. But it was like a hole in my mind—like shock." Lorraine began moving away from the corner toward Paul. "Then after you got big, the endorsements from McDonald's, Gatorade, and Reebok brought you so much attention."

"That's what the phone stuff was about?" Paul asked, not quite understanding.

"The girl, Crissy, her mother got our number and started calling here threatening me and telling me how I was going to have to pay for her little girl's death since I let her killers get away."

"How'd she find you?"

"Apparently she had seen our picture together in the newspaper." Lorraine began sobbing. "Then it all came back. I couldn't stop thinking about it. For the last few months it's like I've been possessed. One night I got home late—I told you, a little boy had come in on a drive-by. It's been hell ever since. Between the phone calls, the memories, the guilt—I think I'm losing my mind.

"I don't know what to do now, Paul. Just getting the number changed isn't going to stop Crissy's mom from harassing me. Hell, I don't blame her for calling me out. If Crissy had been my little girl, I'd probably be doing the same thing. There was no reason that her murderers should have ever walked the streets again," Lorraine said, looking at Paul for the first time.

"Let's notify the police," Paul said.

"No way! I don't want to call the police on that poor woman! She's been through enough," Lorraine said vehemently, shaking her head.

"Not on her. Maybe you *did* have a reason not to report them years ago when you and your mother's life could have been in danger. But what's stopping you from reporting them now? Didn't you say you knew all of their names?"

"First, middle, and last names, those details all came back—and I can't forget them," Lorraine said, glancing up at Paul.

"There's no statute of limitations for murder. Report the bastards now. The police will track them down, if they're not already dead or in jail. But at least this way, you're doing the right thing. They can't hurt you now," Paul said, grabbing Lorraine's hand.

"But what about us, Paul? What if the Disciples try to come after us?" Lorraine asked, concerned.

"Come here, woman," Paul said, pulling Lorraine into his arms. "Do you think I would ever let anybody harm you?"

"But what if they—"

"They're not gonna do anything to either one of us. That gang probably isn't even together anymore, and even if they are, they're not getting near us. Trust me on this." Paul took his wife in his arms and finally embraced her.

"It's hard, huh?" Casey said as Trina ended her phone call with Rick.

"The hardest thing I've ever done in my life." Trina's voice was shaky. "I need to run upstairs and check on Monica and her friend. They're a little too quiet. If the buzzer rings, take the cake out of the oven for me, will ya?"

As Trina hurried out of the kitchen, Casey could not help but marvel at her for-titude. With two chil-dren, another one on the way, a husband who could offer only problems, no support, and the challenge of a new business, Trina was holding up well. What amazed Casey the most were the changes she saw in Trina. With all the ambivalence Casey felt about her own marriage, she never actually visualized asking Brent to leave, and being able to stick to such a decision.

Casey looked up as Trina returned to the kitchen with a bemused expression on her face. "Monica and her little friend were on the bed kissing the pillows—like they were making out with boys. I don't know where she gets that stuff," Trina said, looking at the oven timer.

"Yeah, kids are like sponges."

"Well, she must have gotten that from school or one of her friends' houses, 'cause she ain't never seen me and Rick kiss the way she was kissing that pillow. I feel sorry for her life-size Barbie doll; no telling what she does to her."

The aroma of the baking cake permeated the air as Trina removed it from the oven and placed it on the island counter. She seemed to go far away for a moment, then she returned to their earlier conversation.

"The hardest thing about all of this is that I really miss him . . . in a different way than when he's just on the road. You know what I mean?"

Casey slowly nodded her head. But inside, she couldn't imagine it. As much as Casey was perceived as independent by the other Flyers women, she knew that she was definitely no pillar of strength. She never even considered asking Brent to leave after finding out he had gotten another woman pregnant. In fact, the only thing she had done over the last three years was beat herself up for remaining in the marriage.

Sitting on the barstool in Trina's kitchen, Casey realized that she had been in a holding pattern of uncertainty since Brent's infidelity. Watching a determined Trina as she spread the thick, sweet glaze over the warm cake, Casey envied Trina's decisiveness about her children and her business venture; but what she admired most of all was how she had handled her husband. Trina had asserted herself in her marriage and had made her decision out of love for her family and herself.

Trina suddenly glanced up at Casey and waved the spreading knife in the air. "I had no other choice, though."

Casey leaned her head to the side as she looked at Trina. "About what?"

A serious expression clouded her face as she stared at Casey across the counter. Trina began to speak and stopped a couple of times before finally uttering a word.

"Something just snapped in me . . . what I was feeling about my . . . my and Rick's baby. Like, he didn't want another child. That's why it took me so long to finally break it to him. But you see, there was still this part of me that believed he'd react differently if I told him I was pregnant. I guess I kind of had my hopes up that he would secretly be happy . . . you know, that he might accept it." Trina shook her head. "I'd been disappointed by him before, but nothing like that. No, nothing where he had rejected our family. I knew I still loved him and that I still wanted to be his wife, but I wasn't going to let him do anything to destroy our family."

Casey wondered whether she could somehow apply what Trina was saying to her situation with Brent. "So what did it come down to, Trina?"

"My children. It was my children. He wanted me to back down from something that was against everything I stand for, questioning my own pregnancy, . . . and you know the funny thing about it, Casey? I didn't even know how important my own beliefs were to me until I was up against the wall."

"So you chose your children over him?" Casey asked.

"I chose my children and myself. Both are part of me. I know I did the right thing, and one day we may even be a family again."

"What makes you want that so badly? I mean, how do you know that Rick wouldn't just disappoint you again if you got back together?" Casey asked.

"I don't know anything for certain. I guess that's why I told him to leave in the first place. I only knew that he wasn't happy with 'having another mouth to feed,' as he put it. That didn't make no sense to me. Not to be able to accept your own child? I couldn't understand that. And then for him to say that it all came down to money, with all that gambling he was doing; it just wasn't right."

Casey loved Brent with every ounce of her being, but why couldn't she figure out what to do about her relationship? There was an inner tug-of-war going on, and she wanted desperately to come to peace with her situation. She recognized that Brent was a good man, but she was stuck like a record replaying his adulterous act. She just couldn't forgive him.

"Why do you think I never made Brent go?" Casey asked, feeling confused.

Trina looked at her and then said, "What do you mean?"

"I mean, I certainly had plenty of ammunition to send his ass packing. Why didn't I kick him out and be done with him? I must be a fool."

"What are you talking about? Every time I've seen you and Brent together, I only wished Rick would be that sensitive and loving toward me. He's so sweet on you."

Casey revealed more of her private life to Trina than to any other person—except Remy. She had always been careful to be the model wife in the circle of Flyers women—except for Alexis, of course. With everyone else she was always ready to listen. She was the one to whom everyone entrusted their deep, dark secrets. Not only did she choose to keep her personal issues private, she also somehow believed that since everyone thought she was strong, she had no place to take her own weaknesses or those of her relationship.

"He's done some things." Casey hesitated. "Brent's done some messed-up stuff, you know what I mean?"

"When, Casey?" Trina skeptically said.

"A while ago, recently . . . Hell, I don't know. It's just hard for me to forgive him," Casey said, standing up and walking to the window.

"Casey, most of us know about the little girl. And I know that must have been hard for you to go through. But it's also clear how you two love one another *and* like one another. Brent respects you and appreciates you. And I can tell, no matter what's happened between you, that you feel the same way toward him." Trina approached Casey.

"What if I can't ever trust him again, and what if trust is not enough to make a difference?"

"There's no doubt he made a mistake and that he hurt you. But perhaps there's a way to forgive him so that you two can focus on the good stuff you have."

"But he fucked everything up!"

Trina threw the knife in the sink as she finished icing the cake. "Is that right? Well, tell me why—no, tell yourself why you're still with him."

Trina wasn't holding back. She was asking questions Casey hadn't had the courage to ask herself. Adultery was at odds with every image she'd had of marriage growing up as a child. Monogamy was supposed to be a given. The fact that infidelity had entered her marriage had rocked her belief system to the core. And then to learn he had lied again.

"Casey, let's just say that there's a chance the two of you can work things out. What does he have to do to win back your trust?"

Casey continued looking out the window watching the drizzle, the indecisive prelude to the rain that refused to come. "Well, how do I know that there's a chance for us to get it right?"

"How do you know there's not? Have you even given it a chance?"

"I don't know what to do. It's like I can't even make a decision to stay or leave."

"Is there something else you're waiting for Brent to do to prove his love to you? If you love him, why can't you forgive him?"

"Trina, love's not all there is to a relationship . . . a marriage. You've got to have trust."

"Sometimes it's a leap of faith you gotta take. But you want to know what I think? I think you *can* put your faith in Brent," Trina said. She removed her apron, revealing a full, rounded belly beneath a snug velour shirt.

"How can I forgive him? How can I forget what he's done when his daughter is a constant reminder of his infidelity?"

Trina walked up to Casey and rubbed her thin shoulders. "Sit down, Casey. I want to tell you something that I've learned in fourteen years of marriage." She led Casey to the kitchen table. "I'm gonna be blunt with you, just like my aunt Thelma had to be with me a short while ago. Casey, there comes a time when you have to be a woman. You have to make decisions, not just for yourself, 'cause that's a given. But you know what else you gotta do? You gotta make decisions for your family and about your family, whether you like it or not. And if you don't think you can do that, you know what you gotta do? Casey, you need to shit or get off the pot, for everyone's sake. Right now, whether you realize it or not, Brent is your family as well as Brent Jr., and now so is his daughter. For better or worse, that's part of the commitment you made to him when you committed to be his family."

Casey shook her head. "Well, that commitment didn't include him cheating on me and fathering a child in the process."

"But you're still married to him?"

"Yes."

"Well, is he sorry?"

"He claims he is."

"Is he good to you?"

"Yes."

"How do you feel when you're with him?"

Casey thought about repeating the first word that came to her mind at Trina's question, but she was almost embarrassed to say it for fear that she would sound foolish.

"Well? How do you feel when he's with you, when you're with him? What's it feel like to you, girl?"

"It feels . . . I guess the best word to describe it is . . . is 'divine,' " Casey said, feeling her cheeks flush.

"Then you have your answer. I don't know what you're gonna do or what you want to do, but what you need to do is choose. Stop all this back-and-forth stuff."

"But he's done—"

Trina interrupted Casey. "You either commit yourself to be his wife and put all of your love and faith into it or maybe you should leave. Three years is a long time to be in a holding pattern. That was a four-teen-year lesson for me firsthand. And I'm not saying that I won't take Rick back, but a decision had to be made. It had reached that point. I may let him come back, but only if he comes back right. Brent's a good man. And I think in your heart of hearts, you know that better than anyone."

"Is that enough?"

"Only you can decide, but I think you already know. You're right, Casey. What he did three years ago was wrong, but he's tried to make amends—you've said so yourself. Forgiving is hard, but it's worth it."

"Yeah, I found out he's been seeing his daughter after promising he'd cut off all contact except financial support. The disgusting part is, it was Alexis who told me."

"Yeah, good 'ol Alexis. Come on, how could you expect a man like

Brent not to want to have a relationship with his own flesh and blood? Would you rather he be like Rick—able to jet out when blood ties aren't convenient? No matter how she came into the world, I don't see Brent turning his back on that responsibility." Trina got up from the table. "Lucky you."

Suddenly Casey felt ashamed looking at Trina, pregnant, alone, with two other young children to care for. "Any sign of him softening up about the baby?" Casey asked.

"Well, it's not like he's overjoyed now, but since he heard it was another boy, he seemed to get a little excited. But what if the doctor made a mistake and it's really a girl? Then what? I don't know, Casey. I'd have to be sure he's grown before I open that door back up for him."

Trina shook her head and walked toward the cordless phone as it started to ring. She looked a bit weary as she lifted the receiver.

Casey wanted to be sure about her marriage with Brent too, but she wondered if that was possible . . . if certainty in a relationship was ever truly attainable. Should she simply be grateful for the loving bond they shared and enjoy it, or constantly rehash his wrongs?

"Thank you! Thank you! Thank you!" Trina excitedly said as she hung up the phone.

Casey watched as Trina did a little dance, pushing her hands against the sky and wiggling her wide-set hips.

"They approved it, Casey! They approved my application for a small-business loan!"

"Congratulations!" Casey said, mustering up as much enthusiasm as possible under the circumstances.

"I got to call my aunt Thelma and tell her," Trina said, picking up the phone again and quickly punching in the numbers.

Casey smiled. Trina was right; Casey did have to stop riding the fence. Her relationship could not bear the strain of it much longer.

After three years of holding a silent grudge against Brent, was she finally ready to remove the scab over her heart?

"Damn, Coach, what are you trying to do, kill us?" Rick gasped as Coach headed off the court.

That's exactly what he's trying to do, Brent thought, watching all of his teammates heaving. The excruciating practice was unheard-of for a game day, doubly so considering it was the morning of the last game in the championship series. Tonight was it.

Coach walked quickly toward the locker-room area. Most of the other guys were still panting. The Flyers and Lakers were tied at three games apiece and the title was on the line. It was all or nothing, but the way Coach just had them playing, Brent felt as if he might not have enough energy to last through the actual game tonight.

Coach had had the team racing through unnecessary drills and playing one scrimmage after the next. None of the guys had been prepared for such an intense practice, and many had not even bothered to tape their ankles to protect against injuries. Brent had assumed they would just be shooting around, which was the team's normal practice routine for game days. He should have known better after everything that had been going on. It defied logic for Coach to have them practicing so hard the day of the final game. No matter how Brent looked at it, Coach's actions did not add up.

Now Brent had a good idea of what was really going on and he was determined to get to the bottom of it before tonight's game. Shaking his head, he still couldn't get Steve's words out of his mind. It was so hard to believe—impossible to believe. But as Brent replayed the reel of the last few weeks with Coach and Jake, as much as he hated to admit it to himself, Kelly had probably been telling the truth to Steve. There was too much at stake to delay confronting Coach.

Paul slowly dribbled the ball over to Brent with a look of exhaustion on his face. He began to shake his head in disgust. "We gotta make Coach talk to us, Brent. He still hasn't given Steve the game plays and he obviously has no intention of doing it."

"I know. He's still not gonna put Steve back in the lineup."

"And what the hell was he trying to prove with this marathon practice? We're all gonna be dead tonight. There was no reason for us to practice that hard—unless it's really true, but it's . . . it's so . . ."

"I know, I know. This has gone too far. I wish we had lit into his ass before practice," Brent said, throwing down his towel and storming off the court.

He was fuming as he made his way through the tunnel to Coach's office. This might be his only opportunity to ever win a championship, and he wasn't going to let anyone jeopardize it, especially his own coach.

Paul caught up with Brent. "What if he won't talk to us?"

"He's gonna have to. I'm not giving him a choice," Brent said, opening the door to Coach's office without knocking. Brent took a deep breath and looked over his shoulder at Paul. "You ready?"

Paul nodded his head and followed Brent into the office. Brent and Paul walked right up to Coach's desk and sat down, waiting for him to turn around. Coach appeared to be inspecting the aerial-view painting of the Mecca Arena hanging behind his desk.

Coach cleared his throat but remained standing with his back turned. "Since when don't we knock before entering my office?"

"Ever since you stopped acting like our head coach," Brent quickly shot back.

"I see." Coach turned around toward Brent and Paul.

"That's all you have to say?" Paul asked.

"Why would I have anything else to say to either of you about anything I do?" Coach smugly began as he took a seat behind his desk. "I've already explained my reasons for the new rotations, which was more than I was obligated to do in the first place. If you think—"

Brent interrupted, "We're not only talking about that. Why do you have us practicing this hard the day of the final game? You know that doesn't make any sense. Most of the guys are gonna be too exhausted to play tonight."

"Look, I don't have to answer to either of you. But let me remind you of something for the record. I've never followed anyone's coaching rules except my own, and if I happen to decide on a new tactic on the morning of the NBA championship, that's my prerogative. That's what I get paid to do. I'm the coach, and you two get paid to play by my rules."

"You got me pegged wrong, Coach," Paul began as he sat forward, meeting Coach head-on. "I get paid to win, and if I'm not mistaken, that's supposed to be your objective too."

"Winning has always been my objective in this game. One look at my coaching record and anyone can see that. How do you think we made it to the finals in the first place?"

"We didn't make it this far with what we're doing now, that's for damn sure. With Steve and Collin on the bench, we're lucky to still be alive in this series," said Brent angrily.

"Steve and Collin put themselves in their predicaments, not me."

"Whatever predicament you may think they put themselves in is irrelevant now because it's affecting the whole team," Brent said.

"Well, they should have thought about that before they acted. Shouldn't they?"

"Come on, Coach, we all know that's bullshit. The charges against Steve have been dropped. They were bogus from the beginning. You should know that, of all people. You have no objective reason not to play him tonight," Brent insisted.

"Well, the damage has been done now. Everyone thinks that Steve beat the woman anyway and that he just paid her off to be quiet," Coach said matter-of-factly.

It was astounding to Brent that a man he had respected so much as a coach could transform before his eyes.

"You're not making any sense," Paul said. "Kelly didn't simply drop the charges against Steve for money. She admitted to the press that she had lied about the whole thing. Come on, Coach, I know you've got to realize how preposterous you sound. There's no reason in the world why Steve should not be back in the lineup. Or is there? He's been exonerated and he shouldn't have been taken out in the first place." Paul threw his hands up in the air.

"Look, the two of you have no place questioning me. I already told you how hard Commissioner McDeavitt and the sponsors are coming down on me trying to protect the image and integrity of the league. It's out of my jurisdiction."

Brent looked skeptically at Coach and wondered if he even realized how much he had contradicted himself just in this short conversation and the previous one in the sauna. It was obvious that Coach was lying, but as Brent thought about it, he realized two could play at this game.

"So it's out of your hands, huh?" Brent asked.

"Out of my hands," Coach said, wiping his hands together in the air.

"Hmmm. So what's the reason behind you benching Collin, then?" Brent said.

Coach began to shuffle the papers in front of him. "Same reason."

"You can't not play a guy because he's gay," Paul blurted.

Brent looked at Paul to quiet him. Coach needed to be strung along just enough to hang himself.

"Pressures from the powers that be? Commissioner McDeavitt and sponsors again?" Brent pressed.

"Precisely," Coach said, placing the papers on top of his desk in the drawer. "So I think that should cover it. Now, if the two of you will excuse me, please."

"You know, Coach, I find it a little strange that not five minutes ago, you were damn self-righteous about how much control you have as the coach of this team. Wouldn't it stand to reason that you could play exactly who you chose to play if that were the case?"

"I . . . My control is of this team . . . not of the whole NBA. I can't do anything to contradict the NBA's overriding standards."

"Those standards and rules have been met as far as Steve and Collin are concerned. And anyway, I thought you followed your own coaching tactics. Why such deference all of a sudden?"

"It's not all of a sudden. Like I said, I told you guys this when they handed me the orders."

"Coach? You're taking orders from Commissioner McDeavitt? Brent, have you ever known Coach to take orders from the commissioner?" Paul said, turning toward Brent.

"Never. I didn't know he took orders, not even from Hal," Brent responded sarcastically. "Coach, please tell me something. How stupid do we look to you? Just tell me that. Your whole story is so full of holes you're getting us wet with your slop."

"What story? I'm just following orders. Now, why don't you get out of here and rest up for the game. You're wasting my time."

"I'm disappointed in you, Coach. You never follow orders," Paul said as if on cue.

Brent sat staring at Coach, trying to figure out his best angle of attack. Paul had already planted the seed. "Especially since you never got any orders in the first place. At least not from who you say you got them from. Isn't that right?" Brent said.

"I don't know what you're talking about," Coach said.

"Don't you?" Brent began as he rose from his seat and began walking around to Coach's side of the desk. "You see, Coach, I've been making some calls of my own . . . talking to people . . . to companies . . . specifically to Flyers sponsors, and I even had some business partners conduct a little due diligence on the whole team's behalf. I also had a few calls put in to good old Commissioner McDeavitt. And you know what I found out? You've been feeding us a crock of shit. Guess what. The commissioner doesn't have a problem with a gay player; he just wants the most competitive series possible. In fact, the commissioner is a little gun-shy of being targeted by gay activists. The last thing he wants is for the NBA to be labeled as homophobic. They'd break all kinds of equal protection laws by not allowing Collin to play."

Coach's face was turning whiter by the second. Brent could see Paul's look of surprise, but he didn't want to lose the momentum of his story.

"And you know what else I found out? Not one sponsor planned on pulling their advertisements after the story in the *Post* about Collin. In fact, according to a friend of mine at NBC, the ratings for the finals skyrocketed to an all-time high after that piece ran." Brent leaned against the desk inches from where Coach was sitting.

"I . . . I didn't . . . I said it was the powers that be . . . not the . . ." Coach stammered.

"Save it. You've obviously got your own agenda," Brent said.

"Yeah, and the powers that be are somebody else or—" Paul chimed in.

"Some other corporate entity," Brent interrupted.

"You guys are talking nonsense."

"Are we? I don't think so. How bout you, Brent?"

"I know we're not. In fact, we're right on the money. Aren't we . . . Coach? I know we are. And you know what sealed it for me?" Brent began, but caught himself. He had assured Steve he wouldn't use Kelly's name in this. Steve was afraid for her safety if it came out that she was the leak. Apparently Hightower's henchman had contacted a number of people associated with the Flyers. Steve didn't want it coming back on Kelly, even though it would probably serve her right.

"What sealed it for me was when I received a phone call confirming everything about your—how should I put it—'subversive activities' maybe. You've been trying to make us lose. It's only been by sheer will and a little luck that we won the three we've won so far in this series. You sabotaged us. I know you, Coach; well, at least I thought I did. Even if I hadn't gotten confirmation of my hunch, I know what the team winning means . . . meant to you. But now I know something else means a hell of a lot more to you."

Coach shifted uncomfortably in his wing chair on wheels as he attempted to roll away from Brent.

"How could you sell us out like this, Coach? Why'd you do this?" Paul asked.

"Nobody would be sold out, fellas," Coach started. "It could be a win-win situation for all of us. Moving to Albany is a small sacrifice in exchange for all of the other benefits."

Brent felt as if he had just entered the twilight zone with a dagger stuck in his back. Actually hearing Coach admit that he had been maneuvering against the team the whole time was more hurtful than he imagined.

"Come on, you guys. Don't you realize what it would mean for Hightower Enterprises to own the team?" Coach said, a stiff smile on his face as he looked back and forth between Brent and Paul. "The Flyers as a ball club would blow all the other NBA organizations to shreds. The private MGM Grand–caliber airplane would just be the small potatoes in this package. It would mean contract extensions for both of you, more lucrative than you could ever imagine, a brand-new state-of-the-art arena, and first class of everything."

The hurt was quickly turning to rage. Son of a bitch, Brent thought, and then looked at Paul, who shook his head.

"And would you finally get to be the highest-paid coach in the NBA?" Paul asked.

Coach hesitated.

"Well, would you?" Brent began. " 'Cause we need to know that."

"That's not all this is about, but . . . but . . . that would be one of the benefits," Coach said, very quietly. And then with a little more spark, "You gotta listen to this, guys. The Hightower boys make great deals. They even promised me an ownership interest in the team. What do you guess they'd do for you?"

Brent stood up, feeling fury and weariness simultaneously wash over him. "The almighty dollar," he said, shaking his head. "The almighty dollar. So that's what this is all about to you, huh? You disgust me, Mitchell."

"It's not only about the money. I want control of my team— deserve control. I don't need management meddling in how I run my boys. It's my show. Or at least that's how it's gonna be, and as far as money is concerned, you guys fight over your contracts all the time when you already have more cash than God. Don't try and act like you can't understand my position. And this could mean even more money for both of you . . . if . . ."

"If what?" Paul contemptuously said.

"If the Flyers lose tonight."

"Wasn't that your plan already? For us to lose so Hal would be forced to sell the team." Brent towered above Coach.

"Yeah . . . but do you know what would be in it for you two if you made certain that happened?" Coach said softly.

Paul pushed back his chair, knocking it over in the process. "Other than being owned by a racist bastard?"

"And coached by a moneygrubbing, sell-out, control-freak bastard? I'll fucking pass."

Brent looked at Coach, and the sight disgusted him. Pointing his trembling finger in Coach's face, he said, "You're finished, Mitchell. You'll never work in the NBA again. After winning the championship tonight, I'm making that my number one priority."

"What do you mean I'm finished? You'll never be able to prove anything, Brent, either of you!" Coach said, rising and brushing past Brent.

"Well, we'll just have to see what Hal has to say about it. And don't even think about showing your face at the game tonight. You're constructively relieved of your duties, effective immediately," Brent said.

"What do you mean? Are you crazy? Hal will never believe you two dumb black jocks. You two boys are going to regret this! I'll be a coach forever, making and breaking careers like yours. You can't play in my league! Just get the hell out of my office!" Coach shouted as Brent and Paul left the room. An ugly yellow cloud of epithets and threats followed them down the corridor.

Brent wiped the sweat off his brow and exhaled as he and Paul headed to their next stop. Pressing the up button on the elevator, Brent looked at Paul, his partner in crime. Now he only hoped Hal wasn't a part of this nightmare.

"Shaq elbowed him! Are you blind or something, Ref?" Trina screamed as Rick visibly cringed on the court after a hard brush with Shaquille O'Neal.

Casey, Remy, and Lorraine had watched an excited Trina jump up and down in her seat throughout the entire game. Casey was worried that Trina was going to hurt the baby in the process.

"Don't do it, Rick! Don't give him the satisfaction!" Trina hollered as Rick charged toward Shaquille and took a swing, narrowly missing his face by inches.

The crowd in the Mecca rose as one; Brent and Paul physically restrained Rick from striking Shaquille. Unfortunately for Rick, Shaq shoved him so hard that he lost his balance and landed bottom first on the court floor. Paul and Brent, although gripping Rick's arms, could not stop the force of impact as Rick fell to the ground with a dazed expression on his face.

Casey and Remy reflexively ducked to the side as a plastic beer cup flew between their heads. The fans were crazed with outrage. Before Casey realized what was happening, Trina started to run out onto the court.

Casey jumped up, Lorraine joined her, and together they blocked Trina's path. "Trina! What do you think you're doing?"

Trina did not respond and continued trying to push by Casey and Lorraine.

"Trina, calm down now. You think you're bad enough to jump Shaquille?" Lorraine said in an attempt at humor.

Trina, breathing heavily, stared out onto the court, shooting daggers with her eyes.

"Just sit down and relax. You're going to get the baby stressed out," coaxed Lorraine.

Trina remained standing as the referee handed down his judgment.

With a wave of the hand, Rick and Shaquille were both ejected with only two minutes remaining in the game, and the Flyers were down 90–94. The crowd roared with fury at Rick being ejected except for the small sound of a few jubilant Laker fans—. It had been his first solid effort against Shaquille in the entire series. Steve Tucker, the usual starter, had returned to the lineup tonight, along with Collin DuMott, but Steve was obviously having a difficult time getting his rhythm back. Rick had taken up the slack and had been able to limit Shaquille to only thirteen points.

In a fit of anger, Trina kicked an empty popcorn box at one of the referees as Rick and Shaquille were reluctantly escorted off to their respective locker rooms, hollering back and forth at each other the entire time.

"Trina, the refs are going to eject you if you keep it up," Casey said, noticing one of the referees eyeing them. They were sitting together in Casey's seats just one row behind Star Row. Robert DeNiro turned around to high-five Trina as Jack Nicholson glared across the court at them.

"I don't give a damn! Rick's been gettin' knocked around all night. Shit, half of the Lakers should've been ejected in the first quarter alone," Trina spat out.

"Come on, Trina, we don't need two of you getting kicked out tonight," Remy chimed in. "I could just see the headlines now. 'Pregnant Flyers Wife Thrown out of the Mecca—Injured Referee Seeking Ten Million in Damages.' " Remy was clearly trying to make light of the media's overzealous involvement in all of their lives.

Casey glanced at Remy. She knew how difficult it was for her friend to even show her face at the Mecca. But when Collin had called begging her forgiveness and support, Remy had been unable to refuse him. Underneath the rawness of her hurt and anger, Remy loved Collin and wished the best for him, no matter what, and she was relieved to see him back in the starting lineup.

"Well, it's true," Remy said sheepishly, lifting her shoulders and chuckling as she looked back up at Trina, who was quite a sight standing near the edge of the court with her protruding stomach. She looked like she was ready to attack one of the referees.

Casey pulled at the back of Trina's sweater in an attempt to coax her back down. "You want one of the players to knock you out when they get started again?"

Trina looked over her shoulder at Casey. Finally settling down and sitting in her seat sandwiched between Lorraine and Casey, she crossed her arms over her stomach, a grimace on her face.

Casey had invited the group of women to sit with her for the last game as one final act of camaraderie. They were not usually together since the players' seats were scattered throughout the arena, with the most coveted locations given to the team's franchise players, the rest by seniority on the team. Casey did not know what next season would hold for any of them, including their men. The ties these women and men shared were uncertain ones, determined by the seasons they experienced together. Casey knew how indefinite their relations were, thinking of the recent breakup of Michael and Dawn and the banishment of Kelly after her trumped-up charges against Steve. And she knew something more: no matter who comprised the Flyers next year and where they went, Coach Mitchell would not be with them. Brent had called her after he and Paul talked to Hal; his sense of betrayal and hurt had reached over the lines and touched her. She assumed Lorraine also knew the whole sordid story and how Hal had socked Mitchell, though they hadn't discussed it. The lives of the men and women of the New York Flyers intersected over the course of a basketball season. One day they were thrown together with the expectation of behaving like a big, happy family, and the next day they were parting ways, strewn about like dandelion fluff.

The Flyers could be relocated to Albany, Paul could be traded, Brent could suffer a career-ending injury, Rick could be forced into retirement by the team's unwillingness to sign an older player, and Collin, being a free agent, could end up playing ball just about anywhere in the world. They all lived an existence plagued by a tenuousness that not only pervaded their careers but trickled down into their relationships as well.

Even though a breakup had been inevitable for Remy and Collin, Remy's love for him as a friend rose above her broken heart and disappointment. Remy had put her raw feelings aside and decided to stand behind Collin in what could be his last game in a Flyers uniform, or in any team uniform for that matter. She had told Casey that she intended to give Collin her support, especially since so many of his alleged friends had turned their backs on him after the *New York Post*'s exposé article.

Casey watched as the ball boys mopped up the wet floor and removed the debris littering the court. The announcement asking the crowd to refrain from throwing items onto the court was barely audible over the chants of "Bullshit" echoing throughout the arena. The fans were close to rioting, with Rick Belleville ejected and the Flyers down four points.

Steve Tucker ripped off his sweats and began jumping up and down in an effort to loosen up as he prepared to take Rick's place on the court. Casey watched across the court as the acting head coach, Bob Stillman, whispered in Steve's ear. Casey imagined Steve had to be grateful that Shaquille had been ejected as well. When Steve had initially entered the game in the first half, he had struggled trying to hold on to the ball. The same had been true for Collin as he unsuccessfully tried to get one three-pointer after another to sink. Yet somehow the Flyers had managed to stay in the game, despite Steve and Collin having a difficult time trying to get back into their grooves.

When a few of the wives had questioned why Coach and Alexis

were absent, Casey had made up something about a death in the family, crossing her fingers so God wouldn't punish her for the lie. No one seemed to mind much, including the fans, since Mitchell's strategy had been the object of much talk and speculation in the media. During the last game, Ahmad Rashad had wondered aloud over the air whether Mitchell had lost his sanity. The fans had been ecstatic when Stillman put Steve and Collin back into the rotation. Postgame stories would no doubt probe into this detail, but as for now, Ahmad Rashad just kept mentioning his absence, playing speculative games when there was nothing else to say, telling the fans the media had to improvise. Tomorrow would be feeding-frenzy time for the sports press.

As Collin inbounded the ball to Paul, Casey's mind wandered. She felt a tug at her heart. She had rushed in and out of her apartment to change from her work attire before the game tonight. As had become her routine, Nikki had been waiting at the door. She had begged to accompany Casey, but Casey had refused her, not wanting Nikki to stay up past her weekday eight-o'clock bedtime. When Nikki had finally relented, she made Casey promise to kiss her when she got home, no matter how late; and oh yeah, Daddy too. As much as she had been fighting it, Casey had to admit to herself that she had fallen in love with the little girl.

"Yes, Collin! Hit another one, baby!" Remy uncharacteristically screamed as she jumped out of her seat when Collin hit his first three-pointer of the night, putting the Flyers within one point of the Lakers.

Casey noticed that the people sitting around them were staring at Remy with looks of confusion on their faces. Since Collin and Remy were such a well-known couple, the general public was engaged in a mission to figure out if the *New York Post* article was really true or if Collin was straight and he and Remy were still an item.

As Kobe Bryant of the Lakers attempted to inbound to Eddie Jones, Paul Thomas stole the ball out of Jones's hand and made an easy layup, putting the Flyers up by one point. The entire Mecca was on its feet. Trina seemed to have forgotten that she was angry about Rick's ejection as she frantically jumped up and down, waving a purple and black Flyers towel in the air.

With forty-six seconds left in the game, the Lakers called a time-out, probably hoping to diminish the Flyers' momentum after Paul's steal and easy basket. As Paul ran to the sidelines, the guys were bumping chests and slapping each other on the butts in frenzied excitement.

When the guys left the huddle and resumed their positions on the court, Brent quickly winked at Casey and mouthed the two words "Thank you."

As Brent stayed glued to his man on the court, guarding his every move, Paul followed suit and shut down his man as well. The twenty-four-second clock expired without the Lakers ever getting a shot off. The Flyers regained possession with twenty-two seconds remaining in the game and a one-point lead.

The tension and excitement was so thick in the Mecca, it made the hairs on Casey's neck rise. Michael Brown inbounded the ball, passing it to Paul, who guarded it as he was double-teamed with intense full-court pressure. He dribbled down the court as if his life depended on it; the seconds took an eternity to pass.

Brent was open and waved his hands in the air for Paul to pass him the ball. Casey could see the burning desire to win in Brent's eyes. She could not recall seeing such a fervent expression on his face except on one previous occasion—when he had asked her to marry him.

Casey felt a sudden surge of forgiveness toward her husband. For the first time in three years she felt a freeness in her love for him. She was not encumbered by the weight of his past wrongs. Instead, she felt a receptiveness to his love descend upon her.

As Brent caught the pass from Paul with four seconds remaining in the game, he went up for a ten-foot jumper. Just as the ball was released from Brent's hands, Casey tightly shut her eyes and hoped for the best outcome of the game and their marriage.

Epilogue

"Come on, Mommy! Daddy said they gonna have a merry-go-round!"

"Yeah, Casey. What are you doing in there? You drown in the tub or something?" Brent said as he banged on the bathroom door.

"Can a woman get a moment's peace around here?"

"Hurry up, Mommy," Nikki begged.

Listening to Nikki on the other side of the door, Casey knew without a doubt that she'd created a wonderful little monster despite her initial apprehension. She'd indulged her to the point that she could coo and whine and not irritate Casey in the least bit (unless she was waking her up at six o'clock on a Saturday morning). That night on her doorstep several months before, it had not occurred to Casey that Nikki would turn into a surprise package that she could never fathom returning.

"Five minutes, I'll be out in five minutes. You two act like you haven't seen me in years." She laughed thinking about the father-daughter duo.

The directions written in bold letters on the back of the box stated that it should only take a couple of minutes for the results, but it

330

seemed as if hours had passed. Casey's two big babies impatiently hovering at the door didn't help matters. They seemed to have forgotten that she'd spent the whole morning romping around Central Park with them. Sometimes Brent acted like more of a kid than Nikki, but Casey suppose'd she was the one to blame for that since she'd been incessantly spoiling both of them over the last five months.

After the final game of the play-offs, a welcome calm had begun to descend upon their lives. A calm that Casey allowed to enter into her marriage. She had been fighting it for so long—to the point of mental exhaustion. The seesawing had not done either of them any good, especially their marriage. The truth of the matter was that she loved Brent and she wanted to spend the rest of her life with him. Although he had made a huge mistake, Casey felt he was trying to rectify his wrong. He was genuinely trying to make amends. She wanted to give him another chance—really give him another chance this time, not just pay lip service to trying to make their marriage work. Casey knew the infidelity was inexcusable but it was time to move on. She not only believed, but she knew in her gut that Brent had totally re-committed himself to their marriage. It had become her turn to decide whether or not she wanted to be committed again. And she had decided—for better or for worse, Brent was her man. Finally, she truly believed the worst had passed for them.

In July, they'd gone on a vacation with Nikki and Brent, Jr., to a family resort in Hawaii. In August Brent and Casey had driven around the coast of the Italian Riviera. She could not quite pinpoint when the transition occurred, but everything had begun to fall into place for them as a couple and as parents about the same time they got settled back in their Virginia home. Casey was actually a parent—not only a stepmother to Brent, Jr., but a mommy to Nikki. She'd officially adopted her two months ago.

Apparently, ever since Nikki was born, her mother had been shuffling her between various relatives' homes until they got tired of caring for her or the money she gave them ran out. She'd never had any interest in being a mother in the first place and had readily relinquished all of her parental rights, claiming that Nikki cramped her style. The child support she'd been receiving from Brent had been squandered on exotic vacations for her and her string of boyfriends. Brent's money fit into her plans, but Nikki did not.

Brent had been worried about Casey's reaction to Nikki moving in with them permanently; he'd assumed that Casey wanted more than anything for Nikki's mother to change her mind somewhere down the line and take her back. When Casey had not only agreed but suggested adopting her, Brent had been floored. With Trina's voice in her head, she'd known she wanted her marriage to work above all else. The picture for them was almost complete, personally and professionally. Casey wanted Nikki in their lives as much as Brent wanted her, and she knew he understood her final forgiveness.

Oddly enough, the Flyers beating the Lakers in the last game had been almost anticlimactic for Brent with all the controversy surrounding the whole series. Which was not to say that he wasn't excited to finally win an NBA championship. He strutted around wearing his championship ring, flashing it like a woman with a new huge diamond engagement ring. But still, the fallout after the win cast a shadow over the Flyers' success for him.

When Hal, along with Commissioner McDeavitt, had told the entire Flyers/Coach/Hightower saga, the fans had been great—though the vote wasn't in on whether Stillman would coach. New York was glad to have their team, swept clean.

Soon the NBA investigation had exposed Mitchell's and Jake's activities and they were both banned from working with the league. Jake's agency license had been revoked and he'd been disbarred by the State of New York from practicing law. The last Casey had heard, Jake had tried to negotiate a deal with a publishing house for the rights to his story, portraying him as a victim in the entire debacle. Jake claimed to have been framed as the fall guy by the good ol' powers that be. Who are these powers, anyhow? Casey wondered. As far as she knew, Jake's proposed story had not been bought by a publishing house (even publishers like basketball) or the public, so he'd decided to publish and distribute the book himself.

Mitchell had had better luck than Jake. He'd signed a contract to coach a basketball team in Turkey, and reportedly he would be the highest-paid person associated with basketball in all of Europe and the

Mideast. From what Casey understood, Alexis and their daughters had chosen to remain in the United States and had relocated to Palm Beach, which was probably a wise decision on Alexis's part. With the language barriers and all, teaching the wives of Turkish players about proper etiquette would probably have proved too challenging a task even for her.

Now, in the aftermath of the scandal that had rocked the Flyers, the threat of the team being relocated to Albany was gone. Just last month the city had made good on its promise to absorb a substantial amount of the operating costs for the team and the necessary financial bonds were issued, enabling Hal and his family to keep the Flyers in their rightful home.

Casey was happy that everything had worked out for Brent and the team, but she couldn't help but be saddened that Trina and Remy weren't going to be back when the season began. Even though Rick had contributed to the Flyers reaching and winning the championship, management still decided that he was too old to re-sign. From what Trina had told Casey, Rick wasn't very disappointed. Actually she said he'd spent the summer going to Gambler's Anonymous meetings every week, and so far it was helping. Since Trina had given birth to their little boy last month in North Carolina, Rick had taken over the parenting responsibilities of all three kids and had become a regular Mr. Mom. His new domesticated role gave Trina free reign to concentrate on her growing baking business. She'd just landed a national distribution contract for her miniature peach pound cakes, with plans to open her own bakery in order to accommodate the growing demand for her culinary delights.

Even though Remy and Collin had committed to being friends forever, the hounding paparazzi constantly trying to figure out the status of their relationship had taken their toll on her. She'd just signed on a yearlong concert tour of Europe, Asia, and the Caribbean.

True to public speculation, Collin had not re-signed with the Flyers. Instead, he'd inked a lucrative four-year deal with the Golden State Warriors. Phil had also signed a contract with an ABC affiliate in San Francisco as a sports commentator. The two men had moved in together and bought a Great Dane puppy, and Collin was now the first openly gay player in the NBA. Ironically, according to the latest media accounts, Collin was quickly becoming the darling of the Warrior's fans.

As for the hot young rookie Michael Brown, he was only getting hotter. He'd ended up winning Rookie of the Year, had landed a starring role as an action hero opposite Sylvester Stallone, and had been named one of *People* magazine's "Fifty Most Beautiful People." But all this had come at a steep price. He'd lost Dawn. In a recent interview, he swore to remain a bachelor until he retired from the NBA unless he could win back his college sweetheart. Judging from Casey's most recent lunch with Dawn, it seemed that Michael was going to remain a bachelor for a while. She was dating a gorgeous young resident who treated her as if *she* were a star.

Dawn wasn't the only one being treated well by her man. When Brent and Casey had attended Sam Perkins's celebrity basketball tournament over the summer, they'd bumped into Kelly. She'd obviously recovered from her very public, very scandalous breakup with Steve and had managed to hook another young NBA player. Her latest victim was a rookie with the New Jersey Nets who barely looked legal. When Casey had seen them together at the Hotel Nikko in Seattle, he'd been carrying Diamond around and following behind Kelly as if he were her personal valet. But Kelly, thank goodness, was staying sober. Steve was just relieved that he had been able to work things out with her so he and Stephanie could pursue their relationship . . . undisturbed. Casey kind of felt bad for the new young buck, but he was bound to learn the hard way; they all did, most later rather than sooner.

"Mommy. Daddy said five minutes is up. Come on."

"Yeah, Casey. We're gonna miss the groundbreaking ceremony, and I promised Paul we'd be there."

Casey tuned them out as she looked down at the faint blue line appearing on the rectangular stick and was determined not to get excited, yet. As she glanced at her watch, she knew Brent was right. They had to hurry if they planned on making it in time for the groundbreaking for the Crissy Jackson Community Center. Paul and Lorraine, in conjunction with the city of New York, were opening a youth center, devoted to keeping the children of Harlem safe, in memory of the little girl whose gang-related murder Lorraine had witnessed in high school. Lorraine had finally contacted Crissy's mother. It had taken a lot of talk, more than one conversation, but finally Lorraine had told Mrs. Jackson the whole story of that night. And Crissy's mom, though not ready to forgive, at least had stopped wanting to do damage. Casey would meet Mrs. Jackson that day at the center's opening.

When Lorraine had reported the identity of the murderer and his accomplices to the police, they'd discovered that he had been killed two years before in a prison fight while serving a double life sentence. The two others were serving time, but both were about to be tried for Crissy's murder.

"You promised, Mommy," Nikki cried into the door.

"You're right. I did promise and I'm coming out now," Casey said, taking one last look at the unmistakably solid blue line.

Holding the stick behind her back, she pulled the door open, and Nikki and Brent almost fell into the bathroom. She was so excited, she could scarcely suppress a scream from escaping her mouth. The result of the pregnancy test defied her doctor's prognosis and confirmed a dream she'd no longer dared to think possible.

"Well, it's about time," Brent began as he kissed her on the forehead. "If you were trying to make yourself look beautiful in there, you did a good job."

"You look pretty, Mommy," Nikki cooed as Brent picked her up with one arm and led Casey out of the bathroom with the other.

"So it's me and my two girls today. I'm the luckiest guy in the world." Brent beamed looking at Casey and then Nikki.

"Brent . . ." Casey glanced at Nikki. Yeah, she was old enough. Casey tried to keep a lid on her emotions. "I have to tell you something and I can't wait." She pulled the stick from behind her back and held it up for them both. Clearly they were clueless.

"What's that?" Nikki asked, scrunching up her face.

A light dawned in Brent's head, "Is that what I think it is?" he asked, a grin developing on his handsome face.

"Yup," Casey answered quickly.

"And does it mean what I think it means?"

"Yup."

"What is it, Mommy?"

Brent lifted Nikki above his head and spun her around in a circle. "What it means is that you are going to have your very own little brother or sister and that I am beyond the luckiest guy in the world. I'm the luckiest guy in the galaxy!"

"Yaaaay," Nikki screamed as Brent and Casey joined her, all of them hollering at the top of their lungs as if there were no tomorrow.